PAINTING THE MISTS, BOOK 6

PATRICK G. LAPLANTE

Published by: Patrick G. Laplante
Editing and Interior Design by: Crystal Watanabe
Cover Illustration and Design by: Petros Stefanidis

First edition, 2019
ISBN: 978-1-989578-00-1

Other Painting the Mists Books:

Clear Sky
Blood Moon
Light in the Darkness
Pure Jade
Corrupted Crimson

Dedication

To my fiancée, Xing Wen. For saying yes.

Author's Note

As I write this note, I realize how much time has passed since I started writing *Kindling*. The book took two and a half months to write and one month to review before it even got to Crystal, my editor. It's been a difficult book to write for many reasons, but I'm confident that it was worth the wait. This book is a turning point in the series for both Cha Ming and myself.

The original title was meant to be *Bridge of Stars*, but after some careful thought, I felt that *Kindling* better reflected the mood of the book. More to the point, it best reflects the theme of fire that it tries to portray. But what is fire? Is it just a physical process, a chemical reaction that reduces wood to ash? Or is it something more?

To me, fire is hope on a cold winter day. It's the joy in all our hearts as we bubble with excitement. Fire is also the warmth in love. Hope, joy, and love—these are all choices. And these choices are what *Kindling* is all about.

Prologue

A generous portion of black fish simmered as Yu Wen looked on in rapt attention. "The key to proper Devilish Noodles is dipping the freshest fish into boiling broth and letting it cool as the fish cooks," the kindly old man in front of her said. "I know this because it is what my grandfather told me, as did his father before him. People flock from all over Silverstream just to have a bite."

Yu Wen drooled as her noodles cooked within the steaming broth in the bowl. Her chopsticks were ready to pounce. "So many people come here. Why don't you raise your prices?" she asked. "I waited outside for three days just to get in."

"If I raised the prices, then how would the common people eat the continent's best noodles?" the shop owner said. "Our family came from humble origins. How can we turn our backs on the community after digging ourselves out of poverty?" He sighed. "Though, I won't have much choice in the matter if things keep going the way they are. Taxes have been going up every year. It's only a matter of time until I have to raise my prices or close up shop."

A delicate aroma filled the air as the noodles approached perfection. The owner waited patiently before scooping up the bowl with a practiced hand and deftly placing it before Yu Wen. Her curly locks bounced as she ate the fish and noodles with inhuman speed and drank the steaming broth in a single gulp.

"These are the best noodles I have ever tasted!" she said, sighing in satisfaction. "The prince who raises your taxes is just a crook who wants to keep them all to himself."

After she said this, the noisy restaurant quieted substantially. People began speaking in hushed whispers, and many customers around Yu Wen finished their conversations and left the restaurant, leaving their payment and a generous tip on the table.

"You'd best be careful with your words," the owner said. "The prince has ears everywhere."

The chatter in the restaurant began picking up where it had left off—save for two people, who dutifully relayed what they'd heard through their communication devices.

"Those are the prince's men," the shop owner whispered, pointing them out with his eyes. "You should leave now while you still can. The prince's uncle is a mighty martial artist. We lowly commoners can only obey."

"Let's see if he dares," Yu Wen said with a sniff. "By the way, I want another ten bowls."

"*Ten?*" the owner exclaimed. "A pretty young girl like yourself shouldn't eat so much."

A dreadful chill suddenly washed over him.

Yu Wen looked at him with a pleasant smile that belied her dangerous aura. "Would you care to repeat that?" she said.

"I mean... you have such a healthy appetite for a young lady," the owner said nervously. "Eat up, eat up, it's on me!"

A small white-jade creature popped out of her travel bag as they waited for the next bowl. "You really shouldn't eat so much," the creature said. "You should also stop causing so much trouble wherever you go."

"But I can't help it." Yu Wen pouted. "They're so delicious. You should try some."

"A jade rabbit eating meat?" the creature asked. "Maybe when hell freezes over. Speaking of which, we should go. That mighty martial artist isn't powerful, but he can blow our cover. I don't mind dying, but I really don't want to break my moon-cake-eating streak."

"How many are you on now, Xiao Bai?" Yu Wen asked.

"This one makes fifty-seven million five thousand and forty-six," Xiao Bai said, popping a yellow cake into her tiny mouth. "Over fifty-seven million days without gaining weight and still perfectly healthy. The moon cake diet is the future, mark my words."

Yu Wen chuckled as she prepared to dig in. But at that moment, a tall man wearing a white cloak burst in with a half dozen armed guards. The two gentlemen who had been communicating earlier stood up to greet him. The remaining customers in the restaurant ceased eating.

"Is there anything I can help the crown prince with?" the owner said from behind the bar.

The prince ignored him while looking Yu Wen up and down. "This is why I keep telling you to restrict your clientele," he said to the owner. "If you did, you wouldn't have to deal with these pesky unregistered guests."

I told you we should have registered at the city gates, Xiao Bai said to Yu Wen. *But you never listen. All you think about is food.*

He would have caused trouble anyway, Yu Wen said. *Look at his eyes.* She gestured to the prince, whose faint yellow aura caused both the woman and the rabbit a large amount of discomfort. His eyes were filled with a familiar look of uncontrolled lust and greed. She met people like this wherever she traveled.

We should run, Xiao Bai sent to Yu Wen as the prince and the guards drew their weapons and rushed toward them.

Just a minute, Yu Wen said.

Ripples of gray energy surged around her and encompassed the entire room. They continued until they formed a mile-wide bubble that caused everyone to freeze in place. Only Yu Wen, Xiao Bai, and the noodles were unaffected. The piece of devilfish reached perfection a few breaths later, and Yu Wen rapidly gobbled it down.

She then looked toward a handsome man she'd been eyeing the whole time. His body was muscular, and his jaw was sharp, like chiseled marble. She ran a finger across his forehead and watched as his life's memories were displayed in a fast-moving projection.

"Why do I have such bad luck with handsome men?" she said as she saw the good, the bad, and the ugly. "Most of the ones I meet are terrible, and all the nice ones go away."

She scooped up the tiny rabbit and disappeared from the restaurant. A few breaths later, the prince and the owner moved again, quickly realizing that the young woman had vanished before their very eyes.

"I want everyone to fan out and find her!" the crown prince yelled, startling the nearby guards.

They rushed to obey his commands, but in the process, many of them tripped. Meanwhile, the crown prince didn't notice the contents of his bag of holding spilling out onto the ground as he ran out of the building. Some customers, who were less than pleased with the prince, rapidly snatched them up. They then approached the owner and placed all the spirit stones in their possession on the bar.

"Thank you, everyone," the owner said, teary eyed. He knew these customers by name, and they all had one thing in common—they were the poor who everyone else had forgotten, the downtrodden in this oppressive country. They were the dregs of Silverstream City.

"Why is everyone around me so lucky, but I always get discovered?" Yu Wen moaned. "Why is fate so unfair?"

"Who knows?" Xiao Bai said. "Luck aside, you shouldn't use your Grandmist powers so often."

They ran across a ten-mile bridge that connected two giant mountains floating on a sea of mists. Nine gigantic liquid metal rivers ran beneath them; they reflected the light of the planet's three suns, bringing color to an otherwise drab and uninteresting world.

"If I hadn't used them, I couldn't have eaten the noodles," Yu Wen said. "Besides, it's not like they can do anything to us anyway.

Those slowpokes couldn't stop me if their lives depended on it."

The duo leaped over a crowd of guards and rushed over to the second island, where a large platoon stood ready for them.

"What now?" the Jade Rabbit said nervously.

"Watch this," Yu Wen said. She grabbed the rabbit and jumped off the bridge. At the same time, she threw out a small jade object that floated in front of her. It returned after letting out a soft click. She looked at the resulting picture in satisfaction. "My camera always takes the best pictures. See how it perfectly caught the reflection of the silver streams on the mist and caught the fear and hesitation in their eyes?"

"This is the most wasteful use of a soul-bound treasure I've ever seen in all my lifetimes," Xiao Bai said dryly.

"At least you remember your lifetimes," Yu Wen muttered.

They dodged the spirit ships that chased them and landed on the silver streams. The rivers rippled as they ran, causing the lights they reflected to shimmer and scatter. A large gate appeared in the distance. It was nine miles tall and three miles wide, the large opening in its center filled with a hazy gray substance.

"You think I'll let you escape through the planar portal after the ruckus you've caused?" a voice called out of nowhere. A man in a golden robe appeared before them. The space around him was filled with sharpness, as though anything that entered this domain would be reduced to mincemeat.

"You're awfully brave for a rune-carving cultivator," Yu Wen said as she and Xiao Bai stopped.

"How can I not be brave with the generous bounty on your head," the man said. "I only need to force you or your rabbit to use your powers, and my soul will be reincarnated into a life of luxury. This is enough to make anyone go crazy. I'm fortunate that my stupid nephew happened to stumble on you."

This older man was surrounded in a thick ochre glow, and a large apparition with gold-and-ochre wings stood behind him. Its large claws held the man's domain firmly, reinforcing it with the power of sin.

"Let's see if you have the skill," Yu Wen said as she quickly analyzed the route to the planar gate.

Silver strings burst out around her and shot toward the old man. Meanwhile, the meek Xiao Bai underwent a startling transformation. Her eyes turned red while her two front teeth grew into vicious hooks that could decapitate gods and devour immortals.

The girl and the rabbit darted out in opposite directions. The golden-robed man grunted and chased after Yu Wen. His devilish speed caused even the Silver Streams to churn. Seeing this, Yu Wen raised her fist and struck out against the man's domain, which shuddered under the impact.

The man coughed up blood but cackled as he pulled out a black spike. The sinister object immediately disintegrated and fed the ochre glow in his devilish apparition. The phantom of a second pair of wings appeared behind it, which in turn caused his domain to almost double in size.

"Damn it all," Yu Wen said as her skin began suffering various cuts and lacerations. Although they were healing rapidly, they were incredibly painful. She tossed out dozens of silver threads to fight against the many blades surrounding her. Unfortunately, they couldn't stand up to the ruthless assault; the silver threads became silver dust that scattered into the rivers below.

Just as she was about to activate her own domain to counteract her opponent, she received a mental message from Xiao Bai. The small rabbit appeared behind the ochre avatar and took a large bite out of it. It roared in pain and threw the white animal to the floor. Ochre blood oozed out from the apparition's strange wound.

We can't beat them without unlocking at least a tiny bit of our power, Yu Wen sent. Her eyes turned cold as they locked on the golden-robed man. *We might as well make it worthwhile.*

"For your information," she said, "your employer withheld some information from you."

"And what might that be?" the golden-robed man said, stalling for every scrap of time he could.

"He might have promised you eternal life, but if your soul is destroyed, then even the supreme ruler of Hell can't reincarnate it for you," she said.

A gray cloud oozed out from around Yu Wen and expanded unreasonably quickly. Despite its gaseous appearance, it weighed more than the heaviest metal. Spatial cracks appeared around the oozing fluid, completely shattering the golden domain. It was as though the transcendent plane couldn't bear the weight of the mysterious substance.

Bit by bit, the energy that comprised his domain was absorbed into the expanding gray cloud. It formed a domainlike sphere that encapsulated him before he had a chance to resist.

"No!" he yelled as his body, devilish avatar, and soul were consumed by the gray barrier in a fraction of a moment. Then, the gray cloud vanished as though it had never existed in the first place.

"Let's go!" Yu Wen said as she joined up with Xiao Bai, who was completely unharmed by the devilish apparition's strike. They floated toward the gray gate that hummed after sensing their presence.

"Where to this time?" Xiao Bai asked.

Yu Wen thought for a bit before her expression brightened. "The Bridge of Stars will be opening soon," she said. "It's the perfect place to lay low. Let's go see if we can make some new friends."

The portal shimmered slightly as they entered it. Unbeknownst to them, a black-cloaked figure appeared behind them just before they finished passing.

"I've finally found you," the figure said as he raised his hand.

Time seemed to flow in reverse as the ghostly images of Yu Wen and Xiao Bai appeared just in front of the gate. Their lips moved slightly before the technique collapsed. Several bolts of lightning rained down on the figure, who accepted the plane's punishment without complaint.

As the bolts struck him, his barely visible face was revealed. It was gaunt and pale, and his hair was white as fresh winter snow. His eyes were black.

"Just what are those devils up to?" Yama muttered as he looked through a literal mountain of ledgers.

He was currently at a repository company called Iron Planet. According to the Underworld's accounting regulations, every company operating in Diyu was required to keep a minimum of 10,000 Underworld years' worth of records. His findings thus far were infuriating.

"Han Yu, come here," Yama said. His assistant instantly teleported to his side. "I want you to look through this small pile of documents and investigate the individuals who issued them. If you do this well, you'll get a raise."

Her bright smile made him immediately regret his brash decision.

"I think five percent would go a long way," he added.

The comment instantly doused the fire in her eyes. It was replaced with frustration and indignation, and most importantly, unwillingness and stubbornness.

A good sign, he thought. *You need to keep them hungry or they won't work hard.*

"Am I looking for anything in particular?" Han Yu asked stiffly.

"Connections to devils," Yama said. "Investments, relatives, friends, roommates of a third cousin. No matter how obscure they are, I want them found. I don't particularly care that we sell edicts to devils, but everything must be balanced. We are a nonpartisan, nonprofit organization, not a custom reincarnation company that supports the cosmos on the side."

"Then what about our participation in the election?" Han Yu asked.

"That's different!" Yama said. "It affects the very survival of our universe." He looked into the void. "Lily, come join us as well."

A second woman in a suit appeared beside them. While Han Yu sported a navy outfit, Lily wore a white one, complete with white bordered glasses.

"What can I help with, Your Eminence?" Lily said. A hint of flirtation appeared on her otherwise deferent expression.

"For the last time, 'boss' will do fine," Yama said sternly, hiding his pleasure. "This pile of documents shows that our edict sales have been heavily favoring devils. In passing, I've also noticed some disturbing financial details. Our sales group has been booking sales before delivery and has been refusing to write off bad debt. As a result, our numbers have been inflated by thirty percent over the past century. As our company's controller, I need you to perform a full internal audit and get back to me with suggestions for further accounting regulations."

Lily's eyes brightened at the prospect. "I'll be suggesting the most comprehensive, most ironclad management recommendations possible!"

Yama massaged his brow. "I just want reasonable, incremental regulations that can prevent this *specific* problem. Why do all you accountants go on a crusade every time someone steps out of line?"

"With all due respect, sir," Lily said, "if people can't do anything, it's impossible to make mistakes."

Yama groaned inwardly as he flew off the small storage planet and into the chill of empty space. He didn't dare admit that she had a point, lest it get to her head.

By the way, sir, you have a guest waiting in the lobby, Han Yu sent via SpiritChat, a new messaging service that was taking the Underworld by storm. You could do everything with it, including paying, phoning, and messaging. If you paid for the add-on, it could even take your kids to school. *It's the Jade Emperor. He said you didn't accept his SpiritChat invite.*

"Why does everyone expect me to answer these SpiritChat messages right away?" Yama grumbled. "If it's really important, can't they just call me? Or send an email with an urgent tag followed by a second email reminding me to read the first one?"

He swiftly teleported to his office, the only location he could teleport to within Diyu. After straightening himself out, he walked out to greet the ruler of Heaven.

"My friend, Yama, it's been ages!" a graying man with jade robes said as soon as he entered the lobby. He wore a thin jade crown on his head. "I'm here to ask about my—"

"Your daughter," Yama cut in. "Yes, I know. It was the same last week and the week before that. I still haven't seen her, and if I did, I'd inform you immediately." Just as the stately king was about to protest, Yama continued his tirade. "You've lived for aeons, but you still can't let her wander off for a millennium without getting antsy about her. Are you a king or a housewife suffering from empty nest syndrome?"

"This is different," the Jade Emperor said indignantly. "I have a foreboding feeling. I feel like our father-daughter karma is about to expire. And when you didn't add me to SpiritChat, I started to worry."

"I just added you, so you can stop worrying," Yama said. He shuddered as he rapidly swept through the man's profile. It was filled with pictures of him and his daughter, some as much as a million years old. "If you're so worried about her, why did you lend her your soul-bound treasure, the Jade Moon Cloak? You can't even keep tabs on her when she wears it. If I were you, I would have placed her under house arrest in the heavenly courts. None of this 'you're your own person and you can do whatever you want' nonsense."

"How could I do that to my own daughter?" the Jade Emperor said, taking a seat. He sniffed the tea Yama offered him, making sure that the man wasn't drugging him with Meng Po's tea. "She has such a free spirit, and if I don't let her wander, the cosmos would have made something happen. Traitors would have appeared within our ranks and would have tried to kill her from within the palace. Flaws would have appeared in our defensive formations. Rebellion would have fermented in the heavens and lured me away." He sighed. "It's not easy being that girl's father."

"If you can't even bear to put her under house arrest, how will you deal with her two reincarnations from now?" Yama said.

A pained expression appeared on the Jade Emperor's face, causing Yama to regret his words.

"I don't know," the Jade Emperor said. "I can only live in the present. In this lifetime, she is my daughter, cosmic balance be damned."

"You know of cosmic balance, yet you've spoiled your daughter," Yama said. "It's brought the heavens untold fortune, but you know full well that when the cosmic scales shift, you'll reap what you've sown. The heavens will experience unprecedented disaster, and countless mortals will get caught up in the resulting storm. Hell, I'm experiencing it right now. The Yellow River is flooding, and Heaven and Hell's policies are forcing me to get involved in politics again. Meanwhile, I'm pretty sure the devils have been tampering with my edict system."

The Jade Emperor shook his head. "You know I can't budge on this. My hands are tied. Not only are Heaven's policies good for Heaven, but if I don't do this, my senior statesmen will push for Heaven to go on the ten-thousandth-and-eighty-third crusade against the devils. I absolutely loathe our two-party system sometimes."

Seeing Yama's downcast expression, the Jade Emperor's softened his stance.

"I can lend you Fuxi for some pro-bono work," the Jade Emperor conceded. "Maybe he can think of something that will increase the efficiency of the Yellow River system as a whole."

"Thanks for doing what you can," Yama said. "The fate of the universe is at stake. Don't worry, I'll let you know as soon as I catch a whiff of your daughter."

After exchanging a few more pleasantries, the Jade Emperor left. Yama's gaze wandered over to Iron Planet, where his two assistants were hard at work. He hoped he was reading too much into the situation. As the CEO of Samsara Incorporated, he was karmically responsible for the actions of his employees.

Chapter 1: Kindness

A fresh spring wind blew past Cha Ming as he meditated in a forest clearing. He was surrounded by five energy-gathering formations that were slowly but surely bolstering his cultivation. High-grade spirit stones were rapidly ground to dust as the energy in his body intensified. He wasn't short on cash like before—the money he'd left in Wang Jun's care had already netted him a tidy profit.

The five-element qi circulated through his body before entering his dantian, where a small cracked core was greedily absorbing energy. The process was extremely inefficient; a third of what poured in leaked outward and had to be reabsorbed once more.

Cha Ming let out a deep sigh, exhaling all sorts of impurities from his body. Then, he directed his attention to a nearby cave, where his three prospective disciples were eliminating a group of devilish cultivators.

One of the disciples, Zi Long, wielded a large purple staff. He used a familiar style, one inspired by the many pointers Cha Ming had given him. Unlike his teacher, however, he didn't use soul pearls to complement it. Instead he used his qi to incorporate more lethal moves into his arsenal of staff arts and movement techniques. He used talismans to jam his opponents' movements and deflect incoming attacks.

Yue Bing, on the other hand, used a completely different style.

She wielded a sword with deadly grace while using her qi to bolster her movements and entrap her foes. Her defensive swordsmanship incorporated offensive talismans to make up for her deficiencies. She danced between Zi Long and their enemies, using his strong battlefield presence as a springboard. The duo worked in tacit understanding to fight off most of the weaker devilish cultivators.

While his two companions focused on the small fries, Ling Dong fought against the leader and elites. He used Earth Wall Talismans to lock himself and his enemies within a large cage. His qi covered him in a five-element shield as he slashed away with his heavy saber. One gash after another covered his refined body as he fought. He ignored these nonlethal injuries while trading blows with his enemies, whittling down their qi before cleaving through their defenses.

"Why us?" the leader said as his last elite fell. "There are plenty more out there who've done worse than us."

"They'll get what's coming to them," Ling Dong said. "You can ask them when you meet each other in the Yellow River."

Seeing that his defeat was inevitable, the leader burnt his blood essence. His strength surged by a half rank as he abandoned all defenses to concentrate his energy in a single strike. Ling Dong crumbled a defensive talisman, and an icy shield deflected the enemy's sword. He then cleaved down with his greatsword, cutting the man's body in half.

His enemy defeated, he banished the earthen walls and climbed out from the makeshift cage. He was greeted by Yue Bing, who immediately got to work healing the many gashes on his bare chest. Unbeknownst to them, jade merit poured into them as the ochre glow surrounding the devilish cultivators dissipated.

"Where to next, fearless leader?" Zi Long said as he wiped the blood off his staff. After recording their kills on a jade slip, he rapidly burned the corpses. A wicked stench filled the air as they turned to ashes.

Ling Dong winced in pain as a dreadful cut on his arm stitched itself together under Yue Bing's careful guidance. "We still have four more missions. We'll finish two of them on our way to the Western

Wall, and the final two on the other side. My goal is for us to finish them within two weeks' time."

"Two weeks?" Zi Long complained. "You're such a slave driver."

"If we're lucky, we can catch them before they hurt anyone else," Ling Dong said. "The kingdom didn't issue these missions because they were lazy, they issued them because there's a lot of work to do, and there are people dying every moment. It's worth it to go the extra mile, even if that means we suffer extra injuries in the process."

"I think the kingdom had more than efficiency in mind," Zi Long said, shaking his head. "They could have solved these small problems by dispatching core-formation cultivators, but they've sent us out instead. These missions were issued to have us personally witness these atrocities and grow closer as a country. Strong cultivators will emerge from the survivors and become our new foundation in the war against the south."

"I wish I was half as smart as you," Yue Bing said. "Or half as brave as Ling Dong," she added. "Truth be told, I'm extremely scared to be out here. My dream is to help people, not kill them."

"Sometimes, it's one and the same," Ling Dong said, inspecting the arm she'd just healed. "In fact, healing the righteous will bring harm to sinners. You're a vital party of this team, Yue Bing, and don't you forget it."

"You shouldn't fight so recklessly," Yue Bing huffed. "It's very draining to heal such deep wounds."

The two men laughed and allowed her to work in peace.

Cha Ming retrieved his resplendent force as the trio set off. According to his calculations, these four additional missions would grant them merit glow. After that, they would be ready to accept Fuxi's legacy.

He brushed himself off before walking through the forest at a leisurely pace. Every so often, he discovered ripe medicinal herbs and other oddities. He encountered no beasts as he traveled. They were subconsciously repelled by his presence.

As he walked, Cha Ming's features slowly changed. His steps became short and labored, and his hair turned gray. His face morphed and became covered in wrinkles. His clothes became nothing more than rags. Finally, he slashed his side open and allowed blood to soak the rags he wore. He collapsed a short distance away from the traveling trio.

Yue Bing sighed in exhaustion as they walked toward their next destination. Despite her minimal combat participation, the healing that came afterward thoroughly drained her. It was something that couldn't be recovered with cultivation—only sleep would make her feel refreshed, despite her peak-qi-condensation cultivation.

A cry rang out overhead as an eagle swooped down and perched itself on Zi Long's arm. His contracted spirit beast cooed softly before opening its beak expectantly. Zi Long fed it pieces of smoked meat, which it greedily gobbled down before flying off once more.

"Ziying says there's a wounded man up ahead," Zi Long said. "He doesn't think it's a trap, and there are no other cultivators for several miles."

"We should take a look," Ling Dong said, shrugging. "Maybe we'll be able to help someone in passing."

They ran down the road until they saw an unconscious man wearing nothing more than rags. He didn't even have a bag of holding—his only possession was a third-grade spirit sword, which was fastened to his thin body with a hempen rope.

Yue Bing rushed toward the man and infused green runes into his body. The gash on his abdomen gradually began to close under her supervision. It then stubbornly refused to heal any further, despite her intervention, continuing to leak blood onto the forest floor.

He's only at the sixth level of qi condensation, she thought. *Why would such a weak man be wandering out here, where even the weakest beast could kill him in a few exchanges?*

The results of his expedition were self-evident. If he didn't get proper healing soon, he would die of blood loss. She looked at the man uncertainly before firming her resolve.

There's still one thing I can do, she thought. *But who would have thought the first time I would use it would be with a stranger?*

She took out a golden ankh, a relic she'd inherited from the family she never knew. As she began pouring qi into the mystical object, Ling Dong grabbed her wrist.

"Are you sure he's worth it?" he asked. "He could be a complete scumbag for all we know."

"There's only one way to find out," Yue Bing said coolly. "And this isn't your decision to make."

"Carry on, then," Ling Dong said, releasing her wrist. "It's your life."

As he walked away, Yue Bing focused on the mystical runic characters on the golden ankh. It was only after she'd met her teacher that she finally understood what they meant. Her spiritual force and qi traced the runes, and so too did her life force.

A bloody glow encompassed the ankh as her blood coursed through it. The wounded man stirred uncomfortably as she worked.

Perhaps he's not so far gone, she thought as she stopped pouring in life force. She then took the ankh in both hands and uttered an incantation.

Bloody light flowed into the man, and the gash on his torso vanished. Color returned to his face as he woke. His eyelids fluttered, and an intense spiritual force covered the three. Before Yue Bing knew what happened, her surroundings changed, and she was now in an open meadow.

"That was a very kind thing you did," a voice said. "But you should care more for your life, or you'll find yourself with very little time remaining."

Yue Bing turned around and saw an older man dressed in a regal robe. His eyes contained a piercing jade glow that shone far brighter than her teacher's purple-and-green irises. A golden sword hung at his waist, and his gray hair was tied in a knot like a Confucian scholar.

"This junior greets senior," Yue Bing said, moving quickly to bow. The man suddenly appeared before her and stopped her midway.

"I can't bear my savior abasing herself in such a way, especially after she's lost so much," the man said. He reached out with his bony hand and pulled a few strands of gray hair from her head for her to see. She gasped when she saw them. "Your ankh is powerful; it can make you an unprecedented healer, but it can also drain you dry if you try to heal someone beyond your capabilities."

Yue Bing gulped. "I'll be more careful in the future."

"Then I am relieved," the man said. Then, he tapped his finger on Yue Bing's forehead. A stream of information poured into it, and an aged voice whispered inside her mind.

Devil-Sealing Scripture
A single scripture to seal all evils in the realms.
Can you see what I see with these eyes of pure jade?
Only those who share my will can understand my resolve.

She felt a sharp, debilitating pain in her eyes. It felt like a thousand needles were blinding and piercing them simultaneously.

"The pain only comes once, when the technique confirms that you've slain a devil," the man said. "From now on, you'll be able to see merit and sin as well as angelic and devilish endowment. Beware the color ochre."

Then, as suddenly as the pain had come, it vanished. Yue Bing gently opened her eyes and saw an entirely different landscape. The meadow was gone, and two jade-colored figures approached her position in the spirit woods from a distance.

"Yue Bing?" a familiar voice asked. Both Zi Long and Ling Dong walked out of the woods wearing relieved expressions. "What happened? Where did you go? Where's the old man?"

"You wouldn't believe me even if I told you," Yue Bing said, rubbing her eyes. Despite having exhausted her energy healing the man, she now felt fully invigorated. Her qi seas were full, and her body felt spry and refreshed. She reached beside her ear excitedly but was disappointed to discover a few strands of gray hair.

Did I go too far? Cha Ming thought as he reviewed the sequence of events. If he'd known about the ankh, he'd have played his cards differently. *How are things on your side?* he sent to Huxian as he followed the trio.

Things are productive but worrisome, Huxian said. *There are many fiendish demons on the mountain, so we're on our way to find the source.*

Fiendish demons? Cha Ming asked.

They're like devils, but they're demons instead of humans, Huxian replied. *Saint beasts occupy the other end of the spectrum. Both are very rare—demons prefer to stay neutral.*

Cha Ming observed his students as the three defeated another group of devilish cultivators. Then, under Yue Bing's guidance, they saved the prisoners and defeated the disguised wind devil using fire-affinity talismans. Due to her disproportionate contribution, her merit increased until it condensed in a light-jade glow around her, making her the first to succeed in the trial he'd set for them.

I felt you giving the Devil-Sealing Scripture to someone earlier, Huxian said. *Who was it?*

It was Yue Bing, Cha Ming said. *I like her personality the most. I admire her kindness, though she's a little bit naïve. In a way, she reminds me of myself.*

I like Yue Bing, Huxian said. *She always pets me. By the way, what do you think of the diagram we got when our Devil-Sealing Scripture broke through to the third stage? Do you think you can build it?*

Cha Ming shook his head. *It'll take ten thousand years. We just don't have that much time. Other than that, I'd need to build a massive grand formation with a central node and twelve peripheral nodes.* He shook his head. *Somehow, I can't shake the feeling that I've seen the formation before.*

Maybe you have ancestral memories like me! Huxian exclaimed.

I don't think that's the case, Cha Ming said. *I'm human through and through. Perhaps I've just seen something similar. Even a cultivator's mind can play tricks on them.*

Cha Ming's watched the trio for two more days. They finished the last of their missions within the Song Kingdom before proceeding to the Western Wall's fortress. They didn't linger long before entering the wilderness.

They're in your territory now, Cha Ming said to Huxian. *Take good care of them, but don't coddle them.*

No problem, Huxian sent back.

Satisfied with how things were going, Cha Ming flew over to the Western Wall. He used a different entrance than his students, one that led him directly to the main fortress.

A man with a billowing black-and-gold cape welcomed him. "You're always hiding and never come to drink with your old friends," Feng Ming said as Cha Ming landed.

"I'm just too busy," Cha Ming said. "Cultivation and developing professions are both very time consuming. I'm not like you, a freak who can stumble forward without even trying."

"Let's be fair, I've had my share of difficulties," Feng Ming said.

Remembering that the man's father had passed away recently, Cha Ming could only nod and follow Feng Ming into the fortress.

"This time I'm supervising a few juniors near the walls as they exterminate some aggressive demons," Cha Ming said. "Will it be a problem to grant me gate access in case I need to leave quickly?"

"Not at all," Feng Ming said, tossing him a black token. "In the meantime, I need your help with something."

The black-armored man led Cha Ming down a series of corridors to a shimmering blue shield.

"During my time in this fortress, I discovered that the Western Wall used to be known as the Westvale Wall. It's a transcendent treasure that predates the Song Dynasty. I stumbled upon this shield through sheer luck. This blue shield has a flaw in it, and it's coincidentally the entrance to a command center not unlike the one at Southhaven Fortress."

They crossed the shimmering blue barrier, and an immaculate room filled with various empty projections surfaced. A thin sheet of blue material with white lines was sprawled on the table. Cha Ming was amazed to discover that it contained an intricate runic diagram that exceeded his comprehension. Here and there, small pieces were highlighted with yellow coloring.

"Where did you find this?" Cha Ming asked.

"When I entered the room, the system came to life for a brief moment," Feng Ming explained. "Using the last of its energy, it materialized this runic diagram. I can't understand any of it, but I figured you could."

"It's a blueprint," Cha Ming said, looking it over carefully. "A blueprint of the chamber we're in. It's the most complex formation diagram I've ever seen. In fact, I feel like just reading this for a few days will help me break through to grandmaster level in formation and talisman arts."

"Lucky," Feng Ming said. "Can you fix it?"

Cha Ming stared hard at the white lines and glanced at the yellow portions. He then walked over to a corner of the room and formed some hand seals, which revealed complex white lines on the walls. Only the lines highlighted in yellow were missing.

Thinking for a moment, Cha Ming summoned his Clear Sky Brush and poured creation qi and pure liquified elemental essence into it. Then, seeing that the white coloring of his own ink wasn't as intense as that of the wall, a thought occurred to him.

Cha Ming's mental avatar appeared in the Clear Sky World and walked over to the seven pools of elemental essence he had created. Then, he withdrew a small glob of each of the five element pools and tossed them together. They didn't mix and remained in their own separate compartments.

Not willing to admit defeat, he grabbed a glob of wind essence and tossed it into the pile. To his surprise, the five pools didn't merge, rather they separated. The elemental essence began transferring from one pool to the other as though guided by the wind essence, slowly forming a white circle. Wood fed fire, which birthed earth, gold, water, and back to wood once more.

This cycle repeated itself twelve times before the five pools suddenly glowed white and combined into a large pool of the purest white ink he had ever seen. Despite its liquid appearance, Cha Ming could sense a billowing breeze hidden deeply within it.

"I'll call it creation essence," Cha Ming thought out loud.

He then repeated the same process with five-element essence and lightning essence. This time, a black star cycle formed, and after twelve revolutions or sixty transfers, it condensed into a small black pool.

"And this one is destruction essence." The destruction essence gave him a peculiar feeling. This ink could never make a talisman or formation—it could only destroy.

Cha Ming awoke from his trance to a bored-looking Feng Ming. He rapidly summoned the entire pool of creation essence and completed a few dozen white strokes. The glowing white lines snapped into place beside the older ones and formed a seamless whole. The blueprint on the table glowed slightly. The yellow lines Cha Ming had corrected had turned white.

"It looks like I can fix it," Cha Ming said cautiously, "but I'm going to need a *very* large amount of elemental evanescence and liquified elemental essence."

"How much are we talking?" Feng Ming asked.

"One million two hundred thousand jin of liquified elemental essence and twenty jin each of wood, fire, earth, gold, water, and wind evanescence," Cha Ming said after reviewing the blueprint. "And I'm not even taking a commission."

Feng Ming hissed through his teeth. "That's an enormous sum of money for such a small kingdom. How confident are you?"

"I'm one hundred percent confident I can fix the runic lines," Cha Ming said. "The real question is, do you feel lucky?"

Feng Ming thought for a moment before nodding. "I'll get you that elemental essence. You can count on it."

Chapter 2: Valor

Large obsidian rocks crumbled to powder under Huxian's heavy paws as he and his two friends made their way up a large black mountain. Not a single living thing could be seen in this ravaged land. Streams of lava burned deep canyons into the mountainside as they meandered up its steep slopes.

Have you spotted anything on the lower half? Huxian asked as he continued his arduous climb. Lei Jiang was lazily seated on his back, occasionally sending out bolts of lightning to deflect rocks that flew toward them from the peak.

Negative, Silverwing said. *I can't fly any higher because of the clouds.*

Likely demon-bone ash, Huxian said. *Even the lava's been manufactured. This mountain isn't a volcano—it's a lair that's been camouflaged as one. Come back down. I'll get us through this smoky mess.*

Silverwing let out one last cry before landing on Huxian's back. He shrunk his size down until he was a dozen feet wide, which was a pittance compared to the fox's enormous three-tailed frame. Lei Jiang was perched between his large ears. He looked around the mountain with great interest.

Huxian's Eyes of Pure Jade and Demon-Subduing Eyes were both active. A subtle purple and ochre glow emanated from the peak of the mountain through the ash-gray clouds. As they climbed, the glow grew stronger, and a malevolent and wild presence sought to repulse them during every inch of their climb.

Soon they crossed the clouds and arrived at the peak, revealing a plateau obscured by a thick smog. But Huxian was unfazed, as his eyes could see through this deception. They trudged along for a quarter mile before the smoke vanished and revealed a ring of lava, which occasionally spewed excess liquid through channels that led to the mountain below. And within this ring stood a lush island, which could only be accessed by a lone black bridge.

As they approached the bridge, a gigantic phantom appeared before them. It was a bloody, four-headed black dog with fierce ochre eyes and sharp white teeth. "Who dares to intrude upon this mountain without invitation? What brings you to this place?"

Huxian grinned. "We heard that the monarch here was fierce and without equal. We're beasts who like a challenge. That is, unless you're afraid to accept."

The four-headed hound looked Huxian and his two helpers up and down. Huxian was currently disguised as a red-and-white three-tailed fox.

"You must be that bitch's pup," the four-headed dog snorted. "She killed my son when he was trying to steal you in your crib. It seems you were lucky to survive. Are you angry? Do you want revenge?"

Huxian felt a small flame grow within his chest. He violently suppressed it with Devil-Sealing Intent. "You sure can talk a lot for an apparition. So, are you letting us in or not?"

The four-headed dog looked at them uncertainly. "Your offer of flesh and blood is acceptable," it said. "You'd make excellent fiendish demons. But are you sure you want to commit suicide after your mother died to protect you?"

"Cut the crap. Are you accepting or not?" Huxian barked.

"Of course I accept," the apparition said, snorting. "But you need to come in with your two friends. When it comes to parties, the more the merrier."

Huxian hesitated but nodded. "It's a deal."

The three-tailed fox, a falcon, and a mouse crossed the black bridge and entered the woods. A poisonous miasma oozed out from the lava toward them, herding them to the center of the island.

As they ventured deeper, the woods thinned. The trees, which had originally been lush and vibrant, became barren and dry. The leaves beneath them crumbled to dust as Huxian's mighty paws swept across them.

They made their way to a pond in the center of the island, which was filled with black blood containing purple and ochre specks Once they arrived at its shore, a golden contract with black writing burst out from it. It was written in the ancient beast language and contained the terms of their duel. As per the ancient rules, the losers of the battle would be devoured by the winners.

Huxian and the two others sent out a drop of blood toward the contract, which burned with intense purple light. A drop of black blood flew from the pond and entered the contract as well, glowing for a moment before disappearing in a puff of smoke. Then, the blood pond rippled. It grew and grew until it formed a massive four-headed hound. It was a late-core-formation creature, significantly more powerful than the three of them.

"Any last words?" the four heads said simultaneously.

"Yeah," Huxian said. "Now!"

His fur suddenly shifted to black and white, and his three tails lit up with three stars. Domains of devouring and purification were overlaid with the stronger domains of swamp and lightning and the weaker supporting domain of wind. Two of the stars were connected to Huxian's two friends via a gray tether.

"If you think that's enough, you're horribly mistaken," the four-headed hound said. Its four heads roared simultaneously, causing the three of them to shiver down to their bones. Their surroundings began dissolving, flowing back into the bloody black pool. The hound's power was corrosion. It was also clear why the hound wanted all three of them to enter at once—it wanted to catch them all in a dragnet and overwhelm them with its superior power.

Fortunately, Huxian and his friends were playing the pig to catch the tiger. Huxian sent both his friends a silent message, and their eyes glowed jade and purple simultaneously. They combined the thick Devil-Sealing, Demon-Subduing Intent they'd accumulated through killing thousands of fiends. The hound's abilities were reduced by a full sub-realm down to the middle of core formation.

"How can this be?" the four-headed hound roared. "There are only three foxes in the Bagua lineage. How could a fourth suddenly appear?"

Four sets of teeth tried to devour them, but with every exchange, a piece of the fiendish demon's energy was absorbed by Huxian's devouring domain. They howled in agony as they perished, leaving behind only a pond of black blood containing the purest, most concentrated fiendish energy Huxian had ever seen.

A black-and-white funnel appeared over the pond. It lapped up the black blood, purifying its corruption and feeding the refined energy into the three demons. Their bones crackled as they rapidly broke through to early core formation to match Silverwing.

"It's a good thing we managed to get him to sign a dueling contract," Huxian said. "Otherwise more than half of this energy would have gone to waste."

"Boss is definitely the smartest," Lei Jiang said as he absorbed the last of his portion. "Though, I'm a little concerned. I'm already an early-core-formation beast, but I still haven't grown in the slightest. My largest size is still six feet long."

"Maybe you won't grow bigger." Huxian shrugged. "At least you'll be used to your size when you obtain your human form. Silverwing and I will have a really hard time adapting."

Looks of longing appeared in their eyes. They couldn't wait to exit the wilds and interact in cities. Most importantly, once they achieved a human form, their fear of walls would completely disappear. No one could stop them then.

Suddenly, Huxian's ears perked up. "Oh? They're in danger? Let's head out."

The three of them jumped off the black mountain, whose cloud of smoke was dissipating and whose lava was growing hard. They ran twenty miles in a few breaths and stopped a short distance away from three humans who were surrounded by twenty fiendish wolf demons. Their leader was an initial purification beast, a very difficult challenge for them to face alone.

"Let's see how they handle this," Huxian said, lounging on a small outcropping.

Ling Dong, Zi Long, and Yue Bing clashed frantically with the pack of demonic wolves, carefully keeping their backs to each other as they defended against their insidious tactics. Ling Dong smashed down lightly with his heavy sword as a wolf bit toward them, not daring to overextend and fall into their trap.

"I'll create an opening for you to escape," Ling Dong said. "You two are the fastest, and if I stall, you both stand a good chance at escaping."

"We can't leave you," Yue Bing said as she threw out a fire talisman toward another wolf, singing its fur. "How could we ever face Teacher if we did?"

"Silly!" Ling Dong said. "Teacher will understand. Am I the leader, or was that all for show? Zi Long, make us a plan."

Zi Long didn't need to be reminded. His mind raced, computing the various possibilities. "I have a plan, and it gives me and Bing Er a six-out-of-ten chance to live. Since many of the beasts will be distracted, you might have a one-in-a-hundred chance of surviving, but that's being optimistic."

Yue Bing glared daggers at Zi Long as he logically broke down the situation.

"Brother Long, you never let me down," Ling Dong said, laughing. "All right, we'll follow this plan. Don't save your talismans, not even the ones Teacher gave us before we left. I know that magic talismans are precious, but they're only worth money. They can't replace a life. Let's go!"

Despite her misgivings, Yue Bing joined Zi Long in throwing out constricting talismans and techniques. Shards of ice and vines appeared around them and entrapped their foes. The wolves howled as they pounced toward them, only to be stopped by walls of earth and Ling Dong's powerful body. He stood his ground and hacked at whichever beast tried to pass him with his mighty blade.

"Run!" he yelled, not daring to look back.

Zi Long and Yue Bing broke away with ten fiendish wolves in tow. Their leader and ten others were trapped behind Ling Dong, whose impressive defense kept them at bay. His bones creaked with each clash, but he used the heavy blade to his advantage, felling the weaker wolves one after another. He constantly used Earth Wall Talismans to delay them. The larger wolf, fed up with his antics, finally pounced on Ling Dong with the intent of finishing him off.

Seeing the wolf jump toward him, Ling Dong activated his Five-Element Shield Technique and barely managed to resist. A massive blade mark appeared on the wolf's fur, but it barely cut an inch deep before stopping.

The other wolves surrounded him and nipped at his heels as the large wolf circled him. It was only now that he got a good look at them. They weren't like spirit wolves or dire wolves. Rather, their mouths were much larger and their paws more impressive. Their frames were skeletal, and their eyes glowed with a subtle ochre glow. They looked less likes wolves and more like devilish creatures from fairy tales, evil beings whose sole purpose in life was to devour and destroy.

"Just what are you?" he muttered as he batted away one wolf after another. He didn't rush the fight—every second stalled for was a second bought for his companions. Fortunately, whatever creature the demonic wolf had become hadn't lost its fighting instincts. Wolves were cautious, tactical creatures by nature. They would trip him up and grind him down as they waited for an ideal opportunity.

Suddenly, he felt a tug as a wolf bit into his leg. It barely managed to pierce his flesh, but this delay was all the wolves needed. They cackled as they pounced on him all at once, their leader playing the main role in this offensive. Ling Dong grinned maniacally and withdrew a golden talisman, the single protective treasure their teacher had gifted them.

"Just a single least-grade magic treasure," Ling Dong muttered under his breath. "Why did you have to be so cheap? Aren't you a mighty core-formation cultivator?"

The talisman burned away as he poured his soul force into it. As he did, the world turned golden. The wolves' movements turned sluggish and unpracticed. Meanwhile, Ling Dong's senses became quick and calculated. His blade felt incomparably sharp. He wasted no time in rushing toward the larger wolf. His blade carved through its gigantic black body like a knife through hot butter. The wolf's corrupted entrails spilled out as he cleaved through and hacked another wolf in the process.

Ling Dong used his enhanced senses to systematically cut down each and every one of them in as little time as possible. They turned to flee once they realized their leader had fallen, but it was too late.

Ling Dong threw out Earth Wall Talismans and trapped them before finishing them off like fish in a barrel. Then, the golden glow faded. Exhaustion overwhelmed him as he realized that the talisman had pushed him to the peak and suppressed his opponents to bare minimum performance.

There's no way that was only a least-grade magic treasure, he thought as his consciousness faded.

As if Brother Cha Ming would only give them a weak magic talisman, Huxian thought as he walked to Ling Dong. His tails billowed as he approached the young man that hovered on the fine line between sleep and wakefulness. He resembled a fierce Godbeast that could trample mountains and open seas.

"Silly fool," he said. "You know that with your power, you could have escaped instead of your friends. Why didn't you leave?"

Ling Dong's eyes opened slightly as he chuckled hoarsely. "But would that have been a life worth living?" he said.

Huxian grinned. "That's right, it wouldn't. I like your attitude, young pup. You're brave like a tiger and faithful like a fox. For that, I'll give you a gift."

A small black-and-white ball inscribed with purple and jade runes tumbled to the ground just in front of Ling Dong's mouth. The young man hesitated before ultimately eating the strange pill. As soon as he did, his eyes glowed jade and purple as he acquired both the Devil-Sealing Scripture and the Demon-Subduing Eyes. Then, he closed his eyes and fell asleep.

"Are you sure it's a good idea to gift him the Demon-Subduing Eyes?" Lei Jiang asked as he ran up beside Huxian.

"If it was a normal situation, I wouldn't," Huxian said gravely. "A human with those eyes would hold an unreasonable advantage over all of beastkind. However, how long will we remain on this mortal plane? Even fiendish demons have set their eyes on this meaningless mass of land. The humans and demons will have to band together for survival. Even then, who knows how many will survive?"

"Shouldn't you just gift them to demons?" Silverwing squawked.

"And then what?" Huxian said. "Should I give them to someone like the Bear Sovereign, who was willing to betray his people for power? Or to the geomantic boa, whose greed knows no bounds? We entered a dueling contract with a fiendish demon, but you have no idea what they're capable of. They aren't just contagious—they're conniving and seductive. They target a demon's base instinct, and it's something that the mediocre bloodlines of this realm can't resist."

He looked toward the Silverwing Mountain Range in the distance. "The Owl Monarch was willing to bet the future of his people on humanity. I'm just doing more of the same."

An awkward pause ensued. "Boss, aren't you only a few years

old?" Lei Jiang said. "Why are you acting like an ancient, thousand-year-old demon?"

Tendrils of black and white mist reached out and muzzled him. The mouse struggled, but to no avail.

"It's all I can do…" Huxian said in a mystical voice. Although Silverwing felt nauseated, he said nothing. He was far wiser than his rodent counterpart.

Chapter 3: Justice

How are those younglings coming along?" Wang Jun asked as he poured tea for two. The green-clothed man looked substantially more relaxed than a few months ago, largely due to his rapidly increasing fortune.

"You realize we're only a few years older than them, don't you?" Cha Ming said. "Technicalities aside, they're coming along well. From what Huxian tells me, two of them have already condensed merit glow, and the third is not far off. Once they are all successful, I can start teaching them Fuxi's legacy."

"Do you think they'll follow in your footsteps?" Wang Jun said.

"Doubtful," Cha Ming replied. "They've all picked a path that best suits their personality. Although I'll make sure they have a foundation in runic arts, I feel that Yue Bing will focus on healing and may dabble in alchemy, while Zi Long will likely to focus on staff arts, talismans, and formations. As for Ling Dong, I'm not too sure. He can make talismans well enough, but I don't think they suit him."

"Oh?" Wang Jun said, raising his eyebrow. "Then what's the point of teaching him Fuxi's legacy?"

"There are many ways to apply the runic arts," Cha Ming said. "Perhaps he'll learn combat formations, but I have a feeling he'll pursue an entirely different path. Only time will tell. How about you? How has your business been faring?"

"It's been doing very well," Wang Jun said. "The country is recovering swiftly, and the real estate investments are starting to pay off. I can't give you your money back yet, however. I've been using all available funds to acquire many key sectors needed for fulfilling my family's task. Soon, the Wang family will have a dominant position in every corner of the Song Kingdom."

"Take as long as you need," Cha Ming said, taking a sip. "Have you planned your journey to Gold Leaf City yet?"

"Only vaguely," Wang Jun said. "There are too many variables, too many changing conditions. Due to my impending return, my brother has begun to move aggressively on many fronts to lock me out of the market."

"I take it the family's leadership is chosen based on financial performance?" Cha Ming said.

"Current success is the best indicator of future success," Wang Jun said, shrugging. "To be honest, it's not my brother's legitimate financial activities that worry me. A little bird told me about some scattered Wang family business ventures in the south."

"The Wang family does business in the south?" Cha Ming said, frowning.

"Not officially," Wang Jun replied. "And that's what worries me. Hiding is my specialty, so I'm acutely aware of how effective clandestine operations can be. If these businesses are under my brother's control, things could get messy, and fast."

Cha Ming sank deep in thought as he nursed his cup of tea, heating it with qi whenever the temperature dipped below a certain point. Then Feng Ming walked in.

"To what do we owe the pleasure?" Wang Jun asked him as he served a third cup.

"I went treasure hunting and came back with some goodies," Feng Ming said, sitting down. He tossed a ring to Cha Ming, whose eyes widened when he saw the contents.

"So fast?" Cha Ming said. "I thought it would take months to put all this together."

"Fortunately, liquified elemental essence is easy to find, and evanescence is stockpiled by the royal family," Feng Ming said. "My father-in-law has been rather doting on his only daughter. And Prince Lei doesn't seem to mind now that Prince Tian is out of the picture."

"He's lost all motivation," Wang Jun said helplessly. "He helps me out when he can, but he's catching up on all his time away from his wife and kids. He told me he has no interest in the throne, and it can go to the king's grandkids for all he cares."

Feng Ming frowned. "Wait, is this why he started pushing us to have kids all of a sudden?"

Cha Ming laughed. "It's not so surprising. The king still has a few hundred years ahead of him. Why should he care about something like direct succession?"

"Fair enough," Feng Ming said, taking a sip and nodding appreciatively. "Now that the civil war is done, he can take his time in finding an heir and focus on the war to the south instead. Speaking of which, have you thought about my proposal?"

"I find the concept of defense contracting for the Song Kingdom intriguing," Wang Jun said. "Before we proceed any further, I want you to understand that mercenaries can only be so loyal to the kingdom. When it's the choice between their lives and their duty, they'll choose the former without hesitation."

"And that's why I only want year-long contracts," Feng Ming said. "Those who wish to remain on the payroll can join the army, and we have many ways to convince them otherwise once they join. For every mercenary who converts to the army, you'll get a hefty commission. Just think of this as unorthodox recruiting."

"If you're all right with that, I'll start laying the groundwork," Wang Jun said. "You'll need to handle army integration and joint operations, and I can take care of the rest."

"It's a deal," Feng Ming said, finishing his cup of tea. "Cha Ming, you have the goods. When you do you plan on starting the repairs?"

"I'm free right now," Cha Ming said, finishing his own cup. "My students are there, so it wouldn't hurt to work on it while they finish up."

"Well, don't feel obligated to keep me company," Wang Jun said.

"I may not be busy, but I'm not idle, either." The two men left Wang Jun to his afternoon appointments and a mountain of paperwork.

"Such an intricate and complex design," Cha Ming said as he painted what could have been the thousandth line. It was white and curved and connected two functional runes for power distribution and the wall's self-repair capabilities. There were no sudden changes when this line was completed; the formation was a closed circuit, and it wouldn't function until it fully mended.

Having depleted most of his mental energy, Cha Ming took out *Samsara*, Jun Xiezi's painting, and focused on replenishing it. He focused on the life-filled portion of the polarized painting and ignored the death-filled portion that would wear away at his soul. The dual mysteries of life and death eluded him as he watched, taunting him with the splendor inherent in the painting.

One thousand down, fifty thousand to go, Cha Ming thought.

He began painting once more while simultaneously studying the complex design. He focused on the smaller details first, and when he understood them, he linked them together. There was a logic to their structures, and although the rules weren't explicitly stated, they could be deduced with enough effort. As he painted, his repertoire grew from linking a few runes together to linking hundreds. His progress only slowed once he reached a thousand.

With every line he painted, he realized there were some mistakes in his original thinking. Every new insight allowed him to add more lines to the diagram in his mind. One thousand became one thousand and fifty, which soon turned to one thousand and seventy. The toll on his mind grew until he could no longer perform the repairs and could only sit in contemplation. A week passed before he finally opened his eyes.

"It wasn't one thousand and eighty like I thought it would be,"

Cha Ming muttered as he imagined the completed diagram. "But that all makes sense now. One hundred and eight is perfection, while twelve is just the beginning. Therefore, 120 runes are the foundation of core arrays, and these runes are connected with twelve hundred runic lines. As for Gong Lan's 10,080 rosary, that must be unique to the Buddhists."

After this sudden epiphany, he continued painting the remaining lines in the fortress. His progress was swift, as his soul had grown much more corporeal, and his resplendent vestment much brighter than before. Unknowingly, he had broken through to the middle of the resplendent soul realm.

Soon, he was finishing off entire walls. It wasn't long before he finished the final character on the final wall, causing the pattern to glow slightly before fading.

It's deficient in energy, Cha Ming determined. He tossed a pile of high-grade spirit stones onto a dedicated energy-gathering formation. It activated instantly, and white lines began glowing around the small mound of crystals. The lines expanded until they encompassed the entire command center.

Feng Ming walked into the room after sensing the disturbance. Projection screens and diagrams lit up wherever he looked, and on the table where the blueprints once lay, a different diagram appeared. It was a blueprint of the entire wall, whose runic lines were mostly destroyed. Despite this heavy damage, they were being rapidly regenerated, starting with those nearest to the central fortress.

"It should only take a day for the wall to completely recover," a voice said from behind them.

Both Cha Ming and Feng Ming were surprised to see a middle-aged man in strange robes. His hair was cropped short and his figure semitransparent.

"Are you the custodian of this place?" Cha Ming asked.

The man looked at him in surprise. "Yes, I was sent from a transcendent realm to preside over this fortress. How may I address these two masters?"

"Please call me Cha Ming, and this is Marshal Feng Ming," Cha Ming said. "Do you have any instructions for us?"

"None," the man said. "This fortress was sent down from the transcendent realms ten thousand years ago to defend the World Tree against a tide of fiendish demons. Once the fiends were defeated, the fortress's purpose was fulfilled. My instructions were to pass on command tokens to those with sufficient merit if the fortress was repaired in the future." He flicked out his sleeves and sent out blue tokens to the two of them. "What are your orders?"

"Are you able to help us against the current tide of fiendish demons?" Feng Ming asked. The custodian closed his eyes, and the view on the projection screen changed to that of the mountain range. Small ochre dots appeared near a large mountain.

"The fiendish demon origin has been defeated, so there is no need for me to intervene," the custodian said. "While I can prevent them from breaching the wall and can easily clear out all of the remaining fiendish demons, your juniors seem to have the situation under control."

"Then let's let them take care of it," Feng Ming said after thinking for a moment. "While some of them might die, we need to be strong to fight against the Southern Alliance."

"I'll leave these military matters to you," Cha Ming said. "Custodian, do you mind if I take a look at the fortress's array diagrams once more?"

"It's not a problem," the custodian said, summoning the blueprint. This time, it was a three-dimensional structure that could be manipulated at his leisure. "If either of you need anything, let me know." Then he vanished.

"So, was it worth it?" Cha Ming asked Feng Ming.

"We'll see," Feng Ming said. "I still need to evaluate its defensive measures, and I need to see if the wall can be integrated into the

Southhaven system. I know next to nothing about this type of mystical equipment."

"Let me know if you need any help," Cha Ming said. "I'll be studying this diagram in the meantime."

He had barely taken a few steps before he received a mental message from Huxian. "On second thought, I need to take care of something."

He swiftly disappeared from the room, leaving Feng Ming alone with the central display.

"They're in an interesting situation," Huxian said to Cha Ming as he flew up beside them. "I thought you'd like to see how they do." He and his two friends were eating large slabs of roasted meat. "Watching juniors fight against each other is the best."

"You know you're only a few years old, right?" Cha Ming said.

A few miles away from them, a group of peak-qi-condensation cultivators were fighting against a larger group. From what he could tell, one group had discovered a valuable medicinal root, while the other had attacked them out of jealousy. While there were no deaths yet, many of the cultivators had been grievously wounded.

Meanwhile, his three students were rapidly approaching the two groups. Cha Ming noticed that although Zi Long hadn't yet condensed a merit halo, he had already advanced to foundation establishment before the others. His foundation consisted of five pillars, surrounded by five qi seas, but in between these seas, wisps of black and white had begun to accumulate.

"Interesting," Cha Ming said, taking out one small cup and three big ones. He filled his own with a peculiar blend of Pu Er tea while he filled the others with Demon Soothing Tea. "Let's see how they choose."

"There's a fight up ahead," Zi Long said as they abruptly changed course. He used his aura to repel many lesser beasts as they moved through the forest. "There they are," he said as he landed. The three walked toward a large group of people. Half a dozen cultivators were huddled in a tight circle with their backs to the center while twenty ragtag cultivators encircled them.

"You'd better hand over the Foundation Spirit Root," an ugly man covered in scars said to the smaller group. "Even foundation-establishment experts would fight over such a treasure. Do you really think you're worthy of it?"

A younger man leading the smaller group gritted his teeth before pulling out an orange root. It was brimming with heaven and earth qi, to the point that it made Zi Long's heartbeat quicken.

Should we take it? Ling Dong said. *It's not a treasure either of their groups can protect.*

Zi Long pondered the matter before entering the fray. He walked slowly as he expanded his aura, causing the aggressive group to cower in fright as the purple-robed man walked toward the central group. "Thank you for finding the root for us," he said, holding out his hand. "I'll be delivering what I promised once we return to Songjing."

The leader of the smaller group gulped. His hand trembled as he reached out and placed the orange root in Zi Long's hand. The purple-robed man looked behind him toward the ruffians.

"They didn't cause you any trouble, did they?" asked Zi Long.

"It's nothing worth concerning yourself over," the leader said, gritting his teeth.

The leader of the bandits is an atrocious excuse for a human being, Ling Dong sent from the outside of the encirclement. *Just how many atrocities did he commit to accumulate so much sin?*

I'm more concerned about the woman beside him, Yue Bing said.

Yue Bing's eyes glowed with jade light as she inspected the beautiful lady. *She's different from the others. She glows ochre, much like the fiendish demons we've fought. The rest can leave, but those two should both stay.*

Zi Long's eyes narrowed. He looked to the bandit leader and his assistant coldly, and his figure blurred before appearing right next to the scarred man and the beautiful woman. He struck out with his purple staff, expertly slicing them both in two despite the staff's blunt nature. While the man's corpse fell to the ground, the woman's body disintegrated into sawdust. Their ochre and yellow auras dissipated and converted to merit, which joined together with Zi Long's and formed a jade glow surrounding him.

"The rest of you may leave," Zi Long said to the group. "I'd suggest you stop robbing people, or you'll end up like your two companions."

"Thank you for your mercy, Elder," the remaining eighteen cultivators said one by one, leaving behind their leaders' corpses. Only the six cultivators who'd gathered the spirit root remained. Zi Long tossed him the orange root before walking back to his companions.

The leader ran up to him, confused. "Many thanks for your assistance," he said. "We'd like to offer this spirit root in repayment."

Zi Long looked back and shook his head. "It's your root. I'm not a robber." Seeing the man glance uncomfortably toward the wall, he looked toward Ling Dong and Yue Bing, who gestured for him to do as he saw fit. "But it's a long way to the wall. How about this: My companions and I will accompany you there. In exchange, we'll take a quarter of the spirit root. The rest is yours."

Their leader let out a sigh of relief. "Then I, Ding Shen, am eternally grateful. Those bandits were right—it's not a treasure we can protect."

"It's not unusual for weaker people to hire mercenaries and guards," Zi Long said indifferently. "Just consider this a simple business transaction."

After cleaning up the battlefield, they left together toward the wall. They weren't bothered by man or beast, though several groups of adventurers didn't leave before probing their group for weaknesses. As for the others that didn't bother them, suffice to say that Huxian and his friends returned to the fortress with full bellies.

Yue Bing and Ling Dong closed themselves up in meditation soon after arriving, leaving Zi Long to guard them as they broke through to foundation establishment. He sat outside their rooms patiently, keeping a careful watch on his surroundings.

As the sun set, an aged figure in tattered clothes appeared in the fortress. He had a kindly expression and eyes that shone with pure jade. He slowly walked up to Zi Long, who opened his eyes as he approached.

"Teacher, are you not embarrassed when you wear such an obvious disguise?" Zi Long asked.

Cha Ming coughed awkwardly and quickly transformed to his normal appearance. Huxian also appeared beside him. "What gave me away?"

"You mean the random gestures of goodwill, and our eye colors suddenly changing to match yours?" Zi Long said. "Or maybe the fact that you happen to have a fox that has three tails accompany you everywhere?" He shook his head. "You really ought to put more effort into your disguises if you want to remain anonymous. Like that time when you planted the body-cultivation technique for Ling Dong. You made some mistakes, but it wasn't so blatant."

Cha Ming sighed and sent the Devil-Sealing Scripture into the air, which quickly shot into the man's glabella. Despite the immense pain in his eyes, Zi Long didn't even blink as they gained a jade coloring.

"You've proven to be a just man, and all three of you have accumulated merit halos. Since you've passed the test, you are now my disciples," Cha Ming said, tossing three jades to Zi Long. "Keep one for yourself, and give the other two to your disciple brother and sister. Come see me in Songjing once you're done here."

"What's inside it?" Zi Long asked as he dripped his blood on it.

"A foundation," Cha Ming said. "I'm not sure about Yue Bing and Ling Dong, but I'm confident you'll be able to fully learn everything on this jade slip. When the time comes, I'll give you another."

"Master, I have a question," Zi Long said. "Why are you being so nice to us when we haven't done anything for you?"

"The first reason is that I owe karma," Cha Ming said, chuckling. "As for the second reason... can you tell me why you protected those cultivators and didn't take their treasure? Or why Ling Dong was willing to sacrifice himself to save you? Or why Yue Bing is always willing to help strangers, even at the cost of her lifespan?"

Zi Long nodded slowly. Seeing that the younger man was itching to study the jade slip, Cha Ming chuckled and walked back to the command room to study the blueprint.

Chapter 4: Debt

Two thousand three hundred and forty-eight, two thousand three hundred and forty-nine... twenty-four hundred!" Cha Ming said as an assortment of runes and runic lines snapped together into a complete initial-grade core formation. He'd holed himself up at the Westvale Wall for two weeks to try and replicate its runic array diagrams. While they weren't very useful to him on their own, they were a convenient way to break through bottlenecks in runic arts. He was now much more confident in his ability to create core-grade formations and talismans.

After recovering his qi and stamina, Cha Ming pulled out three sheets of paper. He painted a Flow Talisman, a Matter Talisman, and a Shape Talisman. All three sheets were a mixture of light and dark colors, a harmony of creation and destruction. After completing them, he pulled out a batch of poetic talismans he'd produced earlier. He poured his emotions into them, and they transformed until they became mid-grade core talismans. His work complete, he summoned *Samsara* and used it to temper his soul and recover his soul force.

Life and death, Cha Ming thought as he observed the painting. *How can I possibly fathom life and death at my young age? Jun Xiezi could do it because of his long life, his experience, and his travels. Although I've been reborn once, it wasn't a true death. At most, it gives me insight into how the two are related.*

Seeing that he would achieve nothing on the road of life and death for the time being, he turned his attention to some verses brewing in his mind. He imagined fire embodied by kindling and dousing but couldn't put it into words. Was kindling embodied by joy? Or was it embodied by passion and love? And if so, wouldn't the opposite be heartbreak, misery, and depression? He had no desire to experience such things.

While he thought, he sensed movement in the fortress. *Are they already leaving?* he thought.

His three disciples, who were currently making their way to the gate, had all broken through to foundation establishment. They all had the same five elemental pillars and the same black-and-white mist hovering in their centers. In addition, Ling Dong had also broken through to initial bone forging.

How long do you need to clear the mountain range? Cha Ming asked Huxian as he brushed himself off.

We have three more mountains to explore, after which we'll go see the hole in the back, Huxian said. *But I have a bad feeling about it. I figure it will take us two weeks to uproot everything else before taking a peek.*

All right, Cha Ming sent back. *I'll be in Songjing tying up loose ends. Let me know if you need help.*

He packed his things and exited his chambers. He left the wall soon after alerting Feng Ming.

The breeze was significantly warmer than it was two weeks earlier. Spring was fading into summer, and farmers were busy sowing crops and tending to newborn cattle. Meanwhile, ducks were busy leading their young onto ponds and teaching them to swim. It was a race against time, as only the fittest would survive the journey south in the fall.

As he approached Songjing, things became increasingly lively. Farmers were busy buying and selling seed, and the first of the spring vegetables had made it to market. These were rapidly snatched up by customers who'd eaten nothing but rice, meat, and preserved vegetables for the past month. The apples and potatoes had long since run out.

Cha Ming walked through the city gates without much fanfare. After signing in, he walked straight to the Jade Bamboo Auction House and to Wang Jun's office. The door was open and ready for him, and tea had already been poured.

"Have your prophetic abilities improved?" Cha Ming asked as he sat down and grabbed a cup.

Wang Jun smiled. "I had a small breakthrough this morning. Much of what was unclear is no longer muddled, and I now have 100% assurance in completing my family's task. I'll return your spirit stones in a year." He took a sip from his cup. "I take it you'll be leaving in two weeks or so?"

"As soon as Huxian and his friends are done exploring the western mountains," Cha Ming said. "In the meantime, I'll help Feng Huoshan by teaching some classes before I leave. I'll be taking my three new apprentices with me."

"I told you they would pass," Wang Jun said. "But let's discuss urgent matters before pleasantries. I need you to pass along a message to Huxian. Tell him he can peek in the hole, but he must not set foot in it. There is an evil being slumbering there that exceeds my comprehension."

Cha Ming frowned but quickly passed on the message. "I've confirmed with him—he won't set foot in there." Seeing his friend relax visibly, he sipped his tea and moved on to the main reason he'd visited. "Have you looked into my request?"

"I'm afraid I can't help you," Wang Jun said. "Treasures that heal souls are extremely hard to come by, even in transcendent realms. We wouldn't be able to obtain one with all the wealth on the continent. But I did hear some good news from our patriarch. Every sixty years, the Alabaster Group sends out core-formation cultivators into a secret realm. They all return with extremely valuable treasures. While he isn't qualified to know much about it, perhaps Lu Tianhao in the Alabaster Group can help you."

"Thanks for looking into this," Cha Ming said. "A friend's life depends on it."

"Not a problem," Wang Jun said. "It's interesting to see that the patriarch is now willing to speak with me. Perhaps he's finally realized that I'm not a pushover."

They drank tea in silence for some time before Cha Ming straightened up and headed for the door.

"I'll come and see you before leaving," he assured him.

"You'd better," Wang Jun said. "It'll be years before we meet again."

Cha Ming traveled through the unusually hot city toward the Talisman Artist Guild's new location in Central Square. They had taken over one of the many abandoned storefronts and started a thriving business, catering to adventurers and the military. He walked through the storefront, whose shelves were now fully stocked with all types of talismans. Many of them had been provided by Cha Ming himself, and he was relieved to see that their popularity hadn't waned.

He passed through a door at the back and entered a special section of the building dedicated to Hua Dong's own brand of healing talismans. He smiled as he saw his friend's apprentices experimenting with cost-effective talismans that could compete with alchemical products and spirit-doctor medicine. The approach reminded him of Li Yin, who was now the kingdom's chief medical officer.

And like Li Yin's Royal Medical Office, Hua Dong employed mortals to complete ordinary tasks that otherwise wasted their artists' time. It was the beginning of a harmonious relationship between mortals and cultivators.

"You've finally come to pay us a visit," Feng Huoshan said as Cha Ming entered the main workshop and approached his workstation in the back. "How long has it been? A month?"

"Something like that," Cha Ming said. "In a couple of weeks, I'll be heading back to Quicksilver. It'll be quite some time before I come back." He took a seat in front of his friend, who smiled wistfully.

"What are your plans?" Feng Huoshan asked. "You're a popular teacher, so I hate to see you go. On top of that, you're the only one who teaches light and shadow talismans in both the Quicksilver Empire and the Song Kingdom. What will your students do?"

"I can only leave some instruction jades for them," Cha Ming said. "If they want to learn more, they'll have to go elsewhere. I have my own life to live, and I can't spend it chained to my students. As for everyone else? I'll be holding a ten-day lecture for everyone who wants to take part, including you, Hua Dong, and Luo Ming."

"What could you be lecturing on that would take so long?" Feng Huoshan said.

"Everything," Cha Ming said. "From start to finish, everything I've learned. Those who have too much sin need not attend. Whatever people can grasp is up to them. I'll start in three days."

"All right, I'll make it happen," Feng Huoshan said. "I'll let our clients know that we'll be closed for an unforeseen amount of time. Though, I'm sure the blacksmiths and many cultivators will want to attend."

"It will be an open lecture," Cha Ming said. "I'll teach anyone the venue can accommodate."

"Good, good," Feng Huoshan said. "Perhaps I can ask the king for funding. But before that, I have some doubts I'd like you to address." He took out a piece of paper containing the rough prototype of a talisman. "I've been giving a great deal of thought about fusing fire and earth talismans, and I think this one has potential. Can you spare a moment?"

"Sure," Cha Ming said. "Anything for a friend."

He spent hours discussing talismans with his first friend from Quicksilver. Three days passed by in a flash.

Cha Ming walked through the palace gates under escort of a royal guard. The black-armored man guided him to a large open courtyard where thousands of cultivators were seated in cultivation. Cha Ming thanked the man before walking onto a small stage at the front.

He looked over the audience, which was packed with professionals, both runic and otherwise, as well as young and old martial artists. Ling Dong, Zi Long, and Yue Bing sat at the front row with Feng Huoshan and many other master-level professionals. Many of the kingdom's top core-formation cultivators were also in attendance. Every cultivator bore not a trace of yellow sin—which wasn't surprising, given that he'd installed a formation to ward off evil not too long ago. Having confirmed this basic requirement, he began his lecture.

"Runic arts and martial arts," he said. "Is there a difference?" His voice projected directly to everyone's ears. He summoned the illusion of a scroll in the air, a replica of Three-Layered Burst Steps, a fire-based movement technique. He did the same with the remaining four elements as well as wind and lightning, light and shadow. Phantom cultivators appeared in the air and began displaying the elementary techniques.

"You can see the qi pathways being used by these phantoms, as well as the nodes they pass through, the meridians," Cha Ming said. "But if we twist these images, you'll see that our qi pathways resemble runic lines, and our meridians resemble focus points. By activating techniques, we become formations, and we channel runes. That is my understanding of martial arts."

The nine apparitions became transparent, leaving behind only the outlines of their utilized qi pathways. The lines shifted and contorted until they all became flat diagrams with twelve key points. Some of them had additional lines and extraneous points. Cha Ming erased these with a swish of his sleeve, and the diagrams shifted until they became basic runes.

"In qi condensation, we approximate runes," Cha Ming continued. "The more complex and appropriate the runes, the better the technique." The runes transformed and displayed many potential characters. Their complexity increased until they reached top-tier runes used in mortal-grade talismans. "To my knowledge, this is the limit of qi-condensation techniques."

"But as master artists, do we not use runes as nodes and join them together with formation lines? Why can't we do the same with our bodies and martial techniques?"

The characters multiplied, and many other characters appeared to complement them. Three-Layered Burst Steps sought to superimpose burst steps three times with explosive runes. The others also underwent similar transformations. "As the techniques progress through foundation establishment, the formations become increasingly intricate."

Lines were added on by the dozens, and the key runes went from twelve to twenty-four, from twenty-four to thirty-six, from thirty-six to seventy-two, and finally, from seventy-two to one hundred and eight. After this final transformation, they contorted and morphed, their lines curving in certain places and straightening in others.

Before long, they transformed into the original phantom cultivators. The transparent people's qi pathways were seemingly fully utilized and operating using their element's fundamental laws. The phantoms then flew up and began sparring against each other, displaying their movement techniques to their fullest. Water-based techniques moved smoothly while earth-based techniques moved stably and stiffly. The spar in the air continued for a few breaths before the phantoms dissipated.

"I confess: I do not know what happens in core formation," Cha Ming said. "I have an inkling, but I will display it near the end. Until then, I'll display every rune I know, followed by various ways of linking them into formations and techniques. I'll show you sigils and display runic diagrams with thousands of lines. Whatever inspirations you gain are yours and yours alone. All I ask is that you use them to fight against the south and protect your homeland."

Cha Ming then summoned a phantom brush in the sky and painted a simple character, which imprinted itself onto an illusory sheet of paper.

"The first character, mountain," he said before proceeding to the next one. No one dared look away as he demonstrated. As he painted, some people would gain immediate enlightenment while others achieved breakthroughs and perfected techniques. A few tried to persevere, aiming to absorb as much knowledge as possible to perfect their craft.

One by one, the people could no longer take the strain and sat in silent meditation. One by one, they sat down to collect their harvest. Soon, nine days had passed, and the only ones still watching were Feng Huoshan, some master professionals, and various core-formation cultivators.

At this point, Cha Ming began delving into the mysteries of the Westvale diagram and his speculations on core-formation runic arts.

The rocky ground crumbled to dust as Huxian crossed to the other side of the mountain. He was cautious, carefully flitting from shadow to shadow as he ventured toward the dark indentation in the ground. While it was day outside, the mountains prevented the sunlight from reaching the desolate area. Moss and fungus grew sparsely on the scattered remnants of trees that had tumbled down from the surrounding peaks. A poisonous miasma oozed from the swampy ground as he approached the gap in the landscape.

Are you all right, boss? Lei Jiang sent mentally.

I'm fine, Huxian replied. He'd left them behind for this scouting mission. Although he wasn't the fastest, his concealment abilities were the best in the group. Slowly but surely, he crept up to what seemed like a violet-and-ochre hole in the ground. As he drew nearer, he heard shallow but powerful breathing drawing in the nearby air. He heard no exhales.

How am I supposed to figure out what it is without seeing it? Huxian thought with disdain about Wang Jun's warning. What could a human know about demons? He inched toward the pit before finally seeing the tip of a black horn that blended in with the shadows.

No, that isn't right, Huxian thought as he observed it. *The shadows are blending into it.*

He observed it for a while longer before noticing that with every breath, the shadows quivered around the horn. Not only was the creature breathing in the air, but it was breathing in the shadows.

What could it be? Huxian thought, wracking his ancestral memories for details. Try as he might, he couldn't think of anything that was weak enough to be on a material plane but powerful enough to devour shadows. *Unless… could it be an egg or a baby?*

His heart skipped a beat as he thought of a possibility. Memories of a powerful eight-tailed fox and a painter surfaced in his mind. They were fighting a horned creature made of an empty void. Everything around it was being devoured, and despite their best efforts, the fox and the painter were at a disadvantage. They fought for centuries before finally calling the Jade Emperor, who joined forces with them and slew the creature.

How could this be? Huxian thought. *Even a transcendent plane can't contain such an evil being.*

He trembled as he approached the pit. It was a risky action, but he had to be sure. Horns appeared one after another, as did flimsy formation lines that had outlasted their usefulness. They were peak-core-grade formation lines that could seal away anything in a mortal realm for ten thousand years.

Ten thousand years, Huxian thought. *Isn't that how old the wall is? Didn't they say they'd defeated the fiendish demons?*

It suddenly occurred to him that the humans were simply ignorant. A newborn of this variety could swallow time itself for sustenance. How could sealing it for ten thousand years possibly kill it off? He crept a little closer, and the horns expanded as he approached until they finally joined together with a glistening black shell. The horns were protrusions, and the breathing was coming from the shell itself. It had no mouth. In fact, its entire *being* was a mouth. After confirming this point, Huxian backed off as silently as demonically possible.

"How did it go?" Silverwing asked as Huxian appeared beside his companions.

"We need to get strong, and fast," Huxian said solemnly as they retreated. "Once that thing hatches, the entire continent—no, the entire plane—is doomed."

Chapter 5:
The Red Dust Pavilion

Hong Xin looked out the window into the courtyard, which was filled with students of the Red Dust Pavilion. Several of them played instruments while others danced. Others practiced their posture while a few even played *Angels and Devils*. Laughter filled the courtyard despite the chilly wind from the north. It was a paradise, a dream she wished she'd never wake from.

"When do you think they'll see us?" a girl asked.

Her name was Bai Ling, and she was only a year younger than Hong Xin. She and several other girls were waiting in comfortable accommodations for the biannual recruitment event. Each of them possessed superior charm, grace, and disposition.

"It should be any day now," Ji Bingxue said. Her skin was fair as snow and her voice pleasant like a songbird's. "They always hold it within three days of the fourth moon of the year, when hope fills the air and the cold weather begins to fade away."

"I can't wait for summer to come again," Bai Ling said longingly. "I've had enough of this winter."

Hours passed as they waited patiently. That afternoon, the silence of their accommodations was broken by gentle footsteps and the careful sliding of their living room door. A beautiful woman who appeared to be in her midtwenties entered the room. She wore a red dress with long sleeves, and her long black hair was carefully woven into a complex braid around a red hairpin.

"Welcome to this year's biannual selection," she said. "You may call me Mistress Yan. Please follow me, and I will guide you to the headmistress for selection."

Each of the young girls breathed in deeply and followed the woman's graceful steps, seeking to imitate her poise and grace. Each of their backs straightened as they filed out from the room in an orderly manner. Only one person seemed out of place—Hong Xin's relatively heavy footsteps and awkward posture drew glances from the many students they passed as they walked through the courtyard.

It wasn't long before they reached a bright-red building with a conical top. It was clearly the focal point of the pavilion. The other buildings and even the walls surrounding them seemed like accessories to it. And so, too, did the crimson-leaved trees inside and outside the courtyard. Hong Xin wondered if the arrangement was cosmetic or if there was a purpose behind it.

As they walked into it, they were amazed to discover that it was much larger on the inside than the outside. It opened up into a large hall with gilded walls, whose shape was perfect for carrying sound.

"Welcome to the first biannual selection of the year," a sweet voice said. A lady that appeared to be in her midforties walked onto the stage. Like Mistress Yan, she was dressed in red. But she wore a phoenix coronet on her head, and the charm she exuded far exceeded Mistress Yan's. It was a disconcerting charm that put Hong Xin's mind at ease and compelled her to let her guard down.

"You may call me Headmistress," the woman continued. "The selection will take place using the usual rules, where each participant will go up on stage and demonstrate their talent. I will be the sole judge of the selection, which will depend on the performer's grace, disposition, beauty, and other characteristics. Who would like to go first?"

Grace? Beauty? Disposition? Hong Xin groaned inwardly. She wasn't so attached to this place, but it would be embarrassing to fail considering that Hong Yinyue had suggested that she come here.

She bit her lip as the headmistress stepped down, and one of the candidates took her place on stage.

Ji Bingxue, the peerless beauty, appeared like a fairy maiden from a dream. Snowflakes sprouted where she stepped, their color matching her fair skin. A lonely song filled the air, causing the snow to tumble around her slender figure as she walked. Hong Xin was immediately captivated, and as the song continued, she saw snowflakes dancing around the beautiful woman. They were tears, frozen solid by the coldness of the singer's yearning heart. But as the song continued, the temperature rose. Snowflakes melted as her music changed pace. Misery turned to joy as the singer found her true love.

How can true love be so simple? Hong Xin thought involuntarily. As she did, the snowflakes melted and turned to rain, tears of sadness for her true love as he was sent to war. The tears rained down for what seemed like an eternity before they finally dried up and turned into a piercing fog that made it impossible to keep warm. It caused Hong Xin to shiver and lose hope.

Finally, a mournful wail erupted from the cold. Ji Bingxue kneeled down on the floor in sorrow as she discovered that her love had fallen in battle. Her heart died with him, and the snow began falling once more. It piled up six feet high, completely burying the woman in her sadness. It even suffocated Hong Xin, who desperately tried to breath. She struggled for what seemed like an eternity, and just as she was about to faint, the snow suddenly disappeared. The stage's warmth returned, and Ji Bingxue bowed before walking off stage. The sadness left with her.

"If she doesn't get in, I don't know who will," Bai Ling whispered as another girl walked up. This one summoned a guqin and played a graceful melody. Having heard Hong Yinyue play before, Hong Xin was unimpressed. And so was the headmistress, judging by her pursed lips.

"You can stop now," the headmistress said after one minute of performance.

The woman cast her eyes down and stepped off the stage. She was replaced by a flutist, who was shooed off the stage after a minute-long lackluster performance. Then came another guqin player who was accepted, followed by three rejected singers. Most people couldn't seem to tell who would pass or fail, but Hong Xin could: Only people who could move her emotionally would get accepted.

Maybe I stand a chance, she thought. *Maybe that talk about beauty, grace, and disposition was a smokescreen.*

Soon, it was Bai Ling's turn to go on stage. To Hong Xin's surprise, she didn't summon an instrument. Instead, she gently kneeled on a cushion and pulled out a gorgeous *Angels and Devils* board. She motioned to the seat in front of her.

"My talent requires an opponent," she said with a fiery gaze that made Hong Xin feel fear.

"Mistress Yan, you may go," the headmistress said.

The woman floated up onto the stage and sat before Bai Ling, who didn't bat an eyelash at having a core-formation cultivator before her. She motioned to Mistress Yan, who made the first move. Bai Ling played each move fiercely but rapidly became disadvantaged.

Everyone around Hong Xing began to murmur. "What does she think she's doing? She can't even play, yet she dares fight against a mistress?" one girl said.

"Why doesn't the headmistress just end it?" another said.

Though the game was being played at an abnormal speed, a half hour passed easily as they watched. Still, Hong Xin was unconvinced by their meaningless chatter. She felt the urge to scold them, which was odd, given her severe lack of knowledge about the game.

Suddenly, the atmosphere changed. "What was that?" a girl yelled. "That move changed everything!"

Excited whispers ensued as what seemed like a disadvantageous board position changed drastically. The whispers turned to murmurs, and before long, they were shouting excitedly as they watched Bai Ling pulverize Mistress Yan. Finally, the last stone was played, sparking cheers from the audience.

"You let me win," Bai Ling said as she bowed to her opponent and pulled back the board.

Mistress Yan smirked to the cheering audience as she walked away, pouring cold water over their joyful attitude. Only Hong Xin, Mistress Yan, and the headmistress had been more or less unaffected by the performance.

"Hong Xin, you're up next," the headmistress called.

She nodded and walked up onto the stage nervously. Her average looks and unrefined posture attracted snickers from the audience. Hong Xin didn't care, however, as she'd suffered much worse catcalling.

She began her dance, which was clumsy and plain, but as she performed each movement, doves appeared around the stage and danced around the audience playfully. It was a dance of innocence, a dance which everyone could relate to. And as she moved, ravens appeared. They fluttered alongside the doves playfully, and the pace of her dance quickened in tandem.

The doves joined the ravens, and soon they were flying side by side. They flew high and low, in circles and spirals. They flew to the heavens, and the stars in the sky formed a bridge that could reach out across time itself to connect their loving hearts.

Unfortunately, all good things come to an end. Out of nowhere, a crow cawed at an innocent dove before flying into the starry bridge. Other crows soon followed, and before the doves could join them, the bridge shattered and crumbled into nothingness.

Seeing that the crows had flown off, the doves hid themselves in frustration. They hid in thorny rose bushes, not daring to appear before the various other birds flying outside. But as they hid, they cut and scratched themselves. One of the doves, having had it with the rose bushes, flew into nearby tree.

Unfortunately, the tree was already occupied by a dozen magpies. They pecked at her until she was barely able to fly. Fear filled the air as she struggled against her aggressors, who taunted as they wounded her. When it seemed like the she was about to die, she lashed out at the magpies with a mysterious hidden strength, sending tongues of flame out to burn their bodies.

The dove flew away, but as she did, the bleeding continued. She kept flying until she collapsed in a farmer's field, where a kindly old couple found her. They nursed her back to health until she was finally able to fly again. Uncertain of the future, the dove flew off to a nearby tree. Life was nice there, and the other birds didn't fight with her.

However, she felt the world had more to offer. She flew around every day until she discovered something peculiar—a strange red fruit had appeared on her tree. It taunted her from the top branch as she flew around day in and day out. She resisted the temptation for a few days before her curiosity finally got the best of her. She swallowed the fruit, and something inside her ignited. Her white feathers burst into flames as she realized she wasn't a dove, but a phoenix.

Hong Xin's movements grew erratic and fierce, joyful and unhindered as the fiery phoenix above her flew out above the audience. Their hearts beat faster as they admired her graceful and unhindered movements on stage. After making its rounds, the phoenix returned and merged with her figure as she wound down the intense dance. She was dripping with sweat, but the audience could only applaud her hard work for such a stellar performance. Their minds wandered as their hopes and dreams resurfaced.

"So young and able to perform a heart kindling," the headmistress said, quieting their applause. "Do you have a teacher?"

"I am self-taught," Hong Xin replied, as per Hong Yinyue's instructions. After all, she wasn't here for pleasure. This was a difficult and dangerous test that would be extremely beneficial to her dancing and cultivation. She felt the headmistress's soul probe hers slightly before pulling back.

"Hong Xin, you are formally accepted as a member of our Red Dust Pavilion," the headmistress said. "Ji Bingxue, you are formally accepted as a member of our Red Dust Pavilion."

The names continued in reverse order of performance. Hong Xin looked toward Bai Ling. Although the young girl seemed calm and composed, Hong Xin could sense great anxiety from her direction.

"Bai Ling, you are formally accepted as a member of the Red Dust Pavilion," the headmistress finally said.

The young girl let out a sigh of relief as she climbed onto the stage and joined her eleven new sisters.

The twelve students followed Mistress Yan out of the pavilion and into the nearby dormitories, where they saw ladies studying, practicing, and dressing. No one was resting, despite the late hour, but this made sense to Hong Xin, as sleeping was optional for cultivators.

"Each of you will share a room with a senior sister," Mistress Yan explained. "You are to wear your uniform at all times, though you may wear makeup or style your hair however you choose. Your clothes must always be clean and tidy, and inspections will be performed daily. If you have any questions, you can ask your new senior sisters."

Hong Xin knocked on an oak door, which opened and revealed a red-dressed woman wearing her hair up, fastened by a black pin with two red stripes, signifying that she was a second-level student. "Junior Sister Hong greets Senior Sister," Hong Xin said, bowing.

"Call me Sister Ying," the woman said warmly. She returned to what she was doing previously: applying makeup that contained exotic ingredients. Hong Xin could see faint runic lines disappearing under her skillful brushstrokes. "Do you have any questions?" Sister Ying asked as she worked.

"If it's not too much trouble, could you tell me what classes I can expect?" Hong Xin asked.

"Every student starts without a hairpin," Sister Ying said as she applied her makeup. "To obtain yours, you will need to achieve passing marks in posture, etiquette, dressing, and makeup. You will also need to take a hobby class."

"Oh?" Hong Xin said. "What's your hobby?"

"I play the flute," Sister Ying said, smiling. She picked up a black flute, which she blew into. As she played, a school of silver fish began swimming around them. They filled Hong Xin with a sense of wonder. She began dancing with the fish and complementing the melody, adding waves to the small school with her movements. The flute music stopped suddenly, and Hong Xin couldn't help but feel inexplicably disappointed.

"It's getting late," Sister Ying said to Hong Xin, placing the flute back onto the bed. "How about I help you get dressed for tomorrow? Our uniform is difficult to wear the first time around."

Hong Xin nodded and followed the woman's lead. To her surprise, the seemingly simple dress was composed of twelve pieces, which were fastened with invisible threads from behind to promote its bewitching shape. Each piece contained hidden runes within its red fabric. Thin golden embroidery provided stunning highlights.

"We'll have to braid your hair since you don't have a hairpin," Sister Ying said.

"No need," Hong Xin said. "I have a hairclip." She took out a purple clip, the same purple clip she had worn on her many dates with Wang Jun. She hadn't worn it in a long time, but it seemed appropriate to do so now.

"You should hide it if you like it," Sister Ying said, her eyes shifting awkwardly. "Things people like have a tendency to disappear around here."

The words sent chills down Hong Xin's spine.

"What do you mean?" Hong Xin said.

"I mean that nice personal possessions grow legs around here," Sister Ying said cheerfully. "What else could I possibly mean?"

Hong Xin was unconvinced. She suddenly had a foreboding feeling about tomorrow's classes.

"What about your flute?" Hong Xin asked. "Should you be keeping such a beautiful instrument lying around?"

"This?" Sister Ying said, looking at the black flute. "It'll be fine where it is. No one will take it." She finished braiding Hong Xin's hair before walking toward the door. "I'll be outside practicing if you need me," she said, summoning her flute. "Make sure you get enough rest. The first day of classes is always the hardest."

"Sure thing," Hong Xin said. She looked at her bed and her dress briefly before giving up on the idea of sleeping. Instead, she walked in the central courtyard, where students practiced martial arts, dancing, singing, and other hobbies. They all wore cheerful smiles on their faces, and they laughed as they saw their fellow classmates. Superficially, there was nothing wrong. Yet she couldn't shake the feeling that something was amiss, that something insidious was lingering within the courtyard.

She looked at the central pavilion and the tall red walls but found nothing peculiar. She looked at the students, whose smiles seemed to lessen with each passing moment. Finally, she looked at the crimson-leafed trees. The eyelike pattern on their trunks stared back at her eerily, as though evaluating her as she evaluated them.

Finally, she walked back to her room to cultivate. After much effort, she slipped into a trance as Hong Yinyue had taught her, consolidating her kindling foundation one flame at a time. She woke when dawn arrived.

Chapter 6: Dousing a Flame

"Who could have known that there were so many things to consider when applying makeup," Hong Xin said to Bai Ling as they walked out of their first class. "And this isn't even considering glamour arts. They won't let us touch those until we've mastered basic cosmetics."

Bai Ling chuckled. "I've heard that even mortal courtesans could woo kings by using their body as a canvas. We're cultivators, not mortals. How can we not exceed those standards?"

Hong Xin agreed with her assessment. A mere two-hour class had overthrown her notions of what she'd previously thought was a mundane field.

She and Bai Ling followed the other ten students to their next basic class: posture. A young woman with a red pin welcomed them into the class. The room contained no chairs, only cushions. Hong Xin and the others awkwardly kneeled, imitating the instructor's position as closely as possible.

"You may call me Mistress Meng," the young woman said softly as everyone settled down. "And you should all be ashamed of yourselves. Imitating someone else's posture shows lack of confidence and diminishes your status."

Everyone's previously cheerful disposition was immediately quashed. Sensing blood in the water, the instructor continued her assault. "The one who performed the best out of all of you was Hong Xin, but this is only because she is lacking even the barest fundamentals on posture and doesn't have the skill to imitate me."

Even her praise is a form of mockery, Hong Xin thought, though she didn't adjust her posture despite the scathing words.

Mistress Meng stood up gently, her long legs moving beneath her red dress as she gracefully walked around the new recruits. "A person's posture is very telling—this applies both to both women and men," she said in a voice that came from all around them. "It can seduce, inspire confidence, and show strength and domination. It can kindle a flame in a person's heart, pulling them out of their darkest nightmares. Conversely, it can show weakness and lack of initiative, and repulse even the most desperate men."

Her lithe footsteps changed slightly, but Hong Xin's impression of Mistress Meng changed drastically. She was now utterly horrified by the woman, who now seemed like a hungry ghost wearing the skin of a woman as a feeble disguise. The horrendous woman's steps changed once again, and she now looked like an adorable, innocent girl. Hong Xin felt an overwhelming urge to fawn over her.

"These are all higher-level skills," Mistress Meng continued. "To achieve this standard, you must build a foundation. For Hong Xin, with no foundation whatsoever, this will be easiest. As for the rest of you, I will break you and mold you. Only after I've hammered out these massive imperfections will I guide you and shape you like a precious vase made from earthly clay."

With a snap of her fingers, various gold weights, sticks, and books appeared around them. Mundane and deadly obstacles now littered the room, which now seemed much smaller than before.

"All of you grab a stick with fifty jin of weights on each side. You'll be carrying it with you as you walk. Whoever makes a mistake will receive one lash." An ominous black whip appeared in one hand, while a green bottle appeared in the other.

At least she has medicine, Hong Xin thought as she walked through the obstacle course. The tricky maze of barbed wire forced her to contort her body at awkward angles as she avoided their sharp thorns. Her spine slouched slightly as she maneuvered through a small opening, and pain wracked her body as she avoided harm from the obstacle but was rewarded with a quick strike from Mistress Meng's whip. It left a shallow gash on her back that healed over after three seconds. The fabric also mended, but the bloodstains remained, blending in with the red fabric of her uniform, adding a slightly wet spot on the vivid material. As she sighed in relief, she noticed the whip heading toward her once more.

What did I do this time? Hong Xin thought as she adjusted her posture. She pushed the pain of the lash to the back of her mind and continued down the treacherous walkway.

The other eleven tried their best as well, but the whip struck them swiftly and seemingly at random. After an hour and a half of grueling torture, a student finally couldn't take it and collapsed. She was rewarded with ten lashes before being removed from the course, twitching and moaning. The remaining students joined her one after another.

"How was that even a class?" Hong Xin asked in a bristly tone as they moved to their next destination. Their entire group was nervous and fidgety.

"Do you really want to know?" a beautiful woman with raven-black hair and alabaster skin said as she walked up beside them. She wore a pin with two red stripes. "I can tell you, but it will cost you a secret."

The memory of the dreadful pain suddenly surfaced in Hong Xin's mind, and she couldn't help but shudder. "I'll do anything to avoid more pain," she blurted suddenly. Surprised by her sudden willingness, she sealed her lips. However, she felt crimson chains dig into her heart as the woman spoke.

"Do you love a man? What's his name? Where did you learn to

dance? Who sent you?" the woman said. Hong Xin felt the world blur around her as the chains dug deeper into her heart, demanding an answer.

"I do," Hong Xin blurted helplessly. "His name is Wang Jun. I learned to dance in the Song Kingdom."

Suddenly, she realized that the chains were no longer binding her. As she was no longer obligated to answer, she bit her lips before she could blurt out anything more. Then, she bit back at her assailant.

"How are they teaching us? What is the school's goal? How will they accomplish it?" She unleashed the three questions simultaneously, urging the fire in the woman's heart to grow. She exerted no pressure on the other woman but rather fed her bewildered emotions.

"They are teaching you by breaking you," the woman said quickly. "You will instinctively know what a good posture is after they are done, if you can stand the pain. Their goal is for you to obey. They will accomplish this by taking what you—" She suddenly caught herself mid-sentence and looked at Hong Xing coldly. She pursed her lips and stormed off, leaving Hong Xin deep in thought.

"That was amazing," Bai Ling said as they walked to their next class. "You were able to manipulate a second-grade student! Can you teach me how you did it? Was it a glamour or a movement art?"

"It was none of those," Hong Xin replied as they walked. "When someone affects another's heart, they have to open theirs in turn. I simply made hers waver when she least expected it." Inwardly, however, she was shocked at the other student's behavior. *It seems I'll need to keep my guard up while I'm here.*

Bai Ling nodded, and they soon took their seats in etiquette class. Fortunately, it was boring and uneventful. They simply learned the various rules of the continent, absorbing them like a dry sponge would water. But Hong Xin performed poorly, her mind preoccupied by the strange student and those crimson chains.

Just what is she after? Hong Xin thought. *And what will we have to lose? Why would the pavilion want to control us?*

Despite brooding over the matter for a full two hours, she couldn't think of any reason. Likewise, she realized she'd sorely underestimated Hong Yinyue's warning about danger. Her sense of foreboding grew as their next class approached. Her eleven classmates also seemed uneasy as they cautiously entered a black door that opened into a small performance hall.

As they entered the hall, a wonderful melody flew around them. It was a flute melody, and it took the shape of a small firebird that whizzed around excitedly. Hong Xin's spirits lifted when she saw it. A feeling of pure joy enveloped her and brought a smile to her face. Her concerns and the concerns of the others vanished as they followed it through a playful garden of fire.

They couldn't resist chasing the bird, which hurriedly led them to a woman who sat cross-legged on the floor. Her long black hair was fastened with a red pin, and the black flute she played with was covered in golden runes. Her fingers moved swiftly and joyfully. At first Hong Xin sensed happiness from her. But she soon realized that this was a disguise, and that the woman was actually sad and alone.

Hong Xin's classmates were oblivious. They sat down and enjoyed the music, awaiting the end of the amazing performance. The woman gently opened her eyes and looked at each of them. Her phoenixlike gaze warmed their hearts as she inspected each of them.

"Welcome to hobby class. Unlike the other classes, which are superficial, this class will delve deeply into matters of the heart."

Hong Xin bubbled with excitement. This class was the one she'd been waiting for all this time.

"But before we begin, do any of you know *why* I'm so good at playing the flute?" the woman asked.

One of the girls raised her hand, the effects of the posture training already showing. "Is it because you love playing the flute?" the girl asked.

Hong Xin and the others nodded in agreement. Only with pure love for a hobby could one play so passionately.

"You would think so, wouldn't you?" the woman said. "I, Mistress Huang, am a very accomplished flutist. I once bewitched an emperor and extorted the wealth of his nation with a single performance. Dozens of kings have sent me marriage proposals, and men fall at my feet whenever I play. But for the sake of your education, I will tell you a secret."

The students involuntarily inched forward.

"I hate the flute."

Everyone suddenly became aware of a few simple tells. Mistress Huang had discarded her disguise, and they could now see that she held the flute gingerly. A hint of disdain was present in her eyes as she looked at the object, as though she wanted nothing more than to throw it away.

"My true passion is the zither," Mistress Huang said. "But I haven't played the zither in decades. I cast it away to learn something greater. I lost the music I loved but was rewarded with control and power. This is the allure of the Red Dust Pavilion, and the reason we are such great performers. To control the hearts of men, we first douse our own."

Her expression suddenly hardened as she uttered these words. "Each of you will now be assigned a hobby. From this moment forward, you are all forbidden from practicing your original hobbies.

"Bai Ling, your passion is *Angels and Devils*. No more. From now on you must play and learn the zither. Ji Bingxue, you are now prohibited from singing. From now on, your hobby is also the zither." Mistress Huang listed off one name after another, and the expression of each student paled when they heard her instructions.

Finally, Mistress Huang's gaze lingered on Hong Xin. "Hong Xin, I will personally teach you the flute," she said softly. "You will hate it, but you will not pass this class until you convince me that you love it." A black flute with crimson runes appeared before her. Likewise, two black zithers appeared before Ji Bingxue and Bai Ling, as did various black shoes, instruments, and collars. "Should any of you be caught performing your old hobbies, the consequences will be severe. Expulsion will be the least of your worries."

Hong Xin's previous positive mood was put out like a weak campfire. She was overwhelmed with dread and disgust as she glanced at the black flute floating before her. She wanted nothing more than to cast it away and leave the pavilion.

But to her horror, she involuntarily reached for the loathed instrument. When she tried to pull away, she felt a stinging pain in her heart and crimson chains tightening around it. The more she pulled, the more they constricted.

I might die if I refuse, she realized. She struggled one last time before finally giving in. She grasped the black flute, and the moment she did, the intense fire in her heart dimmed and grew cold.

Hong Xin shuddered as crimson chains shot out from her instrument and wrapped around her core, replacing the chains that had coerced her into picking it up in the first place. The flames in her kindling foundation retreated little by little, until finally it was covered in a thick layer of frost. Her eyes glazed over, and so too did those of her eleven classmates.

"Your minds are free, but your hearts now belong to the Red Dust Pavilion," Mistress Huang said. "That is all for today. I expect great things from you."

The students filed out of the classroom one after another. They exited the building directly into the courtyard, where various people were practicing their skills. These students were no longer cheerful, their masks were gone, revealing their cold hearts and icy dispositions.

On their way back to their residence, Hong Xin saw the young woman who had compelled her to speak. The woman smirked as they passed. "See? You ended up just like us all the same."

The twelve students walked back to their residence without a sound. As Hong Xin entered the room, she saw Sister Ying looking at her pityingly.

"I'm sorry," Sister Ying said. "I was barred from saying a thing. We're the same now. Two snowflakes floating in the wind, looking for sunshine." She sighed. "We'll never find it. Not even if we look for our entire lives."

Sister Ying soon left for supper, leaving the exhausted Hong Xin to rest. While she knew she had complete freedom and could dance whenever she wished, the thought of being expelled from the Red Dust Pavilion frightened her. If she didn't graduate, she wouldn't be able to help Hong Yinyue or Wang Jun. She would continue to remain useless while everyone around her outpaced her. She also felt that the consequences weren't limited to expulsion. Her previous enthusiasm had waned, and only fear of failure continued to motivate her.

"How bad could it be?" Hong Xin muttered as she grabbed the revolting flute. Her first few notes were nothing but screeches, reminding her that she had little talent for the musical instrument. As she struggled to make the barest sound, she felt the crimson chains around her heart dig deeper and deeper, settling into every nook and cranny. As they dug in, she noticed her skills improving, and little by little, the screeching sounds turned into a soft, soothing melody. Before long, a dove appeared in the room and circled her as she played. The white bird was cold and had a heart of ice.

The more she played, the more it froze, until finally it revealed its true form. It was an icy phoenix, the embodiment of winter misery. She shuddered as a gust of freezing wind blew around her, bypassing her defenses and heading straight into her dantian.

The hidden embers in her frost-covered kindling foundation froze over until they were nothing more than lumps of charcoal.

Chapter 7: Obligation

Sweat rolled off Cha Ming's brow as nine runic projections shifted before him. There were much fewer people in the royal courtyard, as the basics had already been covered. What he now shared were speculations on core-formation runic arts. Only master-level professionals and core-formation cultivators could benefit.

"I only have one last thing to share," Cha Ming said to the two dozen people seated before him.

He waved his hand and banished eight formations, leaving only a golden one. It twisted and contorted until it took the shape of a human body. It was filled with golden qi pathways that circulated qi in the same way he did.

"Let us suppose that this golden sigil is the human body. All qi pathways are utilized. So how can we expand it?" He covered the diagram of the body in a golden film, after which many runes and runic lines appeared on it. They covered every inch of its skin as they imitated the runes he'd seen in Westvale two weeks prior. "We all know that rune carving is the next stage for cultivators after core formation, so why not carve runes onto our bodies?"

The small crowd murmured before a powerful individual, the king's protector, spoke up. "Most of us have practiced a core-formation martial art before, and it's nothing like what you describe.

You might be a cultivation genius, but I would hate to see you heading down the wrong path."

"Then what path is the right path?" Cha Ming asked.

The red-robed protector stepped forward, and fire left his body and surrounded him. It took the form of a flaming dragon that threatened to consume anyone who approached him. "In qi condensation, qi can barely leave the body, while in foundation establishment, roughly half of a cultivator's qi can leave the body. In core formation, this figure exceeds nine tenths. This phenomenon is what makes flight, among other things, possible."

"Then what if I do this?" Cha Ming asked, taking a small step forward toward the protector.

Golden runes lit up on his body, and three-dimensional runic lines appeared in the air. Little by little, a thin halo surrounded him. A few seconds later, the halo grew to three feet wide as the runic lines expanded outwardly. Finally, it expanded to ten feet wide before stopping. Although it didn't seem as threatening as the flaming dragon, the air surrounding Cha Ming was sharp and incisive.

"This self-made technique seems very draining," the royal uncle remarked. He retracted a portion of his qi, leaving a quantity similar to Cha Ming's. The dragon floated around the man within a hundred feet, gently dancing as it pleased. Meanwhile, the runes around Cha Ming remained static—they could only remain in the vicinity of his body. "It's also immobile. But what about its power?"

The fiery dragon slowly flew toward Cha Ming at the behest of its master. It surrounded him, gently probing the golden sphere. After a few probes, it opened its mouth and tried to give it a vicious bite. To everyone's surprise, however, the flame dragon collapsed. It was as though the golden bubble around Cha Ming couldn't tolerate intruders, despite its obvious elemental disadvantage.

"Interesting," the royal uncle said. A second dragon, twice as large as before, left the man's side. It dove for Cha Ming's golden bubble, crashing into it before vanishing in a puff of smoke. A few small cracks spread across Cha Ming's barrier, but they rapidly healed. The man's fighting spirit was kindled, and an even larger dragon appeared. Its power reached the middle core formation and flew out at a much slower pace.

Cha Ming gritted his teeth as the dragon slowly flew toward him. He mobilized his qi to mend his receding territory. But try as he might, he couldn't hold on. Little by little, cracks propagated inside the golden bubble. Lesions appeared on his skin, and blood spewed through the open wounds. He struggled to hold on as even his bones began to show signs of strain.

Finally, the bubble burst, and the dragon disappeared. He caught his breath as the cuts on his skin healed using the power of his initial-marrow-refining cultivation.

"Not bad," the royal uncle said, nodding in appreciation. "It's like a transcendent domain, but much weaker. Despite its obvious flaws, its power is much greater than your cultivation should allow for."

Cha Ming wiped a trickle of blood from his lips. "It's also very difficult for someone who isn't a body cultivator to fully utilize it. It will take much more work to make it a viable technique."

"Then I look forward to it," the royal uncle said. He clasped his hands together and bowed. "Many thanks for the lecture. Be sure to visit in the future."

"Many thanks, Brother Cha Ming," Feng Huoshan said. "I now feel much more confident in reaching the peak of master rank."

Several other professionals, including alchemists and spiritual blacksmiths, did the same. As these powerful figures left, Cha Ming's three apprentices roused from their extended meditation. While their cultivation realms had not progressed, Cha Ming felt that their foundations had quickly stabilized, and their souls had grown more powerful. It was only a matter of time before they became master talisman artists.

"Are you ready?" Cha Ming said.

The three nodded, allowing Cha Ming to sweep them up. They traveled straight from the palace to the Jade Bamboo Auction House, where Wang Jun was waiting for them, carrying a small wooden box in his hands.

"I prepared a gift for you," Wang Jun said as he handed the

wooden box to Cha Ming. "It's a twelve-year supply of Demon Soothing Tea and Red Jade Tea," Wang Jun said. "Fate is a funny thing; although I tried to divine when we'd meet again, my results were inconclusive. Should you run out before then, don't hesitate to give me a shout, and I'll send some over.

"With any luck, I'll run out before an all-out war begins," Cha Ming said.

"Who knows?" Wang Jun said. "But I hope you're right. For all our sakes."

"Thank you for everything," Cha Ming said, hugging his friend firmly.

Wang Jun awkwardly hugged him back. It was the first time Cha Ming had ever seen his friend surprised by anything.

"Come meet me in Gold Leaf City when you get a chance," Wang Jun said.

"It's a promise," Cha Ming said.

"What up, wait up!" a voice suddenly called out. Cha Ming looked over in surprise as the leader of the Jin family dragged his youngest son, Jin Huang, over to them. "Your promise still holds, right?" the man said.

Cha Ming focused on the fifteen-year-old boy who hadn't yet started cultivating. His jade glow hadn't lessened in the least—in fact, it had thickened.

"I naturally keep my promises," Cha Ming said. "However, I'll be leaving the city for the foreseeable future. If he wants me as a master, he'll have to come with me to the Quicksilver Empire."

While the father looked uncertain, the boy looked at Cha Ming with shining eyes. "This disciple greets Master," he said, falling to his knees and kowtowing. The father rolled his eyes before pulling his son up and hugging him tightly. The young man then scampered off toward Cha Ming's group.

Cha Ming then swept up his four apprentices and flew through the city gates. A few moments later, a larger bird with a wingspan of two hundred feet appeared before them. A small fox was sitting on its back. Cha Ming and his four apprentices hopped on while strands of air reached out and secured them. The gigantic bird flapped its wings, and they became a silver streak that flew across the Song Kingdom.

As they flew, they saw fertile plains stretching across the horizon. These plains turned to woods and mountains guarding a lone pass to the north. After crossing the loosely guarded border, they entered a vibrant empire filled with industry, technology, and most importantly, hope. It wasn't long before Quicksilver City appeared before them.

Cha Ming, his four apprentices, and the three small beasts walked toward the gigantic city walls. The fox, the bird, and the mouse glared at the huge stone structure in defiance as they registered with the city guard.

"This will be your home for the next year, everyone," he said. "Quicksilver is a wonderful place, but remember one thing: Beware the color ochre. This is a city where angels walk in the light, but devils lurk in the shadows."

"You're back much earlier than I expected," Lu Tianhao said as Cha Ming entered his office. "Are you in such a hurry to pay back your debt to Mo Tianshen?"

Cha Ming was surprised to see that the man had started a miniature garden. A large variety of strange plants now filled the empty spaces on his bookshelves.

"Why the change?" Cha Ming asked, ignoring the previous question. "It's not like you to decorate the place."

"I'm helping out Mo Tianshen by growing some supplementary herbs," Lu Tianhao said. "It won't be long before the entire Alabaster Group is filled with them."

"Does that mean we'll be receiving a large batch of main herbs soon?" Cha Ming asked.

"Yes, but the source of the herbs is divulged on a need-to-know basis," Lu Tianhao said as he continued watering the plants.

Cha Ming approached a peculiar-looking herb that resembled dancing flames. Despite the various protections on his soul, he couldn't help but be entranced by it. As he walked closer, he felt his soul growing stronger by the second. The feeling only stopped once a barrier appeared between him and the flower. Despite the lack of physical intervention, he was sure that Lu Tianhao was responsible.

"Does there exist an herb that can heal a wounded soul?" Cha Ming asked. "A powerful one?"

Lu Tianhao arched an eyebrow before walking over to the bookcase and retrieving a thick dusty book. He leafed through it before handing the open book to Cha Ming, showing him a beautiful red-and-white lotus. Nine drops of pink dew occupied its center, complementing its nine red and nine white petals.

"The Burning Samsara Lotus is a rare herb that only grows in transcendent realms or higher," Lu Tianhao said. "The dew that gathers on the flower is one of the few things that can heal a soul. Beyond that, I can only think of a few other remedies, like Phoenix Source Blood and a Bodhi Tree's life core. Extracting them results in their death, so I don't recommend these options. They are holy creatures, so killing them incurs substantial sin."

"I have a friend who needs this flower," Cha Ming said, touching the picture of the lotus. "Where can I find it?"

"With your core in such a state, you're still caring for your friends?" Lu Tianhao asked gently, closing the book and placing it back on the shelf.

A sphere appeared in front of Cha Ming. It was a projection of his runic core that glowed with the five elemental colors and black, white, and gray. It was covered in many thin cracks. "With your core like this, it's impossible for you to complete a rune carving. These cracks will interrupt the carving process and likely obliterate your core and end your life. I suggest you fix this before worrying about anything else."

Cha Ming shook his head. "That's a problem for later," he said.

"My core can wait, but my friend cannot. Besides, I can still cultivate."

"You call that cultivating?" Lu Tianhao said sternly. "I doubt your core could handle more than the pressure of a mid-core energy-gathering formation. If you tried using medicinal pills to cultivate, the cracks would widen and worsen your situation. Sure, it's possible—if someone customized some pills and rendered them gentle enough. But even then, the materials to make such pills are far too scarce and the skill level required far too high."

"Like I said, I can worry about that when I get back," Cha Ming argued. "The Burning Samsara Lotus is a priority."

Lu Tianhao sighed. "I don't want to discourage you, Cha Ming. The world is filled with many possibilities that I can't even imagine." He pointed to the various plants growing in his office. "For example, these plants are grown in preparation for our harvest from Jade Moon Planet. With any luck, we'll find ample herbs and lucky chances to promote some of our members from the peak of core formation to transcendence."

"Is Jade Moon Planet where I can find the lotus?" Cha Ming asked.

"Yes," Lu Tianhao said. "Jade Moon Planet can only be accessed through the Bridge of Stars once in a sixty-year cycle. It contains plenty of herbs, ores, and lucky chances. Perhaps you can even find a solution to your predicament there. Unfortunately, we can only send ten people there every time it opens. I don't believe you have what it takes to earn one of these spots."

"What do you need me to do?" Cha Ming asked.

"I need you to show me your resolve," Lu Tianhao said. "I need you to prove to me that you can continue down this path. Using the energy-gathering formations the basement, you have fifteen months to reach early core formation. If you can't do that, there's no need for you to keep trying. Not only will you need to give up on the lotus, but you'll need to scrap your cultivation and start over. I know your cultivation method is special, but there's a war brewing, and I can't waste resources on wishful thinking."

Cha Ming rapped his finger on Lu Tianhao's table as he mulled over his options. He thought about his mysterious inheritance, his runic pillars, and his sigil core. He thought about the many advantages he had over other cultivators.

At the same time, he thought of all the help he'd received from Sun Wukong. He thought of the formations in Fairweather, their sparring as the monkey taught him staff arts, and the Creation Qi Manipulation Technique he'd used to heal his severed meridians.

Finally, he thought of the time when Sun Wukong defended him and Huxian from the Heavenly Tribulation. The memory of the Monkey King's imposing figure and jade-white runic circle caused what remained of his hesitation to disappear.

"All right," Cha Ming said. "You have yourself a deal."

Cha Ming knocked on a wooden door. It opened, revealing an overjoyed Mo Tianshen.

"You came back much earlier than expected," he said. "And not a moment too soon—the launch of the ninth-generation pill was a smashing success, and I already have a plan for developing the next iteration."

Cha Ming chuckled. "There wasn't much sense in me staying in the Song Kingdom any longer. I won't be able to relax until I pay off my debt."

"Very good," Mo Tianshen said. "But we'll be approaching this next batch much differently than the last."

"How so?" Cha Ming asked, taking a seat. A large variety of herbs were piled up on the table next to a messy stack of paper.

"There are just too many possible variations to account for," Mo Tianshen said. "Even if I work you to the bone for fifty years, we'll never get a chance at creating a better version. I've determined that brute force is not the answer. Therefore, we need to pursue theory and understanding."

Mo Tianshen waved his hand, and an image appeared between them. Multiple compounds that Cha Ming was familiar with were there. With another wave of his hand, the compounds began mixing and mingling in the old way, forming an inferior pill.

"According to normal alchemical rules, this is how the pills should be formed," he said.

Then he summoned the original illusion once more. This time, the liquids and solids formed runes that interacted differently. The diffusion rates were controlled, and their reactions occurred in different ways. Cha Ming had never looked at the process in depth, as they'd used a statistical approach to create the ninth-generation pill.

"As you can see, the interaction is completely different. Normal alchemical rules can't explain it, which means that my current knowledge on alchemy is insufficient this project. Therefore, you need to learn enough to become a master alchemist as soon as possible," Mo Tianshen said gravely. "As a core-formation cultivator, I'm confident that you can do it in less than half a year. After that, we'll work together to alter the standard alchemical theories up to the fourth grade. That should be enough to give us a direction, enabling us to conduct a batch of experiments before your time is up. Any questions?"

A million, Cha Ming thought as Mo Tianshen dropped a pile of jade slips and books before him. He also handed him a bag of holding containing alchemical ingredients, several alchemical furnaces, and a pass to an explosion-proof laboratory in the basement of the Alabaster Group building.

One ruined furnace later, Cha Ming thanked his lucky stars that he hadn't neglected body refining.

Snow covered the ground in the Red Dust Pavilion. The trees in the courtyard were slumbering, their weathered limbs covered in a few inches of delicate white frosting. Unlike the trees outside, their branches weren't bare. Instead, their crimson leaves clung tenaciously to their branches, making one wonder whether they were living or dead.

In the courtyard, a lone figure in a red dress and a black braid stood playing the flute. She played a mournful melody that inspired sympathy from her surroundings. It caused the wind to slow and the snow to pepper her frail figure. But this small luxury was far from enough to ease the sadness in her heart.

Three other red-dressed women sat around her as she played. They'd lost themselves in her tune long ago and were now covered in a foot of snow. The usual mesmerizing fire in their eyes had vanished and iced over with nothing but regret. Unlike the woman playing the flute, these women all wore hairpins with one or two red stripes. But this distinction in rank meant nothing. They were mere children before her song.

"How long do you plan on keeping them here?" a woman asked as she walked over. It was Mistress Huang, her teacher. Seeing her superior arriving, Hong Xin finished her song and set down her flute. Her initial discomfort at the object was no longer apparent.

"I'm not keeping them here," Hong Xin said, smiling. "They came to visit me but couldn't help but stay and listen. That's what happens when you love what you do." Her face betrayed no animosity or dishonesty. Instead, it was as if she spoke from the bottom of her heart.

"You and I both know that you hate playing the flute," Mistress Huang said, sweeping her hands toward the two women. She frowned when she noticed that they didn't wake from their stupor.

"You're letting your eyes deceive you," Hong Xin said gently. "Their look is cold and dull because the song is sad. However, their hearts are joyful. Kindling their hearts can't do anything. Let me play them a dousing tune so that they can come back to their senses and greet you."

Hong Xin's fingers fluttered as she played a light tune. A

colorful songbird appeared out of nowhere and danced about. The temperature within ten feet soared, and the snow melted. The eyes of the two women turned joyful, and they suddenly woke from their stupor.

"Thank you so much for your song," they said, bowing. Then they noticed Mistress Huang standing beside them with a quirked eyebrow.

"My apologies, Mistress Huang," the most senior sister said hurriedly. "It's our fault for not noticing your approach."

"That's quite all right," Mistress Huang said. "Please leave Hong Xin and I to discuss things in private."

"As you order, Mistress," the senior sister said. They both bowed and departed.

"How did you do it?" Mistress Huang said as she reached out and touched Hong Xin's flute. Its original black-and-crimson appearance had completely vanished. The flute was now black and gold, and it let out joyful vibes as she handled it. "After so many months of putting up with your lies, I'd just about given up on you. Yet now your flute has turned golden, something that should only be possible with true love for your instrument. But I know that's not the case."

"I think the results speak for themselves," Hong Xin said sweetly.

"Indeed," Mistress Huang said. "Although I don't know what you did, results are what matters. Before I can give you a pass, however, I need to inspect your foundation."

"As you wish," Hong Xin said. She let down her defenses and allowed Mistress Huang's resplendent force to peer into her dantian. Her foundation had grown substantially over the past year. Nine pillars reached all the way from the top of her dantian to the bottom. These charcoal pillars were covered in ice and snow, a steep departure from her original fire-based cultivation. Her original fiery qi seas were filled with frigid waters.

"It's amazing that you were able to transform your kindling foundation into a dousing foundation so easily," Mistress Huang said. "I must confess, I envy your talent."

"Many thanks for your compliments, Mistress," Hong Xin said.

"They are well deserved," Mistress Huang said. She held out a hairpin with a single red stripe. "You may rejoin your classmates once you break through to core formation." Hong Xin accepted the hairpin and retreated while Mistress Huang stood in a courtyard with a complicated expression on her face.

Hong Xin maintained her mask of ice as she sat meditating within the cultivation chamber. While this might have been the safest, most private location in ordinary sects, the opposite was true in the Red Dust Pavilion. The same applied to her sleeping quarters and the woods. Privacy was an illusion here.

Why did she have to harp on me so much? Hong Xin thought as she adjusted her cultivation base. *She didn't break any of the others. Rather, she made it look that way and let them preserve some semblance of a heart. So why treat me differently?*

Not only had her methods been different, but her criteria for evaluation was as well. The others had already moved on to their second year, but Mistress Huang had held her back and zeroed in on Hong Xin's lies. She was punished for every lie she spoke, and after months of trying to fool her, Hong Xin had decided to pursue a radical approach—she had become two people at the same time. She'd buried her sweet, warm persona behind a golden mask of arrogance and ambition. It disappeared, little by little, until finally, not even the headmistress could find it.

Hong Xin carefully kept an icy layer on her dantian as she absorbed the frost qi from her qi seas into her qi pillars. Then, she slowly melted them from the outside in. They produced drop after drop of frigid water until finally, a reddish glow peeked through. She carefully separated the icy-cold portion of her foundation, then proceeded to melt the kindling portion. It poured into a pool of red liquid, which coexisted with the nearby ice.

After completing this first step, she began forming her core. But instead of forming a single ball like most would, she started by forming an inner core with her kindling qi and covered it in a shell made from her dousing qi. The center of the sphere was red while the shell was blue. It felt unstable and unpredictable, but this was something she'd expected. She'd rather die than lose herself.

Hong Xin compressed the liquid core and used her resplendent force to ensure that both layers were kept separate. With each step in the compression process, a wave of turbulence mixed increasingly large amounts of red and blue qi together. The process caused her mind to waver and her emotions to blur. It caused her blood to boil and her skin to freeze solid. Her two separate personalities clashed as her kindling and dousing qi mixed, threatening to tear apart her facade with each exchange.

Will I even be able to form it? she thought as crimson chains dug into her heart. *Will I be able to survive core formation?*

She pushed once more, and a small eruption went off inside her mind. She sat, dazed, as fire and ice comingled and solidified. Everything snapped together like a puzzle as her core crystalized and wisps of blue and red qi rushed in. She trembled as she controlled her raw emotions while they reassembled themselves, much like her core did. And then, all was quiet.

Hong Xin peered within her dantian and saw a sparkling blue core. It was covered in a thick layer of frost that completely hid away the presence of the embers in the center. And so, too, did her frosty persona completely mask the warmth within her. No one would ever know the difference.

No one *could* know the difference.

Chapter 8: Cooperation

Cha Ming focused carefully as he manipulated a wisp of blue flame, urging it to regulate the temperature and control diffusion between three intersecting runes. These three-dimensional structures were formed from the juices of three low-grade herbs. He patiently waited for thirty breaths before adding a solid gold rune to the three, catalyzing the reaction at a key step. The four runes liquified under the aid of a second flame, this one red, producing a thick purple blob.

He willed the blob into a sphere before grabbing three more vials of liquid and using them to draw a multicolored pattern on it. He summoned a green flame and reduced the temperature slightly. Its runic pattern grew as it took nourishment from the flame and expanded across the surface of the sphere. Then the blob began disappearing as it was consumed by the green runic network.

Once the purple liquid was fully absorbed, a golden flame appeared and minced the green runic structure while heating it. A brown flame joined the golden one and pressed the melting green substance into a spherical shape while simultaneously roasting it. Another sixty breaths passed before a golden seal appeared on the hardened green orb.

It's a success, but is it useful? Cha Ming wondered. *Only a fifth-grade alchemist who cultivates five elements and knows runic characters could make this pill.* He shook his head before dusting himself off and cleaning the room with a flick of his sleeve.

"Greetings, Grandmaster," many junior alchemists said as he passed them to Mo Tianshen's laboratory.

"I'm not a grandmaster yet," Cha Ming said, rebuking them.

Lu Tianhao had made things difficult for him. Since his abilities had transcended that of ordinary formation masters, he had gifted Cha Ming with an honorary grandmaster medallion.

The juniors excitedly continued their work. Cha Ming was living proof that one didn't need to spend their entire life locked up in cultivation to achieve the illustrious title.

Cha Ming soon arrived at Grandmaster Yao's office. He knocked three times before the door opened, revealing the branch president and Mo Tianshen drinking tea. Outside the laboratory, of course. The first time Grandmaster Yao had come, he'd severely reprimanded his student over his disorderly conduct.

Everything is as it should be, Cha Ming thought, grabbing his teacup and Wang Jun's red tea.

"How was your latest experiment?" Mo Tianshen asked Cha Ming, who produced a small vial. The older man unstoppered it and observed the pill before sniffing it carefully. "A fifth-grade gold-seal pill? Not bad. They're tough to make."

"Now we only need a five-element cultivator who simultaneously practices talismans and alchemy," Cha Ming said sarcastically. "It's hardly a practical pill to make."

"But it's a step in the right direction," Mo Tianshen said. "That aside, the greater your skill in runic alchemy, the easier it will be to conduct our experiments."

"And how are those going?" Cha Ming asked.

"I gave them a new batch of experiments this morning," Mo Tianshen said. "They should be succeeding any moment now."

Suddenly, they heard a soft bang from the workshop below. "Let's go take a look firsthand," he said.

The three men flew out of the office and down the stairs. They passed a crowd of fledgling alchemists before arriving at a blackened corner of the laboratory.

The qi-condensation cultivators retreated as Mo Tianshen, Cha Ming, and Grandmaster Yao made their way to the back. Cha Ming and Mo Tianshen bent down to inspect the wrecked furnace while Grandmaster Yao used his secondary discipline as a spirit doctor to rapidly heal the injured juniors.

"What do you think?" Mo Tianshen asked as he picked up a furnace fragment.

Cha Ming swept away some dust and picked up another. He tasted the residual powder, testing its effects on his sensitive but durable body.

"The composition is correct, it's just that some elements are unstable," Cha Ming said. "For us, it's nothing major. In fact, it wouldn't even register as a problem if they were two fourth-grade professionals. But your requirement for third-grade or lower professionals makes things difficult."

"The cost doubles otherwise," Mo Tianshen said helplessly. "Mass production will be difficult without this final step."

As Cha Ming pondered the problem, dozens of illusory models appeared in the air. The previously disgruntled alchemists and talisman artists were now glad they had been injured, as it granted them the opportunity to see masters work up close.

"What if we use an icicle rune here to moderate the power of the melting rune during catalysis?" Cha Ming asked. Twelve different models showed a variety of methods of doing so. Unfortunately, they all ended in failure.

"The icicle rune creates another point of instability by increasing diffusion in the overall pill," Mo Tianshen said. "We need to modify another component if we want to make it work."

"How about we add fossil grass again?" Cha Ming said.

Mo Tianshen moaned. "But the cost will increase by ten percent!"

"If we don't do something, we can't produce it," Cha Ming said. "You're the cheapest man I've ever met. Why don't you just donate a million spirit stones to make up for the shortfall? I'll tell you what,

I officially donate a million spirit stones to the cause. Do you dare match them?"

Mo Tianshen turned red with rage. "Of course I match them, but throwing money at a problem won't solve it." Then, after looking at the many components and runes, he shook his head. "Fine, let's do it your way. A ten-percent increase it is."

"Perhaps we can mitigate the costs in another way," Cha Ming said carefully. "Let's try with third-grade alchemists and then see if second-grade alchemists can make them with moderate success. We're already bare bones on the talisman artists, so we only need second-grade artists for half the runes and first-grade artists for the other half."

"We can't have two alchemists working on the same pill," Mo Tianshen grumbled. Then, a thought occurred to both of them simultaneously.

"Or can we?"

"What if we have the talisman artists assist the alchemists?" Cha Ming said. "Instead of just producing materials, they'll also stabilize the runes as they react. They're better at it than alchemists anyway. Then the alchemists can relax and focus on maintaining the temperature."

"If we do that, I think we can cut back on a few materials," Mo Tianshen said.

"Stop cutting everything all the time," Cha Ming snapped. "Let's see if it works first before cutting."

"Fine," Mo Tianshen said. "You two, are you all rested up?"

"Yes, sir!" they immediately said, for fear of being caught in the crossfire between the two bickering core-formation cultivators.

"Good," Mo Tianshen said. "Li Xuan, I want you to forget about stabilizing the runes from now on. That's talisman artist work, and you're much better than that. Let those glorified scribes do the dirty work and focus on controlling the temperature."

Meanwhile, Cha Ming turned to the talisman artist. "Fu Xing, those alchemists are just brutes, and they can't do this without us. He needs your help because he doesn't know the first thing about runes.

Heck, I'm not even sure he knows how to write. Make sure you help him stabilize the runes while he works so the pill furnace doesn't blow up in your face."

Soon, the two professionals nervously began processing materials. The talisman artist carefully drew out ink for the seven materials present and formed twelve different runes, which he handed over to the alchemist, who held them in the furnace. Then he created five other runes and held them in midair while the alchemist worked. He kept a careful eye on the runes that were blending and dissolving together in the cauldron.

After an incense time, an orange blob appeared. The alchemist passed the blob to the talisman artist, who reshaped it into a rune and threw it, and five other runes, into the cauldron. This time, he carefully maintained their shape as they combined, and the alchemist carefully controlled the temperature. The various liquids leached into each other and reacted as they pushed closer and closer together.

The second-grade talisman artist paled as he struggled to maintain the shapes of the unstable runes. Fortunately, he didn't need to do so for long. The components soon perfectly melded together into a red blob, which the alchemist roasted patiently. Instinctively, the talisman artist helped him control the pill as it rolled in the furnace. The grateful alchemist was then able to maintain a better control over the temperature until finally, a silver seal appeared on the pill. They both wiped the sweat off their brow as Mo Tianshen retrieved the final product and inspected it.

"Now *that's* what I call teamwork," Mo Tianshen said. "Now that we know it's possible, we should give them a bonus if they make silver-grade products." He looked to the young professionals. "As a reward for being the first, you'll get a hundred-spirit-stone bonus each."

The two professionals' eyes glowed when they heard this.

"Do you think we could cut back the grade of the alchemist?" Cha Ming commented. "I think it's possible."

"Are you blind?" Mo Tianshen said as they left the workshop and a bemused Grandmaster Yao behind. "The kid was clearly exhausted.

You just noticed it with Fu Xing because the brat's weak as hell."

"Now who's wasting money?" Cha Ming bit back. They traveled upstairs, where they carefully observed the junior alchemists, who rapidly produced some prototype pills. Hours passed, and soon they were rewarded with a large container of red pills. A quarter of the seals were silver while the rest were bronze.

"What do you think?" Cha Ming said as Mo Tianshen looked them over.

"I think it was a very productive year," Mo Tianshen said. "The pills are twice as effective as the originals, half the cost, and contain very little pill toxicity. It's too bad I don't have you for longer."

"I don't think I would make a big difference," Cha Ming said. "We've figured out the basics of runic alchemy. Will you be working to perfect it further?"

"Absolutely not," Mo Tianshen said. "Runes aren't my strong suit. It's enough that we've gotten this far. Soon the streets will be overflowing with fledgling cultivators. They won't be strong, but they'll be able to defend themselves if we're ever invaded. They'll be able to grow herbs, drive locomotives, heal mortals, and live a better life." He teared up slightly. "I just expected it to take twenty more years to achieve my goal."

"What will you do next?" Cha Ming asked.

"I'll work on my next project: cheap cure-alls for the masses," Mo Tianshen said.

"You know what they say about cure-alls…" Cha Ming started.

"They cure nothing, I know," Mo Tianshen said. "But it's worth a shot. And I really don't want to go back to making pills for arrogant cultivators. I'll just make some for the Alabaster Group when they ask me, but that's it."

"Fair enough," Cha Ming said. "I, on the other hand, don't have much time to waste. I need to break through to early core formation within the next three months."

"Why the rush?" Mo Tianshen asked. "You're already cultivating very fast, given your condition. Can't you just take a break?"

"And miss the opportunity of a lifetime?" Cha Ming said

cryptically. "I'll pass." He sighed and walked to the door. "It was nice working with you. See you in a few months."

The familiar pounding of metal on metal was a common occurrence in Quicksilver's industrial district. This was especially so due to the train lines that were being built. It was the dawn of an industrial age for cultivators, and only time would tell if it made a difference in the war against the south.

Cha Ming slowly made his way to a smithy, where Ling Dong had apprenticed himself to a spiritual blacksmith. The profession was a good fit, given the man's strong body and stubborn temperament. But it was something Cha Ming couldn't help him with, given his limited time.

He carefully spied on Ling Dong and the aged blacksmith. The younger man was carefully shaping a large greatsword while the old man grumbled about the shoddy workmanship while simultaneously complaining about his arthritis.

Is arthritis even possible? Cha Ming thought. The man's body cultivation was no joke. *Regardless, Ling Dong seems to be getting along well.*

He slid a letter beneath the door, informing his disciple that he would be cultivating in seclusion. With the young man's temperament, it wasn't likely that he'd come visit anyway.

After visiting the smithy, he flew to the hospital. Yue Bing was busy applying a runic bandage on a patient afflicted with a poison injury. Her spirit-doctor mentor guided her throughout the process while praising the quality of her healing runes.

As she worked, Cha Ming inspected the public board of student rankings. Not surprisingly, Yue Bing was first in her class. Seeing that she was busy, Cha Ming left a letter at the reception and made his way back to the Alabaster Group. On his way, he walked into a tavern, where he saw Zi Long chatting up Luo Xuehua.

"The fiendish boar was chasing after us, and its skin was so thick that we couldn't hurt it no matter how hard we tried," Zi Long said. "We were out of options, because even Brother Dong's greatsword couldn't do anything to it. I'd yet to break through foundation establishment, and the boar was much too fast. And that's when I had an epiphany."

"What did you do?" Luo Xuehua asked.

"You see, I suddenly remembered Brother Dong's words from earlier," Zi Long said. "He was so hungry he'd even eat fiendish demon meat. Now, you and I both know that their meat is poisonous to humans, and I hadn't yet had a chance to call him out on it. The thought of making him eat his words again inspired me to try something crazy—I painted myself as a target and had it chase me down an alley of earthen walls. It was just me and the hog, and I was going to be crushed if I didn't do something quickly.

"As it caught up to me, it opened its fanged mouth and tried to bite me. I quickly threw up my staff and wedged it open. Then I threw an Earth Spear Talisman on the wall up ahead and directed it to skewer the boar straight down its throat. The spear went in one end and came out the other. I used the chance to throw a few Ruby Flame Talismans down its mouth, roasting it from the inside out. Then, I climbed out of the hole while dragging its smoking carcass. I threw it at Ling Dong, who stared at me slack-jawed. 'Here you are, sir,' I said. 'Dinner is served.'"

Luo Xuehua and many other eavesdropping adventurers burst out laughing. "Did he try it?" she asked, wiping tears from her eyes.

"Of course not," Zi Long said. "The guy acts dumb, but he's smarter than he looks."

Cha Ming, who was listening in at the entrance, chuckled before retreating. He left his disciple a short message on his core-transmission jade, instructing him to take care of Jin Huang, his youngest disciple from the Song Kingdom. Then he entered the cultivation chamber in the Alabaster Group's basement for his last bout of secluded meditation.

He tossed a small mountain of high-grade spirit stones on each of the formations before breathing in deeply and circulating his qi. A sharp pain lanced through him as the formation hummed to life.

How long has it been? Cha Ming wondered as his consciousness returned. *Has it been a few weeks? A few months?*

Regardless of the amount of time he'd spent, it didn't matter. He hadn't yet reached early foundation establishment, so there was no point in stopping. He turned his attention back to his core, which had barely grown since he'd last checked. It was stuck at one and a half times bigger than when he'd first formed it.

So this is what cultivators experienced before medicinal pills were created, he thought. *Endless dullness and endless solitude.*

There was no rushing the process. Without medicinal pills, he could only constantly wear away at the bottleneck, refining the energy within his core until it reached the next stage. It was even possible that his cultivation would halt entirely, forever stagnating at his current realm. Therefore, he wore away at the barrier like a millstone, slowly but surely polishing away the invisible impediment.

Days passed before he finally felt a light tremor in his core. A warm, joyful feeling spread throughout his body as he realized that his long-anticipated breakthrough was imminent. His core pulsed and began expanding crazily while filling his meridians with higher-quality qi. His joy turned to horror, however, as a massive burst of pain assaulted his mind.

Why is the pain so bad? he thought as one pulse after another appeared. His core constantly crackled as it expanded violently. He twitched as the breakthrough, which normally occurred with a single pop, completely disabled him.

He lay incapacitated in the center of the five formations. Meanwhile, his body automatically cultivated as his core rapidly grew to two times its original size and the mountains of spirit stones disintegrated. The process only stopped after an hour, revealing an eight-colored core with a smooth surface. A crack appeared on it, causing him to swiftly lose consciousness.

"Now do you know why I told you to start over again?" Lu Tianhao's voice said.

Cha Ming opened his eyes and noticed he was in a small bed in the older man's office.

"That was the worst thing I've ever experienced," Cha Ming confessed.

"And it will only get worse," Lu Tianhao said. "While it's possible that you can keep cultivating, it's also possible that the trauma will destroy your soul." He sighed. "If you recultivate, I'll grant you a slot in sixty or a hundred twenty years. However long it takes."

Cha Ming shook his head. "I don't know how long my friend has. I can't risk it."

"Can you move yet?" Lu Tianhao asked.

Cha Ming clenched his fists and stood up. His body was unharmed, and his core felt the same as before he lost consciousness, save for the much greater concentration of qi within it and its expanded capacity.

Lu Tianhao passed him a jade slip. "This slip contains our accumulated knowledge on Jade Moon Planet and the Bridge of Stars. Our group leaves tomorrow. Try to get some rest before you leave."

Cha Ming bowed and accepted the jade slip. "Thanks for keeping the spot for me. I owe you a favor."

"You owe me medicinal herbs, and lots of them," Lu Tianhao said sternly. "Truth be told, I'm ripping you off. The cultivators we send only need to give us a quarter of their herbs, and the rest is theirs to keep. I'm simply placing a lucrative bet on your ungodly luck."

We're heading out soon, Huxian, Cha Ming sent to Huxian. *Make sure to be back in the morning.*

Sure thing, Huxian sent back. *We're all packed up and ready to go. What will you do until then?*

I'll try one last thing to get stronger, Cha Ming said.

As he reviewed the jade slip's information, he realized that he'd been naïve in thinking that he could just waltz over to a garden and pick whatever he wanted. Cha Ming secluded himself in his bedroom before lighting a thick gray candle. He closed his eyes, and when he opened them, he was dreaming. He was surrounded by gray mist, and around him, he saw ten doors. There were two for each element, one pale, and one dark. There were also two doorways beneath him, one black and one white.

"What is this place?" he wondered aloud.

He walked over to two brown doors that were clearer than others. One of them contained a dream of crumbling and the other of hardening. He then walked over to the blue doors, which contained his dreams of momentum and resistance, before proceeding to the gold doors, which held his dreams of sharpness and dullness.

Four closed doors remained, and these didn't contain dreams. The light-red door felt warm, like a small campfire, while the dark-red door felt cold, like a small flame on the verge of being snuffed out. The light-green door was filled with vitality while the dark-green door was filled with death and decay. The four doors felt alien to him, unreachable.

Confused, Cha Ming headed toward the first door, the light-red one. A warm sensation filled him as he reached for its ember-colored handle. His blood boiled and his heart raced as he did. Yet as he tried to enter, he heard the soft voice of an old man.

"Why the rush?" the voice said.

He turned around but saw no one, and when he turned back, the door had disappeared. There were no red doors or green doors, no gold, brown, or blue doors. The black and white doors on the floor had disappeared, and only endless gray mists remained in the mysterious space.

The dream ended soon after, and when it did, he looked down at the gray candle and saw that only four uses remained.

Am I lacking in experience? Cha Ming wondered. *Am I lacking inspiration?*

He sighed before climbing into his bed. That night, he dreamed of fire and clouds of gray.

Interlude: A Heavy Burden

Gong Lan lit up a joss stick, filling the candlelit room with gray smoke. Though it was the largest room in the monastery, it felt tiny due to the many people crowding it. Each and every monk on the mountain peak had come to lay Master Zhen's soul to rest. As his successor, Gong Lan presided over the lengthy funeral.

She let out a soft hum, the primal mantra. The others followed in cadence as she ran through all 108 verses. Their words spoke of Master Zhen's beginning and his end, his life and his death. It ended on a soft note, which naturally led into the Mantra of Forgiveness. As they hummed, they begrudgingly forgave those who had harmed him, bringing a modicum of peace to their hearts and souls. Such was the way of the Buddha, the embodiment of compassion toward all beings.

The Mantra of Forgiveness soon led to the Mantra of Purification. The monks sang in unison, using their Buddhist souls to wipe out as much residual karma as possible for their deceased leader. Their song wore away at the crimson strings on his burial plaque. It continued until, one after another, they could do no more for their exalted leader.

Gong Lan ended her chant last, causing a reaction in the burial plaque. It shook for a moment before a golden glow surrounded it. It flickered a few times before the glow poured into the writing on the plaque, illuminating Master Zhen's illustrious name. And then, it vanished.

The ceremony continued as the many monks burned incense and bowed, sending their prayers out to guide Master Zhen's reincarnation. They wished him a virtuous journey and a swift path to Buddhahood before filing out of the prayer room one at a time.

Soon, only Gong Lan and Master Zhen's few personal disciples remained. She led them to place a plaque in the mausoleum. Like the ones who came before him, Master Zhen left no body. All he left behind was his name, his memory, and a heavy burden for Gong Lan to bear.

"Brother Shen, how are the juniors coming along?" Gong Lan asked when they left the mausoleum.

"We're training them as quickly as we can," Brother Shen said. "But you know what they say: Haste makes waste."

"They're trainees, not dishes," Gong Lan said. "Still, I see what you mean."

She looked out toward the woods, where the demonic beasts had grown increasingly vicious. They'd begun assaulting the mountain's defensive formation, and while these attacks accomplished nothing individually, they wore away at it like a steady trickle of water.

"I want you to take a group of monks to recruit externally," Gong Lan said after a moment of silence. "Recruit in the Song Kingdom, the Quicksilver Empire, and anywhere else in the north that permits it. Recruit from the rich and the poor alike. Anyone suitable for the Buddhist ways will do."

"Such unbridled preaching might irk the Church of Justice again," Brother Shen warned. His voice was filled with warmth and concern. After all, Gong Lan might be the World Tree Master, but she was still his junior sister.

"If they are irked, I will show them my resolve," Gong Lan said. "A storm is coming, and I will *not* let the plane fall into depravity because I'm afraid of some brutes waving their swords around. If there are consequences, I will bear them."

"What should I tell them if they press me for answers?" Brother

Shen said. "You know their type. They can be quite aggressive at times."

"Remind them that it was *us* the World Tree chose, not them," Gong Lan said. "And if they have a problem with that, they are welcome to ascend to the monastery and petition it directly. That is, if they have the courage to do so."

"That ought to rile them up," Brother Shen said, laughing. "Though, given their character, I'd prepare a few extra beds just in case."

"Noted," Gong Lan said. "I'll also prepare a few robes. It wouldn't be the first time we've converted some of their members."

"Now *that* would be an inspiring sight," Brother Shen said, bowing. "I'll get right to it."

"Let me know when you need to leave," Gong Lan said. An ominous glint appeared in her eyes. The beasts had established a toll to cross their territory, and she would pay it in blood.

Chapter 9: The Cowherder and the Weaver Girl

Cha Ming woke to the quiet chirping of birds in the Alabaster Group courtyard. He stretched his relaxed limbs as he climbed out of bed. After tidying up his room and retrieving all his possessions, he walked outside to the courtyard, where he was greeted by his four disciples.

"How did you all know I was leaving today?" he asked as he sat on a bench in front of them.

"Brother Long heard it through the grapevine," Yue Bing said. "As a senior member, he gets news much faster than us."

Cha Ming glanced at Zi Long in surprise. Obtaining an upgrade in membership required significant contributions to the Alabaster Group. This requirement increased with strength, and the only senior member he had met before was Luo Xuehua.

"It's good to see you're all progressing smoothly," Cha Ming said. "Now we have a spirit doctor, a spiritual blacksmith, and a formation master. Jin Huang, which path will you choose?"

The youngest of them had not even broken through to foundation establishment. A small visitor badge was pinned to his blue cultivator robes.

"None of their paths interest me," Jin Huang said, shaking his head. "I suppose I'll continue studying talisman arts. Perhaps I'll dabble with alchemy and see if I like it."

"It's a good field," Cha Ming said. "Perhaps Mo Tianshen will teach you something if you beg him."

He took out a jade slip from his bag of holding and quickly imbued it with his knowledge of runic alchemy before passing it to Jin Huang. The younger man's eyes brightened when he saw the contents.

"It's only the beginning, but maybe it will be useful to you," Cha Ming said.

"Many thanks, Master," Jin Huang replied, bowing.

"Do you all have any questions you need me to answer before I leave?" Cha Ming asked. They shook their heads. "Then I'd better head out. It'll take some time to get to the meeting point."

"Have a safe journey," Yue Bing said, tearing up.

"Why are you crying?" Cha Ming said. "You practically never see me anyway. I barely show my face, and I only give you casual pointers whenever I feel like it." He sighed and pulled out a few wooden slips from his bag of holding. "Here's a gift before I leave. They're obligation tokens from Mo Tianshen. If you supply him with materials or pay his material costs, he'll craft a batch of pills for every slip. But remember, don't spend these chances easily. It's practically impossible to commission his services without selling yourself into servitude."

"I heard that!" came a shout from Mo Tianshen's laboratory, which wasn't far away.

The shout was followed by a loud explosion and a cloud of smoke, which prompted laughter from their entire group. They chuckled as they walked to the outskirts of the city. Cha Ming spoke to Jun Xiezi and Grandmaster Yao through thought transmission as he passed their respective buildings.

After exiting the city, heavy flapping noises alerted them to Silverwing's arrival, who landed and allowed Cha Ming to hop on beside Huxian and Lei Jiang.

"I'll be back in a year," Cha Ming said to his four disciples. "Take care of each other."

A few flaps took them miles away, and Quicksilver City soon faded into the background. "So what did you guys do while I was locked up inside Quicksilver?" he asked Huxian.

"More of the usual," the fox said. "Bullying demons, raiding mountains, and setting up the foundation of our future beast empire."

"We're sowing the seeds of rebellion!" Lei Jiang squeaked. "Down with the humans!"

Huxian quickly slapped Lei Jiang upside the head. "It's just rhetoric we tell the beasts to rile them up," he said quickly. "It doesn't really mean anything."

Cha Ming rolled his eyes. Hours passed as they traveled north over the fertile farmlands that grew wheat and soybeans. The land became increasingly rocky and barren as the farms gradually disappeared. The land became an infertile plain where demon beasts roamed in a tense balance with the cultivators who hunted them.

Soon, trees began appearing across the landscape. The tiny green specks grew increasingly dense until they finally joined together with a hilly forest. These hills grew in size until they gradually merged with cloud-covered mountains of fire and ash. All vegetation disappeared as the giant volcanoes spewed endless lava onto their surroundings near the northern border of the Quicksilver Empire.

Silverwing let out a piercing screech as he rushed into their thick gray clouds. They passed through miles of smoke before finally reaching the empty sky above them. There, they saw a peak jutting up like the tip of a sword. It was the tallest mountain on the continent, far taller than the lava-gushing mountains below it. It was the legendary Sword Peak, located in the middle of the Fire Mountains at the edge of the Huoshan Kingdom.

A quarter hour passed as they slowly approached the massive peak. Though it looked sharp from a distance, a smooth plateau was located at its tallest point. Three miles away from the platform, they arrived at a transparent membrane that glowed brightly with all five elements and threatened to destroy them should they intrude.

Cha Ming supplied a jade slip, causing a large doorway to appear within the elaborate formation. They flew through the opening and landed beside nine people sitting in meditation.

"It's about time you showed up," one of them said grumpily. His name was Han Jiling, and he was one of the oldest core-formation cultivators in the Alabaster Group. "You've obtained such a precious opportunity, but you can't bring yourself to arrive early?"

Cha Ming frowned but didn't reply. The old white-cloaked man was much more powerful than he was.

"There's no need to bully juniors," a black-haired, middle-aged woman said. "Despite his young age, he's accomplished many amazing feats. He's also contributed the Devil-Sealing Scripture to the Alabaster Group. He deserves the quota."

"What does deserving have to do with anything?" Han Jiling said. "We only have ten positions every sixty years. People who venture to Jade Moon have a much higher chance of transcending compared to other people. It's a waste to send anyone other than peak-core-formation cultivators there."

"I'll make sure I don't weigh you down," Cha Ming said sincerely. Han Jiling snorted but didn't say anything further. "When will we be leaving, Junior Partner Song?" Cha Ming asked the middle-aged woman, who was the leader of the group.

"Soon," she said cryptically. "You should sit down with your contract beast and have him dismiss his friends. Otherwise the Bridge of Stars will pick up random passengers."

Cha Ming nodded and sat down cross-legged with the others. Huxian stowed Silverwing and Lei Jiang in his tail and sat on Cha Ming's lap.

"We'll be separated when the Bridge of Stars arrives at Jade Moon Planet," Junior Partner Song said. "Everyone here will do their utmost to reach the Jade Moon Garden after passing it. If we're lucky, we'll gather enough herbs to craft a batch of rune-carving pills."

The other eight cultivators' eyes glowed when they heard this. Among them, not a single one was less than a few hundred years old.

Cha Ming and Huxian sat in silence as they waited on the mountain. They admired the lava flowing beneath the clouds as day turned to night. The red streams meandered randomly down the mountainside, pooling into makeshift lakes in the valley below. They contrasted the starry sky, which seemed to grow closer with each passing moment.

Brother, the stars are getting brighter, Huxian sent.

Cha Ming looked up and saw a curved line of stars growing out in the distance. It resembled a transparent strip of silk gauze floating in the wind. The jade-colored constellation grew until it encompassed half the starry sky, spreading out from one end to the other. Cha Ming now understood why it was called the Bridge of Stars—it looked like an endless flat river that meandered across the universe. He didn't know its origin, but he could see its destination— the moon in the sky. But the moon was different from the one he was used to seeing; it was milky white, like a smooth piece of white jade.

"They say the Bridge of Stars was built by the Jade Emperor for his daughter," Song Min said as the bridge descended. "Others say it was built for the Weaver Girl and the Cow Herder to reunite them every sixty years. Their love was forbidden, so they were separated by countless worlds. However, the heavens never bar all exits. Their longing for each other was so strong that it invoked the Heavenly Dao's pity. Every sixty years, the Bridge of Stars appears so the two lovers can reunite on Jade Moon Planet."

One mile, half a mile, a quarter mile—the bridge approached quickly but erratically. Once it breached the quarter-mile mark, it quickly scooped downward and encompassed their group of eleven in white light. It hovered around them as though probing for information before coiling around them like a comfortable blanket.

Then their surroundings lurched. The world rapidly shrank behind them, exposing Cha Ming to the true shape of the Ling Nan Plane. Unlike Earth, it was a small world, with only a single continent. It was flat and completely detached from its surroundings, like a miniature universe that maintained an isolationist policy against the unknown void. The Jade Moon wasn't a part of their world. Rather, it was a giant light in the firmament that illuminated every night sky across the universe.

Seeing their world fade away, Cha Ming turned his attention

toward the stars in the sky. Despite traveling faster than light, he could see everything clearly. He took everything in stride, as each new experience unshackled his limited worldview and opened him up to countless possibilities.

As they traveled toward the increasingly large jade moon, they passed many wondrous sights. In the distance, two golden giants battled for the leadership of a large plane in the shape of a mighty palace. A little further out, another plane took the shape of a coiling serpent.

"In the mortal realms, the planes vary in size but are ultimately small," Junior Partner Song explained as they flew. "They say that mortal realms are only unstable fragments of higher-level planes. This instability is why the will of each plane cannot abide the existence of powerful cultivators. Transcendents usually choose to leave their world due to its oppression."

"And what would you choose?" Cha Ming asked. "Would you leave?"

"The plane is my home," Song Min said. "I don't want to leave it, but how can I be certain? Ten thousand years is a long time to live. Perhaps I'll feel differently once enough of my loved ones pass away. But enough of that, why don't you take a look at this wondrous miracle?"

Off to their right, a beautiful red lotus was blooming. It had 108 petals that reached out into space, sucking up every bit of golden sunlight it could lay its hands on. Just like there was only a single jade moon in the mortal realms, there was only a single golden sun. It was the last remaining member of the golden crow family, the single sun that Houyi spared.

A full day passed as they traveled. They lost count of the wonderful worlds they saw. Even Cha Ming remembered only a few dozen of them. The top three didn't resemble worlds, but animals. One was a flying rainbow fish whose every scale housed a shifting continent. It danced through space, absorbing small mortal planes like food as it traveled.

The second world was a maelstrom of lava that housed a single flame the size of a mortal house. The gray flame constantly absorbed energy fed to it by its ever-expanding lava. Curious creatures lived in this world, and they all obeyed the plane's will, constantly laboring to transport energy and material back to their home plane.

The most impressive world, however, was a ball of silver water. The world was oceanic, and all its continents were below sea level. Each creature on the planet had a high affinity to water and an abnormally strong body. Just the fact that they could survive the pressure of the hundred-mile-deep ocean spoke volumes. They domesticated giant sea creatures whose lengths spanned hundreds of miles, establishing cities on their thick shells, housing billions of people.

"We're here," Song Min said as their speed finally slowed.

Jade Moon Planet loomed up ahead, and over a hundred million life-forms waited patiently on a jade platform that orbited around it. They were connected by a starry bridge, the only entrance to the lush planet. Yet no one was in a hurry to cross it. Instead they waited patiently for the Bridge of Stars to completely retract from the various mortal realms.

As Cha Ming gazed at the many cultivators on the platform, he noticed that nine out of ten were human, but many demonic beasts were also present. Among the humans, most of them had straight black hair and brown eyes, like the Asians of Earth. However, he also saw many people with fair features and others with black skin. Some people had fur and resembled beasts while others had gills. The majority had at least a light merit glow, but a good tenth of the humans were devilish cultivators.

"Didn't the jade slip mention that the odds of surviving the journey through the Bridge of Stars were ten times lower for devils?" Cha Ming said. "Why are so many of them here?"

"Although there are more than usual, it's not so surprising," Song Min said. "Those despicable creatures cannot help but lust after the Jade Emperor's inheritances. Our speculations are that it's a honey trap, leaving barely enough survivors with rich rewards to tempt countless elite devils to attempt the trial every sixty-year cycle. Overall, the devils lose an astronomical amount of resources in the exchange; only individual greed keeps them interested."

"What a frightening scheme," Cha Ming said, hissing between his teeth. "Every sixty years, the Jade Emperor can take the chance to eliminate millions of enemies."

"It's only a drop in the bucket, but every little bit matters," Song Min said. As she spoke, the bridge began turning corporeal. The many transparent supports glowed with white runic patterns. It extended toward them as millions of tendrils converged as it approached Jade Moon Planet. "Steel yourself, as we'll soon be separated," Song Min said. "You and your fox friend are no exception."

Cha Ming, who was already aware of this fact, calmly allowed himself to be transported to the bridge's surface.

Cha Ming observed his surroundings. Instead of thousands of stars, he was greeted by three walls of lightly glowing blue stones and three simple symbols—a vertical stroke, a horizontal stroke, and a dot. The fourth surface consisted of a lightly glowing blue shield that could be passed by him and him alone.

He clenched his fist and noticed a slight distortion in the void. "Such incredible body strength," Cha Ming whispered. He then circulated his cultivation and summoned a thick ball of gaseous qi; it was eight times denser than before he'd stepped into the starry skies. He observed his dantian and saw that it was floating in a thick green envelope covered in mysterious runes. His soul was similarly covered in a jade glow that made its spiritual body more corporeal and his resplendent vestment much brighter.

"The Jade Moon Blessing is truly wondrous," Cha Ming said. "Even a simple ant would be promoted to its mortal limits after setting foot on the bridge."

He summoned his staff and practiced some basic techniques and punching routines, familiarizing himself with his newfound strength. Then he walked through a transparent blue barrier. Each participant started in a similar safe zone that no one else could enter.

He heard a loud crash up ahead as soon as he left the safe space. Weaving through various large blue pillars, he reached an open central area after a few breaths. Two cultivators stood outside a small circle, the inside of which was covered in a dull runic pattern. Three puppets stood guard over three square platforms that each held a green jade rock. A red-robed cultivator was kneeling beside a blue pillar with blood trickling down his cheek. He'd evidently been thrown into the pillar behind him.

"They're much too strong to tackle alone," the cultivator said, looking at Cha Ming and the other cultivator. "I propose we form an alliance to steal the moon stones. As for how we'll split them, that will depend on each person's skill."

"I support your proposal," the second cultivator said. He looked genial and friendly. "How about yourself?" he said, looking at Cha Ming.

"I'm game," Cha Ming said, summoning his staff.

Ten groups of Dao sigils hovered around him, ready to manifest arrays at will. He had four of them transform into two identical formations that resembled icy mirrors and another two that resembled earthen shields. The three cultivators rushed at the inactive puppets, who came to life the moment they entered their surroundings. Cha Ming was overwhelmed by the stifling pressure they emanated.

How can they be so strong? he thought as he used his four defensive formations and the Clear Sky Staff to defend against a strike from above. The puppet he faced wielded a large axe, which crashed through his combat formations like they didn't exist. He didn't hesitate to throw up six more to slow down the strike.

Meanwhile, he used his Gentle Staff Art to sidestep the puppet. Yet as he moved, the strike followed in a seemingly unavoidable manner. Cha Ming could only summon a Matter Talisman. His formations hardened, as did his skin. The axe slowed as it broke through layer after layer of defensive formations and finally struck the Clear Sky Staff. The floor beneath Cha Ming's feet cracked, and his bones and qi shields shuddered as they defended against the firmament-splitting strike.

After deflecting the axe, Cha Ming rushed to the puppet's side and struck out with his Hard Staff Art. Despite being large and extremely heavy, the staff simply bounced off the puppet, who turned around and sent its axe down once more.

I can't defend against this, Cha Ming thought, panicking. He quickly activated a Flow Talisman, which caused the three surrounding puppets to sink into a quagmire while Cha Ming's speed was unaffected. He pushed off his assigned puppet and dove toward the central platforms.

"I'll switch you!" the white-robed cultivator said as he darted past him using an elusive wind-based technique.

Although frustrated, Cha Ming didn't have time to bicker, as a swift horizontal blade slashed toward him. It wasn't slowed by his Flow Talisman in the slightest—the blade's razor-sharp edge cut through their viscous surroundings without hindrance.

Seeing this, Cha Ming summoned ten fire-based combat formations. He didn't attack the puppet; rather, he used his strong body to kick off each formation, taking advantage of the explosions they created to evade the swift blade. As he evaded, he traded places with a blue-robed cultivator, who snatched the moon stone he'd finally managed to approach. He could only grit his teeth and rush toward the remaining one.

Cha Ming felt death looming as he approached the final moon stone. He looked up to see that the last remaining puppet's spear was thrusting—not toward him but at the last remaining platform. Cha Ming threw out a Shape Talisman, sending golden runes out to envelop the sharp spear in a golden bubble. He then sped up and grabbed the moon stone just before the spear struck his chest.

Crack.

He felt his ribcage break as he was struck out of the circle. Fortunately, the spear strike wasn't sharp but dull, courtesy of the

Shape Talisman. White qi oozed out from his marrow and healed his bones as he stood up.

The information I received wasn't exaggerated in the slightest, he thought as he crushed the moon stone in his hand. Its power rushed into him, enhancing his body, qi, and soul by a hundredth.

The boost came just in time for him to notice a blade approaching from behind his head. He pushed off the ground sideways and avoided the deadly strike from one of his former companions. Then he used the residual power from his Matter Talisman to strengthen his hands and block an incoming saber strike, sending him back twenty feet.

"Is this really necessary?" he asked the two who'd ambushed him.

"The cultivation world is a cruel place," the white-robed cultivator said. "How do we know you won't do the same? It's best to be rid of you as soon as possible." His genial smile had disappeared.

"You've certainly taught me a lesson," Cha Ming said, inspecting both of them with his Eyes of Pure Jade. "Even cultivators with thick merit halos like yours can be evil to the core."

The blue-robed man shrugged. "It's nothing a few good deeds can't make up for. The end justifies the means. Fortunately for you, we're unable to deal with you in a short time."

Cha Ming shrugged. "There's no need to deal with me. I'll be going back to my starting point. Enjoy the competition."

A few quick steps brought him back through a blue shield and into the blue stone chamber where he'd started. After some time, the two cultivators proceeded to the next part of the trial.

Chapter 10: Foundation

Time trickled by, and soon two weeks passed. During this time, Cha Ming mulled over the disparity between himself and the other cultivators on the bridge. It was a difference in essence, a difference in skill. Due to his forceful promotion to the peak of core formation, his combat experience and techniques were sorely lacking compared to the others traveling to Jade Moon Planet.

"It's unbearable to cultivate here without doing anything else," he said as he struck out with his Clear Sky Staff for the thousandth time.

The square space he occupied allowed him just enough room to practice martial arts. He used the opportunity to imitate one of the three marks on the back wall—the single vertical stroke. He swung his staff down over and over, like a solitary wood cutter in the mountains. He only stopped after swinging it ten thousand times.

Just what am I missing? he thought as he looked at a vertical line on the wall. As he did, he remembered the vertical axe strike that had nearly killed him in the runic circle with the three puppets. He was convinced that the strike and the stroke were related, but replicating them was easier said than done.

Maybe I need to look at them from a different angle, he thought. He walked up to the lone line and traced it out with his finger. *Is it a staff strike? An axe strike? Or is it a brushstroke?*

On a whim, he summoned the Clear Sky Brush and lightly

painted in the air. A thin white line floated there before dissipating. A twinkle appeared in his eyes. *It resembles the simplest brushstroke.*

He summoned the Clear Sky Brush in its large form and repeated the original process. He painted a vertical line ten thousand times in various elements, and the duration it remained in the air increased progressively. Surprisingly, though each element was effective, none of them seemed to fit it perfectly.

I'm still missing something, he thought before sitting down and continuing his cultivation. The thick ambient qi rushed toward him and nourished his core. As he cultivated, he imagined the vertical strike over and over. And the more he visualized it, the more it reminded him of Pangu shattering chaos at the dawn of time. If it was a staff strike, it was a bold one that crushed anything in its path, even the path itself.

Cha Ming ended his cultivation and struck out a few more times with no progress. Seeing that he was going nowhere fast, Cha Ming moved on to the horizontal stroke. He visualized the swift sword he'd experienced from the puppet. Despite mobilizing his full physical strength, and even manifesting a blade of metallic qi on the staff, he couldn't achieve a tenth of its speed. Still, he didn't despair. He performed tens of thousands of staff strikes and tens of thousands of brushstrokes in various elements before cultivating and pondering its mysteries.

A week later, Cha Ming switched to the single dot. He thrust out with his staff and used it like a spear. He used his brush to make single points in the air. Yet no matter what he did, nothing yielded any results. Helpless, he could only shift back to the vertical stroke. He casually struck down with his staff, but this time he noticed a small amount of gray light trailing behind it.

Is it really a staff strike? he wondered as he struck ten thousand more times. Each time, the afterimage grew stronger and remained longer than before. *Or is it a blade strike?*

He slashed out with a blade of qi and then switched back to his brush, leaving a thick line of ink in the air, but the effect was the same. Repetition caused the afterimage to deepen and focus.

Ten thousand times turned to twenty thousand. Twenty thousand turned to thirty thousand. He soon lost himself in the process. One hundred and twenty thousand brushstrokes later, he reached a bottleneck in the vertical stroke and shifted to the horizontal one. Then, after reaching his limit in the horizontal one, he perfected the simple dot.

Before long, a full month had passed. Although it initially seemed like he was getting nowhere, Cha Ming realized that his horizontal, vertical, and stabbing staff strikes could generate a frightening amount of power. They greatly outstripped his initial self-made staff arts. In fact, he felt that they wouldn't lose out to the royal uncle's techniques.

Unfortunately, I've reached a bottleneck, Cha Ming thought. *It's time to face the puppets again.*

He walked toward the central circle and observed his surroundings. Any damage that had been dealt to the blue stone walls from their previous efforts had long since healed over.

"Strange," Cha Ming said as he observed the markings inside the runic circle. The three puppets still stood guard like the moon stones had never been stolen. Yet the places where they stood was exactly where the strangeness lay. The floor within the circle was covered in runic lines, but the location where they stood was strangely empty. His instincts as a formation master itched when he saw three clear imperfections that he'd missed before.

Cha Ming summoned ten combat formations and calmly stepped inside the circle. The first puppet's eyes lit up as it hefted its axe and struck down toward him. The other two puppets didn't move an inch.

As I suspected, Cha Ming thought. *There's more to these guardians than meets the eye.*

Although he spotted an opportunity to act against it, he used ten defensive combat formations and his Clear Sky Staff to defend against the puppet's axe. He coughed up blood as he was thrown outside the circle with half his bones broken. Yet there was a sparkle in his eyes now. He allowed his wounds to regenerate before executing the vertical strike with his Clear Sky Staff once again. A faint trace of gray caused the line to linger in the air for a full five seconds before finally disappearing.

Cha Ming's eyes sparkled once more. *This is what I've been looking for.*

One strike after another, the line deepened. One-tenth, one-fifth, one-half... the trace of gray grew until it almost encompassed the entire afterimage. Finally, Cha Ming approached the circle once again. The puppet gripped its axe and prepared to bat him away once more, but Cha Ming was faster. He struck down with his Clear Sky Staff, executing a perfect strike that glowed with a gray light. His staff crashed down onto the puppet, which shattered into thousands of pieces.

The residual vertical line plunged into the floor and completed the diagram where it once stood. The puppet's body burst into motes of light and agglomerated into a green jade stone and a gray runic fragment. The stone added onto his aura while the runic fragment plunged into his spiritual sea. He flew out of the circle and struck out vertically—the technique resonated with the runic fragment in his spiritual sea and greatly increased its might.

Having experienced such ample rewards, Cha Ming recuperated before facing the second puppet. It slashed out with a swift and unforgettable horizontal slash. Instead of blocking it forcibly like he did before, he used his own version of the horizontal strike in an attempt at parrying it. He was knocked back fifty feet, but the blow deepened his understanding of the strike.

Instead of crushing chaos, it feels more like splitting heaven and earth, Cha Ming thought.

"Again!" he yelled, executing the technique once more. This time, he was only forced back forty feet. He continued to trade blows until finally, his staff quickened. It became faster and faster until a gray beam bisected the guardian puppet before plunging itself into the floor beneath it. A second moon stone and runic fragment rushed toward him. He wasted no time and flew toward the third guardian, which was already ready for him.

Cha Ming traded blow for blow, using formations to strengthen his defenses as they both stabbed at each other. If the previous strikes embodied Crushing Chaos and Splitting Heaven and Earth, this one resembled chaos itself, the origin of the universe.

With this thought in mind, his staff strikes grew increasingly strong, and before long, he could trade blows with the puppet without needing to rely on formations. It wasn't long before his staff left a small gray mark on the puppet's chest. Gray tendrils spread out from this initial point until they fully encompassed its sturdy body. The puppet broke apart, and the gray spot fell into place within the runic circle.

A glowing runic fragment and a moon stone rushed toward Cha Ming and entered his spiritual sea. At the same time, the formation circle where the guardians once stood glowed brightly. It shone with a blinding light before fading.

Ten gray line groupings appeared where the puppets and the platforms had once stood. Like the three strikes he'd seen in the starting area, these groupings also appeared like runic fragments. And like the three before it, each of the ten fragments contained their own unique charm.

Do I need to learn these to pass the next phase? Cha Ming thought.

His heart bubbled in excitement as he realized that snatching treasure wasn't the only way to obtain rewards on the Bridge of Stars. Moon stones aside, these mysterious staff arts were worth their weight in jade.

Huxian sniffed around curiously as he appeared inside a small room. He glared menacingly at the walls before stepping outside a transparent blue membrane. More walls greeted him.

"Do you think you can confuse me with these petty minions?" he said. "Do you think I don't know a clear path to the center when I see one?" he asked a blue stone pillar. It didn't respond.

"Fine, wait here all day for all I care," he said, strutting away proudly. He continued walking toward the center, where two cultivators appeared. One smelled nice, while the other didn't. They were separated by a small runic circle filled with three statues. In the middle, he discovered three delicious-smelling stones.

Those must be the moon stones Cha Ming told me about, he thought.

Without waiting for the two cultivators to introduce themselves, Huxian quickly spread his dual force field of light and shadow. He used his powerful teeth and claws to bat away the three annoying puppets that barred his path before gobbling up the three shining objects. They melted in his mouth in a symphony of runic flavor.

"Just how I remember them." He sighed as he licked his lips. The two cultivators looked at him liked they'd seen a ghost.

"The one on the right can scram," Huxian said, looking toward a gentle pale-skinned woman. "The one on the left can stay."

He pulled back his ears and bared his teeth as he walked toward a cultivator with an ochre aura. The lone man didn't stand a chance before being devoured whole. Or almost whole. Huxian made sure to collect his spatial artifacts. It was a hard world out there, and one didn't just throw away perfectly good lunch money.

Huxian rolled his eyes as he saw that the beautiful white-skinned cultivator had fainted. He ignored her and proceeded back to the statues.

"If I recall correctly, these are made of moon stones as well," he said. His frame grew until it spanned 333 feet, the maximum length he could grow to before surpassing core formation. Then he opened his maw and rained light and darkness down on the runic circle.

The guardian puppets tried to fend him off, but he pressed two statues down with his two massive paws and bit down on the third one. It resisted for a moment before crumbling into moon stone fragments that were quickly gobbled up by the black-and-white fox. He then ate the second and the third in quick succession.

Finally, the circle on the floor glowed and revealed three gray runes. Huxian sniffed at them suspiciously.

"Runic fragments in the air, are you tasty, are you bare?" He licked his lips before cycling his black-and-white aura around him like a vortex, dragging the nearest runic fragment shaped like a log into his mouth. To his surprise, it couldn't be crunched. He swallowed it whole without any hesitation and was rewarded with a warm, delicate flavor.

"These fragments are far too tasty," Huxian thought out loud. "I dare the others to try taking them away."

He immediately sucked up the last two before sitting for a whole week to digest them. After completing the process, the dissolved runic fragments floated outside him like some sort of protective talisman. Yet he instinctively knew that it was far more than that. Rather, he sensed this his ability to utilize demonic qi had increased substantially. All his domainlike techniques had received a healthy boost.

Wait until Cha Ming learns about this, Huxian thought as he trotted toward the next room. This time, he didn't wait to digest the fragments after stealing all the moon stones, eating the guardians, and absorbing the fragments. There were snacks to be had, and he'd miss them if he didn't hurry.

Chapter 11: A Familiar Face

"Get 'im. He's just one demon,'" Huxian said, rolling his eyes. "Can't these guys come up with something original?"

He carefully organized his loot and stowed it into his collar before devouring the puppets and runes. It was the second batch of cultivators he'd run into—one of the side benefits for hurrying rather than taking one's time like Cha Ming did. After absorbing the next group of runes, he ran through the blue corridor toward the next location. As a Godbeast, it took him only a few hours to cross it. When he arrived, he was surprised to discover an empty room with a small white rabbit. It was carefully mixing ingredients in a large cauldron, and one of the ingredients was moon stones. A bunch of them were piled up on the side.

"What, you want a go?" the white rabbit said as Huxian approached.

Huxian frowned. "I don't want to fight, but to be fair, shouldn't we at least split these moon stones fifty-fifty?"

"Why should I split them?" the white rabbit said, placing a small paw on her hip in a very humanlike pose. "I got here first, fair and square."

Huxian was caught off guard. "Maybe we could share the next batch," Huxian offered.

"And why should I share what I can take by myself?" the white rabbit said.

"I could say the same," Huxian replied, casually walking over to the runes. Shadow and light danced around him, forming a small maelstrom that swiftly devoured the intangible objects.

The rabbit's eyes widened. "So you have a bit of skill," the rabbit said. Her ears twirled, and the contents of her cauldron floated into the air. Space distorted as a yellow batter was pressed into tens of thousands of small cakes. Their smell wafted to Huxian, whose mouth watered.

"You wouldn't mind sharing some of those, would you?" Huxian asked. A glob of saliva dripped to the floor.

"What a rude kid," the rabbit said. She flicked a small cake over to Huxian, who gobbled it up and looked at her once more with a pleading expression. The rabbit's eyes narrowed. "You want *more* moon cakes?"

Huxian nodded expectantly. The rabbit looked at him strangely before tossing a thousand over. Huxian ate ten before burping loudly.

"These are so delicious, but so filling," Huxian said with satisfaction. He tossed the rest into his collar. "I'll have to save the rest for later."

"You *like* my moon cakes?" the rabbit asked. She tossed the remainder of the cauldron of moon cakes to Huxian.

"I really like moon stones, but I'm willing to trade them for moon cakes," Huxian said. "They're the most delicious thing I've ever tasted."

"No need," she said cheerfully as she retrieved her cauldron and loot. "Since you like them, I'll make as many as you like. But moon stones are moon stones, so we'll need to rely on our respective skills to compete for them. Let's see if you can keep up, slowpoke." She left behind a white afterimage as she left the room through the shimmering blue portal.

Huxian immediately chased after her. Seeing that she was slightly faster than his raw speed, he channeled light and shadow to catch up.

They were soon neck and neck, and nothing either one did could break the ongoing stalemate.

"Okay, so you're fast," the white rabbit said. "But let's see who can fight faster." They crossed the blue corridor in half the time Huxian usually took and entered the next room.

The fox didn't hesitate. He split into light and shadow doppelgangers and dashed toward the pile in the middle of the ten puppets. He weaved through them in a confusing pattern, joining and splitting as he pleased.

The rabbit, on the other hand, bounced off the puppets like a pinball. After a few quick dodges and deflections, they reached the pile at exactly the same time. Seeing this development, Huxian sent out a mouth of shadow and a mouth of light that tried to swallow the pile in a single gulp.

The rabbit, not wanting to be outdone, sent out a gray cyclone that perfectly countered Huxian's devouring force. A black, white, and gray wave front moved back and forth, oscillating between one-third and two-thirds of the pile.

"You think your brute force can outdo my skill?" The white rabbit chuckled. "You're a million years too early."

"You think your skill can outdo my appetite?" Huxian barked back. "You might be the best cook to have ever existed, but I was born for eating."

The pile of moon stones shifted back and forth between them, with neither of them gaining the advantage. Then, to their mutual surprise, the pile of moon stones broke apart, exactly in half. Huxian swallowed his while the rabbit combined hers with her aura.

Now for the guardians, Huxian thought. He leaped up and increased in size, using his paws to crush two puppets while devouring another. He then picked up the crushed puppets and tossed them in his mouth before approaching two that he had already bound in shadows. He lashed out with these three massive tails, and the three successive blows rapidly demolished the fourth and fifth puppets, whose moon stones he immediately devoured.

"How will you deal with that?" he barked, glaring at the white rabbit. To his surprise, she too had demolished five puppets. The formation activated and revealed ten glowing runes. Huxian swaggered over to the mysterious images and swallowed them without restraint.

"Fine," the rabbit said. "We can split them fifty-fifty. To save energy."

"What about human cultivators?" Huxian asked anxiously. He didn't want to pass up any delicious evil cultivators or their loot.

"Only if they attack us first," the white rabbit said. "And then fifty-fifty. That's my bottom line."

Huxian relaxed. "My name's Huxian," he said excitedly. "What's yours?"

The rabbit rolled her eyes. "I'm Xiao Bai, the one and only Jade Rabbit."

Huxian blinked in confusion. However, he soon saw the rabbit glare and understood what he needed to do. "Ah, yes, the Jade Rabbit. I've heard so much about you."

"And what exactly have you heard?" Xiao Bai asked. "I love hearing about myself."

"Ahem, in a second," Huxian said quickly. "Cultivators are coming."

They immediately collapsed on the ground with open wounds, adopting an appearance of easy prey as twenty cultivators walked near them. To their surprise, however, the cultivators took the long way around and proceeded toward the exit.

"Isn't that cute?" a female cultivator said in the distance. "A wounded fox demon and rabbit demon are helping each other as a team. They're much nicer than most cultivators on this bridge."

"You're right," an elderly cultivator said. "We should take this lesson to heart." Then they disappeared in the distance.

Both Xiao Bai and Huxian gaped at their behavior. "My baiting isn't working anymore," Xiao Bai said.

"Neither is mine," Huxian said. "Humans usually can't resist attacking a wounded demon."

They both scratched their heads for several moments before Huxian had an epiphany.

"I've got it!" he said. "Next time, I'll hide in the shadows while you do your thing. Not only will they take the bait, but we'll have the element of surprise!"

"Isn't that entrapment?" Xiao Bai asked.

"Isn't pretending you're wounded entrapment?" Huxian pointed out. "Actually, what they do when we're wounded and alone is much more telling about who they are as people. I'd say we're just screening the good from the bad much more harshly." He grinned ear to ear as he recited his idea.

"I like it," Xiao Bai said, leading him toward the blue tunnel. "Now let's beat that group of cultivators to the next batch of moon stones."

Cha Ming shook his head as he observed a large runic circle. Its runic patterns were much sparser than the original, and it was occupied by ten puppet guards. While they were substantially stronger than the first three, he'd managed to strengthen himself using the forty-three moon stones he'd gained before. While he couldn't defeat the guards, he could hold his own against them as he gained enlightenment on their techniques.

He summoned a Stormchaser Formation before rushing into the circle. The puppets responded in an instant, forcing Cha Ming to use quick strikes to deflect their blades, swords, axes, and staves. His feet left behind runic fragments with every step.

One of the puppets predicted his movements and struck out with its own runic fragment technique. Cha Ming used Splitting Heaven and Earth to parry the blow and continue his footsteps. He painted a beautiful runic pattern as he danced with his ten opponents. When they came too close, he used Crushing Chaos to repel them or Origin

Strike to interrupt their techniques midway.

My staff strikes are runes, and so are my movement techniques, Cha Ming thought as he fought in their midst. *My body is a rune, my mind is a rune.*

The floor lit up bit by bit. Sometimes he left runic fragments, and at other times he left line fragments. Some were straight while others were curved. Some were deep and others shallow. Bit by bit, he formed the outline of a complete formation that only lacked ten pieces.

"It's time to end this," Cha Ming said as he summoned the Clear Sky Brush. He kicked off one of the guardian puppets and used the momentum to paint a hook. After that, he painted six consecutive brushstrokes that formed fetters and momentarily bound the puppets. Then he swiftly painted out five runic fragments—three were numbers, one represented a woman and another a child. The meanings of these runic fragments were ambiguous and multipurpose.

Seemingly enraged by his actions, the puppets doubled up their efforts. Cha Ming threw out a Flow Talisman and used their difference in speed to paint the last four fragments. The components shot out toward four locations on the runic circle that immediately glowed with a gray light. The ten puppets shattered and reassembled into ten moon stones and runic fragments that added to Cha Ming's already impressive aura.

After collecting these pieces, Cha Ming sat in the middle of the formation and meditated on the ten new fragments that appeared. Some seemed to combine previous radicals while others were entirely new. His experiences aided him greatly, allowing him to reach a bottleneck in each of them after only two weeks' time.

How long will it take to catch up? Cha Ming thought as he walked through the light-blue corridor. Its bare blue walls soothed his mind and nourished his soul during the calming journey.

A full day passed before he reached the next chamber. Like before, it only contained ten puppet guards, but these were much stronger than the ones in the previous room. However, the podiums contained twice as many moon stones. Blood and ashes littered the floor, which had not yet healed over, remnants of the intense battle prior to his arrival. Regardless of the outcome, the cultivators who'd attempted had either died, moved on, or left the Bridge of Stars of their own accord.

His gaze lingered on each puppet and the runic patterns on the floor as he formulated a plan to solve its puzzle. After a half hour, his train of thought was rudely derailed by a piercing shriek.

Twenty figures suddenly rushed into the chamber, chasing a woman wearing a green cloak. "Give back what you've stolen, you thief!" the lead cultivator shouted. They unloaded a salvo of strikes at the petite figure.

Only half of these cultivators are strengthened with moon stones, Cha Ming thought. *Judging by the strength of their auras, most of those who do only have one, while three of them have ten moon stones each.*

"You're all just bullies," the green-cloaked woman said as she used silver strings to deflect the various techniques and weapon strikes. They twirled around her opponents, who carefully avoided them as they closed in on her.

She must have about thirty moon stones, Cha Ming thought. *And her pursuers aren't good at all. Three of the twenty are devilish cultivators.*

He hesitated, however, as his prior experience with meritous cultivators had dampened his expectations. As though reading his mind, the woman sent him a mental message.

If you help me fight them off, I'll give you ten moon stones!

Cha Ming sighed. While he couldn't easily be bought over, his instincts told him that the twenty cultivators were in the wrong. Unfortunately, he couldn't see through this woman with his Eyes of Pure Jade. Her face, her merit, and her sin were all completely hidden from him.

Fine, he sent back. *But I'll only protect you and force them to leave to the next chamber. What you do after that is up to you.*

Good enough, the woman said.

Cha Ming hefted his staff and quickly summoned 1,080 Dao sigils.

Instead of morphing into his usual combat formations, they hovered around him in the shape of fifty-three different runic fragments. They rapidly reorganized into an incomplete gray formation whose style closely resembled the formations in the room.

"You should just move on to the next room and save us both a great deal of trouble," Cha Ming said to the cultivators as they approached. The woman landed beside him, just outside the range of the mysterious gray formation circle.

"With just you?" a skinny man in a black robe said. "This viper killed four of our companions and stole our moon stones. I suggest you don't meddle in our affairs." Despite his strong words, the man didn't intrude on his formation.

"That's not true!" the woman said. "I snuck behind the guardian puppets and took the last batch of moon stones from under their noses. The puppets ended up killing them. It's not my fault their skills were lacking."

"I've already given my word," Cha Ming said cheerfully to the skinny man. "Once I've promised something, I don't go back on it easily."

"Boss, let's just fight them," a diminutive man said. "How strong could a single man possibly be? Looking at the chamber, he's just the leftovers from a group of cultivators who failed to take any moon stones."

Their leader looked Cha Ming up and down. Then he lifted his sword and pointed toward Cha Ming. "Kill!" he yelled.

The cultivators rapidly surrounded him and unleashed a salvo of techniques. Golden phoenixes danced and lightning clouds raged. Several of the cultivators who focused on hand-to-hand combat rushed toward him with heavy weapons.

"Noisy," Cha Ming said as he stepped forward. His runic circle instantly doubled in size and encompassed half the cultivators and suppressed them. Then Cha Ming rushed toward a cultivator surrounded by an ochre glow.

"Crushing Chaos," he said, cleaving downward with his staff and leaving behind a trail of gray light. The devilish cultivator tried to evade but couldn't even take a step back. His body crumbled into a pile of ash.

To everyone's surprise, instead of evading the attacks, Cha Ming rapidly recalled the runic array he'd deployed. Ice, fire, wind, and lightning exploded around him, filling the room with smoke.

"It's too bad you found such an unreliable helper," the leader said to the green-cloaked lady. "I'll tell you what, why don't you give me all your moon stones and all your treasures, and we'll let you stay behind after we plunder this stage?"

"Did I really choose badly?" the woman said playfully. "I happen to think that I'm a very good judge of character," she said.

Suddenly, dozens gray strings burst out from beneath her cloak and entangled the leader and his strongest helpers. Cha Ming burst out from the cloud, expanding his array to encompass all of them. The runic fragments suppressed their power and entangled them further.

Meanwhile, Cha Ming used his Clear Sky Brush to paint large characters in midair. He painted one runic fragment after another, which soon formed a complete rune that rushed out to a devilish cultivator, who collapsed into a puddle of water. He then continued sending out runes, and with each rune, one of the opposing cultivators fell.

"Rush to the next level!" their leader suddenly said. Seeing their intent to retreat, Cha Ming halted his assault. The green threads binding the cultivators broke, and the eight remaining individuals rushed through the barrier to the next level.

"It's very silly to let them go," the woman said, approaching him. "They might find more allies in the future and fight against us."

Cha Ming shrugged. "Our aims are different. Besides, how do I know you're not just manipulating me to fight? For all I know, you're the one at fault in this whole mess."

"You haven't changed a bit," the woman said, chuckling. "Still too nice for your own good. But I like that."

Ten jade stones floated out toward Cha Ming, who caught them and immediately integrated them into his aura.

"Have we met before?" Cha Ming asked as he looked her up and down.

"Naturally." The woman giggled. "But I'm hurt. It seems you've forgotten me so quickly." She pulled back the cowl of her cloak and revealed a familiar head of curly black hair.

He remembered those curls—they were the same as the first time he'd seen them inside Fuxi's Library, and they belonged to the same mysterious person he'd met there, Yu Wen.

Chapter 12: Company

Ten puppets crumbled under the pressure of the completed formation, transforming into twenty moon stones that rushed to Cha Ming. Combined with the twenty stones the puppets had been guarding previously, there were a total of forty. He passed twenty to Yu Wen without hesitating,

"I didn't do anything," Yu Wen protested. "I don't deserve these."

Cha Ming shrugged. "If this trend continues, your strength won't improve while mine will grow. What if I'm entangled and can't protect you? What if others attack us with overwhelming numbers?" He shook his head. "Keeping all these moon stones for myself isn't only selfish, it's stupid."

"Then I'll be impolite," Yu Wen said. "What next?"

"Now I study," Cha Ming said, looking at ten runic fragments that appeared above the platform. He summoned the Clear Sky Brush and began painting them piece by piece.

Seeing his focused expression, Yu Wen sat in meditation and waited.

A week and a half passed before Cha Ming finally stopped. Despite his promoted cultivation, he was tired and mentally exhausted. He looked to Yu Wen as he sat down to recover. Her beautiful curly black hair hadn't changed a bit. She sat in silence, peering intently at a large jade tablet that floated at eye level. Only after some time did her eyes flicker toward him, causing him to look away hurriedly.

"Are you hungry?" Yu Wen said. "Why don't you have a moon cake? Don't worry—it's made of vegetables."

A small yellow pastry imprinted with the character for longevity appeared in her hands. Curious, Cha Ming waved it over and took a bite. A strange, horrible taste filled his mouth, and while he didn't want to swallow it, he forced himself to do it all the same.

A surge of energy instantly filled him, revitalizing his qi, body, and soul. To his surprise, his soul grew a little clearer, and his soul's vestment became a shade more resplendent.

"What a powerful pastry," he said, nodding appreciatively. Not wanting to appear rude, he hesitated before eating the remainder of the cake. Unfortunately, much of the energy was wasted in the process.

"Is it delicious?" she asked, looking at him curiously.

Did she make it herself? Cha Ming thought hurriedly. *Should I tell her the truth? No, only a fool would tell a woman her baking is terrible.*

"Very," Cha Ming said with a smile.

"That's good. My friend will be relieved that *someone* likes her baking," she said. "I personally can't stand it, but you looked exhausted enough to eat anything."

Cha Ming nearly puked blood at the revelation. Unfortunately, he was committed to the lie. "Different people have different tastes," he said. "If I had one every day, I'd eat one every day."

She can't have more than a few such precious things, he thought. *Even a grandmaster alchemist would struggle to make such a powerful pill.*

"That's great!" Yu Wen said. She quickly tossed a bag to Cha Ming, who peered inside. He paled when he saw the large spatial treasure that contained over ten thousand cubic feet of space. It was filled to the brim with what seemed like a million moon cakes. "Eat as many as you like," she said sweetly.

"I'll have to limit myself to one a day," Cha Ming said. "After all, a cultivator's life is extremely long, and the effects of a single cake are so potent."

"It's too bad I don't have more with me," Yu Wen said. "Otherwise, I'd give you more. Truth be told, I only took them to avoid hurting my friend's feelings. But one cake a day sounds just right. She says that even gods and immortals only need a single moon cake a day as nourishment. They'll also maintain a slim, healthy figure."

Cha Ming let out a sigh of relief as he dusted himself off. "We should head over to the next runic circle," he said, looking at the corridor where the cultivators had escaped to.

"Give me a few moments," Yu Wen said, nodding. Her eyes returned to the jade tablet, where they reflected flickering lights.

Is she studying a technique or scripture? Cha Ming wondered. He pondered peeking behind her before pushing this thought out of his mind. *Everyone has their secrets. There's no sense in prying into hers.*

A half hour later, they headed down the silent, empty corridor. Normally, such a silence would be suffocating. This time, however, it was a warm and comfortable interlude that passed by all too quickly.

"I'm so bored," Xiao Bai said for the twentieth time that day.

Huxian yawned as he lounged. "It could be worse," he said as he chowed down on a small moon cake. "We could have nothing to eat."

"You're eating too many!" Xiao Bai said. "I gave you a hundred-thousand-year supply, but at this rate, it won't even last ten thousand!"

"Can't you just make more?" Huxian said as he ate yet another one.

Xiao Bai glowered at him. "You're wasting my work."

"I'm appreciating your good work," Huxian said in a wounded tone. "It'd be different if I was faking it, but I just can't stop myself from eating them." On impulse, he ate yet another one.

"Fine," Xiao Bai said. "I just wish we had dramas to watch or something while we wait for the next batch of cultivators."

"What are dramas?" Huxian asked.

"They're moving pictures," Xiao Bai said. "You watch all the interesting moments in a person's life and pay attention when they get angry, feel sad, or something bad happens to them. It's therapeutic. It makes you feel much better about your own life."

"Huh," Huxian said, eating another moon cake. "Sounds boring."

"You're boring. Your whole family is boring!" Xiao Bai said aggressively.

Huxian lowered his ears in submission. Hours passed, until suddenly his ears shot up. "They're here!" he said, slinking into the shadows.

A few dozen cultivators advanced from one of the two hallways. Half of them looked like vicious killers while the other half looked like decent human beings.

"What a cute little rabbit," a young lady said, skipping out up front. "Can I play with her?"

"Must you?" an older gentleman said. "Haven't you had enough fun?"

"No, I haven't, you old geezer," the lady said. "Come here and play with Mommy!" She looked at Xiao Bai with charming eyes. If Xiao Bai and Huxian were newborns, they'd definitely have been fooled by her act. Fortunately, they were demons and could sense the thick killing intent hidden behind her facade. That, and they could see the giant saber hidden behind her back.

Why do we get all the lunatics? Huxian said as his shadow snuck up behind them and devoured the back-most cultivators. They disappeared without making a sound.

It's either the lunatics or the Goody Two-shoes, Xiao Bai sent back. *Take your pick.*

A half hour later, they finished splitting the spoils and went along their merry way.

Maybe lunatics are best, Huxian thought as he counted his share of the loot.

"Why are these connecting hallways so long?" Yu Wen said as they walked.

"To be fair, we're literally walking to the moon," Cha Ming said. "I'm amazed it's not taking much longer than this."

Yu Wen shook her head. "With the Jade Emperor's might, it would have taken a snap of his fingers to shorten the distance. Yet he chose to make the rules rigid. Even a powerful being from the heavenly courts would have his cultivation suppressed to the peak of core formation if he wandered in."

"Then I have no idea," Cha Ming said helplessly. "You clearly know more about this place than I do. The sect you come from must be very powerful."

"Sect?" Yu Wen said, shaking her head. "I simply stole an entrance token and snuck onto the Bridge of Stars."

Cha Ming's curiosity was piqued. "I take it you had a good reason for stealing it?"

"How did you know I wanted to tell you a story?" Yu Wen said. "It's like you can read minds." She ignored Cha Ming's eyeroll and began her story. "Although I don't belong to a big sect, I have a special and coveted skill."

Her figure blurred before she appeared several hundred feet away. She returned before he could even blink. "I have a fierce movement technique. So fierce, in fact, that I can easily hop between worlds. I've been to more mortal planes and transcendent planes than you can imagine."

"What for?" Cha Ming asked.

"Sightseeing, mostly," Yu Wen said. "Doesn't everyone with enough money want to travel and broaden their horizons? Aren't the best things in life seeing new things and eating good food? I happened to be traveling in a mortal realm when the Bridge of Stars was drawing near.

"There, ten cultivators were waiting for the bridge to descend. I originally wanted to walk past them, but I heard a scream. To my horror, one of the cultivators happened to be 'hungry' and fetched a snack before stepping onto the bridge. The 'snack' was a sixteen-year-old girl."

Yu Wen's gaze hardened. "This type of devilish cultivator was very common in this world, and even good-aligned cultivators had developed a tolerance for such acts. However, I couldn't stay back and do nothing. I rushed up and snatched the girl and conveniently killed the cultivator."

"You managed to do that in the presence of nine other cultivators?" Cha Ming said.

"They were just a bunch of brutes with no skill," Yu Wen replied. "Unfortunately, such brutes do have some strength. They trapped me with their boorish techniques, but before they could do anything to me, we were swept onto the Bridge of Stars, where I made my escape."

Cha Ming rubbed his forehead. "What does that have to do with the twenty-man group you were with when I saw you? Everyone was transported to random locations on the bridge."

"Oh, them?" Yu Wen said. "One of them tried to take advantage of me, so I killed him and his three helpers while I was at it. It's a much less exciting story than the one before."

"It seems like you attract a lot of trouble," Cha Ming said while secretly swearing never to offend such a vicious woman.

"You don't know the half of it," Yu Wen said. "I'd tell you more about it, but I think we have company."

The sounds of blades clashing and the familiar hum of Daoist spells caught their attention. Cha Ming and Yu Wen rushed toward a blue barrier that opened up into a familiar room filled with a few dozen cultivators. They stopped just before the entrance to observe the situation.

"These moon stones aren't something you three can keep," a black-robed cultivator said to three white-robed ones. The black-robed cultivator was accompanied by thirty accomplices.

"We competed for them based on our strengths," the white-robed man said. "Are you going to let your greed cloud your judgment? If you dare point your sword at us, I'll gladly keep you company. But don't say I didn't give you a chance."

"Greed?" the black-cloaked man said. "You three have gobbled up half the moon stones we've encountered in the last three locations. It's not us who are being greedy, but you."

"Brother Fei, this is why I said it was best to draft a contract when we started," a skinny, short-haired man said. He, too, wore white robes. "With a contract, we wouldn't need to worry about enforcing justice—it would enforce itself." He then looked to the leader of the black-robed men. "Speaking of fairness, however, we left you plenty of opportunities to grab stones for yourselves. You just weren't competent enough grasp them."

"Kindness is a virtue, Brother Li," the white-robed woman said. "People often act unreasonably when provoked like this."

"I concede to your wisdom, Sister Qianlin," the man named Li said.

"Are you three just going to ignore us like we don't exist?" the black-robed leader said. His face was red and his fists were clenched in rage.

"I don't want to look down on you, but you won't be able to do a thing to us," the man called Fei said. He then looked toward Cha Ming and Yu Wen through the blue barrier. "There's no need to involve yourselves, friends. You can come once they leave."

Cha Ming felt a resonance when he looked at the man. He quickly realized that although his blond hair and heroic demeanor were unfamiliar, his irises were jade green. Activating his Eyes of Pure Jade, Cha Ming noticed that the three white-robed experts each had jade auras that converged into a pair of wings at their backs. These wings resembled Lu Tianhao's, though the runic patterns covering them differed slightly.

Just as Cha Ming was about to rush out to help them, Yu Wen stopped him. "There's no need," she said. "Unprincipled rabble like them won't even be able to touch their robes."

As she spoke, the blond-haired, jade-eyed man plunged a golden sword into the ground. Red flames emerged from the sword and suddenly entangled the thirty cultivators. They patiently floated around them as they awaited an answer.

"Anyone who chooses to attack from now on will have crossed my bottom line," the man. "This is the third chance I've given you. Think it over well."

The black-robed men hesitated for a moment before speaking.

"He's nothing but a paper tiger," the leader said. "Otherwise, there's simply no reason for him not to butcher us and take our spirit stones." He struggled against the flames briefly before they dispersed. Seeing his success, the others did the same. "Let's see if you have the strength to back up your words," the man said.

Just as he was about to resume his offensive, however, the flames returned. This time, they appeared in the form of red swords of justice. The black-robed man paled, and even Cha Ming, who was far away, was frightened by the eruption of power.

"Quickly, crumble your tokens!" the man yelled. He crushed a jade slip and turned toward motes of light that rushed out from the Bridge of Stars. Five moon stones tumbled to the floor.

Half the cultivators promptly crumbled their tokens, but another half hesitated when they saw the many jade stones tumbling on the floor. Greed filled their eyes as they dove down toward them. Like sentient beings, the swords followed and surrounded them. They barely had a chance to scream before the swords of flame turned them to ashes.

The white-robed, blond-haired man motioned to the moon stones and split them in three portions, one for himself and one for each of his companions. "There's no need to be scared," the man said in Cha Ming's direction. "We don't bite. That is, unless you bite first."

To Cha Ming's surprise, Yu Wen stepped out without any hesitation. He followed suit, and the two arrived before the three white-robed cultivators.

"My name is Zhang Fei, and this is my brother Fang Li and my sister Mu Qianlin."

"My name is Cha Ming, and this is Yu Wen," Cha Ming said.

"It's nice to meet you," Yu Wen said to them. "Decent people are hard to come by these days."

"Indeed," Zhang Fei said. "These cultivators say they're principled, but when they chase treasures, they're nothing more than glorified robbers." Then he looked at Cha Ming with his jade-green eyes. "You should have noticed it too. Only a few devils have entered because the Bridge of Stars is unforgiving to them and prevents them from transmitting them off the bridge. But that doesn't stop the remaining cultivators from succumbing to their greed." He then looked to the group of ten puppets. "What are your plans now?"

"We have some business in this room," Cha Ming said. "No need to mind us." He then stepped toward the runic circle containing the puppets.

"It's not wise to challenge the puppets on your own," Zhang Fei warned.

However, Cha Ming had already entered the circle. The ten puppets instantly charged toward him, unleashing techniques that were several times more powerful than the last time.

Why is their strength so great? Cha Ming thought as he swept his staff in a skillful arc. His strike left behind a runic fragment that hovered in the air. However, this fragment was rapidly decimated by the combined assault. Cha Ming swiftly stepped across the floor, sending runes into it as he stepped.

Three puppet strikes bounced off his two hastily summoned formations, but a fourth one broke through. Cha Ming was forced to throw out a Flow Talisman to dodge their encirclement.

"Just what is he trying to do?" Mu Qianlin said from the side.

"He's trying to solve a puzzle," Yu Wen said. "He just doesn't realize that the puzzle is a lot harder when there are three more people in the room."

"A puzzle?" Mu Qianlin said. "Can't we just get a bunch of moon stones if we destroy the puppets?"

"And how many precious talismans and single-used treasures do you plan on using to do that?" Yu Wen said with a raised eyebrow.

"Are you saying there's a way to avoid it?" Zhang Fei asked.

"Cha Ming has a way," she said. "Though he'll expend a lot of resources if you all linger here. I don't suppose you're willing to move to the next room?"

"It's not only moon stones that are precious," Zhang Fei said, shaking his head. "How can we gain enlightenment on rune carving if we don't defeat them?"

"So that's what you're after," Yu Wen said. "How about this: If you help Brother Cha Ming fight them, we'll split the moon stones sixty-forty. Sixty for us, forty for you. Both our sides won't need to expend consumables."

"Sixty-forty is a bit steep," Fang Li commented. "That aside, can we sign a contract?"

"Mid-fight?" Yu Wen said. "Maybe for future rooms, but I'm helpless at this point."

"Let's just do as she says," Zhang Fei said. "Cha Ming's going to suffer if we don't hurry. Besides, they don't seem like the ungrateful sort."

Though Cha Ming was managing to cope with the aid of his talismans and combat formations, his situation was becoming increasingly dire.

Chapter 13: Goals

I can't hold out for much longer, Cha Ming thought as he fought off the puppet onslaught. Just as he was about to catch a glimpse of his target technique, an ominous sensation forced him to dodge a blade before it could slash his back.

How much time and talismans will I have to waste at this rate? He slashed out with Splitting Heaven and Earth, quickly deflecting yet another blow aimed for the back of his head.

Cha Ming locked onto his target once more, but just as it was about to execute its signature technique, another puppet rushed beside him. Before he could dodge, he noticed green vines wrapping around it.

Good! he thought, summoning his combat formations to defend against the strike. *What a powerful fragment,* he thought as cuts appeared all over his skin.

Fortunately, his physique had been strengthened by moon stones, and the cuts regenerated instantly, leaving not a single drop of blood to moisten the floor.

Another two puppets appeared before him, but a gentle wind brushed up against them as the Mu Qianlin flew up beside him with her Exorcist Staff. The four puppets that took their place were repelled by Zhang Fei and his flaming swords. They joined his golden sword in striking the puppets, stunning them for a brief moment.

Seeing that he was now free to do as he pleased, Cha Ming struck out against his target puppet using his own version of the runic fragment technique. They clashed, but Cha Ming took the brunt of the assault.

Again! he thought. He rushed toward the puppet and executed a five-stroke fragment that lingered in the air for a moment longer. It was quickly destroyed by the puppet.

One last time! Cha Ming struck out five consecutive times. They superimposed over each other before sinking into the floor. The puppet, which was substantially more powerful than the ones that came before, barely resisted the runic attack. Having accomplished his goal, Cha Ming sought out another target.

"I'll switch you," he shouted as he tackled a puppet controlled by Yu Wen's gray strings. As he ran, runic lines lit up on the floor and filled in the missing gaps. Each runic line was composed of the sixty-three he'd learned before. He rushed up to the puppet and clashed against it a few times before abandoning it for another one. Although their three new companions were perplexed, they waited to see the end result.

Before long, the entire floor was covered in gray runic lines. Cha Ming flew up above the circle and lashed out five times with his staff. Each stroke left a gray imprint in the air that bound the puppet's movements. Once the fifth stroke was completed, all five lines combined and rushed into the floor, which glowed brightly after receiving its final component. The ten puppets instantly disintegrated and transformed into twenty moon stones.

"Many thanks for the help," Cha Ming said, sending twelve stones to Zhang Fei's group.

"Too much," Zhang Fei said, sending four stones back. "We made a fair deal, sixty-forty. This saves us much time and consumables and provides us insurance against other groups."

Surprised, Cha Ming sent six stones to Yu Wen, who didn't reject them. With the disappearance of the ten puppets, ten runes appeared in the room. Cha Ming and the three angelic cultivators began focusing on the runes while Yu Wen took out the same jade tablet she'd been studying since he'd encountered her.

Cha Ming's trance ended ten days later. He looked around and was amazed to see everyone lounging about. "Weren't you very excited to study these runes?" he asked Zhang Fei and Fang Li. The two were playing cards while sipping wine.

"Inspiration only goes so far," Fang Li said, shrugging. "We aren't trying to memorize these runes. Rather, we're trying to gain inspiration for rune carving. We already know which ones we'll carve, so our scope of study is rather limited."

"You've already decided?" Cha Ming asked. "Is breaking through to rune carving really so simple?"

"How can it be simple?" Fang Li said, shaking his head self-deprecatingly. "Out of the three of us, we'll be lucky if one succeeds. And that's considering that we were lucky enough to come to the bridge and belong to a powerful sect with dozens of suitable rune-carving diagrams. Cultivators with no background aren't so lucky. They can only rely on the most basic runic inspirations."

"What are their chances of success?" Cha Ming asked.

"One in ten," Fang Li said. "Assuming they've reached the grandmaster level in a supporting profession."

Unease filled Cha Ming's heart as he realized how difficult cultivation truly was. Thus far, he had experienced relatively smooth sailing along this journey. "Shall we continue?" he said to the two, looking toward the exit anxiously.

"We can leave after this game, assuming the ladies are free," Fang Li said.

"Can't we just call it quits now?" Zhang Fei complained.

"And let you take back your wager? Ha!" Fang Li said. "That aside, I figure the ladies still have fifteen minutes before they need a break."

"A break?" Cha Ming said. "Aren't they studying a technique?"

The two men looked at each other before bursting out laughing.

"What's so funny?" he asked.

"It's nothing," the two men said, wiping tears from their eyes. "But if you're interested in studying the technique, you can go ahead and admire it. Yu Wen already sent out an open invitation."

Frowning, Cha Ming walked toward the two women, who were gazing intently at the jade tablet. Cha Ming sat down just in time to catch an amazing saber strike, which was rapidly deflected by twin swords.

"Good technique," he whispered. Sensing irritation from the two women, he quieted down and watched the two men battle.

As time passed, he became perplexed. *Isn't this fight a little too unrealistic?* he thought. Although the combat was fast-paced, the two fighters showed far more openings than normal. He began to suspect the fight was staged. Then the scenery switched. A teary-eyed woman looked at the two fighting men in confusion before speaking a few words.

"Please don't fight," she said. "I'll never forgive you if you hurt each other."

Cha Ming trembled. A dull tremor spread through his mind as he finally realized what was going on.

Are you kidding me? he thought. *They're watching wuxia dramas?*

His glorified view of the cultivation world suddenly crumbled to bits as he realized that, despite the temptation of eternal life and deeper truths, cultivators would still choose to watch dramas if given the opportunity.

"What's wrong?" Yu Wen asked Cha Ming, who was still in a daze after they'd packed up.

"Nothing," Cha Ming said as he brushed himself off. "Everything is as it should be."

He popped a moon cake in his mouth. The bitter taste and plentiful energy soothed the pain deep within his soul.

"I was only a piddling foundation-establishment cultivator when the war began," Zhang Fei said as they walked down the blue stone corridor. "The mad king Long Tian plunged four nations into turmoil. They fought tooth and nail, and being a hot-blooded youth in the prime of my life, I left with the army to fight in the vanguard. My Dao companion begged me not to go, but I knew what had to be done. If good men didn't bleed, the entire continent would suffer.

"Despite my weak cultivation, I fought with everything I had. Years passed by in a flash. As my cultivation improved and my battle merit grew, I was quickly promoted to captain, then colonel, and finally, general. The war ended after ten years of brutal slaughter. I was one of the lucky few to land a hit on the mad king, so I was promoted to honorary marshal and given a hefty retirement package.

"I knew the reason behind the package. I wasn't a fool. The army had grown too large for the kingdom's own good, and they had to downsize. Given my achievements, I would have had far too much sway in the capital, so they chose to bribe me into retirement. Still, that satisfied me. I'd fought with my life on the line for a decade and deserved a rest. Therefore, I grabbed a flight treasure and flew off to my hometown, where my Dao companion was waiting for me. Or so I thought.

"The love of my life had disappeared, and everyone I knew refused to tell me where she'd gone. Only after a week of constant hounding did they relent and tell me the truth. Seven years ago, she and my best friend had fallen in love and traveled to another kingdom. They were happy together, and the villagers didn't want me doing anything rash. My family urged me to remain calm, but the rage in my heart was difficult to ignore. I rejected their advice and rushed across the continent. By then, I was a middle-core-formation cultivator.

"I fought through swampy land and flew through demon-infested skies. I scaled mountains and fought mighty elementals when they prevented me from crossing their territory. It took me two weeks to arrive in the Soulfire Kingdom, a rich and prosperous nation unaffected by the war. I seethed as I walked into the city they inhabited and scouted their residence. Then, ignoring the many warnings from the city's protector, I flew up above their home with my sword held high. I gathered flames around my blade as I prepared to unleash my mightiest techniques on my former Dao companion and former best friend. I looked at their three older children and newborn baby with cold fury in my eyes. They should have been mine, but now they were his."

He looked to Cha Ming and the rest, the raw emotion in his voice apparent. They were all breathless, waiting for the terrible story to end. "And that's when I did the single most satisfying thing in my entire life," he said softly.

His fiery demeanor calmed and was replaced by the patient man they knew. "I forgave them. I bottled up my rage and put it in its place. Then, I followed the protector to his manor. We talked for a while, and after some brief negotiations, I sold him my sword for a rock-bottom price. It was my lifelong companion, but after aiming it at the people I'd known and loved, I couldn't bear the sight of it. I wrapped up the spirit stones I sold my sword for and placed them in front of their house with a teary note of congratulations. Three days later, I received my angelic endowment."

Cha Ming frowned but said nothing.

"You look confused," Zhang Fei said gently after sensing his dissatisfaction.

"I just don't understand how abstaining from a despicable act would lead to angelic endowment," Cha Ming said. "Don't get me wrong, I love your stories. You've accomplished may great deeds in your life. But to me, *not* killing a half dozen innocents pales in comparison to the many villains you've killed and the justice you've upheld."

Zhang Fei nodded. "Yes, it does. But sometimes it's not the deeds of a man that matter but the man himself." He looked at Cha Ming with his jade eyes. "Despite having accrued more merit in your young age, you've yet to gain your wings. And haven't you seen merit-imbued people perform despicable acts on this bridge? Ultimately, it isn't a matter of quantity but of essence. For that, you need to look within. We're sharing the stories we feel are most important to your development, but it's up to you to glean your own lesson from them."

"Now it's your turn to share a story," Yu Wen said from the side. "Even though they aren't as interesting as my travel stories, I like them just the same."

"All right," Cha Ming said. "Since we're almost there, I'll keep it short." The light-blue glow leading to the next room was approaching swiftly. "There was once a man who taught me staff arts. Although we met under unusual circumstances, he gave his all to teaching me. He gave me advice whenever I needed it; he taught staff arts when I needed to fight and runic arts when I couldn't save others on my own. Life was truly relaxed under his care. One day, however, my brother and I encountered something that was completely beyond us: a Heavenly Tribulation when I was only a late-qi-condensation cultivator."

"A Heavenly Tribulation during qi condensation?" Fang Li asked. "How is that even possible?"

"What do you guys know?" Yu Wen said. "There are countless things that can cause the anger of a plane. It could be something like transcendents fighting or the birth of a soul-bound treasure. It could be the appearance of a mysterious natural treasure or the evolution of a powerful demon beast." After scolding them, she turned to Cha Ming. "But I'm more interested in this teacher of yours. Where does he live now? Is he still on your mortal plane?"

"Unfortunately, he was gravely wounded by the tribulation," Cha Ming said. "He painted a mystical white formation to shelter us from the lightning, but it placed a great burden on him. All that's left of him is his wounded soul. I've journeyed to Jade Moon Planet in the hopes of finding a Burning Samsara Lotus."

"A Burning Samsara Lotus," Mu Qianlin said, pondering. "It's

– 142 –

difficult, but not impossible. In the long history of my sect, three people have seen and recorded it." Cha Ming's eyes lit up at the mention. "But it's very difficult to obtain, and only by passing the Jade Moon Garden trials can you hope to have a chance at collecting it."

"I can only try," Cha Ming said. "And I'm willing to exchange half the herbs I pick for this one item."

"I'll be sure to pass this news along to my team leader," Zhang Fei said.

"I'll do the same," Fang Li said.

"As will I," Mu Qianlin said. "But I'll leave out the part about how desperate you are. I'll just let them know that you're willing to pay a high price."

Cha Ming nodded. They entered a room devoid of moon stones and filled with guards.

"It looks like we're a little late," Cha Ming said. "But that's all right. Let's get started."

Time flew by, and before long, they arrived at the second to the last group of guards. Their experienced group showed no hesitation when they charged at the thirty guards that stood within the runic circle. The blue stone floor they guarded was mostly empty, save for thirty types of runic fragments. The remaining empty spots were up to Cha Ming to complete as he saw fit.

He took a deep breath before rushing headlong into the runic circle. Blades of elemental light attacked him and his four companions. They tumbled carefully and deflected countless techniques while fighting against the much stronger puppets.

Cha Ming laid down runes with his steps as he executed various staff arts to deflect the puppets. Yu Wen's strings, combined with Fang Li's constricting vines, greatly restrained their movements.

This allowed Mu Qianlin and Zhang Fei to repel any unneeded interference away from Cha Ming at their leisure.

One, he thought as he completed a perfect ten-line radical and rushed to his next opponent. *Two, three, four, five.*

The floor rapidly filled with gray runic fragments until only a few empty spots remained. Cha Ming rushed toward two puppets simultaneously. He used intricate staff movements to draw two fragments while deflecting both techniques the guards had unleashed. *Eight, nine.*

Yu Wen and the other three moved quickly to keep away the nine nearest puppets as he worked.

Fast! Cha Ming thought as he dodged twelve consecutive strikes. He raised his staff just in time to deflect these twelve blows once again. Each blow he parried caused the image in his mind to grow clearer and clearer, until finally, it clicked.

Cha Ming swiftly took three steps back and lashed out three times with his staff. Three lines floated into place. He then lashed out four times, and they superimposed into a seven-line fragment. Finally, he unleashed five more rapid staff strikes. The completed twelve-line fragment rushed to the floor, and ten guardians burst into moon stones.

Cha Ming rapidly split these seventy moon stones and flew toward the last twenty puppets. He clashed with them time and time again as the group stalled for time. Runes filled the circle one after another, until finally a bright glow enveloped them.

The guardians shattered and transformed into moon stones. Then the large runic circle fully activated and projected the remaining thirty runic fragments. He didn't immediately proceed to studying them, however. Instead he absorbed the moon stones he'd just obtained to nourish his body, qi, and soul. His perception also improved in the process.

Combined with the various moon stones he'd acquired by dispatching ambushing enemies, he'd accumulated 711 moon stones. According to the Alabaster Group's introductory slip, this was enough to exchange for seven herb-gathering quotas.

"All that remains is the final trial," Zhang Fei said as he absorbed his share of moon stones. "What are your opinions on this competition?"

His eyes were filled with battle intent—it was clear that he wanted to participate in this struggle.

"My sect normally advises participants to avoid the competition," Mu Qianlin said. "Unfortunately, it's always accompanied by a grand melee where everyone kills each other to snatch moon stones. It's rather despicable if you think about it."

"But our strength should be much stronger than most participants," Fang Li said. "Most people won't destroy the guardian puppets, and most allied groups will gather at least twenty members before arriving at the final trial. That means that we should have around four times as many moon stones on average. Most of the remaining cultivators will exit before challenging the final stage, and a few million will exit without obtaining any moon stones. In the end, perhaps only 300 to 400 confident cultivators will participate in a final bloodbath."

"Although the guardians are much stronger, they'll be keeping 30,000 moon stones in total," Cha Ming said. "Even grabbing a thirtieth means an extra herb-picking quota."

"That's not counting the many moon stones these participants will have in their possession," Zhang Fei said. "Many people will court death by trying to rob others. Although I won't go out of my way to attack them, I don't mind collecting a tax from those who try to kill me."

"Fair enough," Cha Ming said. "Though I'm curious as to whether or not there will be even more runes after the guardians are dispatched."

"It's difficult to say," Zhang Fei said. "The puppets are said to be impossible to destroy. But that was before we were introduced to your method. Perhaps it's possible to defeat them by activating the formation. In my opinion, it's worth a try."

Cha Ming shook his head. "It's all moot until I actually solve the formation. And judging from the past trend, I'll need to memorize these runes and draw the formation up from scratch without any reference points."

Cha Ming walked over to the runic fragments and began studying them. Yu Wen went to sit by him while the three others kept a respectable distance. Thirty days passed before Cha Ming stowed away his staff.

"It's almost been a full year since we entered the Bridge of Stars," Cha Ming said as he stood up. "How about it? Are you all willing to join me in the final struggle?" He had mastered 303 runic fragments—only the key essence of the final thirty remained.

"Of course," Yu Wen said, stowing her jade tablet.

"I was born ready," Zhang Fei said.

"I'm in," Mu Qianlin said.

"We won't know unless we give it a shot," Fang Li said, shrugging.

"Then let's see what these sects are made of," Cha Ming said as he crossed the blue boundary.

Chapter 14: Building a Fire

"Lin Xiu, wait up!" Hong Xin said as she ran down the hallway. She feigned catching her breath, causing the other woman to slow down and wait for her. Then she started walking again at a deliberately slow pace. The group Lin Xiu had previously been walking with moved on without her.

"How have you been?" Hong Xin said as they walked toward lying class. The unusual class took place in a small patch of crimson-leafed trees outside the red pavilion. It was one of the few classes that took place outside the central courtyard.

"I've been very well. Thank you for asking," Lin Xiu said.

Hong Xin picked up notes of interest and anticipation. She stoked those flames and caused her heartbeat to quicken.

"Of course, things are always better when you're around."

"Things can't be all that bad," Hong Xin said in a bewitching voice. It took yet another layer of frost off the woman's guarded heart.

"No, I mean it," Lin Xiu said wistfully. "It's been so boring ever since…" She looked off to the side.

"There's no need to talk about the past," Hong Xin said. Meanwhile, she sent a different, unheard message. *No one will hear us if we don't speak out loud.*

"You're right, it's better to talk about the present," Lin Xiu said. She bent over to pick up a few scattered violets. She led them to her nose and closed her eyes as she inhaled their delicate scent. "I like these purple flowers. Although they're not roses, they have their own charm."

I just miss dancing, Lin Xiu sent. *Life isn't the same without it. The zither pales in comparison, and I hate to even look at it.*

"Quite right, but you shouldn't pick so many flowers," Hong Xin said, looking at the violets in her hands. "They last much longer when they're in the ground." *What if I told you I had a place where we could practice unsupervised?*

"But I can't help it," Lin Xiu said. "They're so pretty." *Is that even possible?* Her eyes shifted.

"Come now, just show a little self-restraint, and you'll be able to come see them every day," Hong Xin said.

We'll be gathering tonight, Hong Xin sent. *In Mistress Huang's classroom one hour after sunset. Use glamour to hide your traces.*

"All right, I'll try," Lin Xiu said. "Anyway, I should really hurry to class. Otherwise, Teacher will scold me again." *What if I can't come?*

"I understand," Hong Xin said. "She scolds me every so often as well. Her punishments are the worst!" *Then don't. We understand.*

Lying class passed by uneventfully. Afterward, Hong Xin returned to the courtyard to practice the flute. She didn't go out of her way to attract a crowd or punish passersby as she used to. Instead she practiced with her usual elegance in the routine she'd established for the past several weeks: three hours of playing followed by three hours of cultivating. It was the same every day, forever unchanging. And given her previous pattern of revenge for the slightest grievances, everyone made sure to avoid her precisely at these times.

Three hours trickled by before she stowed her flute and walked back to her deserted chambers. Although she still had to share a room, her roommate made sure to avoid her whenever possible. Hong Xin sat cross-legged as she always did and cultivated peacefully. She waited for the usual wave of spiritual force to wash over her before picking up a brush and a pallet of makeup. She copiously dabbed the white paste on her face, her hair, and her red clothes. Soon, every inch of her body was covered.

Hong Xin walked out from the cloud of makeup, leaving an illusory replica of herself. It matched her cultivation, her aura, and her appearance. It was a complex glamour that, in theory, greatly exceeded her level. After inspecting it for a few moments, she brushed a different kind of makeup on. This time, she infused it with her resplendent force and caused it to shimmer vaguely. She then disappeared without a trace.

Hong Xin walked out from the room soundlessly, using her knowledge of posture and balance to avoid any sounds on the intentionally creaky flooring. Several students passed by her as though she didn't exist. She walked unimpeded to the teachers' quarters, where she waited for a familiar figure to make an appearance.

Mistress Huang, her flute teacher, walked past her without noticing anything and approached a small chest. She traced a mysterious pattern on it and placed a red slip inside it. The slip was a key, and she left it there during her three hours of cultivation every day in case anyone needed it. No one ever did.

Hong Xin waited as Mistress Huang walked away from the box. Like clockwork, Mistress Meng also arrived and picked up a pile of papers. She leafed through them before leaving to teach a class. Although they'd walked all over a relatively small area, Hong Xin hadn't moved a bit. She stood slightly off center, positioned in such a way that they wouldn't walk near enough to detect her. After Mistress Meng left, Hong Xin walked up to the wooden box and traced the familiar pattern. The box clicked open.

"What are you doing open?" a voice suddenly said.

Hong Xin's heart leapt. She quickly stepped to the side as an assistant teacher who wasn't often there walked into the work area. She rifled through the chest and pulled out a white slip before leaving.

Hong Xin let out a sigh of relief. She waited for a few moments before opening the box once more and retrieving the key.

Just when you think you have a system figured out, someone comes in and upsets the balance, Hong Xin thought. Her heart still racing, she rushed out of the teacher's area and headed toward Mistress Huang's classroom.

The large hall was a flurry of activity. Nine women danced, sang, and played musical instruments they hadn't touched in many months. Their tender nerves relaxed as their activities brought a modicum of warmth to their cold hearts. Little by little, they felt the daggerlike tendrils of the Red Dust Pavilion easing out of their souls, making breathing just a little bit easier.

"I thought I'd lost myself," Bai Ling said as she lounged in a relaxed posture. "My personality was beginning to change. It was icing over, to the point that someone could spit in my face and I wouldn't even react."

"That's what they're looking for," Ji Bingxue said, grimacing. "My original pride and indifference can't hold a candle to the way I was just a few hours ago. You have our thanks, Hong Xin."

Hong Xin shook her head. "It's too early to thank me. We have a long way to go till graduation." Although she had quickly caught up to her peers, less than a year remained before the two-year deadline. "Furthermore, I think we should save more sisters. We don't want what happened to Lili repeating itself."

The cheerful atmosphere immediately turned gloomy.

"Aren't we nine enough?" Ji Bingxue said. "I want revenge as much as you all do, but the mistresses scare me. Given how quickly our cultivations increase in the Red Dust Pavilion, won't those hags be unfathomably strong?"

"How strong could they be?" Hong Xin pressed. "There are only a dozen of them, but there are hundreds of sisters. We're all prisoners here. We all saw Lili's corpse the next day after she tried escaping."

"Many of the mistresses have been around for decades," Bai Ling interjected. "I'm not against revenge, but we need to be smart about this. We need some tangible advantages before we act, or we'll be nothing but fish on a chopping block."

"But what *are* our advantages?" Hong Xin said. "I know my talents, and a sharp mind isn't one of them."

"You don't need to worry about that," Bai Ling said. "I'll lay it out for you. If we cause a rebellion, as you are hoping, we have two advantages. The first is manpower, the second is morale."

"We have an advantage in potential manpower, but morale?" Ji Bingxue said, lifting an eyebrow. "Pardon me for being blunt, but our group of nine young women is barely able to keep themselves from crying to sleep every night."

"Just let me finish," Bai Ling said grumpily. "We have an advantage in *potential* manpower and *potential* morale. Hong Xin has a strange talent—she is able to thaw the hearts of the students in the Red Dust Pavilion and enable them to find the joy that's missing in their lives. Anyone who gains this sort of energy will want to join our group and save the other sisters. If we carefully screen recruits, that means we can outnumber the mistresses at least ten to one.

"The advantage in morale is also obvious," she continued. "We got in by following our hearts, and in turn, they taught us to be cold and manipulative. Our ability to rouse emotions is top notch. If we time things right, we could potentially turn uninvolved students and even teachers to our side."

"It's not that I don't want to help, but I'm worried about lapsing back," Lin Xiu said. "Their methods are persuasive and make you lose hope. You were able to draw us out this time, but what about next time?"

The other women nodded in agreement.

"That is the second reason I brought you all here," Hong Xin said. "Currently, everyone practices the Frozen Heart Sutra." She pulled a black book from her bag that chilled the air around it. "The sutra invades the heart and soul of the cultivator practicing it. An icy disposition is etched into one's cultivation. After reaching perfection, it completely transforms the cultivator. At this point, I believe it's irreversible without causing great damage to one's heart realm."

"It's irreversible?" Lin Xiu asked sadly. "Can we at least stall the inevitable?"

"I only said it was irreversible upon reaching *perfection*," Hong Xin said. "None of you have reached this realm." She then summoned a tiny flame that floated above the book's chilly aura. It shrank until it became a small red ball that kept its warmth tightly bound.

"Today, I will begin teaching you about heart kindling," Hong Xin said. "I can't show you the original scripture, nor can I show you the step-by-step method. What I *can* do, however, is share with you a story of a girl who lost everything only to find it again once after all hope had faded. I can tell you the story of a girl whose heart was broken but mended. Only those who have felt the chilling cold of loneliness and despair can truly kindle a person's heart. You have all felt that chill, so I'm confident that you will succeed. The first step to kindling another heart is to kindle your own."

As she spoke, the eight other women felt their confidence and joy increasing. Their heartbeats quickened, to the point that they thought they were doing vigorous exercise or meeting their first lover. It was at this moment that they truly felt the power of kindling.

They will be the flames that light up the Red Dust Pavilion, Hong Xin thought as she saw them desperately struggle for enlightenment. *From these eight, the fire will spread and dispel every inch of cold that pervades this place. The Red Dust Pavilion will burn.*

Hong Xin recast her glamour before soundlessly exiting the room in the dead of night. The floor creaked slightly as she misjudged her posture.

Calm down, Hong Xin, she told herself. *Icy disposition, icy disposition.*

Her posture gradually adjusted until finally, no more creaking could be heard. She headed to the teachers' accommodations where she waited for two mistresses to finish what looked to be a long conversation.

"And the nerve of this student," Mistress Yuan said. "She had the *nerve* to say that I was mistaken. I almost lost my cool before realizing that she was goading me. I made her kneel on broken glass for half a day as punishment."

"We sometimes get pigheaded ones," Mistress Shan said. "But they all learn in time. Let me tell you about a silly girl who…"

Hong Xin looked around nervously as the clock on the wall ticked. Only a quarter hour remained before the punctual Mistress Huang returned to take her key.

Should I do something to distract them? she thought.

At this moment, a familiar figure walked up beside the two women. It was the loathsome Mistress Meng. "Talking about pigheaded students, I see," she said. "I had an especially difficult one this past year."

"Is it that girl Hong Xin?" Mistress Shan said. "The one you had publicly flogged?"

"The very same," Mistress Meng said. "In the first week of classes, she had the nerve to glare at me. But let me tell you, when I see fire in a girl, it excites me. I paid special attention to her, and within three months, she was my best student."

"What did you do?" Mistress Yuan said. "I mean, aside from the public flogging."

"Well, you know what they say—that warmth comes from within, right?" Mistress Meng said wickedly. "One day, I was so fed up with her that I decided to try something… experimental. I threw her in an icebox and forced her body temperature to drop quickly."

"You can kill a student that way," Mistress Yuan said, concerned. "Every seedling we have is a rare talent."

"But a bad seed isn't worth growing," Mistress Meng said. "So I kept her there for three days and three nights. During that time, I discovered a light flickering in her foundation. Not only did it keep her warm, but it kept her heart from icing over."

"You mean she'd worked heart kindling into her foundation?" Mistress Shan said, startled. "I didn't think that was possible. I mean not since…"

"You should be careful of what you speak," Mistress Meng said. "But yes, it was a similar case to that one. I used my own qi and the cold in the room to gradually make her kindling die down and frost over. I snuffed the flame of her heart out, and she's been as cold as ice ever since. And surprisingly, her foundation has morphed into a perfect dousing foundation."

"Amazing," Mistress Shan said. "It's no wonder that the headmistress made you the disciplinary elder."

"You'd better remember it," Mistress Meng said. "Now then, we should get out of here. We wouldn't want to bump into *her*."

"No, we would not," Mistress Shan said. "In some ways, she's worse than the headmistress.

"You'd better be careful about what you say," Mistress Meng said dryly. "The last mistress who spoke ill of her still hasn't recovered."

The other two glanced around worriedly before departing. Then Mistress Meng walked over to the wooden box, took out a token, and left to teach her class.

Hong Xin heaved a sigh of relief as she saw that an incense time still remained. She carefully traced open the wooden box and replaced the token in the same order she'd found it. Finally, she crept out of the teachers' area, dispelled her glamour, and began walking to her bedroom.

"Already done your cultivation for the day, I see?" a voice suddenly said from behind her.

Hong Xin gulped before turning around. "Greetings, Mistress Huang," Hong Xin said, bowing. "The stars are very beautiful tonight. Have you had a chance to see them?"

"Yes, the stars extend across the moon like a small bridge," Mistress Huang said. "These days have been rather chilly. It's best to keep inside lest you catch a cold."

"But we don't feel the cold," Hong Xin said.

"I didn't mean physical cold, child," Mistress Huang said, stepping closer.

Hong Xin felt a warmth surging from the depths of her core.

She hurriedly froze it over, preventing any trace of heat from being exposed.

"Is there something you need?" Hong Xin asked.

"Nothing," Mistress Huang said. "I'm just surprised to see that you've reached the first level of the Frozen Heart Sutra."

The compliment welled up inside Hong Xin, threatening to burst the thick layer of ice protecting her core. She firmly contained the surge of joy.

"Many thanks for the compliment, Mistress," Hong Xin said. "I'll be sure to continue working hard."

Mistress Huang frowned slightly before stepping back toward the teachers' residence. "Off you go, then, child. I'll make sure the headmistress knows of your success."

"You're too kind," Hong Xin said, bowing. She waited a few moments for Mistress Huang to disappear. Then she returned to her residence and continued cultivating, ending her false session before returning to practice the flute. Snow fell as she played, further deepening the layer of ice on her heart and core.

That was far too close, she thought. *I'll need to give up a little warmth in favor of concealment.* As she thought this, the red part of her core shrank by a quarter while the cold exterior took over the abandoned space. Her body temperature plunged in response, leaving her white skin feeling smooth and cold as marble.

It recovered moments later. As her body changed, so did her temperament. She was now cold and logical, a beauty with a heart of ice.

Chapter 15: Struggle

The light-blue glow of the barrier faded, revealing thousands of cultivators patiently waiting in a massive chamber. Its ceiling was transparent, revealing the nearby Jade Moon Planet's exterior. Half its surface was covered in oceans while the other half contained lush forests, rich mountain ranges, and verdant plains that did not lose out to any mortal plane. This otherworldly paradise was only one quick jaunt away through one of the chamber's ten teleportation arrays.

"That's a lot more than five hundred cultivators," Cha Ming noted as they entered the large hall.

Tens of thousands of humans were gathered near the teleportation arrays in informal groups—some had set up stalls while others were drinking. They stood in stark contrast to the few hundred cultivators sitting near a large circle, surrounding thirty massive puppets. These constructs were several times larger than the ones they'd faced before. And according to the runic fragments he'd seen previously, their techniques were much deadlier.

"I wonder why they haven't started plundering the moon stones," Yu Wen said as they approached the center.

The outer circle contained dozens of small piles of one hundred or so jade rocks, while the middle area contained ten mid-sized piles of about a thousand each. The inner circle contained three piles of ten thousand moon stones each, an astronomical amount compared to what they'd obtained thus far.

"It's not because they don't want to but because they can't," Zhang Fei said, shaking his head. "Although they've acquired enough cultivators to challenge the puppets, there are still too many cultivators casually lurking about. Since the time limit for crossing the bridge is one year, they're waiting until the end to plunder the remaining moon stones. This way, they can casually chase out the remaining cultivators before advancing."

"But what are all these cultivators doing?" Cha Ming said, surveying those near the teleportation gates. Most of them had less than twenty moon stones.

"They're trading," Mu Qianlin said. "Each influence will send a large amount of resources with their strongest members. They'll trade these resources with miscellaneous cultivators who haven't gathered enough moon stones to trade for anything. Each group will bid for the moon stones before sending the cultivators on their way. With any luck, they'll manage to get some extra herb-gathering quotas or even some techniques or treasures."

"Fair enough," Cha Ming said. He looked out toward the few hundred cultivators near the central circle and spotted Song Min, who looked at him in surprise. She waved and flew over with Han Jiling from the Alabaster Group.

"I thought you'd already left the bridge along with the others," Song Ming said as they landed. "But that's good. Our group of fifty is lacking members. If you participate, it's possible for us to earn an additional half share of the moon stones. That could be anywhere between five and ten moon stones once everything is said and done."

"My apologies," Cha Ming said, shaking his head. "I've already made an agreement with these four companions. We won't inconvenience you."

Due to their large number of moon stones, Song Min couldn't accurately determine their individual strength. Meanwhile, Cha Ming could tell that she and Han Jiling had each collected a hundred or so moon stones.

"A half share would be doing you a favor," Han Jiling said, staring at him coldly. "You wouldn't be able to obtain so many without Song Min's connections and recommendations. In the end, your actions not only make you lose out but the Alabaster Group as a whole."

"I understand your concerns," Cha Ming said. "I think we'll be able to obtain a harvest with the five of us. This will naturally benefit the Alabaster Group."

"There's no need to press him," Song Min said. "If he's agreed to join these people, then so be it." She then headed back toward the fifty-man group along with Han Jiling.

"I don't like her," Yu Wen said as they sat in an empty area. "I can tell that while the older man is fuming, she's actually happy that you didn't accept. She only invited you out of courtesy."

"So you can read minds now?" Cha Ming said, chuckling.

"Would you believe me if I said I could?" Yu Wen said, smiling sweetly.

Their three companions rolled their eyes. They'd grown used to such banter after almost a year of traveling.

Cha Ming didn't respond. He looked over to a group at the opposite end of the circle. There, Huxian, a small jade rabbit, and several dozen peak-core-formation demons were waiting lazily. Unlike the human participants, whose moon stones were more equally distributed. Cha Ming discovered only a few moon stones on each of the dozen beasts. Huxian and the rabbit, on the other hand, had accumulated thousands.

Just how many moon stones did you swallow? Cha Ming sent to Huxian.

I don't know, maybe five thousand? Huxian replied. *Xiao Bai and I kept getting attacked by cultivators, so we kept their things and sent them packing. That aside, those tasty puppets seemed to contain a lot of moon stones.*

Is Xiao Bai that jade rabbit beside you? Cha Ming asked.

Yep, and she's very fierce, Huxian sent back. *I don't mean to brag, but we can probably demolish half the cultivators in this room without breaking a sweat. Godbeasts are already quite fierce compared to cultivators, but now that we're almost three times stronger? We're basically wolves in a flock of sheep.*

Cha Ming paled. *Please don't kill all of them. Not unless they attack you.*

Sure thing, Huxian sent. *But we've only had a single group of humans steer clear of us yet. It's discrimination, I tell you. Speciesism at its finest.*

Cha Ming sighed and prepared himself mentally for the impending carnage. He only hoped that the cultivators had the presence of mind to crumble their tokens and escape while they still had the chance.

"I just got in touch with a friend of mine," Cha Ming said to Yu Wen and the other three. "We should have no issue capturing moon stones, but we'll have to negotiate splitting them after the fact."

"You too?" Yu Wen said. "I bet you my friend is fiercer."

"We'll have to see," Cha Ming said. He highly doubted that her friend could be stronger than a Godbeast.

"The both of you seem so confident," Zhang Fei said. "Unfortunately, all three of our sects have already moved on. We'll have to trouble your friends if any issues come up. It isn't unheard of for people to rob each other during the final melee."

"Noted," Cha Ming said. They sat down and waited. Little by little, the main area emptied out. The traders gradually left the premises, leaving only five hundred or so cultivators to fight over the central prize. Time trickled by, and soon only half an hour remained before the bridge's closing. Finally, a gong sounded. The many cultivators and a minority of demonic beasts floated in the air and prepared to tackle the deadly puppets.

"Charge!" an impressive cultivator at the front said. He wore a set of resplendent golden armor and wielded a powerful white sword. The power it emanated reminded Cha Ming of Lu Tianhao.

Is that a transcendent treasure? he thought.

Thousands of cultivators rushed to the guards, who swiftly struck out at them. Their every strike bore the charm of runic fragments, and judging by the power they delivered, it was impossible for anyone to contest them head on.

Seeing the golden-armored man and affiliated groups rush toward the center, Cha Ming's group kept to the outskirts. While the larger groups were busy dealing with the medium-sized piles, they would aim to secure as many small ones as possible.

Cha Ming ducked plumes of fire and shards of ice as he closed in on an outer platform. As he approached the guardian puppet, he felt an extreme constriction. A fifteen-stroke runic fragment appeared around the guardian. Cha Ming's staff was a blur as he fought back with several fragment techniques.

Seeing the guardian being repulsed, various cultivators rushed in. Cha Ming snorted and sent out 1,080 Dao sigils to form a runic fragment formation. They halted in their tracks while Cha Ming swept in and conveniently captured a pile of a hundred jade rocks.

"He's just one person!" a cultivator shouted. "Get him!"

Instantly, a small group of people threw out a dozen techniques toward him. Cha Ming didn't dodge. Instead, he gathered his Dao sigils around him and shrank the formation. The guardian puppet also reactivated and began attacking everyone at random.

"You want to kill me?" Cha Ming said. "Fine, if that's how you want to play, but don't blame me for being merciless." He had already evaluated these cultivators—one was a devil while eleven were normal cultivators. However, he loathed these despicable people, those who would kill others for their possessions. Competition was one thing, but murder was unforgiveable.

Dozens of techniques bounced and exploded off Cha Ming's protective formation. Just as the twelve cultivators were reveling in their success, a large staff reached out from the cloud of smoke surrounding Cha Ming and struck four of them, killing them instantly. A gray horizontal line traveled toward them as Cha Ming executed Splitting Heaven and Earth. He then followed up with several staff strikes, and gray light rushed down toward the floor, causing it to glow.

Cha Ming rushed out of the cloud of smoke and rapidly executed ten more runic techniques that crashed into the cultivators, who fell to the floor, wounded. Some of them rapidly crumbled their tokens and were whisked away from the Bridge of Stars, barely avoiding Cha Ming's expanding Dao sigils. Hundreds of moon stones floated out to Cha Ming, bringing his total count to 1,400.

His strength was now over double that of a peak-core-formation cultivator. He shook his head at their folly and rushed toward the next pile.

"These humans are all despicable," Xiao Bai said as she kicked an attacking cultivator with her powerful legs. His ribcage shattered, and he crumpled to the ground, dead. Xiao Bai rapidly absorbed his moon stones, but her power only increased negligibly.

"They think we're easy pickings," Huxian said. "It's a good thing I sent the others out ahead of time. They'd be nothing but a hindrance."

His light and shadow domains actively suppressed a dozen-odd cultivators who'd decided to take the opportunity to finish them off. He swatted them away easily, and they crumbled their tokens just before crashing into a nearby pillar.

Huxian and Xiao Bai turned their attention the cultivators' commander, who was fleeing for his life. "You think you can run after trying to kill us?"

Shadows ran out toward him and held his arms and legs. "I'll crumble my token!" the cultivator shouted.

"Too late!" Huxian roared. The cultivator's arms and legs disintegrated and were quickly followed by his body, which Huxian devoured in a single gulp. His power surged from the sudden influx of two thousand moon stones.

"These cultivators are so rich," Huxian said. "I really wish I could just eat them all up and steal their things. These guys are all rotten anyway."

"So do I," Xiao Bai said. "But my friend is too nice. She doesn't want to kill anyone who doesn't attack first."

"I sympathize— Wait, you have a human friend too?" Huxian said.

"Wait, we both have a human friend?" Xiao Bai said. "Which human is yours?"

"The one with the staff and runic fragments over there," Huxian said while gulping a pile of moon stones. "Yours?"

"The jade-cloaked girl a short distance away," she said. "I think they're part of the same team."

"No way!" Huxian said. "Should we tell them?"

"What, and spoil the surprise?" Xiao Bai said, confiscating yet another pile. This was one of the small ones—only medium-sized and larger piles remained. Half of the remaining three hundred or so cultivators retreated to the periphery to observe the situation and take advantage of any conflict in the middle. "The middle looks like fun. Let's go there."

"Let's teach these cultivators that us demons aren't easy to bully," Huxian said, rushing in.

Cha Ming ran up beside Yu Wen, who had just dispatched three cultivators with silver strings. "Hateful fellows," she said, pouting. "They won't even let off a beauty like me."

"They say beauty is a sin that only invites punishment," Cha Ming said.

Zhang Fei, Mu Qianlin, and Fang Li approached from their respective areas. Everyone's aura had stiffened substantially. Cha Ming now possessed three thousand moon stones while Yu Wen had collected two thousand.

"Well, then, shall we rush to the middle?" asked Cha Ming.

"One half of the piles have yet to be claimed," Zhang Fei said.

"But is there a need to be greedy?"

"We're not greedy," Cha Ming said. "It's a fair competition, and we still have an edge. The greedy people were those who tried to kill us and snatch our moon stones."

"You know what I mean," Zhang Fei said dryly.

"I think we stand a good chance," Cha Ming said. "Besides, both Yu Wen and I have friends who can back us up. I don't know about hers, but mine is much stronger than I am."

"I'm sure mine is the strongest," Yu Wen said. "She's one of the top two fiercest in this entire runic circle."

"We'll see," Cha Ming said. He looked at the various fighting groups and carefully selected one far away from both Huxian's duo and his Alabaster Group compatriots. A group of fifty cultivators, half of which had thick ochre auras, were busy fighting two guardian puppets for a pile of one thousand moon stones.

"Those ones will do," he said. "No need to spare any of them. Birds of a feather flock together, and we're better off without those who want to collude with devils."

Both Cha Ming and Zhang Fei projected their Devil-Sealing Intent. Cha Ming spread out his Dao Fragment Formation, supressing those who were busy fighting the two puppets.

"An ambush!" one of the cultivators yelled. "Retreat!"

Cha Ming heartlessly wielded his staff at the ochre monsters who were unable to transform in the Bridge of Stars. Not being able to transmit and not being able to transform—these were the two penalties devil cultivators suffered under the Jade Moon Blessing's suppression.

"You think one of you can kill all of us?" one of the devilish cultivators sneered. He pulled out a long scroll filled with mystical black characters. They peeled off and formed a vicious wolf that radiated a transcendent aura. Cha Ming was forced to retreat a dozen steps as the wolf batted at him with its paw. His runic fragment array shattered, resulting in four deep gashes on his chest.

Powerful, he thought as he sent the array fragments backward into a new one. This time, he used it for support as his Clear Sky Staff grew to the size of a pillar. His joints crackled and his muscles went taut as he struck down with the massive pillar.

"Crushing Chaos!" he shouted as it crashed down on the wolf in a gray blur. Its bones shattered and its fur split, but it still managed to survive.

He swiftly pulled back his staff and urged it to shrink before spinning in a horizontal circle. The slender staff projected a thin blade of white wind that cut halfway through the battered transcendent wolf as he executed Splitting Heaven and Earth.

The summoned wolf howled in pain but lunged forward nonetheless. Seeing that it hadn't yet dissipated, Cha Ming pulled back his Clear Sky Staff and stabbed at the monstrous black wolf. He thrust it like a spear, perfectly executing Origin Strike with the elongated staff. Although the strike drained him, it was the most lethal one in his arsenal.

The wolf dissipated into thousands of black runic fragments as the staff pierced his heart. The devilish cultivator who'd summoned it paled as he realized that his trump card was useless against Cha Ming. He tried to run away but was promptly grasped by Yu Wen's strings and diced to pieces.

Cha Ming didn't stand on ceremony and split the moon stones half and half. They then joined together with Zhang Fei, Mu Qianlin, and Fang Li, who had dispatched the rest of the group. They collaborated and easily robbed the guardian's pile. During this time, Huxian's group had robbed three medium piles as well. Only four groups of fifty or so cultivators remained.

"Friends, I'm afraid that you've been too greedy," a voice said. A golden-armored man appeared in front of him. Judging by his aura, his power was enhanced by at least five thousand moon stones. But the most concerning thing was the sword in his hands.

Its blade gleamed fiercely with the frightening might of a transcendent treasure.

Chapter 16: Essence

W hat's Group Leader doing?" Han Jiling said to Song Min. By now, both had accumulated an extra hundred moon stones, bringing their total to two hundred each.

Song Min shook her head. "Cha Ming's group got too greedy. They took too many moon stones, so Group Leader will rob him."

Han Jiling frowned. "Shouldn't we stop him? He's part of the Alabaster Group, after all. We don't abandon our members."

"No, he was foolish to reject my good intentions," Song Min said. "He can reap the consequences of his actions."

Han Jiling said nothing as he looked at Cha Ming and their group in indecision.

"Jin Tian is right," another voice said. A black-robed woman appeared in front of them. She exuded an unusual charm. Most amazingly, she was floating on a black fan whose power didn't lose out to Jin Tian's sword. "But there's no need to hand over all your moon stones to him. Just give us nine tenths, and we'll protect you from his group."

Cha Ming's frown deepened.

"Don't let them bully you too easily," two more men said as they rushed over. One wore red robes and another blue robes. They each wore a saber at their waist whose power lay somewhere between transcendence and the peak of core formation. "While our group of one hundred cultivators is weaker than theirs on an individual level, we are much fairer. Us two leaders only take fifteen percent of the moon stones each, and the rest is spread evenly across our remaining members. You would all get the same treatment if you joined us, and you needn't worry about these two tyrants. We also won't rob you. You can choose to join us or not join us, but we really can't risk our members lives without enough benefit."

Compared to the previous two, Cha Ming had a more favorable impression of these two. "Many thanks for your concern," he said, bowing to them. "We'll be fine on our own."

At that moment, a white-cloaked figure floated up beside the golden-armored man.

"Could you perhaps show mercy to these fellows on account of our Alabaster Group?" Han Jiling said. "Although we aren't very strong, we have been collaborating for a millennium."

The golden-armored man frowned. "Although we've collaborated in the past, they've accumulated too many moon stones. We could win many wars with such resources. I'm afraid I can't grant you your request."

Cha Ming's heart warmed as he saw Han Jiling, who was usually strict and harsh, sticking his neck out for him.

"I understand," Han Jiling said, nodding. Then he did something that shocked everyone present. He flew out to Cha Ming's group and stood in front of them, sword drawn. "If you wish to harm them, you must go through me. Our Alabaster Group might not be strong, but we have our principles. As long as we stick to them, we will always prevail."

"There's no need to trouble yourself," Cha Ming said quickly. "We can handle ourselves, truly."

"Don't try and convince me," Han Jiling said harshly. "I do what is right, no matter the consequences."

"Is this what you choose?" Jin Tian said. The pressure he gave off mounted swiftly. It manifested in a golden cloud that bore down on Han Jiling.

The older man summoned a forest of metallic shards that fought against the golden cloud. He sank to one knee but didn't drop his sword.

"Then it's decided. From this moment forward, the Radiant Alliance is no longer affiliated with the Alabaster Group."

"Brother Jin, please reconsider," Song Min said suddenly from behind him.

Jin Tian turned around and glared at her. "Are you with them or with us?" he asked.

She averted her eyes. After a moment of hesitation, she clenched her teeth. "With you," she said.

"Good," Jin Tian said. He stared at Cha Ming, who looked at Song Min disdainfully. "Since you don't want to cooperate, then we can only begin."

"Don't regret it," Cha Ming said. He sent a message to Huxian and his five companions. *Go now!*

Runic fragments exploded out from around him, protecting everyone. Ranged techniques and flying swords raced toward them as they rushed toward the central circle. Cha Ming grabbed Han Jiling and dragged him back with them.

There are too many of them for us to fight, but there's still one place they can't breach—the center!

Are you sure that's a good idea? Han Jiling sent back. *The center is incomparably dangerous. If we all rush to the other teleportation arrays, we might be able to make it out alive.*

Don't worry, Cha Ming said. *I have a plan.*

He casually tossed Han Jiling a thousand moon stones. The man's strength rose twofold, and with this increase in strength, he managed to deflect a flaming dragon that was about to overtake them.

"Hateful fellows," he spat as they entered the central runic circle, whose puppets activated the moment they did.

"Everyone, use your all to block them," Cha Ming yelled.

His Dao Fragment Array rotated and became a large shield that blocked the ten puppets. Just as it showed signs of breaking, thousands of silver strings reinforced it from behind. It was joined by thousands of vines from Fang Li.

Zhang Fei, not wanting to be outdone, dropped his sword to the ground. It passed through a spatial slit and transformed into a flaming sword that struck down with world-ending might. Two puppets deflected the sword, which promptly flew back to Zhang Fei's hands. His vigor quickly returned as Mu Qianlin traced mystical runes with her exorcist's staff.

Meanwhile, Han Jiling stood at the vanguard. He deflected the various blows that snuck past their shield. He was an unstoppable guardian, an indomitable bastion. However, it was difficult to hold everything back. He soon began to fall leeward.

"Fall back!" Cha Ming yelled.

"No, I can still hold on," Han Jiling said. He gritted his teeth and moved forward. The skin on his face split as the pressure mounted, but he ignored it. Instead he raised his sword and channeled golden qi into a shield. It lasted five breaths before ultimately shattering, sending golden fragments flying back into his chest and causing him to cough up blood.

The older man wore a satisfied expression as he accepted his impending doom. He chuckled hoarsely as a puppet went in for the kill. As its blade neared his heart, he let out what should have been his last breath.

But just as it was about to land, clouds appeared above them. Cha Ming looked about in puzzlement, but his four companions looked up in reverence. A holy silence pervaded the circle. In fact, the guardians paused as though afraid of disrupting the sacred proceeding. The one who was mere inches away from slaying Han Jiling was no exception; it pulled back its sword and stepped back three paces.

"Angelic endowment," Zhang Fai said quietly. "To think that I would see it again in my lifetime."

The clouds roared as lightning crackled through them. Those

with substantial sin trembled as the heavenly power on the bridge grew increasingly thick.

"What do you all think his principle virtue will be?"

"Without a doubt, sacrifice," Mu Qianlin said. "He's thrown away his life for what he sees as a worthy cause."

"It must be diligence," Fang Li said. "He's as hard as a rock and indomitable like a mountain."

Yu Wen shook her head. "You're both wrong." Everyone looked to her in surprise. "These storm clouds contain more than colored lightning. They contain lightning of judgment. His aspect is, without a doubt, bravery."

Cha Ming's jaw slackened as one lightning bolt after another struck down. They didn't harm Han Jiling. Instead they struck the puppets around him and forced them to back away. The residual lightning accumulated into a hazy shape around the older man.

Then nine bolts of lightning struck down simultaneously. These mysterious jade bolts joined together with the hazy mass of residual lightning and rushed to Han Jiling's back, merging with his substantial jade aura. Two jade wings appeared on his back, and the lightning in the clouds poured into them and formed mysterious runic characters.

"You'll pass over my dead body!" the red-faced Han Jiling shouted. He waved his sword, sending out the accumulated potential toward the nearby puppets. Like frightened rabbits, they ducked and protected themselves from Heaven's wrath. Fragments of blue stone flew off their supposedly unbreakable bodies.

Huxian, now! Cha Ming yelled.

Already on it, Huxian sent back.

The entire central runic circle was suddenly filled with light, shadow, lightning, wind, and swamp. These five elements bore down on the puppets and greatly restrained their movements. Cha Ming sent out his runic fragment array once more, which hovered around the puppets and slowed them by yet another notch. He used the opportunity to grab the pile of moon stones and distribute them amongst the eight of them. Having strengthened substantially, the six cultivators and two beasts regrouped in the center of the puppets before starting a new offensive.

"What happened?" Jin Tian said from outside the circle. He had expected Cha Ming and the others to get repelled from the center. In fact, he'd already prepared his lines to threaten them once more and extort their moon stones. But things had developed much differently than he had expected. Now, a massive fox with three tails stood beside them. On his head sat a jade rabbit, whose aura had merged with the fox in one organic whole.

Due to these overlapping five barriers and the mysterious gray array, the movements of the puppets had greatly slowed and reduced in power. And to his surprise, the two monsters didn't attack Cha Ming and the others. They were clearly allies.

"What are your thoughts?" the black-robed Hei Yin said from beside him. "Is there any way for us to fight that monster?"

"We can only wait from the side," Jin Tian said. "Perhaps we can pay the rest of these cultivators fifty moon stones each for their collaboration."

"That's five thousand moon stones!" Hei Yin exclaimed.

"But we can gain over forty thousand if we're successful," Jin Tian said. "Are you with me? Our odds of success are much greater if you join me."

Hei Yin hesitated. "Fine. We'll do it your way. But why are they wasting their time in the runic circle now that they've already obtained the reward? Don't they know it's impossible to destroy even the outer puppets, let alone the central ones?"

"Who knows," Jin Tian said. "Perhaps their background is insufficient to know such secrets. Regardless, it's to our advantage if they waste their strength." He then rushed toward the smaller cultivator groups.

Only Hei Yin remained, looking at the center with concern.

"Brother Cha Ming, even with the giant fox's suppression, these puppet guardians aren't good to cope with," Han Jiling said as he deflected a puppet's attack. Despite his moon stone empowerment and his angelic endowment, he could barely remain within the central circle. "How much time do you need?"

"As long as you can give me," Cha Ming said as he clashed with one of the ten central puppets. The shadow of a runic fragment appeared in his mind, but it was elusive, difficult to grasp. Just as the essence of the rune was becoming clearer, another strike came his way. Frustrated, he sent ten layers of earth-based combat formations to deflect it. The image regained a modicum of its essence.

Ten strikes. One hundred strikes. Their battle raged, but Cha Ming's comprehension didn't deepen. Three hundred strikes passed, but it seemed that compared to the first three runic fragments and the middle three hundred fragments, these ones were different.

But how are they different? he thought. He repeated this question over and over, but despite his exhaustion, he didn't make any headway.

"We can't support for much longer," Zhang Fei yelled as he fought off his own puppet. His body was covered in cuts, and his qi reserves were frighteningly low. At most, he'd last an incense time.

Is this the end? Cha Ming thought.

The runic symbol in his mind reappeared for the 333rd time. This time, however, he saw a qualitative difference. Instead of a gray runic fragment, he saw a hint of color in the previously plain picture. It was a hint of red. But instead of feeling out of place, it felt like a bit of life had been instilled into it. Color *belonged* with this fragment.

A spark lit up in Cha Ming's mind. *The first three were the core of the runic fragments. All runic fragments stem from these three.*

Then the next three hundred confirmed the shape and flow of the runic fragments. These formations taught me how to manipulate and lay formations one step at a time. However, I've always felt there was something missing. And now that I've seen that glimpse of red, it's clear to me. These thirty runic fragments contain the essence of this runic circle.

The red glow in the runic symbol intensified as Cha Ming continued to exchange blows. Before long, he realized that there was not only color but smell. He smelled fire and burning, ashes and soot. As he focused on the smell, he soon discovered a feeling. It was a warm and comfortable feeling that could intensify at any moment.

It's fire! he suddenly realized. *How could I have been so silly?*

In his journey to grasp the runic fragments, he'd forgotten the core of his cultivation technique in order to grasp them. But didn't runes reflect nature? Didn't creation and destruction exist hand in hand with the five elements?

This sudden flash of inspiration caused the runic fragment to burn brightly in his mind. He slashed out fifteen times with his staff, sending the guardian puppet tumbling back with a red runic fragment. It darted into the floor and glowed with a ruby-colored hue. Cha Ming didn't hesitate to rush to the next guardian.

One strike. Two strikes. Three strikes. Perfect! A green rune appeared on the floor. A gold rune, a blue rune, and a brown rune soon followed.

Following his instincts, he proceeded to the next ten runic fragments. Even without fighting the remaining puppets, the required colors came to mind.

Fire and wood, fire and earth, fire and metal, fire and water... He injected a two-element fusion into each of ten runic fragments, which shot into the floor beneath him. He immediately proceeded to the ten three-element combinations. Following that, he produced five four-element fragments. Each one represented the absence of an element, an incomplete creation.

He then glanced at the floor and noticed that the central circle had already run out of space.

No, that's not right, he thought, looking at it. He looked to the three central platforms, which had previously accommodated moon stones. Now that he had completed the thirty essence fragments, he was very clear that a fusion of four wasn't the end. A combination of five was still possible. Moreover, it could be done in more than one way.

Cha Ming leaped into the air, and the guardian puppets leapt up with him. They bellowed in anger, utilizing every last bit of their power to prevent him from completing the runic array now that he'd discovered the truth. His seven companions fought fiercely to keep them away while his Dao sigils swirled around him, combining and manifesting 360 iterations of the runic design below. Thirty-six formations blocked off each guardian, but time was limited. One formation after another crumbled, and before Cha Ming had time to breathe, five of each formation had already disappeared.

First, destruction, Cha Ming thought. His staff struck down toward the platform on the left. It cleaved downward with unstoppable, world-breaking momentum. Instead of pouring five elements into the runic fragment, he poured the purest, blackest destruction qi. The black line shot out with unusual violence. Space shattered, causing the original black line to split into five, imprinting the platform with a deadly black star. As he did this, the puppets' assault intensified, breaking another thirteen of each formation stack. Only eighteen remained for each guardian.

Next, creation, Cha Ming thought. He swept his Clear Sky Staff horizontally. Pure white creation qi formed a horizontal line. The original white runic fragment wrapped around itself like a snake biting its own tail and landed on the rightmost platform. It left a white circular imprint that glowed with vitality.

Next... Well, I'm not sure what comes next, he admitted to himself. But he didn't stop. As the last few remaining formations around him shattered, he took his Clear Sky Staff and rushed downward, narrowly dodging the ten guardian puppets. Their attacks mutually canceled each other out and propelled him downward even faster.

Cha Ming braced himself as he increased his weight. He poured increasing amounts of five-element qi into the tip of his staff as he approached the central platform and pierced downward with all his might. The world trembled as a glowing gray imprint appeared on the platform. It spat out spatial cracks that shot out toward the ten puppets, and they broke into a hundred thousand fragments that converged on Cha Ming.

His moon stone count skyrocketed, and as it rose, Cha Ming realized that he had reached a hard limit. The first hundred stones had caused his strength to increase twofold, and the next thousand had caused it to increase by the same amount yet again. Finally, the next ten thousand increased his strength to the limit of three and a third times the might of a peak-core-formation cultivator. This was the true limit of mortals—any further increase in strength could only lead to transcendence.

Seeing this, Cha Ming unhesitatingly redistributed his 120,000 moon stones to the remaining team members.

"Cover me," he yelled as he charged toward the middle and outer circles. Twenty guardian puppets came at him from all directions. However, they were much weaker than the central guardians. Cha Ming was able to easily dodge them as he stepped onto the floor. Each step glowed with a gray light as he completed it. As each of them snapped into place, their color shifted to match the flow of energy.

Cha Ming didn't relax his guard as he worked, however. He carefully watched the few hundred cultivators on the outskirts. It would only be a matter of time before they acted.

Chapter 17: Power

"What is he doing?" Hei Yin wondered aloud as she saw Cha Ming hopelessly clashing with the giant guardian puppets.

"He's doing what all mediocre influences do—trying to destroy the puppets using brute force," Jin Tian said. "Only, our transcendent sects know that it's impossible. A fully amplified cultivator with a transcendent treasure can't even crack these puppets."

"But I think something's happening," Hei Yin said. At this moment, a red spot lit up. It was followed by green, blue, gold, and brown, and mixes thereof. Moreover, the disposition of the guardians changed.

At first they were only randomly striking the cultivators. However, they increasingly shifted their attention to the staff-wielding young man, whose techniques were lighting up several runes on the floor. "Perhaps he's discovered a way."

"That's impossible," Jin Tian said. However, his eyes betrayed his uncertainty. They narrowed as a black staff strike, a white staff strike, and a gray staff strike suddenly rushed to the center of the runic array. The colored array glowed brightly, and the ten puppets turned into moon stones and shot into the staff-wielding cultivator and his companions.

"That's impossible!" Jin Tian said, trembling. The first time he said so, it was out of disdain. Now, however, his voice was filled with disbelief.

As Jin Tian struggled to cope with the scene before him, the staff-wielding cultivator rushed out of the inner circle and began tracing additional runic lines. The two demon beasts and five cultivators surrounded him as he worked. They deflected the various puppets while carefully watching out for interference.

"If things continue this way, they may crack open the formation," Hei Yin said. "Who knows what kind of rewards they could obtain?"

Jin Tian's gaze turned cold. "Let's see if they're able to enjoy it," he said. "Tell everyone that the reward has increased to one hundred moon stones each. But to obtain this, they'll have to pull out all the stops."

"Fine," Hei Yin said, sighing. "Let's do it your way."

She looked toward the glowing pattern one last time before going back to her men. After some brief instructions, she retrieved her transcendent weapon, the Black Phoenix Fan, and took out ten small pieces of immortal-jade core. The fan's power increased as the precious jade crumbled to dust.

Cha Ming's feet and staff were a blur of activity. As he deflected the guardian puppets' attacks, one runic fragment after another sank into the floor, causing the small colored circle in the center to expand. The central three runes represented power, while the next thirty were the manifestation of essence. As he painted runes on the floor, the power of essence flowed, as per their instructions, toward the outside. Instead of the initial white-jade coloring, the runic fragments blossomed with color. The power of the formation improved exponentially.

"Yu Wen, drive those three guardian puppets farther away," he said. The floor glowed as he stepped, and although he only painted a dozen runes in the process, many smaller runes blossomed as a result of the energy patterns they created. They reached out and suppressed the guardian puppets, assisting Yu Wen in driving them back.

"Brother Cha Ming, those influences aren't going to leave us alone," Yu Wen said. "I can sense their power accumulating. They're likely going to try to rob us once we succeed."

Cha Ming frowned. "You're very sensitive to power levels. Do you think we'll be able to handle their combined attack?"

Yu Wen bit her lip. "I think so," she said. "I put our odds at eighty percent or more. It really depends on how many trump cards they have. Thankfully, it looks like they're storing up their energy for a single attack. As long as we can resist it, there's no need for us to continue fighting."

"Good," Cha Ming said. "I'll head over to Zhang Fei's side now and let the others know to prepare. Please warn Han Jiling. We still need around an incense time to complete the runic circle."

Yu Wen nodded and flew over to the stoic man. Cha Ming conveyed the message to Huxian, Zhang Fei, Fang Li, and Mu Qianlin. Then he focused on expanding the runic circle. One hundred, 200, 250, 280... Soon he was only three runes short of 300. Cha Ming struck out with his staff, finishing the last three flow runes simultaneously. The twenty guardian puppets shattered, instantly granting everyone in their group as many moon stones as the central ten had.

Get ready to fight off their assault, Cha Ming sent mentally. Huxian and the six others converged and threw up their defenses. Huxian overlaid light, dark, wind, lightning, and swamp suppressions. Yu Wen's silver strings formed a defensive net that combined with the jade glow from Xiao Bai, the jade rabbit.

Meanwhile, Zhang Fei sent his sword through a spatial slit. It transformed into a large sword of holy flame that struck out against hundreds of attacks. At the same time, a fierce gale burst out from Mu Qianlin. It swirled and formed a cyclone around them that defended from every angle. Fang Li's offensive didn't lose out to theirs. The phantom of a giant tree appeared above them, sending out countless vines to form a defensive barrier. They broke rapidly, but for every one that broke, ten more took its place.

Finally, Han Jiling drew his sword. Thousands of black lightning bolts appeared and struck the various magical techniques, one after another. Dragons and phoenixes, ice and flames, sword and saber—nothing could block this lightning. If it was one on one, he would surely be able to dominate his opponents. Unfortunately, the techniques the crowd unleashed were far too many.

The colliding attacks caused space to ripple as they repelled each other. Dozens of cultivators fainted and coughed up blood due to the backlash of their techniques. Yet try as they might, they were no match for the combined might of Cha Ming, Yu Wen, two Godbeasts, and the four angelic cultivators.

Despite being able to repel these attacks, Cha Ming and the others grew solemn as two frightening pressures suddenly appeared. Hei Yin's black fan grew to a width of a hundred feet and swept out, generating devastating winds laced with destructive black lines.

"Summon your defenses," Yu Wen said, paling. "These attacks are powered by immortal-jade core."

The two demons and four cultivators nodded. Their auras surged as they overdrew their strength.

Fortunately, Cha Ming hadn't been idling. As they were repelling the initial attacks, he had condensed his understanding of the runic fragments and infused them into his Dao sigils. One by one, the sigils appeared as 333 runic fragments. These included a gray point, a black star, and a white circle. Myriad colors enveloped their group, protecting them just as the fan broke through his companions' defenses. The transcendent weapon's attack broke against the protective shield like an egg on a brick wall.

Cha Ming didn't relax, however. He continued pouring every ounce of his strength into the small defensive sphere. His efforts were rewarded as a gigantic white sword appeared above them, its transcendent might far exceeding that of the black fan. Moreover, Cha Ming couldn't draw support from his companions, who were already exhausted at having deflected the previous attacks. He didn't hesitate to throw out Flow, Material, and Shape Talismans. Due to his increased cultivation and soul realm, their power skyrocketed, instantly doubling his already-powerful barrier.

Isn't this runic circle the epitome of runic perfection? Cha Ming wondered. *Are emotions really so powerful that an incomplete set of three runic talismans can overcome a perfect runic circle?*

His barrier held firmly against the giant white sword. The transcendent treasure fell toward them and slowed as it hit a viscous layer of air. Finally, it completely stopped as it stabbed through a hard plate of earth in arm's reach of Cha Ming. Seeing an opportunity, Cha Ming caught the powerless sword and immediately stowed it in his Clear Sky World.

Is it over? he thought. Despite having captured the powerful sword, he was suddenly struck with a feeling of foreboding.

Jin Tian's heart grew cold as his connection to his transcendent weapon was severed. Unwillingness welled up in his heart as he lost the one thing that allowed him to run rampant on the Bridge of Stars.

"It shouldn't be possible," Hei Yin said. "Mere mortals should not have power that exceeds transcendence on the Bridge of Stars. Moreover, I fed ten pieces of immortal-jade core to my fan."

Jin Tian was trembling with rage. He had spent twenty pieces of immortal-jade core and still hadn't breached their defenses. "Do I really need to use my trump card?" he muttered. He summoned a black token from his bag of holding before looking at the eight living mountains of moon stones. "It's you who forced me to do this!" he spat as he broke the token.

Cha Ming's barrier fizzled out as soon as the attack ended. He was out of energy and out of options. And so were his companions, Huxian most of all. They each ate a moon cake, replenishing a substantial amount of their energy. To Huxian, however, it was a drop in the bucket.

Then a black cloud began oozing from outside the circle. No, that wasn't right. It was a malevolent ochre so concentrated that even light couldn't properly illuminate it. Its power far exceeded the limits of the Bridge of Stars, which sought to suppress it with all its power. Millions of stars appeared around the cloud to try and contain it, but they were soon engulfed by it.

A lone figure walked out of the darkness. It wore a black cloak that greatly obscured its features, though some prominent ones could still be seen by Cha Ming and the others. Its pasty pale skin, its skeletal features, and its chalk-white hair stood in stark contrast to its pitch-black eyes.

The figure held out one hand and gathered the power of evil surrounding it. The clouds rushed in on a single point and grew from the size of a marble to a full foot in diameter. The devilish figure disappeared as it threw the orb toward them. Cha Ming instantly threw up a multicolored shield with what little power he had.

Huxian drew from his companions and transferred as much energy as he could to Cha Ming in the hopes of stalling the black orb's inevitable onslaught. As it struck the multicolored shield, an intense backlash caused Cha Ming's powerful body and soul to teeter on the brink of destruction.

"Cha Ming!" he heard Yu Wen cry out before losing consciousness.

"Hundreds of thousands of moon stones, and they're all mine," Jin Tian said, licking his lips greedily. Cracks appeared on the multicolored defensive sphere, and before anyone could react, it shattered into millions of pieces. "All mine!" he said once more with madness in his eyes.

Time froze. A woman in a jade cloak floated up, and the air around her turned gray. It became a mist that traveled toward the man unhurriedly. He tried to move his body but realized he couldn't. As the mist approached, a powerful constriction enveloped him. A voice sounded in his mind.

You thought to kill us? Then know the consequences, the voice said. *Your soul won't even reach the Yellow River. It will be decimated for all eternity.* The jade-cloaked woman looked at him coldly.

How can she be so powerful? he thought, panicking. He struggled to free himself, but no matter what he did, he couldn't move. It was as though the space around him had frozen in time.

Little by little, the mist approached him. One by one, those who that had joined him collapsed into pieces that were fiercely devoured by the gray mist. When the mist reached him, he heard another voice in his mind. It was an ancient voice from before creation. His soul began shaking as he heard the dreadful voice.

Many became three and three became two;
All existence a fog of gray.

The moment he heard these words, his soul completely shattered. It joined the gray mist as though it had always belonged there. The last thing he heard was a deep sigh, and the last thing he saw was a receding yellow river, abandoning him to his fate.

Yu Wen sank down on one knee as the cloud receded. Beads of sweat rolled down her brow as she crunched down on a moon cake. Unfortunately, it only replenished a small portion of the energy she'd consumed during the fierce struggle.

How can he be here? she thought as she recalled the black-eyed man's devilish figure. Her surroundings faded as the formation glowed around them and brought them to a hidden place within the bridge.

Yu Wen blinked twice as she appeared within a chamber filled with jade-colored furniture. It was a familiar chamber, one she'd used many times before. Xiao Bai appeared beside her and slumped into her tiny basket at the foot of a large bed.

"I missed my bed so much." Xiao Bai yawned as she sprawled herself out. Yu Wen ignored her and walked over to a jade panel near the bed and pressed it. An elderly lady appeared. "Please contact my father and tell him I'm in danger. Tell him he needs to get to Jade Moon Garden as soon as possible."

"As you command," the elderly lady said before disappearing.

"I shouldn't have used Grandmist Essence so blatantly," Yu Wen said, sighing. "But without it, Cha Ming and the others would have died."

"Why, what happened?" Xiao Bai said, looking at her curiously. "The Bridge of Stars was built by the Jade Emperor himself. What are you so worked up about?"

"He's coming," Yu Wen said, shivering. "I can feel it."

"If he could find you here, he would have done it long ago," Xiao Bai said reassuringly. "Besides, don't you have your father's cloak? As far as hiding goes, I can't think of a better soul-bound treasure in this universe."

"It's different this time," Yu Wen said, pulling at her hair. "He *saw* me."

"Saw you?" Xiao Bai exclaimed. "How?"

"I used my Grandmist Essence to fight him on the bridge," Yu Wen said. "Only a handful of people can use Grandmist Essence in the universe. It won't take him long to figure it out."

A scar on her back began to ache. She shivered as a frightening presence washed over her. "It's too late," she said fearfully. "He's already here."

The elderly lady appeared once more. "My apologies, Princess, but communications don't seem to be working." She hesitated. "Also, the humans and demons on Jade Moon Planet have suddenly gotten restless."

Yu Wen sighed. "Is Cha Ming awake?" she asked. The lady nodded. "Then transfer my moon stones to him and his brother fox and allow those who came with him to cultivate here for two years. I'll give you instructions based on the situation on the surface. Jade Moon Planet is too chaotic to set foot on now."

"What about the cultivators already on the planet?" the custodian asked.

"Inform them to head over to Jade Moon Garden as soon as possible and consolidate our defenses there," Yu Wen said.

"My lady, I advise you to abandon the planet and flee," the custodian said.

"What, and watch the others die?" Yu Wen snapped. "No, not this time. We have what we need to resist him on Jade Moon Planet. We'll be able to hold out until my father realizes something's wrong."

"As you command," the custodian said before disappearing.

Yu Wen and Xiao Bai, exhausted from the intense battle, drifted off into a deep, dreamless sleep.

Chapter 18:
Purging Embers

Greetings, Senior Sister," a student said as Hong Xin approached. "Good day," Hong Xin said with a warm smile that chilled the girl to the bone. "How is your practice coming along?"

"I-I've practiced as you taught me," the girl said nervously. "But it's so cold to do as you say." *I've been giving it some thought,* she sent secretly. *I want to join.*

"Only by braving the cold can we forget our feelings," Hong Xin said. "You will never successfully cultivate the Freezing Heart Sutra with your talent otherwise." *Not just anyone can join,* Hong Xin sent. *Have you done as I said?*

The girl's eyes shifted. She approached Hong Xin and handed her a hairpin with two red stripes. Although it had one less stripe than Hong Xin's pin, it was a grave offense for a first-grade student to steal someone else's hairpin.

I can only give it to you for three hours, the girl sent. *After that, she will begin to suspect.*

Hong Xin infused a subtle charm into the pin. She hid her movements as she did this. For all the girl knew, she'd done nothing. She then handed the pin back. *There's no need,* Hong Xin sent. *This was only to test your devotion. Put the pin back, then come to Mistress Huang's room at the time I mentioned. And remember, tell anyone about this, and you're dead. I'll make sure of it.*

The girl gulped. "I understand," she said before heading back to the dormitory.

"How kind of you," a woman said, stepping out from behind a tree. "One would almost think you've developed feelings for the girls."

Hong Xin shook her head. "Please have a seat, Mistress Huang," she said, motioning to the bench in the middle of the courtyard. It was summer again, but the air surrounding Hong Xin was laced with ice. "To what do I owe the pleasure?"

"Just answer the implied question, dear," Mistress Huang said.

Hong Xin smiled. "I'm just doing what we've been taught in the lessons. I'm garnering support through indebtedness. Even someone with a heart of ice is affected by karma. I'm simply sowing small favors so they might give me back coal in the winter."

"Is that what it is?" Mistress Huang said. "I, too, did similar things, for all the good it did me. My favors were unappreciated, and my efforts in vain. In the end, I was forced to discard everything and subdue everyone with a stick instead of a carrot. You might do well to learn this lesson."

"Different people, different styles," Hong Xin replied.

"Different path, different way," Mistress Huang said. She looked up to the clear summer sky with not a breeze to be felt. "It seems like it might be storming soon. It'd be best not to plan any outings tonight."

"It doesn't seem that way to me," Hong Xin said. "According to my experience, it won't rain for another three days. I spent a lot of time outdoors before I came here."

"Think what you will, but mark my words, it will rain," Mistress Huang said.

"Then I suppose I'll tell the juniors and earn many more small favors," Hong Xin said. "Not that I go outside in the evening. I always seclude myself for three hours. From what I understand, you do the same."

"Indeed," Mistress Huang said. "The timeframe coincides with the best time for clandestine operations. If I lock myself away during this time, people will think I'm up to something. It keeps them on their toes, keeps them wondering what I'm up to."

"You should have told me sooner," Hong Xin said, taking out a teapot. "I went out of my way to frighten everyone off so they wouldn't dare bother me. They all know where I go." She poured them both cups. Mistress Huang accepted it and took a sip.

"They knew in the beginning, but do they know now?" Mistress Huang said. "It's best to remind them periodically, so they wonder as to your whereabouts. It adds variation to their thoughts. Not only will they suspect what you're up to, but they'll also wonder if you're actually doing what you said you were doing."

"Many thanks for the wise words," Hong Xin said. She held up her cup. "A toast to you and your sincerity."

Mistress Huang held up her cup. "Just be careful about the storm," she said, chugging down the cup of tea like it was wine. "It'll be a nasty one. You wouldn't want to be caught out in the rain." Then she stood up and walked back.

Is she trying to warn me about our meeting? Hong Xin thought as she watched her walk away. *But how could she possibly know about it?* The members constantly supervised each other. And they were all very happy to be there. She inspected their hearts during every session.

Hong Xin shook her head and took out her flute, playing gently as she always did. Snow covered the hot grass as she played her frosty tune. Many students exited the dormitory and entered the courtyard, sitting down within the frosty circle. One of them was the student she'd just spoken with. They let the cold wash over their cultivation and their soul, edging ever closer to the Frozen Heart Realm.

Two hours later, she heard a sharp crack. She paused her playing and looked over to one of the students, Ling Xia. Her kindling core was carefully concealed inside a layer of thick ice. Just now, she'd reached the first level in the Frozen Heart Sutra, making her the twentieth student to complete her perfect disguise under her tutelage. Each one of them had obtained some achievements in her personally developed cultivation method—Icy Shell, Molten Heart.

The heart kindling and heart dousing arts complemented each other, making their cultivation advance by leaps and bounds.

"Congratulations, Senior Sister," Hong Xin said.

"Congratulations, Senior Sister," the others echoed. The girl in question was a fourth-grade student who'd been in the academy for six years. Reaching the first level in the Frozen Heart Sutra was a requirement for graduation. Therefore, she'd been stuck in the academy for many years. Now, she'd only need to give a stunning performance at the yearly concert to graduate.

"It's all thanks to you, Junior Sister," Ling Xia said gratefully. "Now if you'll excuse me, I must go cultivate and solidify my foundation."

"Yes, let us all rest for the day," Hong Xin said, stowing away her flute. The cold in the air dissipated, the snow melted, and the students sighed in relief. "I'll be back tomorrow," she said.

She then walked back to her accommodations and began cultivating. After the familiar scan passed over her, she cast a glamour and walked over to the wooden box in the teacher's room. Mistress Huang's token was still there.

Perhaps I'm overthinking things, she thought as she walked over to the usual classroom.

Hong Xin looked at the stage with concern as Ling Xia danced. Her style was passionate, and she danced with a ribbon. An untrained heart would have melted instantly and handed over their life's fortune after seeing only a few movements. Unfortunately, the ones they needed to influence weren't normal people. Ling Xia still needed a qualitative change in her kindling technique to stand a chance at melting the layer of ice on the students' hearts.

"How was it today?" Ling Xia asked expectantly. Sweat dripped off her lovely body.

Hong Xin looked to her companions left and right. All eight

of them looked unimpressed. Although many people in the eighty they'd recruited and were sitting behind them had been affected, it was far from sufficient.

"I don't want to be mean, but the bar is really too high," Hong Xin said. "You've reached the first stage of heart kindling, which is admirable. But only performers at the second stage will be able to have a large effect on the plan."

Ling Xia cast her eyes down. "I just don't know how to do it. I've tried and tried, but to no avail."

Hong Xin sighed. "Let's try it again." She walked toward Ling Xia, her every step causing the fire in the woman's heart to burn brighter, to the point that the external layer of ice showed signs of melting.

"Be careful, Sister," Bai Ling cautioned. "The slightest mistake could destroy her disguise."

"I know what I'm doing," Hong Xin said, taking one step further. A small layer of water appeared between the flame and frigid outer shell. *Do you have any regrets?* Hong Xin sent gently. *One you haven't told us about yet? An unfulfilled desire, perhaps?*

Ling Xia hesitated. *There was once a boy. We spent a month together when we were fifteen. We were inseparable.* She shook her head. *That was before I started cultivating.*

Very good, Hong Xin sent, blowing gently into Ling Xia's ear, causing her to shiver. *Shut your eyes. Think of the yellow flame in your heart as your unrequited love for him. I want you to imagine going back to your hometown. I want you to kiss him and make love to him. Have a baby and live a wonderful life together.*

Ling Xia's body flushed red when she heard this. Her eyelids fluttered, but she bit her lip and did as she was told. The yellow flame in her heart flickered a few times before suddenly shrinking. Ling Xia frowned before sitting on the ground. The yellow flame began fighting an invading chill.

"Will she be all right?" Bai Ling asked Hong Xin as they saw this development.

Their souls kept careful watch on Ling Xia, who was now experiencing an illusion. At Hong Xin's direction, it contained both love and hatred, pain and relief. She was experiencing a lifetime of love and its corresponding suffering in mere minutes.

"She should be fine," Hong Xin said. "I'll stop it if it gets out of hand." She'd tried similar procedures before, but never so forcefully. This was now the third time she'd tried it on Ling Xia, and each time had revealed progressively deeper secrets hidden in her heart.

The yellow flame shrank little by little. They watched worriedly as it became so miniscule that even someone who'd just started practicing kindling cultivation would exceed it. It flickered a few times, almost vanishing. Hong Xin shook her head and moved toward her to stop the illusion. However, she was quickly repelled by the woman, who maintained a bit of her consciousness.

"She wants to fight to the finish," Hong Xin said, looking back toward the five. "I can't pull her out safely without damaging her mind. I say we let her finish."

"Agreed," Bai Ling said.

"Disagreed," Ji Bingxue said.

The rest agreed in sequence. Hong Xin returned to her seat and watched as the flame flickered between life and death. This scene continued for a half hour before finally flickering one last time and returning with an orange coloring. It then grew and grew until finally converging into a molten core. The surrounding ice that had melted healed itself over.

"Congratulations," Hong Xin said.

"Congratulations!" many junior sisters exclaimed.

"Thank you all so much for your support," Ling Xia said. "With me, our odds of success are even higher. We'll rescue many more of our sisters before finally—"

A creak interrupted her. Everyone looked to the lone door at the back of the room, which opened slowly. Hong Xin's face remained unchanged as a new student, Yi Ju, walked through it. The students let out a sigh of relief, but Hong Xin did not. She stood carefully and walked toward the door.

"Why did you do it?" she asked as she walked over to Yi Ju. The many students around her frowned and began murmuring. "Why did you sell us out?"

The murmurs intensified.

"I didn't have a choice," she started.

"That's enough," a voice said from behind the younger student. A red-robed woman with a red pin walked in. Mistress Meng and eight others had arrived. Hong Xin recognized Mistress Shan and Mistress Yuan from before. Mistress Meng's frosty gaze swept across the room before focusing on Hong Xin.

"How ambitious," Mistress Meng said, clucking lightly. "You've recruited a quarter of our students. I confess myself impressed that we didn't discover anything sooner."

"Then you've seen my ambitions," Hong Xin said, staring her down. A fire rose up in her heart, invigorating those around her. These flames joined together and formed a fiery bird that dove down against the mistresses, who summoned an icy shield to deflect it. The shield cracked, causing the small group of mistresses to combust their blood essence and further fuel the shield.

"Don't let up," Hong Xin told the women behind her. "If they escape, we're all dead."

"And what then?" a voice suddenly said behind her. The fire she controlled lessened as the enthusiasm of those behind her waned.

"What will we do if we kill them?" another voice said. "Can we escape?"

One after another, a dozen students from those she'd recruited spoke up. They used dousing magic to demoralize Hong Xin's rebel group, who now fell leeward against the icy shield. The shield then transformed into an icy dragon that rapidly coiled around the weakened phoenix. Hong Xin and those linked to her coughed up icy blood as their combination technique collapsed, and the icy dragon caused the temperature in the room to plummet.

"You came really close to staging an all-out rebellion," Mistress Meng said. "You sowed doubt in their minds but neglected to consider that we could do the same. In the end, you have nothing to blame but your naivety and wishful thinking."

Hong Xin clenched her fists, which were slick with blood that had frozen over. The icy shards bit into her skin as she glared daggers at the evil woman.

"Take them away," Mistress Meng said dispassionately.

The mistresses and the twelve turncoat students shackled the remainder with thin cold chains and icy black collars.

"It's a pity that such an interesting heart cultivation method is incompatible with our organization's requirements," Mistress Meng said as she closed a heart-locking collar around Hong Xin's neck.

The cold seared Hong Xin's heart, but the pain she felt was nothing compared to her feelings of anguish toward her sisters.

"I suppose you'll be taking me to die now?" Hong Xin said as the last of her hope vanished with her cultivation.

"If you're lucky," Mistress Meng said. "The headmistress will be looking into this case personally."

Shortly after, a long train of students walked out from Mistress Huang's classroom and into cells in the punishment hall. Hong Xin cast her eyes down as she passed Mistress Huang, who shook her head in disappointment.

"So," the headmistress said, straightening a pile of papers in front of her. "Manipulating the hearts of over a hundred students, destroying our basis for control. Fooling our teachers countless times. What do you think her punishment should be? And yours, for that matter?"

The teachers in the room shifted uncomfortably. "Headmistress, I believe that we should settle on her punishment first before discussing our own," Mistress Meng said. "Treachery is a far greater crime than incompetence."

"That is allowed," the headmistress said. "Now talk."

"I believe we should kill Hong Xin publicly in a cruel and unusual way," Mistress Meng said. "As a warning to others."

"And admit that a student who's been here for less than two years almost led a successful rebellion?" Mistress Shan asked sharply. "It's better to kill her quietly. And we should do the same for the entire upper echelon in their group."

"But why should we sacrifice the most talented students in our school?" Mistress Ling said. "These students have advanced cultivations and have reached the first layer of the Frozen Heart Realm. By killing them, you're turning our most successful class into a class of weaklings. We might as well just destroy all our students and start from scratch."

The fifteen mistresses began shouting and yelling. Only the headmistress and one other stood by and watched the scene unfold. They exchanged a knowing glance before the headmistress exerted her pressure. The bickering teachers quieted down instantly.

"I believe Mistress Huang has a solution. As my successor, and *that person's* ex-student, I believe there is no one more qualified on matters of the heart."

"Many thanks, Headmistress," Mistress Huang said. "I'd first like to point out the fact that a dual kindling and dousing cultivation can be converted and frozen over."

"That's impossible," Mistress Ling said. "Although we can perform heart kindlings, we're far weaker than a kindling cultivator in that regard. Both their cultivation and soul have been infused with a powerful resistance to dousing that makes it impossible to completely freeze over."

"What if I told you it's possible to convert all of them forcibly?" Mistress Huang said. "In fact, it's even possible with those who've reached the third stage of heart kindling like Hong Xin. It'd be a shame to waste such a great talent. She could cause waves in the greatest empires. She could topple nations in both this realm and the neighboring transcendent realm."

"And what evidence do you have?" Mistress Ling asked. Mistress Huang smiled before holding out a small mirror. "You're telling me a heart mirror is enough evidence?"

"Shut up and use it," Mistress Huang said. Mistress Ling flinched and took the item.

"On whom?" Mistress Ling asked.

"On me," Mistress Huang said, causing no small amount of discomfort in the room.

Mistress Ling frowned before pouring her resplendent force into the mirror. She gasped when she saw what was inside of it.

"I hereby retract my objection," Mistress Ling said, passing the mirror to another mistress.

"I retract my objection," the others said, one after another.

"Please excuse me, as I have a lot of work to do," Mistress Huang said. Many people began to rise as she left the closed chamber.

"And where do you all think you're going?" the headmistress said gravely, causing everyone to pause in their tracks. "We still haven't decided on your punishments. And since none of you are keen on deciding it, I'll do it myself."

Everyone shuddered uncontrollably. They closed their eyes as they awaited their fate.

Hong Xin opened her eyes as the door to her cell swung open. She was suspended by her arms on the wall, and the coldness in the collar seeped down to her very bones. "Have they decided how to kill me yet?" she said.

"What do you think?" Mistress Huang replied as she walked in.

"I think they'll kill me in secret to stop any news from leaking," Hong Xin said. "More than likely, eight others will die, and the rest will live."

"An impressive deduction," Mistress Huang said. "This would likely have been the case. That is, if I didn't have a better way."

"What better way?" Hong Xin said warily. She noticed that

Mistress Huang had summoned a small black box. The box opened, revealing a set of long black needles.

"I happen to have some experience in permanently dousing kindling cultivations," Mistress Huang said. "By the time everything is said and done, you'll be a cold, heartless puppet willing to do our headmistress's bidding. With your talents, you'll be able to accomplish many things."

"It will never work," Hong Xin said. "You might as well just kill me."

Mistress Huang ignored her. She took out a long spike and kneeled in front of her until their faces were level. "As much as you'll hate me, I'm doing this for your own good," she said.

Hong Xin felt a sharp pain as a black needle entered her chest. She let out a wail of anguish as her hopes and dreams began to dull, and her nightmares resurfaced.

She woke a few hours later to a familiar scene. She was in an inn, and a fat man was busy pulling off his belt. She struggled to activate her fire qi and burn him to a crisp. Unfortunately, it never materialized. Hong Xin looked on in horror as the man in her nightmares approached her. She tried to open her eyes but failed.

Interlude:
A Bundle of Joy

The whole experience is a little nerve-wracking," Feng Ming said to Prince Lei as they played cards at a small tea table. He threw a king down, even though an ace would have been a better play. He played to lose, which was always interesting because it was harder than playing to win.

"I remember my first time," Prince Lei said. "I cried afterwards, and my wife asked me whether I was a man or a woman."

"You're making this sound like something else entirely," Feng Ming said. "I just don't know why it's so stressful. It shouldn't be a big deal to me, given that *I'm* not the one having to go through anything."

"But your other half is," Prince Lei said. "And that makes all the difference. Now, come closer and let me show you something." The prince pulled out a large brown bottle. He popped the cork, and an intoxicating aroma filled the room.

"Immortal's Brew," Feng Ming whispered, grabbing the bottle. He sniffed lightly, causing his senses to distort and his balance to go. "They say every bottle is prohibitively expensive, but even the cheapest one could get an immortal drunk."

"That's a little exaggerated," Prince Lei said. "You can get bottles from transcendent realms. Although it's not cheap, many transcendents drink it because they can't get drunk otherwise. But it won't affect immortals. They'd need to drink something far stronger to get inebriated."

Feng Ming poured them two small glasses, then lifted his to Prince Lei. "To luck," he said, clinking his glass against the prince's.

"To luck, indeed," the prince said. "What are your expectations?"

"That's a secret," Feng Ming said. "Though, what I want doesn't really matter."

"That's what always happens with marriage," Prince Lei said, nodding understandingly. They continued drinking one shot after another, and before long, they fell asleep.

A small cry jerked Feng Ming awake sometime later. Prince Lei was still passed out.

"What a wimp," Feng Ming muttered as he waited anxiously. Footsteps sounded outside the living room, and an older man soon entered.

"Despicable," the king said, seeing his passed-out son. He kicked Prince Lei, who immediately tried to fall back asleep. "Wake up for your father!" the king yelled.

Hearing his familiar voice, Prince Lei jolted awake. "I wasn't asleep, I was just pretending," Prince Lei said.

"And I suppose you two weren't drinking, you were just tasting," the king said disdainfully. "Try it," he said to the man beside him. The royal uncle grabbed the bottle and took a swig.

"Immortal wine, aged 1,200 years," the royal uncle said.

"And you kept this from your own father?" the king said, glaring at his son. He immediately grabbed the bottle and took a swig, relaxing visibly. Then he stowed the bottle. "It should be about time."

At this moment, a beautiful woman clothed in white appeared. Princess Song Guo walked down the stairs with a small crying bundle. She walked up to Feng Ming, who excitedly took the newborn baby from her.

"I'm a father," Feng Ming whispered, tears moistening his eyes. He briefly remembered his own deceased father. *Was this how he felt when he held me for the first time?*

The king coughed. Feng Ming ignored him and stared intently

at his newborn son, whose eyes were filled with intelligence. "What should we name him?" he said to Song Guo.

The king coughed once more.

"I think we should call him Feng Yong," Song Guo said, tickling the small child. "In honor of one of our nation's bravest heroes."

"A good name," Feng Ming said, ignoring yet another cough from the king. "And in all fairness, you went through about twelve hours of labor. I think you deserve to name him."

Cough. Cough. Cough. Cough. Cough.

Everyone in the room looked toward the king, who was fuming. "And when am *I* going to get to hold my grandson?" the king said harshly.

Everyone laughed as Song Guo picked up the child and handed him to the king. The older man made very unroyal faces at the small child, who couldn't even see him yet.

Then he eyed him carefully. "A good grandson like mine deserves a good name. Let's name him Feng Yong in honor of one of our nation's bravest heroes."

Song Guo rolled her eyes. "As my king commands," she said. The room echoed her words.

"Now get out of here," the king said to Prince Lei. "You're no longer needed now that I have another grandson."

"But my bottle—" Prince Lei said.

"Bottle?" Song Guo said. "What bottle?"

"Yes, what bottle?" the king said. Everyone swiftly realized that the scent of alcohol was thick in the air.

"We just had a little to drink," Prince Lei said. "But your father has the bottle now."

"Oh?" Song Guo said. "What did you all have to drink?" she asked.

"Nothing much," the king said, pulling out the brown bottle nervously. "But I don't think you'd like it. It's definitely not a lady's drink."

Song Guo ignored him. She grabbed the bottle, bit off the cork, and quickly downed the contents of the half-filled container. She sighed with satisfaction. "Now *that* hit the spot," she said. "I was dying in there. Do you know how painful it is to give birth? Hell, it still hurts."

Everyone in the room looked at her like they'd seen a monster.

How much can you drink without passing out right away? Prince Lei sent to Feng Ming.

I don't know, a quarter bottle? Feng Ming sent back. *You just can't judge a woman using common sense. Anyway, you're lucky she didn't clock us for drinking while she was in labor.*

Fair enough, Prince Lei said. They both looked at the king, whose "we shall never speak of this again" look spoke volumes.

The palace was soon filled with joy and cheer. The king announced a city-wide banquet in honor of the birth of his newest grandson. Everyone, both military and civilian, happily laid down their weapons and tools and toasted in honor of Feng Yong.

In their revelry, they forgot the war that had just ravaged them, the prince who had betrayed them, and the army that was coming for them. They woke the next day rested and brimming with energy, ready to do their all for their homeland.

Chapter 19: Reward

Cha Ming's eyes opened to a gentle blue glow. He looked around a large room and noticed he was lying in a large bed with blue sheets.

I'm alive, he thought as he inspected his body. *Somehow.*

His internal injuries had already healed despite the massive strain his body had suffered from the black sphere. It was as though the clash had never happened, and he had been whisked away to this strange room and this strange bed.

"How long have I been unconscious?" he wondered aloud.

"Only three days," a voice answered. An elderly woman suddenly appeared in his chambers, shocking him. "Relax," she said, looking at his embarrassment in amusement. "As the custodian for the Bridge of Stars, I've seen things that would even make the Jade Emperor blush."

Cha Ming coughed slightly and summoned a set of blue robes before climbing out of bed. "Thank you for taking the trouble to save me, Custodian," he said. "What happened to Yu Wen, Huxian, and the others?"

"They are alive and well," the custodian replied. "They have already accepted their rewards and will be spending two years in seclusion. You will be doing the same."

Cha Ming let out a sigh of relief. "May I speak to them?"

"I'm afraid that's impossible," she said. "Any interruptions will impact their benefits and potentially prevent them from transcending in the future."

"All right," Cha Ming said. "How does the reward system work?"

"It's quite simple," the custodian said. "As one of those who made it through the main array, you will be assigned ten gathering quotas instead of the normal one quota. Each quota enables you to gather 100 points of herbs or ores.

"Then what can I trade moon stones for aside from the usual herb-gathering and ore-gathering quotas?" he asked. Normally, cultivators traded 100 moon stones for these extra quotas. No one from the Alabaster Group had ever captured as many moon stones as he had.

"With 200,000 moon stones, your selection is quite vast," the Custodian said, summoning a jade slip.

"I beg your pardon?" Cha Ming said. His jaw slackened as he observed the contents of the slip with his resplendent force.

"Your companions are all quite righteous," the custodian replied. "They each chose a transcendent treasure and chose to transfer the remainder of their moon stones to you. I'm sure they felt indebted for their unexpected success."

Cha Ming frowned. "Send their rewards back. I don't need them."

"I'm afraid I can't—they've already entered seclusion," the custodian said. "Anything you don't use will go to waste."

Cha Ming rubbed his forehead as he inspected the contents of the jade slip. It contained a comprehensive list of items, including transcendent treasures, alchemy items, formation scrolls, and combat techniques. "You wouldn't happen to have an item that can heal a soul, would you?"

"I'm afraid not," the custodian said. "Only the dew of a Burning Samsara Lotus would qualify, but this is something you need to collect yourself using an herb-gathering quota."

Cha Ming was disappointed but not surprised. "Then are there any items you would recommend?" Cha Ming asked. After all, custodians were an artificial intelligence. Their analytical prowess and powers of deduction were vastly superior to a human being.

"It's good that you asked instead of choosing rashly," the custodian said. "Choosing any formation scrolls, combat techniques, or talisman manuals would be a waste for someone who has already gathered the complete Myriad Truths Diagram."

"Myriad Truths Diagram?" Cha Ming asked.

"Look inside your spiritual sea, and you'll understand," the custodian replied.

Confused, Cha Ming directed his attention to his spiritual sea, where his jade-covered soul sat in meditation. He was surprised to discover an eight-colored diagram floating within it. As he tried to inspect it from one side or another, however, he could only ever see two dimensions to it. It curved as he inspected it, forming a perfect sphere despite its two-dimensional appearance. The contents shifted as he looked. From whatever angle he observed, the three origin runic fragments would always be present in the center, surrounded by thirty essence runic fragments. As such, he could only observe the flow fragments relative to these source items.

Surprised, he observed the diagram for a moment before noticing a peculiar part of it. He inspected a small portion and realized that a perfect formation with 120 nodes had formed.

Isn't that a Fire-Gathering Formation? he thought. Instinctively, he summoned 120 Dao sigils on the outside, easily forming the complex core-formation array. He was surprised to discover that, despite being formed with familiar characters, these characters were naturally formed with runic fragments. His formation now contained the familiar charm of the runic fragments from the Bridge of Stars.

Just as he completed the energy-gathering formation, many runes wandered from other pieces in the mystical diagram and formed a ring on the outside of it. A total of 120 nodes added on, forming the lesser energy-gathering array. Overjoyed, he completed this formation in the outside world. Immediately after forming it, the diagram in his mind expanded to a mid-grade array.

"My apologies, but time is of the essence," the custodian suddenly said, interrupting his experiments. "While you might find it all right to doze off for a week, your rewards will be impacted if you wait for too long."

"One week?" Cha Ming said, shocked. "If I'm not mistaken, the Myriad Truths Diagram is able to help me comprehend runic arts and techniques?"

"Much more than that," the custodian said. "It can be said that every possible formation, runic art, or runic technique is reflected in the diagram. By meditating on it, you'll be able to gain enlightenment on these truths. This is all possible because you first mastered the basics of runic fragments, or runic radicals as we call them, and the Bridge of Stars aided you in condensing the Myriad Truths Diagram as a reward. For these same reasons, the rune-carving enlightenment reward is also a waste of moon stones for you. You'll be able to complete basic-grade rune carving without a doubt, assuming you fix your cracked core."

"So that's how it is," Cha Ming said. "Then what do you suggest I choose as a reward?"

"You have three options," the custodian said. "For ten thousand moon stones each, you could choose transcendent treasures and trade them in the outside world as you wish. You can also choose items that aid professionals for the same value. The third option is to feed your soul-bound treasure."

Cha Ming's eyes lit up. "Is there a way to promote my Clear Sky Brush?"

"There is," the custodian said. "Though soul-bound treasures are ravenous, it's possible to nourish yours into a transcendent treasure by dipping it into a pool of Grandmist Essence."

Cha Ming pondered for a moment. "I have another request. Is there a treasure that will enable me to fix my cracked core?"

"That… used to be possible," the custodian said with an awkward expression. "However, the Nirvana Pill recipe has already been traded for previously. The Jade Emperor only replenishes treasures here periodically, so it will take some time for this to become available again."

Cha Ming shook his head, sighing. "Then do you have any

cultivation methods that match my Perfect Five Elements cultivation technique?"

"I'm afraid not," the custodian replied. "Your core is rather unique, and I've determined that your cultivation requires an initiation by a senior. The senior's level would need to be extremely high to enable him to establish a stable formation in your dantian that is also capable of evolution.

"Then I'll take a transcendent pill furnace, a transcendent hammer focus, and use the remainder of the moon stones to purchase Grandmist Essence," Cha Ming said. He summoned the Clear Sky Brush, which floated about curiously.

"As you wish," the custodian said.

She raised her hand and opened a spatial slit. A furnace and a small crystal ball floated out. Then a viscous gray fog spilled into the room like a stream. It poured for some time before accumulating into a small sphere, which defied gravity. And while the stream continued pouring for an incense time, the sphere didn't grow. Rather, its density increased despite its gravity-defying behavior.

After some time, the elderly woman closed the spatial slit. "You can casually toss your soul-bound treasure into this pool of Grandmist Essence. You should do so as soon as possible, as this is a time-intensive process. With any luck, you'll have a transcendent soul-bound treasure within the next two years."

Her duty accomplished, the custodian vanished. Cha Ming summoned the Clear Sky Brush, which greedily darted into the gray sphere. After confirming that the absorption process was proceeding as planned, he turned to the Myriad Truths Diagram in his spiritual sea. After all, two years might seem like a long time to a mortal, but to a cultivator, it would pass by in the blink of an eye.

"Did he choose as planned?" Yu Wen asked from her luxurious bed.

"Yes," the custodian replied. "The odds of his soul-bound treasure evolving should be at least eight out of ten. With a transcendent treasure, he should have no problem preserving himself in mortal realms. Though he'll have to survive Jade Moon Planet first."

"He'll make it," Yu Wen said firmly. "Although it's currently impossible to transmit people from Jade Moon Planet, my father will soon realize this point. It's only a matter of time until help arrives. How are your emergency preparations going?"

"The Devil-Sealing Array will be fully operational in a year's time," the custodian said. "And while I'm not able to transport anyone already on the planet, I've strongly encouraged everyone to gather at Jade Moon Garden, stating that there would be a special event with increased rewards. Many people have already arrived. The bad news is that half of those who haven't have already perished."

"Very well, let me know if anything changes," Yu Wen said.

The custodian disappeared, and once she did, Yu Wen took out her jade tablet out and began flicking through various images. She passed multiple chase scenes before arriving at pictures of a starry bridge. The next picture was a zoom-in of Cha Ming, who she saw amongst the many gathered cultivators. Then a chase scene with multiple devil cultivators appeared. In this picture, she stole moon stones out from under their noses.

Whoever said having a camera as a soul-bound treasure is a waste? Yu Wen thought. *Who else in the universe can get such high-quality pictures?*

She continued flicking until she arrived at pictures of a growing formation circle. Each step showed five people and a satisfied expression. The circle grew and grew until finally, a fight broke out. It ended with the final impact between the black orb and her Grandmist Essence.

Yu Wen frowned. "It's a good picture, but there's no need to keep it," she said before deleting it. "We wouldn't want anyone getting sad after seeing it." She shuddered as a vision of her doom ran through her mind.

"Perhaps escaping this calamity is impossible," she muttered. She checked the last few pictures she'd taken before going back to sleep.

Huxian looked at the walls curiously. The mysterious runes were useless to him, but he didn't have much else to do. That is, aside from digging through his memories for something useful. After looking for a few hours, he found something inspiring, one that was difficult to build—unless he had Grandmist Essence. This Grandmist Essence had conveniently been made available to him, courtesy of Xiao Bai's moon stones. Therefore, a tiny formation was growing healthily in the center of the room. It contained thousands of lines but only nine focal points—a yin-yang in the center and eight equidistant trigrams. They were connected in various intricate ways with gray lines that caused the energy to flow evenly and equalize between points.

"Who would have thought that I could obtain Grandmist Essence from an old lady on a bridge in the sky," Huxian muttered.

"An old lady, am I?" the custodian said. "Then I suppose you won't be wanting your meals during your stay?"

Huxian paled. "What I meant to say was, 'Who would have thought that such a mystical and beautiful custodian would have such a precious treasure to gift me.'"

"Better," the custodian said. A roasted demon beast carcass appeared on the floor of the room just beside the formation. "Are you sure this is a worthwhile use of Grandmist Essence?" the custodian asked. "Grandmist Essence is an extremely rare treasure. Most demons would use it to refine their bloodline, increasing their potential and combat prowess to the very limits."

"And what would happen to my friends?" Huxian said. "Do I break my contract with them and leave them behind? They'll die if I don't find a way to strengthen them before the next tribulation."

"Everyone dies eventually," the custodian said. "Your father lost countless generals."

"I'm not my father," Huxian said as he observed the formation that was slowly incubating.

It would take eighteen months to complete under the careful nurturing of this small amount of Grandmist Essence. "And to me, they're not generals. Every one of them is an irreplaceable friend."

Cha Ming was a blur. He carefully struck out with a loaner staff as he practiced his newly created techniques. The first technique was called Shape Staff. He thrust out with the butt of his staff, which was covered in a spearlike point of gold qi. It could be used to pierce, slash, or sweep like a genuine spear. He continued until he ran out of gold qi and the complex runes on the tip of his staff faded.

After practicing Shape Staff, he continued on to practice the newly created Flow Staff. The staff became a blur of blue runes that undulated as he moved. His body seemed to distort as his flowing footwork combined with the mirage created by his staff's motion.

Having run out of water qi, he moved on to his latest innovation: the Life and Death Staff. Green runes covered the staff, and every blow contained life-ending energy. The staff art was plain, but its corrosive power was difficult to block and would wear away at the opponent's qi and life force. Meanwhile, as his opponent lost energy, his own energy would be replenished. The vampiric effect was the essence of life and death that he'd gleaned from the painting, *Samsara*.

Once he ran out of wood qi, his plain staff arts became explosive and intense. As he struck out violently and stepped swiftly, his qi drained away four times faster than any other staff art. Energy Staff Art was the culmination of his understanding of fire.

Once his fire qi ran out, he switched to the last staff art, Material Staff Art. While he had many choices to choose from, like vibration and gravity, he chose to focus on the core of his poetic talismans. By using this staff art, his skin was covered in hardening runes. He increased his weight to the limit and covered his staff in crumbling runes, becoming an immoveable bastion of destruction.

"After so much time, I finally have staff arts that aren't total garbage," Cha Ming muttered. *Though it's clear that my water, earth, and gold staff arts are much stronger than the wood and fire ones. It's likely because I infused them from inspirations from my talismans.*

Having finished his practice session, Cha Ming sent out his Dao sigils in five groups of 216 each. They formed perfect energy-gathering formations—at least, as perfect as possible given the number of sigils he had. The next step up was 240, 360, 720, and 1,080 each. Strictly speaking, however, this would require formation flags and other complicated items. For now, he could only utilize combat formations.

His core pulsed as he cultivated. Fortunately, no qi leaked out, as it was protected by a jade membrane. His cultivation session continued for weeks as his instincts urged him to continue. Weeks turned to months before finally, his core broke through an intangible membrane.

A soul-rending pain tore through him as his core rapidly expanded and he broke through to the middle of core formation. New cracks appeared on his shattered core, which was held together long enough by its protective membrane for masses of gray qi to seep between them and solidify.

Even with the assistance of the Bridge of Stars, it will be difficult to cultivate without external help.

After stabilizing his cultivation for some time, he opened his eyes. The custodian was seated before him, pouring tea. "And here I thought you'd never want to leave," the old woman chided.

"On the contrary," Cha Ming said, grabbing a cup, "staying here any longer is useless to me. Any news on my brush?"

He looked to a corner of the room, where the Clear Sky Brush was gently floating. Hints of gray had appeared on its surface, and it emanated a frightening pressure.

"Any minute now," the custodian said. Just as she finished speaking, an undulation of power caused Cha Ming's heart to palpitate. The custodian frowned and put up her defenses, isolating both her and Cha Ming. However, it was useless. The shield broke apart like wet paper, and the blue stone room crumbled.

Cha Ming, however, was uninjured. He walked over to the Clear Sky Brush, which had now transformed into the Clear Sky Staff, and grasped it firmly. "Showoff," he said, quickly retrieving it. A stream of information entered his mind, containing three techniques, one of which would be useful when he returned to the mortal world and two of which were blurred.

"It's sentient?" the custodian exclaimed as she reappeared.

"Of course," Cha Ming said. "Isn't that part and parcel with being a soul-bound treasure?"

"Heavens, no," the custodian said. "At least, not before becoming an immortal treasure. The only exception is us custodians."

"Then I hope you can keep it a secret," Cha Ming said.

"Of course," the custodian replied. "Now that your staff is done evolving, it's time for you to leave. You'll be teleported to the place on Jade Moon Planet that most suits your needs."

"Will I be near the others?" Cha Ming asked.

"Perhaps," the custodian replied. "I'm not a fortune teller." She then motioned to the circle on the floor. "Be careful out there. Jade Moon Planet is much more dangerous than it used to be. I urge you and anyone you find to go to Jade Moon Garden as soon as possible. Not only is the Burning Samsara Lotus there, but any herbs you might ever need are there also. Furthermore, there is a grand competition held only once every hundred openings happening there. Be sure to hurry over. It's a once-in-a-lifetime opportunity."

"Many thanks for the advice," Cha Ming said before stepping into the gray circle. His surroundings changed, and he found himself in a dense jungle. A demonic bear pounced on him the moment he stepped through, its eyes black.

Chapter 20: A Curious Friend

"It's good to be out!" Huxian said, breathing in the fresh air. Silverwing and Lei Jiang burst out of his tails and inspected their surroundings.

"What took you so long to let us out?" Silverwing asked. "I've been dying in there, with only this little mouse to keep me company."

"The Bridge of Stars wouldn't let me," Huxian said. "Now take a look at your cultivation. Does it look any different?"

"Er... my core is a little different," Silverwing said. "It's covered by a weak green layer that's making me stronger." He fanned out his wingspan until it reached 320 feet wide. "It's even affecting my body."

"But I can't get any bigger," said Lei Jiang, who was still only six feet long.

"It's as I suspected," Huxian said. "The blessing's origin is Jade Moon Planet, not the Bridge of Stars. It's related to the protective shield surrounding it." He chuckled. "Good, good, good. As demons, we can't take anything away, but we can eat anything we want!"

"Anything we want?" Silverwing said. His eyes looked around wildly and immediately detected delicious-looking spirit fruits growing in the trees. He reached out with his claw and ate the fruit, which was immediately converted to energy.

"Stop wasting," Huxian said, rolling his eyes. He summoned a complex array made of runic fragments. Two of the eight positions shifted and encompassed Lei Jiang and Silverwing. He alone sat in the central position. Huxian let out a fierce bellow. Two of his tails shone and filled the two side formations with their corresponding elemental light. Then they faded.

"Great!" Huxian said. "I now introduce to you the Friendship Circle."

"What's a Friendship Circle?" Lei Jiang said. "Is it tasty?"

"It's very tasty," Huxian said. "As brothers, neither of us should be weak or strong. I spent two years building this from scratch using Grandmist Essence. It has two functions. First, it uses my powers of devouring and purification to enhance your conversion of external resources to demonic energy. Anything you eat will bring you that much more benefit."

"The second effect is a matter of fairness between brothers," Huxian said. "All of us will split energy according to our needs. When one is stronger, they will stop receiving energy and send it all to their brothers. When we are equal in strength, our cores will grow at the same pace, regardless of how much energy we need individually."

"Boss," Lei Jiang said. "I can't help but feel I'm getting stiffed."

"Nonsense," Huxian said. "As the weakest of us, you benefit the most."

"But Silverwing needs four times more energy than I do," Lei Jiang complained. "I'm usually just lazy and can't grow as fast. And you need ten times as much energy."

"Lei Jiang," Huxian said seriously, "this is a team, and every brother must do their utmost for it. How can you call yourself my brother if you laze around while I toil for your energy?"

A guilty look appeared on Lei Jiang's face. He looked to Silverwing, who looked back solemnly. "Have I really been slacking?" he asked.

"Far too much," Silverwing said. "I just didn't want to say anything. Because... because we're brothers."

"Silverwing..." Lei Jiang said, tearing up.

"Lei Jiang..." Silverwing said, tearing up as well.

The small mouse hopped to Silverwing's talon and hugged it. "You're right. How can I be so shameless? I'll work just as hard as you guys to help promote our group's strength."

"I knew you had it in you, pal," Silverwing said. He and Huxian watched as Lei Jiang darted out toward the trees and began eating spirit fruits like a madmouse.

"Good work," Silverwing said to Huxian. "That guy's been getting on my nerves. And now we can make him work for our cultivation. It's just like taking candy from a baby."

"Indeed," Huxian said. "Now we just need to find six more friends. Preferably those who need less energy so we can slack off."

"I like the way you think," Silverwing said. "But now that Lei Jiang is gone, can we talk about something? This Friendship Circle thing... the name. Why don't we change it to something else? How about Supreme Circle of Mighty Justice or something impressive like that?"

His words fell on deaf ears.

A massive lake loomed in the distance. Huxian sat on a trunk by the river as Silverwing circled above the water. Every flap of his wings brought large waves to shore, and this occasionally brought in beached fish, which Huxian quickly snatched up before returning to his tree.

"Boss, I've collected so many good things today," Lei Jiang said excitedly. "You should have seen the massive pile of seeds I found. Oh, and the grapes! Each of the grapes were bigger than I am!"

"Very good work," Huxian said. He put on a serious face as he watched Silverwing. It was always important to pretend to be doing something. That was why as Silverwing fished, Huxian supervised. He called it lifeguard duty.

"Being a lifeguard sure is boring," Lei Jiang said as he nudged up on a lower branch.

"But it's necessary," Huxian said. "Silverwing might be great in the air, but what about in the water? What if he gets caught by a giant demon crocodile and drowns? Can we call ourselves his brothers if we didn't keep an eye on this small weakness?"

"Boss is the best," Lei Jiang said. "We should all do work we're suited for. I'm much more suited to foraging for resources."

"That you are," Huxian said. "That you are. Now tell me, did you see that strange frog I told you to keep an eye out for?"

"The one who showed up a while ago?" Lei Jiang said. "I haven't seen him at all. Oh wait, he's behind you."

"Wait, what?" Huxian looked around but didn't see anything. Annoyed, he looked back toward Lei Jiang but was surprised to see two large eyes only an inch away from his muzzle.

"Ah!" In his fright, Huxian fell off the branch and landed on a lower one. It promptly cracked, causing him to crash down onto the leafy ground. "Why does falling hurt so much in this world?" Huxian said, gently easing himself out of an imprint in the ground.

"Are you from the outside world?" a voice said. Huxian looked up and suppressed a shudder. What was possibly the most hideous creature he'd ever seen was right in front of him. And to his surprise, it was the same toad that he'd caught a glimpse of the other day.

"My name is Gua, nice to meet you," the toad said. It extended its webbed hand, which was covered in pus-filled warts.

"Gua, is it?" Huxian said, working hard to suppress his disgust. "I'd shake your hand, but I've been a little sick lately. I don't want to be passing it around."

"Heavens, is it bad?" Gua said. "Quick, look at me. I can help you."

Huxian looked at the toad in confusion. Several breaths passed while they stared at each other without blinking. His eyes wandered from wart to wart, wondering what the toad was going to say next.

"There, do you feel better?"

"What do you mean?" Huxian said.

"I find any disease can be cured by gazing at my glorious figure," Gua said. "It's a curse to be born beautiful. Countless ladies prostrate themselves before me and avoid eye contact, for fear of offending me. But I do what I can for the world." His gaze bore no hint of vanity and not a shred of deceit. It made Huxian want to throw up more than Gua's hideous warts did.

"Boss, are you okay?" Lei Jiang said, scurrying beside him. Huxian used the mouse to block out the toad's figure. "Is it just me, or is that toad ugly as all sin?"

"Ugly?" the toad said. *"Ugly?"*

The air shimmered as a sickening pressure surrounded them. They felt as though they were being suffocated in a poisonous swamp that was not unlike the swamp calamity they'd faced together.

"Get out of my sight, you swine-fathered sorry excuse for a mouse. You look like you've been thrown up by an owl, but I didn't say anything. But now, you dare to call your father ugly? Have you no eyes? Have you no shame? Have you considered how poor your mother must feel every day? And now you have the gall to call this father ugly?"

The torrent of insults came swiftly and without warning. Huxian didn't know what to say. He could only hold his jaw tightly shut, for fear that it would drop to the ground near the hideous toad.

I need to run, Huxian thought. *I need a distraction.* "Silverwing!" he said after considering the situation. With any luck, Silverwing would take the hint and eat the toad. Birds did that, right?

A piercing shriek filled the air as Silverwing dove down from above. *Eat him, Silverwing,* Huxian said. *Don't look, just take him down in a single gulp.*

Got it, boss, Silverwing sent back. His massive wings cut down the nearby forest as his beak plunged toward the toad. Huxian and Lei Jiang readied themselves to restrict the toad's movements. As though sensing his impending doom, the toad looked back toward the diving Silverwing. It lifted its webbed hand and hollered.

"Hi! I'm Gua," the toad said to Silverwing. The giant bird's eyes narrowed as they focused on the tiny demon.

"Holy mother of—" Silverwing exclaimed once he got a good look at it. His form rapidly shrunk on instinct to avoid the hideous toad, and he dove into the forest. He smashed through thousands of trees before finally coming to a complete stop. Then Silverwing fluttered back beside Huxian. "What the hell is that?"

"My honorable friend of the skies, my humble name is Gua," the frog said. "You aren't the first to fall out of the skies while admiring my beauty, and you won't be the last."

"Urgh!" the three beasts shouted. Huxian and Lei Jiang hopped onto Silverwing's back. The falcon grew in size as it lifted off and flapped its mighty wings. They traveled all the way across the lakes and closer to a mountain covered in demonic energy. Thousands of demonic creatures milled about its base. Their violet aura was mixed with ochre, a telltale sign of fiendish demons.

"It'll be difficult to fight them all," Huxian said solemnly. "But it's much better than facing that monstrosity. We can only fight tooth and nail for land to call our own."

"I'd rather fight millions of fiendish demons than see that thing again," Silverwing said. "Fiendish demons might taste bad, but they're nutritious."

"That, and they don't make our eyes bleed," Lei Jiang piped in. "So are we really doing this?" the mouse said, looking around hesitantly.

"Silverwing will snipe them from above," Huxian said, nodding. "Meanwhile, you'll be scouting and ambushing as many of them as you can. Make sure to steal any food they try to eat and bring it back to share."

"What about you, boss?" Lei Jiang said.

"Me?" Huxian said. "I'll be doing the most important job of all. Supervising."

Lei Jiang nodded and rushed off to perform his tasks. Meanwhile, Silverwing only rolled his eyes and began floating around the lake as he always had, keeping an eye out for any delicious fish that might make an appearance.

A ravenous crunching sound permeated the valley as a demonic wolf feasted on the decaying corpse of a demonic bear. To the untrained eye, this was a normal occurrence.

Cha Ming knew better. Ochre wisps permeated the demonic wolf. Its body morphed as its paws become much larger and its teeth more elongated. Rather than a self-supporting creature, it now resembled a vehicle of destruction and slaughter. After its body fully transformed, its eyes, which had hovered between purple and ochre, suddenly turned pitch black. They became more subdued and filled with purpose. Contrary to its nature, the wolf immediately stopped feasting and wandered north like the last dozen cases Cha Ming had observed.

Cha Ming moved swiftly and silently; he was surrounded by a makeshift array that emulated the nearby forest and covered his aura. This was how he could remain undetected by the creature, despite being so close.

They're clearly fiendish demons, but there's something different about them, Cha Ming sent to Huxian. *It's like they're being controlled. Are you seeing the same thing on your end?*

Fiendish demons everywhere, Huxian said. *And they're acting strange. They're not aggressive like they should be. It's like they're searching for something. More to the point, fiendish demons aren't native to Jade Moon Planet.*

Be careful, Cha Ming sent. *We can't help each other when we're on different sides of the planet.*

I'm more worried about you, Huxian said. *What will you eat?*

I'll be fine, Cha Ming replied. His stomach growled, so he ate one of the many moon cakes in his bag of holding. It filled his entire body with energy and would continue to do so for a full day.

They might taste terrible, but they're very effective, he thought, grimacing.

Jade Moon Planet was very different than their own mortal plane, the Ling Nan Plane. For starters, gravity was hundreds of times more intense. It was impossible to survive without having an abnormally strong body or qi cultivation. He suspected that this was the main reason for the Jade Moon Blessing. Though they no longer had their cultivation promoted by moon stones, it was more than enough to keep them from being crushed to death.

The most noticeable change, however, was the need to eat to replenish energy. On Cha Ming's home plane, there was no need to eat once a cultivator reached foundation establishment. But on Jade Moon Planet, this need returned. Furthermore, normal food wouldn't suffice. Only food harvested from the plane seemed to be effective. That and the terrible-tasting moon cakes.

I'm in luck, Cha Ming thought as he saw a peach tree with four monkeys at the peak of core formation standing guard over it. Licking his lips, he rushed over to a nearby branch and plucked off a dozen fruits. The moment he did, however, his concealment formation vanished. The monkeys howled in rage and rushed after him.

You have a lot of peaches, Cha Ming sent to them. *I don't want all of them, only a few.* He didn't need to steal peaches, but the moon cakes were just too terrible.

After evading their pursuit for a half hour, Cha Ming sat on a tree branch and bit into a large juicy fruit. His body shivered with delight as it filled him to the brim with energy. Any surplus was directed to his dantian and soul; his body rejected the foreign energy.

It seems I'll need to procure five-element source marrow to advance any further, he thought.

Having fully digested the peach, Cha Ming continued his pursuit of the black-eyed fiendish demons. He landed by a fresh corpse that had been killed but only partially eaten. *Are they in so much of a hurry that they can't spend a few more breaths finishing off their prey?* He looked toward what used to be a demon badger's lair. A crimson flower bloomed above it.

Cha Ming's eyes brightened. As he approached the flower, a jade formation hummed to life. He withdrew an herb-gathering quota from his bag of holding and placed it on a formation eye. Three small dots appeared beside twenty-seven others. Although each herb-gathering quota allowed for 100 herbs to be picked, different herbs held different value. This one was a mid-grade herb and therefore took up three points. As the talisman returned to his hand, the jade formation shrank around the herb and encapsulated it like a jade preservation container. He stored the herb in his bag of holding for future use.

If they're not after herbs, what are they after? Cha Ming wondered.

He continued following the beasts, and as he did, the ground became less densely forested and increasingly rocky. A small mound appeared in the distance. To Cha Ming's surprise, not only were fiendish demons keeping guard but so were a few dozen devilish cultivators. Without exception, each one had pitch-black eyes.

How is this possible? Cha Ming thought. *Isn't it difficult to convert cultivators to the devilish path? How could there be so many on Jade Moon Planet?*

Although the Bridge of Stars allowed devilish cultivators, its rules were extremely unfair to them. Furthermore, they were cooperating with fiendish demons, who were usually so violent that even cooperation amongst themselves was impossible.

Clang. Clang. Clang.

Sounds of metal on stone echoed through the woods. Cha Ming kept careful watch over the group of devilish cultivators and fiendish demons as the clanking continued. Days passed until suddenly a massive demonic badger burst out of the ground. It, too, was a fiendish demon. It patted its giant claws together, letting clods of dirt and rock fall to the ground before placing a small stone the size of a fist before the lead cultivator.

Immortal jade? Cha Ming thought, seeing the opaque stone. On his home plane, such a rock was extremely valuable.

"Still too small," the devilish cultivator said. "I need a piece that's at least six feet long and a foot wide."

"Those are almost impossible to find," the badger roared. "It could take years for us to find even one."

"We only have a few years, and our group needs to find three," the cultivator said. "A fate worse than death awaits us otherwise."

The badger bared its teeth. "Understood, but I need more help."

"We only have so much devilish essence," the cultivator said coldly.

"Then take it back from some of your followers," the badger said. "I'm useful. You're useful. But are they useful? It's all our skins on the line."

The devil and the fiend faced off for some time before the cultivator's hand shot out. Five ochre tendrils flew out past the badger and pierced five unsuspecting cultivators. Ochre light flew from them toward the lead cultivator and accumulated into five small black rocks. The cultivator tossed them to a nearby fiendish wolf.

"Find us more badgers. Or worms. Or anything good at digging."

"As you command," the fiendish wolf said, scurrying off with a dozen of its kind. They didn't notice Cha Ming following them under the cover of his stealth formation.

Chapter 21: Faith

Cha Ming and the wolves ran through the rocky forest like experts, avoiding any unnecessary conflicts with other demon beasts. An hour passed before they arrived at a small clearing with a large burrow. The wolves paused just outside, looking through the dark opening with fear in their eyes.

"After enslaving my brother, you dare come here?" a deep voice said.

The ground trembled and cracked beneath their paws as the being in the burrow spoke. Three of them were thrown up into the air from the shockwaves while five others were pelted with rocks and dirt. A massive clawed paw burst out of the ground and swatted at the lead wolf, who rapidly grew and met the claw head on.

"Just be obedient like your brother and get this over with," the fiendish wolf said. "Life's not so bad as a fiend. You'll realize this in time."

"Over my dead body," the badger snorted. A brown runic field flew out from him, vastly increasing the dreadful gravity and causing the wolves no small amount of discomfort. The badger took advantage of this and slammed its two paws onto the ground. Thousands of sharp spikes burst out of the earth and impaled the many prone wolves. The survivors leaped onto the badger and latched on with his arms, sealing off his movements.

Then the pack leader revealed a black stone in its mouth. "Don't worry. This won't hurt. Much."

Seeing what was about to happen, Cha Ming activated his Fire Staff Art, enhancing his instantaneous movements to their limit. The wolves barely had enough time to react before he appeared in front of their leader and swung with his newly promoted Clear Sky Staff. It sheared through what should have been an indestructible crystal and reduced it to rubble. A thick ochre mist burst out of it and attacked Cha Ming, who instantly activated his Devil-Sealing Intent. The ochre mist shrieked as they mutually destroyed each other.

"How dare you meddle in our business," the lead wolf barked, attacking him. Cha Ming jumped back and activated a Frost Manifestation Formation, stalling the lead wolf just long enough for him to stab out with a Shape Staff. It stabbed through its chest like a spear, allowing Devil-Sealing Intent to burrow deep within the wolf. It howled in pain as its body shriveled into a desiccated corpse.

The badger, seeing that it had a surprise helper, activated a strengthening technique. It used the burst in power to free one of his paws and slash out at the remaining wolves. The two moved in tandem.

Cha Ming used icy formation flowers to stall the wolves as the demonic badger used its superior size and strength to demolish them. Noticing their effective tactic, the wolves changed their target to Cha Ming, who struck out with Splitting Heaven and Earth. He poured both creation qi and fire qi into it, manifesting a horizontal white line of fire that set half of the wolves ablaze. These wolves fell to the ground to extinguish it, but try as they might, they could do nothing against these eternal flames.

The other half of the wolves, seeing that the situation was dire, fled the scene without any hesitation. Before they could run away, however, the ground fell beneath their feet, trapping them within an earthen coffin. Seeing this, Cha Ming flicked his sleeve, and the white flames intensified as they consumed the fiendish wolves before finally winking out once the deed was done. The woods stood eerily silent after their demise.

"It's not safe here, human," the demon badger said. "Your kind should flee to Jade Moon Garden as soon as possible. Did the custodian not tell you that?"

Cha Ming shook his head. "She said this was the place I needed to be," he said. "I saw the fiends in passing and decided to investigate. Do you know what they're looking for?"

"I don't know," the badger said. "What I *do* know is that nowhere is safe. I'm very likely to die or be enslaved before the Jade Emperor comes to save us."

Cha Ming massaged his forehead. "Do you have any elemental lodestones?"

"Of course," the demon badger said. "It's why I placed my burrow here. Why? Do you need some?"

"I can use it to lay you a concealment formation," Cha Ming said. "That way it won't be so easy for the fiends to find you if they come again."

"Good. Very good." The badger laughed. "Since they want me so badly, let's not make it easy. We'll do as you say."

A large fissure appeared, and hundreds of thousands of brightly colored stones appeared in a neat pile. Cha Ming didn't stand on ceremony and stowed them all. He then summoned his Clear Sky Brush and swiftly painted 1,080 pieces and scattered them around the burrow. Then he summoned the Clear Sky Brush's large form and flew above the scattered stones.

He first traced a large white circle, demarcating the formation's boundary. He then painted dozens of lines at a time, which extended across the circle like a rapidly growing spiderweb. Soon, a full 10,800 lines had been painted. Some lines were brown, while others were blue and green. The last stroke activated the formation and mobilized the energy of Heaven and Earth.

"They're coming soon," the demon badger cautioned.

"Let's just rest and see if they can find us," Cha Ming said. As he sat down to recuperate, hundreds of fiendish demons rushed in from all directions toward their fallen comrades. However, they circled around the burrow like it didn't exist.

"Good job, brat," the demon badger said as the fiendish demons retreated. "Although you saved me, it's still very dangerous. You should escape." It pressed its paw on the earth as though feeling for something. "There is another human several miles to the north. Maybe you'll stand a better chance if you run together."

"Many thanks for your advice," Cha Ming said, clasping his hands and bowing. He activated his own concealment formation and slipped past the many hundreds of fiendish demons and flew toward the north at full speed. A lone human wouldn't last very long in this treacherous forest.

"Quickly, don't let her escape!" a devilish cultivator with black eyes yelled. Hundreds ochre-colored figures fanned out into the woods. Yu Wen found her potential escape routes shrinking and her options dwindling.

Did I miscalculate? Yu Wen thought. *Was it worth the risk?*

She pushed the thought out of her mind. Doubt was the last thing she needed now. She expertly ducked under a dozen arrows and darted behind a stone pillar, which was rapidly demolished by the onslaught of techniques. Sighing, she summoned a gray cloud of Grandmist Essence around them. Time stood still as she ran a mile away from her frozen opponents. She then dispelled the draining technique and continued running in the opposite direction.

Why did the Jade Emperor have to be so strict when he made this realm? Yu Wen thought. *Why am I, of all people, getting restricted on this miserable excuse for a plane?*

Despite her exhaustion, the one-mile jaunt gave her the reprieve she needed. She adjusted her direction and continued heading north toward a flowing volcano. Unbeknownst to her pursuers, it was also the location of an impenetrable sanctuary. She would be safe there once she arrived.

While deep in thought, she froze on reflex, barely avoiding a blade aimed at her head in the process. "You think we don't know your little tricks?" a devilish cultivator said, appearing out of nowhere. Two other devils appeared beside him. Their sinister black armor stood in stark contrast to their lightning-filled bodies. Amongst devils, these pride devils boasted the strongest might and were nigh unkillable.

"You think the three of you can stop me?" Yu Wen said, mustering her energy to make another jaunt.

"No," the envy devil said. "But who said there were three of us?"

Out of reflex, Yu Wen unleashed her strongest Grandmist field. Her surroundings distorted as she forcefully broke the illusion surrounding them. Hundreds of blue-skinned devils collapsed under the pressure and splashed down to the forest floor in pools of water. A few stronger ones managed to resist for a moment longer before crumbling to sand.

Even the lazy sloth devils have been mobilized, Yu Wen thought as she bolted in a random direction.

"Get her while she's still weak," the envy devil ordered. The two armored figures beside him ran out with black swords in hand. They struck swiftly and fiercely, like bolts of nether lightning. Yu Wen summoned hundreds of silver strings to block them, but the black swords shredded them in an instant.

Is this where it all ends? Yu Wen thought as the blades pierced the air, moving swiftly toward her.

Cha Ming quickened his pace. He saw a burst of gray in the distance as he approached with fiery footsteps. His staff cleaved through rocks and trees alike as he took the most direct path to a large clearing. It was completely devoid of life, with not even a tree remaining. Outside of the clearing, lush plants were growing at a visible pace. But Cha Ming had no time to ponder the strange mystery. He mustered all his strength to reach Yu Wen, who was desperately fending off two black-armored devils.

Let's hope your strength as a transcendent treasure isn't overrated, Cha Ming thought. His Clear Sky Staff hummed back, reassuring him. One thousand and eighty Dao sigils appeared before Yu Wen as a protective shield of ice, which cracked as soon as the devils struck it.

A transparent devil slashed at Cha Ming with a blade of wind. He avoided the blade and ignored the invulnerable devil, slashing at the two black-armored ones with a Shape Staff. The two devils were cut in two. To his surprise, however, their two halves instantly reassembled.

They're invulnerable as well? Cha Ming thought. Seeing this, he jumped up and struck down with his Clear Sky Staff with Crushing Chaos. He poured earth qi and destruction qi into the technique, making the resulting black line incomparably heavy. The black-armored devils tried to dodge but were unable to shrug off its suppression; the black line crushed their supposedly invulnerable bodies, which transformed to lightning that rushed into the ground.

Cha Ming panted in exhaustion after executing the draining maneuver. He dispelled his fatigue with a healing formation and grasped Yu Wen's tender waist before pushing off toward the north.

As long as we get past that ridge, they can't follow us, Yu Wen sent. He didn't question where she'd obtained the knowledge. Instead, he carefully dodged wind blades and other techniques from the approaching tide of devils, using Dao sigils to deflect those he couldn't avoid.

Hours passed as the devils kept up their dogged pursuit. The trees grew increasingly sparse as they advanced toward the mountains in the distance. It wasn't long before they reached a tall, barren cliff. Their hearts dimmed when they saw an army of a thousand blocking the way. Cha Ming eyed their battle formation, probing for any weakness.

"We can't make it," Yu Wen said. "Just leave me here and save yourself." She slumped slightly in his arms, discouraged.

"You're not being very productive," Cha Ming said as he continued scanning their forces. "Help me find a way through instead. You mentioned before that we're safe past that cliff?"

Not only were they blocked by an army, but tens of thousands of fiendish crows filled the air, preventing them from stepping forward.

"Yes, that same cliff," Yu Wen said. "There is an invisible barrier, which devilish creatures cannot pass. It's one of the few sanctuaries on Jade Moon Planet. I know about it because I came here to retrieve a treasure. If we get past that cliff, give or take ten feet, we'll be safe."

"Then it's decided," Cha Ming said, looking back toward their approaching pursuers. "I need you to hold on tight. We're breaking through the hard way."

He retrieved his Dao sigils and directed them to form a black spiral. The drill-like bubble surrounded them as a protective shield. Then, Cha Ming held Yu Wen close and pushed off toward the devilish army.

"You're using destruction qi as a core-formation cultivator?" Yu Wen said in a panicked voice. "Are you insane?"

Cha Ming chuckled before gritting his teeth and pouring five-element qi, creation qi, and destruction qi into the shield. It expanded just in time to receive a volley of techniques. His body burned under the strain as techniques dissipated and sabers, swords, and staves crumbled to dust on contact. Many of the devilish cultivators and fiendish demons threw themselves at them as they made their way to the cliff, only to be sheared through by the deadly black shield.

I'm reaching my limit, Cha Ming thought as black veins began appearing on his arms.

They were halfway through the devilish army, who had begun to self-detonate in a gambit to stop them. Cha Ming coughed up black blood as the explosion buffeted his shield of destruction. The black veins on his arms spread as he burst through enemy lines and reached the cliff. His bones creaked as they crashed into the rocky surface and worked their way through the dense rock like a knife through hot butter.

Let's hope I was right, he thought as he pushed up toward the surface. They pierced through twenty feet of rock before breaking out from beneath the ground. The swarm of flying fiendish demons shrieked in rage as they saw them exit safely on the other side of the barrier.

Seeing that they were safe, Cha Ming collapsed and allowed his body to regenerate. Yu Wen's grip on him slacked as she too collapsed in exhaustion. As the damage to his body healed, and as the traces of destruction qi were purged from his limbs, he noticed two jade palm prints on his chest that were notably absent of any damage. They covered his heart and dantian, the two most vital places for a cultivator.

A realization struck him. While he was busy fighting for their survival, Yu Wen had been protecting him from himself.

A fire crackled atop the ridge as Cha Ming recovered. He ate what must have been the tenth moon cake of the day before summoning a green sigil formation around Yu Wen. The healing formation gathered energy from piles of spirit stones and poured them into her, replenishing her energy-deficient body. By the time the last of the spirit stones ran out, Yu Wen's pale face regained a trace of color.

Thank heavens, Cha Ming thought before eating another moon cake and sitting in meditation once more. When he opened his eyes, he saw Yu Wen stirring weakly beside the fire.

"Don't move," he said. "You're still very weak. You overdrafted your energy." He walked beside her and took out one of the thousands of moon cakes. "Eat this. It'll help."

"But I really don't like them," Yu Wen protested.

Seeing Cha Ming's raised eyebrow, she closed her eyes and took a bite. Her cheeks instantly regained their rosy hue. She accepted a cup of hot tea as she sat up beside the fire, letting its warmth suffuse her. She hummed appreciatively as she sipped the warm beverage.

"You have pretty good taste for someone from a mortal realm."

"I have a friend who takes his tea hobby very seriously," Cha Ming said. He looked at the flickering flames as he wrapped her in a blanket woven from creation qi and held her for warmth. She nuzzled up to him and let out a deep sigh.

"Fire isn't really a necessity for cultivators, but I like it all the same," Cha Ming said as he noted her demoralized expression.

"You like how it looks?" Yu Wen asked.

"No, I like what it represents," Cha Ming said. "As long as there's fire, there's warmth and light. As long as those two things exist, there's hope. And with hope… well, anything is possible."

Yu Wen nodded and held out her hand weakly. A tongue of flame detached from the fire and danced around in her palm. It alternated between red and yellow, purple and blue. Soon, it turned the color of jade. "Hope is one word for it. Another word is faith."

Cha Ming frowned. "By faith, you mean belief in a god?"

"No," Yu Wen said. "Faith is an ancient concept, but it has far more meaning than you think. By faith I mean belief. Belief in yourself. Belief in others. Belief in a good future. Belief in right and wrong. Every good action stems from these beliefs." She paused for a moment to compose herself. "Faith is like…"

She plucked an ember from the fire. It cooled until it seemed like every ounce of heat had left it. Then, as Yu Wen blew on it, a hint of redness returned to the piece of black coal. It soon lit up with a beautiful orange flame. "Faith is a part of existence, like kindling is to fire. Just like a single ember can create a roaring flame, faith can create waves in people's hearts. It predates the seven virtues, because without it, they would succumb to doubt and fall into depravity."

"I knew there were seven vices, but I didn't know there were seven virtues," Cha Ming said. "I've seen devils and their wrath and lust, their gluttony and greed, and their envy and pride. Though I can't say I've ever seen a sloth devil."

"It's because they're too lazy," Yu Wen said, chuckling. "But when you see one, they're a force to be reckoned with. No, these vices are the antithesis of faith. They are aligned with doubt. Doubt is also the ultimate vice, and it begins with doubt in yourself. Like this ember, doubt will douse the strongest fire. It will dull the sharpest metal and dam the greatest of rivers."

She placed the burning ember on the ground, and the flame receded. It soon extinguished and turned black. All heat had left it.

"Then tell me about these virtues," Cha Ming said. "And do they have something to do with angels?"

"They do and they don't," Yu Wen said. "Angelic endowment isn't something that can be chased after. Many fools try, and that's the reason they fail. Virtues are the core of angelic endowment, but their nature is extroverted, unselfish. The only way to get there is to be a good person, do good deeds, and to be yourself. The rest will follow." Cha Ming held her as they looked up at the sky.

"There was once a painter," Yu Wen said. "He was a powerful man, but he wasn't very good at painting. Fortunately, he had a wonderful brush. It made up for what he lacked and corrected his mistakes. When he painted the mists and created this world, he sought to make it perfect." She shook her head. "Yet nothing can be perfect. The world was centered around seven virtues. Purity, temperance, charity, diligence, patience, kindness, and bravery. Armed with these virtues, the transcendent and mortal planes thrived. Seeing that his painting was beautiful, the painter cast the brush out into the world and left it to its own devices. The world was paradise… for a time."

At Yu Wen's direction, seven flaming platforms appeared in the moonless sky. Beneath them, millions of tiny red flecks came in and out of existence. "The heavens presided over all of existence, and the universe was prosperous. It seemed like a dream come true, but it was too good to last. You see, the brush paints in both black and white, Cha Ming. It cannot paint good without evil. Within each of the Seven Heavens, within each of the seven virtues, the painter had unknowingly left a small seed of doubt. As the Seven Heavens administrated the realms, they began to argue and bicker. Even the Jade Emperor was embroiled in a massive internal conflict. And as these feelings reached their peak, the Seven Heavens each split in two, creating the seven hells. The angels who fell became devils, and their virtues became their corresponding vices. Charity turned to greed, diligence to sloth, and so on.

"But the battle wasn't over. You see, fate still favored the virtuous. Therefore, the devils declared war on the Seven Heavens. The battlefield was the various mortal and transcendent realms. They fought for aeons, until finally, fortune shifted. The universe changed its mind. Overjoyed with their newfound success, the devils pressed their attack. They continued their assault until they arrived at the Jade Emperor's palace. By then, the heavens were in disarray, and only a few of the most powerful angels remained.

"Yet it was at this moment, when things were at their worst, that the Jade Emperor realized the crux of the matter. If doubt had managed to overturn the world order, what of faith? Why had they lost their way? It was the lack of struggle, the complacence, that led to corruption. This trial was necessary for the heavens to regains their purity. It was a fire that would smelt them; it was a spark that would kindle the fires in their hearts that had been reduced to nothing more than lumps of coal.

"Invigorated, he rallied the ailing forces of good under the banner of faith. It breathed life into their doubt-ridden souls. They discovered that with this newfound hope, they were stronger than the devils. They slaughtered their way back once more, but this time, they only fought until a third of the original hell remained before stopping. The war came to a standstill when they discovered a startling secret."

"What secret?" Cha Ming asked.

"There were two secrets, one of which is widely known," Yu Wen said. "The first is that whoever providence favors will weaken in tenacity. If providence favors faith, doubt is strengthened in balance. If providence favors doubt, faith is strengthened to fight it. As for the second secret... this has to do with the source of providence, and the reason for the shift. But that's something only the heavenly emperors and devil sovereigns know.

"What could be so important as to make the entire universe bend to its will?" Cha Ming wondered aloud. "Is it a mystical artifact? Or a secret scripture?"

I once asked my father the same thing," Yu Wen said. "I'll tell you what he told me. But first, have you never spoken to a lady?" Yu Wen asked.

"On occasion," Cha Ming said, looking at her in confusion.

"And what if this lady asked you who the most beautiful woman in the world was?" Yu Wen asked. She flipped her curly hair back for dramatic effect.

"If such a question did come up, I'd answer that I'd never met a more beautiful woman in my life," Cha Ming said, averting his gaze slightly.

"You're lying." Yu Wen pouted.

"How could I possibly lie to you?" Cha Ming said. "If beauty was ranked on a scale of one to ten, every man would be allowed an eleven."

"And you'd let me take up that precious spot?" Yu Wen said, cuddling a little closer.

"I don't see anyone else on this mountain taking that spot," Cha Ming said.

"I see," Yu Wen, her expression souring. "Are you sure you don't want to rephrase that?"

"I meant that if this mountain were filled with women, the only one I would see is you," Cha Ming said.

"I know it's a lie, but it's a good one," Yu Wen said, tapping him on the nose. "I'll give you a passing grade for good behavior. And now you have the answer you were looking for, the thing my father said. The only thing important enough to bend the universe to its will is me."

They both burst out laughing before lying on the ground to rest. The crackling fire was a soothing melody that lulled them into a comfortable, dreamless sleep.

Chapter 22: Warmth

Cha Ming woke to the scent of smoke. His arm was numb, as Yu Wen's small figure had somehow crawled over from where she'd fallen asleep and was resting on it. Cha Ming began to delicately maneuver the lifeless appendage while considering how ludicrous it was that his arm had fallen asleep in the first place.

My body is at the peak of marrow refining, for heaven's sake, Cha Ming thought. *How is this even physically possible?*

He soon wriggled his way out. A few breaths later, the arm regained feeling. He looked around and discovered a cloud-covered mountain he hadn't seen the night before.

"While it looks like a mountain, it's actually a volcano," Yu Wen said as she brushed herself off behind him. "Those devils were trying to stop me from getting here because they know what I'm after: the fire source within the volcano."

Yu Wen led the way up the rocky slope. It was covered in sharp obsidian fragments that cut at their robes as they traveled. Occasionally they spotted streams of lava that split and combined as they made their way to the bottom. The heat intensified as they approached the distant peak.

Soon they arrived at the gray cloud that filled the air with a poisonous miasma. Cha Ming summoned a simple formation that isolated them from the heavy smoke as they pushed through the dense cloud. Skeletons littered the mountain as they climbed, likely victims of mysterious rocky creatures that waited in ambush for unsuspecting prey. A day passed as they took their time carefully scaling the treacherous peak.

Finally, they pierced through the smoke, revealing a ten-mile-wide lake of lava. The peak seemed like it had been sheared off by a blade to make room for the large pool and a small jade altar at the center. A tiny dirt road connected the fragile outer walls to the central island.

"Let's go," Yu Wen said, hopping onto the dirt road.

Seeing Yu Wen's fearless demeanor, Cha Ming gulped and followed her. The lava bubbled and hissed as they walked past it. Further out, red-scaled fish jumped in and out of the volcano. Birds of flame dove down to catch them with mixed success, and Cha Ming watched them in wonder.

It took them an hour to arrive at the jade altar. Cha Ming was surprised to see that instead of hosting a statue, the altar was actually a throne. As soon as they set foot onto the small island in the center, a loud hiss filled the air. A large serpent of lava emerged from the volcano and coiled onto the giant chair.

"Greetings, honored guestssss," the serpent said. "To what do I owe the pleasure?"

"We've come for the flame source," Yu Wen announced.

"That issss… difficult," the serpent said. "To obtain these resources, you would need special permission."

Yu Wen summoned a jade slip from her robes. While it didn't look any different than his gathering quota, it emanated an inviolable aura.

"Where did you obtain this royal gathering quota?" the serpent asked when he saw the slip. "Who are you?"

"You don't need to concern yourself with that," Yu Wen said. "You just need to obey and deliver the resources to me. While you're at it, fetch me the Flame Essence Core and Flame Source Marrow."

Cha Ming's heart beat a little faster when he heard her mention this vital body-cultivating component.

"You're pushing me too far," the serpent said in an aggrieved tone. "The marrow and the core are one thing, but the source creates all. If you take it away, the volcano will lose its primary source of energy!"

"But I have a royal gathering quota," Yu Wen pointed out.

The serpent's eyes narrowed. "Fine. You have my permission, but you need to gather it yourself. Even I am unsure of its location within this volcano."

"And how are we supposed to do that?" Yu Wen said. "The lava would burn us to death before we even made it a hundred feet deep."

The serpent flicked its tail. Two black stone medallions appeared before Cha Ming and Yu Wen. Their obsidian surfaces felt cool to the touch, and the mysterious runes engraved on them radiated transcendent might.

"These medallions will allow you to swim within the lava unharmed for up to one year," the serpent said. "If you still can't find what you need by then, it's not too late to turn back." Then the snake hissed and plunged into the lake of lava.

"I don't think that snake will make it easy for us," Cha Ming said as his body absorbed the medallion and incorporated it within his body.

"It knows it's difficult," Yu Wen said grumpily. "But we have to try. You can't even imagine what's happening on Jade Moon Planet right now. If we don't get the Flame Essence Source, every person who crossed the Bridge of Stars will die on this planet." She looked at the lake of lava fearfully and glanced at the talisman in her hands.

Rolling his eyes, Cha Ming plunged his own hand into the lava like he would a swimming pool. He immediately let out a bloodcurdling scream.

"Why would you do that? Pull it out!" Yu Wen yelled as she grabbed his robes and threw him to the ground.

Cha Ming burst out laughing as the lava dripped off his hand and onto the island. "Don't worry, he didn't lie to us," he said.

"Come here, funny man," Yu Wen said, walking up to him with a grin on her face.

Cha Ming looked around in a panic, but before he could escape, Yu Wen shackled him with silver strings and flung him into the lava. He resurfaced a few seconds later as though treading water.

"I suppose I deserved that," he said.

Yu Wen sniffed and retreated behind the altar to change.

The world of lava was as beautiful as it was serene. The stream of molten rock parted as Cha Ming paddled his feet, carefully manipulating his weight to maintain neutral buoyancy. As he swam, he made sure to extend his resplendent force into the lava. Though he couldn't see anything, strictly speaking, the wondrous image being transmitted into his mind more than made up for it.

The first things he noticed were the *sounds*. Every wave that struck him, every swirl he collided with, caused a slight tremor in his vast surroundings. As an experiment, he threw an obsidian stone toward the nearby wall. It let out a loud clink that seemed to come from all directions as the dense liquid rapidly propagated the sound waves. Cha Ming continued swimming, and as he did, he heard an occasional pop as noxious fumes traveled between the viscous layers of molten rock.

Do you see anything on your end? Cha Ming asked Yu Wen.

Nothing, Yu Wen said. *I just see a bare, desolate wasteland.*

Maybe we haven't traveled far enough, Cha Ming sent back. As per their original agreement, they dove even further into the giant pool. The pressure increased as they traveled, forcing them to adjust their qi shields to resist it. They encountered little difficulty as they plunged deeper into the volcano.

Ten feet became one hundred feet, and one hundred feet became a thousand. Strange rocks appeared every so often, and so too did curious creatures dwelling in the lava. Before long, they entered a completely alien world. It wasn't devoid of life like the surface.

Rather, it was teeming with it. Magnificent red corals grew on the volcano's rocky walls. They provided food to the many demonic fish that made their home in their sharp, jagged structures. In return, the demonic fish provided fertilizer. Tiny piles of black excrement littered the corals, which greedily absorbed the processed nutrients.

In the distance, a rainbow-colored fish preyed upon smaller silver fish. Their remnant flesh and blood fell near the corals, but before their nutrients could be absorbed by them, they were sucked up by a purple-gold starfish. It extracted the essence before discarding desiccated remnants, which crumbled onto the ground and joined the black sand that covered it. There, tiny white fish used feelers to sift through it in search of nutrients. Nothing was wasted in the volcanic wonderland.

Hours passed as they journeyed deeper and deeper, and a black fissure soon appeared in the distance. It grew swiftly as he approached, and before long, he was floating beside a 100-meter-wide gash. He held out his hand, which was entrained toward the fissure by a swift downcurrent.

I found something interesting, Cha Ming sent to Yu Wen. He waited for a half hour before a lithe figure in a two-piece swimsuit swam up beside him. She looked at the chasm grimly.

Do you think we'll be all right if we go down? Cha Ming asked. *Can we come back up?* Unfortunately, he was far too lacking in many areas of knowledge.

It shouldn't be a problem, Yu Wen sent back. *But it'll be a long journey. It could take us weeks to return to the surface.*

I don't think we'll find what we're looking for up here, Cha Ming pointed out.

Noted, Yu Wen sent. She sent out her space-time camera and posed before snapping a picture of both of them. Then Yu Wen grabbed his forearm and pulled him toward the downcurrent. He grasped her other arm, and they swiftly sank to the depths of the volcano in tandem.

Jagged obsidian corals, schools of fish, and other strange life-forms quickly passed them by. The lava became increasingly bright as they approached a small red circle in the distance. It grew larger and larger, brighter and brighter, until finally they entered a vast red sea with no bottom in sight.

It looks like we'll have to split up and search, Yu Wen said. *But it'll be difficult to communicate.*

Let's find out how deep the bottom is first, Cha Ming suggested. *Once we know that, we can make better plans.*

Agreed, Yu Wen said. *But be careful as you dive. I sense frightening creatures here.*

Cha Ming nodded solemnly as they went separate ways, leaving a spiritual mark at their entry point before diving diagonally toward their perceived bottom.

Cha Ming swam for hours. Not a single wave could be felt or heard in his immediate surroundings, indicating that they were very far from any solid impingements. Cha Ming floated downward in the lonely sea of red. One day. Two days. Three days. A week passed before he finally spotted an obstacle in the distance.

Excited, he quickly swam toward it. A jagged crystal outline slowly appeared in his mind's eye. He approached it slowly, and soon a three-hundred-foot-long object appeared wedged in gritty obsidian sand. It was composed entirely of what seemed like low-grade spirit stone.

Curious, he swam around it while using his resplendent force to fully map out the object. His complexion sank when he finally realized what it was—a skeleton. It was the skeleton of a large lava demon that had previously inhabited the cavern. And judging by the teeth marks and fractures on its bones, it wasn't at the top of the food chain.

I've found the bottom, but I also found a big skeleton, Cha Ming sent to Yu Wen.

No response.

Let's head back and regroup. I don't think it's safe to explore alone.

No response.

Cha Ming cursed as he began swimming back toward his spirit

mark. To his surprise, a warm current buffeted his body and eased his ascent.

One day, two days, three days. Six days passed without seeing the shadow of another creature. He soon saw the familiar twinkle of his spirit mark in the distance. Excited, he increased his speed. But to his surprise, a large shadow suddenly moved between him and the mark. It was a large demon with sharp teeth, and it was swimming toward him at a leisurely pace. Cha Ming swiftly retracted his resplendent force. The world went black as he floated in the dark lava and waited for the giant fish to pass.

Ten breaths, twenty breaths, thirty breaths… after thirty breaths, he felt a hot rush beside him. It flung him backward two hundred feet as the giant demon brushed him lightly. Fortunately, it hadn't noticed him. After waiting for a few seconds, he began reaching out with his resplendent force, only to pull it back once more.

Woosh. Woosh. Woosh.

One beast after another brushed against him. Each brush depleted a large amount of his qi, but he didn't dare fight back. He endured as his qi depleted to a quarter of his total capacity. Finally, when it seemed like he couldn't hold out much longer, the fish stopped as quickly as they'd come.

Cha Ming looked around and saw a retreating school of giant demonic sharks. After quickly looking around for Yu Wen, he followed their plan and caught an upcurrent back to the surface. His surroundings darkened before lighting up again as he reached the surface near the jade altar.

Yu Wen's face lit up as he broke through the surface. "What took you so long?" she asked. "I thought something had happened to you."

"It was a close call," Cha Ming said, shaking the lava from his skin and donning blue robes. "I was almost caught by some lava demons." They walked past the altar, where the lava serpent was lounging.

"No luck?" the lava serpent taunted. "There's no need to stress yourself out so much. If you leave now, I'll give you an obsidian orchid for your trouble. This is a precious treasure that only grows every hundred millennia. It's worth more than a transcendent plane."

KINDLING

"While your offer is tempting, the fire source is irreplaceable," Yu Wen said, causing the serpent to huff in disappointment before heading back into the volcano's depths.

"We should stick together next time we head down," Cha Ming said. "It'll be much safer that way."

They sat down by altar and recovered their qi, and after finishing, Cha Ming pulled out a pad of paper he'd been mulling over.

> *... douses the hearts of the needy;*
> *Man is left...*
> *Kindling the flames ...*
> *Never questioning ...*

He rubbed his forehead as he searched for words. Thus far, he hadn't managed to gain inspiration past a simple structure consistent with his previous runic poetry. Dousing and kindling—he knew the basis of fire he was aiming for. But putting these into words and assigning emotions was easier said than done.

Ironically, Zhou Li wasn't wrong, Cha Ming thought as he looked at the incomplete poem. *My life is too lukewarm. When have I really felt strongly about anything? I haven't loved—at least, not in the romantic sense.*

His eyes flickered to Yu Wen, who was now looking through pictures on her camera. She looked up and smiled. Cha Ming put away his pad of paper and sat down beside her as she browsed pictures of shoals, corals, fish, and serpents.

"Is that what I think it is?" Cha Ming asked, edging closer.

"It is," Yu Wen said proudly, zooming in. She magnified the picture and revealed a fiery decapus, which had perched itself over a school of fish in the shoal. Although it was only a picture, Cha Ming could sense the savageness in its eyes.

"I saw what looked like a school of giant sharks," Cha Ming said.

"Did you?" Yu Wen said. "Show me."

Cha Ming smiled and painted it with the Clear Sky Brush. A large purple shark with bright-red teeth appeared and swam toward them. Dozens appeared behind it and buffeted them with waves of orange-red lava. "They swam right beside me, and I had to hide using my resplendent force. I think I'd be a goner if I hadn't acted so quickly."

"You have to be careful," Yu Wen said. She flicked to the next picture. "This was *my* near miss," she said, revealing a picture of a large volcanic turtle. Its shell was made of obsidian covered in golden runes while its skin was deep purple. Yu Wen's small figure was thousands of times smaller in comparison. Her space-time camera showed a progression of images as she was pushed away by the stream of lava, tumbling uncontrolled toward the unknown.

They laughed as they shared stories, pictures, and paintings. Hours passed by in a flash. "Cha Ming?" Yu Wen said, looking up at him.

"Yes?" Cha Ming said, looking into her eyes.

Yu Wen looked away shyly, causing him to chuckle inwardly. "Come a little closer," she said. "I'm cold. It's not as warm up here as down in the lava."

"Sure," he said, wrapping his arm around her. They continued looking at pictures throughout the night. But Cha Ming remembered none of that. He only remembered his rapid heartbeat, her gentle breathing, and the entrancing smell of her hair.

Chapter 23:
Uphill Battle

"Oh God," Lei Jiang said as they struggled up the steep slope of the mountain. "Leave. Go on without me. I can't take it anymore." He collapsed into a small tubby pile, causing Huxian and Silverwing to slow their ascent. They, too, were covered in a thick sheen of sweat, but it couldn't compare to the puddle dripping beneath the obese mouse, Lei Jiang.

"Tell my family that I love them," Lei Jiang continued.

Huxian rolled his eyes and circled around him before using his muzzle to roll the fat mouse up the steep incline.

"Tell my wives that I'm proud to have fathered so many children with them. Tell my twelve sisters that you'll take care of them, and make sure to find husbands for each of them."

"If you don't shut your trap, I'll have Silverwing throw you off the cliff," Huxian said, instantly silencing Lei Jiang. "Besides, we're here."

The fat purple mouse rolled to a gentle stop atop a large flat peak. Sheer cliffs surrounded them on all sides save the narrow pathway they used to ascend. Atop the mountain sat a lazy-looking hedgehog. Its salmonella-laced spikes, though vicious, seemed like tiny pinpricks when compared to its massive claws and teeth. The hedgehogs' aura was a mixture of purple and ochre, and its eyes were black.

"Why have you come to my lair, little fox?" the hedgehog said.

"Can't you see that we're busy and can't be bothered to hunt down small fries like you?"

"But we like picking fights with other demons," Huxian said with a smile. A jade-and-violet aura swirled around him as he and his three companions revealed their Eyes of Pure Jade and Demon-Subduing Eyes. A thick cloud of devil-sealing and demon-subduing energy covered the mountaintop, causing the hedgehog's expression to grow somber. Hundreds of tiny hedgehogs poked out of the ground and joined their leader in glaring at Huxian.

"You Bagua foxes don't know how to leave well enough alone," the hedgehog said in a deep voice. "Although your father isn't the greatest troublemaker I've ever met, he's definitely in my top ten."

"Then I'm proud to be living up to the family tradition," Huxian said, baring his teeth. An aura of white purification and shadowy swallowing surrounded him. The Friendship Circle appeared around the three demons, allowing them to better redistribute their strength.

"Interesting," the black-eyed hedgehog said. Energy from the surrounding mountain oozed into him, causing him to double in size and sharpening his array of spikes. A nasty black coating appeared on each one.

"Silverwing, suppress the small fries," Huxian said calmly as the hedgehog transformed.

"Roger," Silverwing said. He beat his wings, launching himself several hundred feet into the air. Then he glowed with an azure light, projecting a runic array that spread a full mile wide. Gigantic gusts of wind began to move chaotically, throwing many of the smaller hedgehogs off the mountain. The rest responded by using their sharp claws to dig into the mountain's surface.

"Lei Jiang, give us some light," Huxian said.

"You got it, boss," Lei Jiang yelled. The small puffball, several times smaller than even the smallest hedgehogs, sent out a two-dimensional field formed with purple runic fragments. Dark clouds suddenly appeared above them and summoned lightning onto the densely packed fiends. One hedgehog after another was burnt to a crisp.

"Sixth through fifteenth squads, stop them!" the hedgehog leader yelled. A violet glow surrounded fifty-odd hedgehogs. They doubled in size and flew up toward Silverwing and Lei Jiang.

"Silverwing, Lei Jiang, hold out until I finish off their leader," Huxian said. His large form suddenly split into thousands of tiny black-and-white foxes. They charged at the hundreds of hedgehogs, who unleashed their spikes like volleys of arrows. Half of the small foxes perished in the initial charge; they had only managed to fell a quarter of the hedgehogs.

"Is that everything you've got?" the hedgehog leader said mockingly.

"That was just an appetizer," the remaining foxes said in unison. The corpses of the deceased foxes suddenly turned to motes of light and shadow. They converged on a central point and formed a yin-yang symbol. The symbol tightened, until finally it shattered in the middle and burst into thousands of foxes once more. Their initial number was much greater than last time as Huxian had absorbed energy by devouring the deceased fiends. They clashed once more, and two thirds of the remaining hedgehogs fell.

"How is this possible?" the lead hedgehog roared. "You shouldn't be so powerful at the peak of core formation."

"You believe whatever you like," Huxian said from thousands of mouths. The black-and-white clones swirled together in the shape of a black-and-white maw that began attacking the surviving fiends. Their small spikes were devoured the moment they touched it.

"Why do you have to cause me problems?" the hedgehog said. "Didn't I feed you enough fiendish demons? Didn't I yield many lands to you over the past few months? Those were the richest lands, and I did this all to keep you off my back. Why do you need to betray my kind intentions?"

Huxian grinned. "Which devil sovereign are you, and what makes you think I don't know that you'd devour us all without a second thought? The best time to fight someone like you is when you're still weak and consolidating your grasp on these devil seeds you've sown. After all, it's very draining for you to project so many devils onto a planet protected by the Jade Emperor. It's only a matter of time until you're found out by him, so you're working on limited resources."

"I'm not here for you!" the hedgehog yelled. "In fact, I just need to mine a few resources. You can have anything else you want. Hell, I'll send out fiendish demons to get them for you. Then, I'll even allow you to leave the world by breaking your talismans. I'll even sign a contract with you. You have everything to gain, and nothing to lose!"

"Not here for me, huh?" Huxian said, walking over to the hedgehog, who was bleeding all over. His minions had all been defeated and lay dead beside him. "What are you up to? You must be playing a very big game if you're willing to squander so much of your devilish essence."

"Like I'd tell you," the hedgehog said coldly. "Think carefully about my offer, because I'm only offering it to you once. If you don't take it, you'll experience true despair. I'll send out hordes of fiendish demons to chase you down to the ends of Jade Moon Planet. You'll be buried along with all the others."

Huxian pondered for a moment. "I have a better proposition."

"Oh?" the fiendish hedgehog said. "Do tell."

"You see, I have a huge appetite," Huxian said. "I'm a big fan of eating. You happen to be able to provide something very nourishing for me and my friends, and it requires very little effort on your part."

"And what would you like to eat, esteemed Bagua fox?" the hedgehog said.

"It's quite simple, really," Huxian said. "The best nourishment you can provide me is in the form of devil seeds. This one is a good start. I won't ask for much. Hundreds of high-quality seeds like this one and a million of the others shouldn't be too troublesome for you."

The hedgehog's expression darkened. "I'm afraid that won't be possible."

"I wasn't asking," Huxian said.

Mouths of light, shadow, wind, lightning, and swamp suddenly appeared all around the hedgehog. It howled as the mouths took one bite after another until nothing more than a small black spark remained.

"One more bite, and I'll never let you leave this place alive!" the spark yelled.

Huxian's main body gulped it down without any hesitation. As soon as it entered his mouth, its aura was purified before evening out between him and his two brothers.

"Holy hell, that's a lot of energy," Silverwing said. "In fact, that's much more than all those other fiendish demons we ate combined."

"And the guy dares to threaten us on the Jade Emperor's home turf," Huxian said, shaking his head. "Little does he know they're just giant meal bags waiting to be eaten."

"Where to next, boss?" Lei Jiang said, collapsing on his back. "I feel like I lost 500 jin in that fight."

"You don't even *weigh* 500 jin," Huxian said. "Now let's get going. I think there's a reason the custodian told us to go to Jade Moon Garden. That must be where it's centralizing its defense."

"And how will we get there?" Silverwing said.

"I'm not really sure," Huxian admitted. "But I know someone who does."

They hopped onto Silverwing's back and headed toward a neighboring mountain peak, where they were greeted by an extremely cranky fiendish worm. He didn't give them directions before they swallowed him whole.

"Why are we always climbing mountains instead of flying?" Lei Jiang asked as he collapsed on the steep incline.

"Because we're trying to get you to lose weight," Huxian said. "And until you lose weight, we'll be climbing mountains. Because that's what brothers do. We help each other."

"Boss, you're the best." Lei Jiang groaned. He picked up his four paws, gritted his teeth, and continued the arduous climb.

Do you think we're taking this joke a little too far? Silverwing sent to Huxian. *You and I both know he won't lose weight by doing this.*

All right, this will be the last one, Huxian sent back. *How do you think he'll react when he finds out we made him climb a few mountains for no reason at all?*

Not well, so let's never speak of it, Silverwing said. *I know we're bored, but he'll get fed up soon. That's not how you treat friends. If you're so bored, how about we add someone else to the group for variety? How about that sinfully ugly toad we found that other time?*

Have you heard that monstrosity speak? Huxian said incredulously. *He's toxic. I won't have it.*

I happen to think he's funny in a weird way, Silverwing said. *Besides, he matches one of your elements.*

I'll consider it, Huxian sent. Then, he perked up his ears and looked down into the forest, where thousands of bulls were running at breakneck speed. His eyes followed the current path of the stampeding horde and locked onto two tiny figures running through the trees.

Speak of the demon, he sent. One of the figures was the toad they were discussing, and the second figure was a small white rabbit.

"Lei Jiang, you've lost enough weight," Huxian declared. "Let's hop onto Silverwing's back. We have to rescue a damsel in distress and a friend in need. In that order."

"Salvation!" Lei Jiang shouted. He joined Huxian on the rapidly expanding Silverwing, who zipped across the forest before arriving above the two running beasts.

"I'm not sure how we'll get through all those annoying crows," Silverwing said. A swarm of a million small birds had appeared in the sky.

Huxian's eyes narrowed. "They're not here to stop us. Look at their demonic energy. It's off the charts. They're preparing to do a sacrificial divebomb."

"Then what do we do?" Silverwing said. "We'll be toast if we try to break through."

Huxian frowned. "You and Lei Jiang will need to distract them while I sneak in. Execute Operation Pinball."

Lei Jiang and Silverwing's eyes brightened.

"Do you mean it, boss? Can we really do it?" Lei Jiang said.

"I thought you said it was our trump card?" Silverwing asked.

"We don't have time to think about these things," Huxian said gravely. "I'll be diving down now. Get ready on my mark."

He hopped off Silverwing and spread his four legs out. The wind ruffled his fur as he descended, carefully concealing his presence in shadows.

Now! he yelled just as he passed into the swarm.

On the other side, Lei Jiang and Silverwing had assembled a peculiar formation. Azure and violet runes shifted around a small sphere, enveloping Lei Jiang in Silverwing's claws. Silverwing poured most of his demonic wind qi, leaving just enough from him to stay afloat. "Let's let 'er rip!" he said, launching the small ball toward their flying enemies. It rapidly accelerated until it reached halfway through the cloud of crows. Then a violet bolt of lightning shot out of it and roasted tens of thousands of black birds.

Before the crows had any chance to react, the ball glowed violet and sped into another grouping, rapidly extinguishing them. It bounced from murder to murder, slaying them with impunity. Over half of them died before they realized what was happening. As soon as they did, however, they didn't fight back. Instead, they all dove down in unison toward the jade rabbit and the toad.

While the crows were roasting, Huxian landed in the thick foliage and zoomed through the trees. It wasn't long before he caught up to Xiao Bai and the ugly toad, Gua.

"Fancy seeing you here," Huxian shouted. "Might you be needing a rescue?"

"Possibly," Xiao Bai said. "Though I'm afraid you don't know what you're getting yourself into. It's best if you leave me and hide until this is all over."

"Hi, I'm Gua!" The ugly toad waved.

Huxian ignored him. "Are you the main target?" he asked Xiao Bai.

"One of them," she said. "It's a rather complicated story, so I'd rather not say. But given your background, you must know that a devil sovereign is commanding these annoying pests."

"Why haven't you run back to the shelter yet?" Huxian said. "And how the hell did you meet this ugly mutt?"

"How dare you insult me," Gua said indignantly.

"Boys, now's not the time to be fighting," Xiao Bai said, looking behind. Trees were steadily falling around them as the bulls were gaining ground. "I need to get to the mountains and find an earth source to supplement the defense shield. We can use it to buy us enough time for the Jade Emperor to realize there's a problem."

"Sure, I can help you with that, for enough moon cakes," Huxian said.

"Deal," Xiao Bai said. "I'll give you as many as you'd like, but first you need to get us out of here."

"I have a plan," Huxian said. "But before that, we need to dodge a half million exploding crows. Hop onto my back and support my suppression formation." Xiao Bai nodded and complied. "You too, you unreasonably ugly tadpole."

"How dare you!" Gua shouted.

However, after looking around and seeing the black swarm approaching them from above and the bulls closing in on them from behind, he leaped onto Huxian's back. Five large bubbles immediately spread out from him, encompassing both of them and Lei Jiang and Silverwing. Bolts of purple lightning began zapping various crows, and gusts of wind repelled them. A swampy bog slowed their movements while thousands of tiny illusory black-and-white foxes appeared beside the crows and forced them to detonate prematurely. They squawked loudly upon spotting Xiao Bai on Huxian's back, immediately darting toward them.

"Silverwing, rescue plan!" Huxian barked. "Lei Jiang, provide cover fire. And Gua, for the love of god, I hope I haven't misjudged you. Sign this contract and slow these crows down as much as you can." A golden piece of paper appeared in front of the toad.

"Friends?" the toad said, teary eyed, as he read the writing on the golden document. "You want to be friends?" Two streams of water dribbled down his snotty nose and onto his warty lips. "And we'll be inseparable forever?"

"Oh God, what have I done?" Huxian said, shaking his head. "Just as Huxian was about to retract his offer, the toad spat a glob of source blood on it. As he did, Huxian's runic fragment formation shifted to include him. His murky, swampy demonic qi combined with Huxian's Bagua formation, and the power of Huxian's swamp domain increased fourfold. The air became viscous and gritty. Thousands of crows accidentally collided with solidified chunks of air and detonated.

"Good suppressive strength!" Huxian said in admiration. "What's your lineage?"

"I don't have a lineage," the toad said proudly. "I'm a one-of-a-kind beast with no ancestral memories, but among swamp creatures, I'm unmatched."

"No ancestral memories?" Huxian said, shocked. "With your bloodline density, how is that even possible?"

"Nothing is impossible with the power of beauty!" Gua shouted. He held out a webbed paw, causing the swampy air to reform into a frog avatar. Thousands of crows gasped upon seeing him, choosing to self-destruct rather than be subjected to his appearance. He held out another hand, and this time hundreds of mirage duplicates appeared. Half of the remaining crows instinctively self-detonated before even having a chance to realize what was going on.

Moments later, Silverwing swooped down. Huxian hopped on his back, and Lei Jiang joined them soon after. The bulls chasing them roared in anger as they flew away. "You despicable Bagua fox, how dare you slight me again!" they shouted in unison. "I'll hunt you to the ends of the universe. The ends of the universe!"

"Wow, what did you do to him?" Xiao Bai said.

"We ate a few hundred of his devil seeds and stole some really big immortal-jade stones from him," Huxian said. "And then we ate them so he couldn't even steal them back."

"And you're not afraid because..." Xiao Bai said.

"What's he going to do?" Huxian said. "Send down thousands of devil seeds? Put a spatial blockade on the planet while wantonly destroying all living beings on it because it's convenient?"

"Point taken," Xiao Bai said. "By the way, this silver-winged friend of yours is quite the find. It'd be hard to find someone with a stronger roc bloodline than him in the Primal Demon Realm."

Silverwing screeched with pleasure. Then Xiao Bai looked to Lei Jiang, who looked at her expectantly. "You're okay too," she said to him. "And so are you," she said to Gua, suppressing her disgust at his warty appearance. The toad practically danced with joy at the attention.

Chapter 24:
Kindling

A wave of lava gently rocked Yu Wen and Cha Ming as they lowered themselves into a small forest of lava vents. They meandered among the large plumes that slowly but surely spit ashes into their surroundings. Many tentacled demons latched on to each vent and stuck their mouths over them, filtering out the debris to feed on. Meanwhile, many colorful fish took refuge from frightening predators roaming on the outside. The lava sharks looked at them hungrily, waiting for them to come out to forage.

How long until the next iteration? Yu Wen asked as she looked above warily. Three shadows circled over them, using their strong demonic senses to map the area with echolocation. The fish and tentacled beings cringed as their natural predators combed their surroundings.

Soon, Cha Ming said. His Clear Sky Brush was busy dancing around them and painting runes of fire and earth on their skin. These runes allowed them to move through lava with uncharacteristic ease. They also provided camouflage against the deep denizens of the volcano.

An incense time passed before the runic fragments combined and melted with the formation on their skins. They transformed into a lavalike cloth that covered them from head to toe.

How does it feel? Cha Ming asked.

Yu Wen leaped up from the small "forest" and swam at a rapid pace.

It's twice as fast as the previous one, Yu Wen sent. *And it's much more comfortable. And I think my qi is replenishing. What did you do?*

I added energy conversion runes, Cha Ming sent. *It converts the energy sources into the five elements in equal proportion. Although fifty percent of the energy is lost in the process, it's much easier for us to take in than volcanic qi.*

After ensuring that his qi absorption capabilities and his swimming speed were up to snuff, he warily approached the three lava sharks. After confirming that they hadn't seen him, he crossed the 100-foot boundary they'd previously been able to detect them in.

One hundred feet is still good, he sent. *Get ready to pull me back if things go bad.*

Ready when you are, Yu Wen sent. She held on to her special silver strings that traveled all the way to Cha Ming's location. Having obtained her confirmation, he took a proverbial deep breath before heading toward the nearest shark. He came within fifty feet of the monstrous creature without signs of detection.

I'm going to try getting closer, Cha Ming sent. He edged forward ten feet, carefully timing the lava shark's motions. No response. He edged ten feet closer, bringing him a total of thirty feet away from the shark. Still no response.

You should head back, Yu Wen sent. *Thirty feet is plenty.*

Cha Ming shook his head. *Who knows what kind of dangers we'll encounter,* he sent. *Let's test the limits. Pull me back as soon as you see movement.*

Then he rapidly swam toward the shark. As soon as he passed within ten feet of the shark, it wriggled its body, sending waves of lava toward Cha Ming. He tumbled through the turbulent lava as the fierce wave buffeted his qi shields. The blow caused him to crash down toward a nearby obsidian shoal, whose daggerlike surface threatened to impale him.

Fortunately, Yu Wen was ready. She quickly anchored herself and pulled on the strings with all her might. Then, seeing that she

KINDLING

couldn't stop him in time, she dashed sixty feet over and pulled once more. He avoided the giant obsidian coral by a mere foot and crashed onto a hard sheet of black rock, breaking several of his bones in the process.

Don't worry, I'm alive, Cha Ming sent. *Thanks for the quick thinking.*

You shouldn't have done that, Yu Wen sent. *You could have been killed.*

But I wasn't, and we now have more information, Cha Ming replied. *I think we can go to that place now.*

That place? Yu Wen sent. *You mean the shark nest? Are you crazy?*

I'd be crazy if we only had thirty feet, but it's doable with ten feet, Cha Ming sent back. *Especially if there are two of us. We can use tethers to help each other dodge.*

Yu Wen shook her head. *Let me think about it. How about we search the other place first?*

Fine, Cha Ming sent. *But I don't think it's there. The odds are nine out of ten that it's in the shark nest.*

One out of ten is a good enough reason to check the other place first, Yu Wen replied.

Cha Ming nodded, and they both dove through lava like fish in the ocean. They swam for days before they saw a violet light in the distance. The light glowed stronger until they reached a beautiful crystal arch.

Make sure you don't get too close to any eels, Yu Wen sent as they navigated the field of crumbling crystal columns. A million such structures covered the volcano bed, giving the impression that it was subsea palace. However, they both knew what it really was—a mass graveyard for those demons who fell prey to lava eels. They wandered through the death-filled valley for a full week before admitting defeat and returning to the surface.

Cha Ming smiled as he looked at Yu Wen, who was curled up in a blanket while sorting through pictures on her camera's display. She looked up and smiled back. Cha Ming channeled these warm feelings through his brush and onto paper.

... douses the hearts of the needy;
Man is left...
Kindling the flames...
Never questioning...

While the first part seemed foreign and alien, the second part was starting to surface in his mind. Whenever he thought of these two lines, he recalled the warm feeling whenever he held Yu Wen and they watched pictures together. Or when they held hands while diving in the lava and protected each other from the various beasts. Each experience with her intensified this feeling. To him, this was the essence of kindling.

"But there's still something missing," Cha Ming said, sighing.

"Are you still working on it?" Yu Wen said, stowing away her space-time camera. She approached Cha Ming from behind and hugged his back.

"I'm still missing something, but I don't know what," Cha Ming said. The truth was, however, that he had an inkling. But he was far too cautious about love to mention such things to Yu Wen. Cha Ming knew from his previous life that feelings and relationships could hurt, something that carried through all the way to the present moment. Furthermore, he now had a lifespan of five hundred years. It would soon grow to a thousand. As far as he was concerned, he had plenty of time to ease into anything.

"I think I know what's missing," Yu Wen said. Cha Ming looked at her in surprise. "But you're too scared to talk about it? Why?"

Cha Ming swallowed but didn't reply. He averted his eyes slightly. Yu Wen used her hand to guide his face back toward hers.

"Close your eyes, Cha Ming," she said.

Cha Ming smiled. "No, you close yours," he quipped back.

"As you wish," Yu Wen said. Her eyelashes fluttered gently as she stood still. Although she seemed relaxed, Cha Ming could sense the excitement coursing through her muscles and the irregularity of her breath.

I'm so silly, Cha Ming thought. *You'd think knowing someone for four years and spending two of those years with them would be enough to commit.* He steeled his mind and edged forward. Their lips pressed together gently. After what seemed like too brief a moment, they pulled apart and looked at each other, smiling shyly.

"You're a little slow with things, but I like that," Yu Wen said, blushing deeply.

"We have an eternity ahead of us," Cha Ming said. "Why rush?" Then, he looked to the paper he'd been working on. "But you were right, that was just the inspiration I needed." His brush moved slowly and exquisitely, tracing down his burning feelings.

Kindling the flames of love and caring;
Never questioning his devotion.

Every moment he spent with Yu Wen flashed through his mind as he painted these words. Their initial fumbling meeting in Fuxi's Library. Their surprising reunion on the Bridge of Stars. Her patience as he took his time to ponder the mysteries of runic fragments. Their separation for two years and yearning for each other.

He thought of his worry as he saw her being chased by devils and fiends. He recalled his relief as he held her close during their escape. And finally, he recalled their recent memories. The wonderful sights they'd seen, their impeccable teamwork, and the many times they'd saved each other while searching for the fire source.

The paper turned a vivid red as the ink dried. Although this talisman could be used to burn, that would be far too wasteful. Instead, its true use was to inspire. It could banish fear and kindle hearts. It could fan the flames of faith and annihilate doubt. This was *his* way of fire.

At this moment, a thought struck him. He immediately sat cross-legged. Yu Wen smiled and stroked the side of his face. She kissed him on the forehead before returning to her pictures. He didn't notice a single tear rolling down her check before she wiped it away.

Cha Ming's eyes opened after a week of careful thought. "I've finally figured it out," he said to Yu Wen before approaching her.

"Figured what out?" she said.

Cha Ming didn't answer her directly. Instead he painted a familiar runic diagram. It was their protective suit, which reflected the essence of lava. Yet this time it was different. Many blue lines now accompanied the red and brown ones that represented fire and earth.

"Why water?"

"Because lava *flows*," Cha Ming said, shrugging. "And it likely contains more than these essences. I suspect metal is required to make this perfect. Using water to represent the flow characteristics should make us as fast in lava as we are in the air. Furthermore, it should improve our hiding capabilities. We'll be much safer in the lava shark nest."

Two suits materialized, after which he painted several dozen cables. They dove into the lava, though now, instead of swimming, it felt more like flying. Further, they were now able to push off the lava as though it were solid. The suit could not only cause lava to crumble and harden, but it would also manipulate the viscosity of lava around them, thinning and thickening it as required. What made this all possible, however, was his insights on energy. By incorporating elements of kindling, he was able to provide enough energy to better meld the suits with their surroundings.

Their descent was much more rapid than before. They quickly followed the downcurrent and headed toward the deepest place in the lava ocean. Lava sharks began swimming in pairs, then in trios. Before long, lava sharks of all sizes swam around them. Sometimes they were only able to avoid them by several feet. However, a few feet were enough. The suit's new construction made them practically invisible to lava-dwelling creatures.

They swam unimpeded to the heart of shark territory. The obsidian sand gradually turned to crystal sand as they approached the nest. The violet crystals were the remnants of the many bones the sharks had consumed over the years. In some places, the layer was as much as ten feet thick. But it thinned as they approached territories with larger sharks that tended to swallow their prey whole.

Why are there no youngsters anymore? Yu Wen questioned as they approached an elevated platform at the back of the nest. An eerie red glow emanated from it.

My guess is that it's a restricted area, Cha Ming said. *The outer reaches are used for breeding, while this is the source of their power. It's also why they're the strongest demons in the volcano.* As they spoke, ten massive sharks appeared before them. Each one was two thousand feet long, far larger than any other animal Cha Ming had ever seen. *How can they transcend the limit?* he wondered. *How can they grow longer than 333 feet?*

I think it has to do with the fire source, Yu Wen said. *A fire source contains primal demonic energy. Perhaps it has eroded the Jade Emperor's laws to some extent, but only within the immediate vicinity of the fire source itself.*

Cha Ming frowned. *Do you think we can make it?* he asked, pointing to the red gem in the center of the platform. It released a 20,000-foot aura, giving the sharks barely enough space to swim around.

Perhaps with a distraction, Yu Wen thought. *Quick, make ten more suits.*

Cha Ming rapidly painted ten suits of similar size to those they wore. As he finished, Yu Wen weaved silver strings into puppetlike shapes and sent them into the suits. They moved about the lava swiftly without any external control from the skilled puppeteer.

We'll send them out from above and behind while we approach them from in front and below, Yu Wen said.

Cha Ming nodded. They grasped each other's forearms and entered the 20,000-foot zone. They carefully approached along the sea floor, careful not to make contact, lest the noise alert the large sharks.

They traveled slowly, suppressing their movements to minimize disturbances in the lava. They continued to do so until they were 100 feet away from the glowing red gem.

The moment we grab it, they'll know it, Yu Wen said. *You'll need to store it in your soul-bound treasure space to cut off their senses. After that, they'll likely go berserk. We'll need to leave the 20,000-foot area, or else we'll be crushed to death.*

Cha Ming nodded. They waited as their puppets approached from above. A roar of indignation sounded from five of the sharks, who instantly dove toward the decoys. Yu Wen rapidly controlled the puppets to make evasive maneuvers. Meanwhile, Cha Ming approached the red crystal. It was the size of an adult human head. He quickly grabbed it and urged the Clear Sky Brush to take it in. The moment he did, the senses of all ten beasts locked on to him. Cha Ming swiftly pushed off the lava, grabbed Yu Wen by the waist, and flew through the lava with all his strength.

Swish. A massive, three-layered wave suddenly struck his chest, stunning him for a moment. Yu Wen grabbed his lava suit and pulled him back. The sharks hadn't noticed them, and after crushing the ten puppets, they swam around chaotically, sending powerful waves of lava in all directions.

Cha Ming pulled a Flow Talisman from his Clear Sky Space and activated it. An invisible barrier of lava formed around them, repelling these waves. Unfortunately, this also alerted the lava sharks, who swiftly charged toward them.

They pushed off hardening walls of lava, frantically avoiding the sharks' pursuit. One of them, the largest one, let out a sharp roar, which stunned Cha Ming and Yu Wen, disorienting them. Thinking quickly, Cha Ming pulled out a Matter Talisman. He used it to strengthen their bodies and resist the sound waves. Then he used any residual power to form baffles and divert the oncoming current into a funnel. Power rushed out from his suit to form a platform of hardened lava, which was propelled by the resulting lava stream.

Seeing their attempts were failing, five of the sharks suddenly began glowing. Their energy destabilized as they began self-detonating.

If you have any trump cards, you should use them, Cha Ming said, gulping. He threw up another Matter Talisman and Flow Talisman, as well as a Shape Talisman, and carefully formed a spherical wall to protect them. Then, he summoned his Dao sigils and formed yet another shield within the two. Although he wasn't sure if this was enough, only time would tell.

Boom. Boom. Boom. Boom. Boom. Five consecutive detonations occurred. It severely injured the other five lava sharks but simultaneously engulfed the area in fierce destructive energy. Cha Ming projected his qi into the Dao shield as his Material and Flow Talismans failed. His material barrier crumbled piece by piece, leaving behind only the supporting shape framework. His qi rapidly drained after the initial impact.

Suddenly, a gray light filled the area surrounding them. Cha Ming looked around in amazement as he realized that the source of the gray light was Yu Wen.

Is that Grandmist Essence? he thought as the gray glow intensified. *No, it's not Grandmist Essence but Grandmist Qi.* In other words, she didn't cultivate five elements, creation, and destruction like he did. Instead, she cultivated Grandmist directly. It was a full level higher than his own cultivation method.

Hurry and get us out of here, Yu Wen said weakly. *I can't use this for long.*

Cha Ming nodded. He grabbed her by the waist and pushed away from the general area. The explosion, which had rocked them previously, was frozen in time. He carefully avoided sharp edges and intense turbulent vortexes. Unfortunately, it was impossible to avoid them all, and he could tell that Yu Wen was weakening under the strain. To gain time, he bore the brunt of some weaker vortexes with his body while using his remaining qi to shield Yu Wen.

Finally, after much effort, they left the 20,000-foot area. Time resumed once more, and only the violent remnants of the self-detonation struck them. Cha Ming funneled whatever qi he could into Yu Wen as he brought her toward the surface. Their surroundings grew brighter and brighter, until finally they broke through the surface and arrived at the lava serpent's shrine. They collapsed on the obsidian ground, and lava pooled beneath them as they looked up at the furious fire serpent. The reptile stared at them coldly for a few breaths before speaking.

"Asssss agreed, you may take these three thingssss," it hissed before plunging back into the lake of lava.

Cha Ming sighed in relief when the fire serpent had gone.

"What are these three things for anyhow?" Cha Ming asked as he looked at the red globe.

Yu Wen grabbed it and motioned with her hand. A goopy red liquid film ran off the orb and formed a small blob.

"Quickly, catch the Fire Source Marrow in your brush," Yu Wen said.

Cha Ming didn't hesitate to scoop it up, causing ruby runes to cover the black-and-white artifact.

"It's for you and your body refining. You can also keep the Fire Essence Core. It will come in handy for you in the future." She then pulled a glowing red spot from the center of the sphere that emitted a massive amount of energy. Yu Wen stowed it away in an independent space before too much of the energy could leak out.

"Fire Essence Cores can take over ten thousand years to form," she said. "But fire sources are different—they might take millions before condensing within a Fire Essence Core. Now that we've obtained it, we need to hurry back to Jade Moon Garden. With any luck, we'll all be sent home in five years' time."

As they left the volcanic area toward the garden, a sense of loss filled Cha Ming. *I'll go home, and you'll go home,* he thought. *But what will we do? How will we find each other?* It was a difficult question, one they'd have to face in the next half decade. *But for now, we can enjoy these gentle moments with each other,* he thought as he gripped her hand tightly.

Yu Wen summoned a flying ship, which they used to fly off the peak of the hardening volcano and into the valley below.

Chapter 25: Heart of Ice and Snow

Hong Xin's feelings slowly returned after the latest round of "treatment." The happiness she felt was numb and distant. This was no surprise, given that the process had consumed one twentieth of her inner flame. After much wearing away, the purple flame within her was now only a third of its original size.

"How very resilient of you," Mistress Huang said. She sat down and took a sip of hot tea. "Most people can't resist more than a few treatments before giving in. But you've managed to last dozens. What exactly is it that keeps you going?"

"Just kill me and get it over with," Hong Xin said weakly between strained breaths. "You'll need to force me into the fifth level of the Frozen Heart Realm to succeed, something that's easier said than done. It's a total waste of your time and mine."

Mistress Huang smiled. "How perceptive," she said. "I was the same as you once. So full of hopes and dreams. My first teacher was very different than the current headmistress. Back then, the Red Dust Pavilion's emphasis was on heart kindling. Did you know that?" She didn't wait for Hong Xin to respond. "I was my teacher's personal disciple. I, too, had reached the fourth level of heart kindling before minoring in heart dousing. Back then, we clung to our personal talents like possessive children."

She sighed and placed her cup upside down. A half cup of ice slid out from the cup, which was still warm. "But that didn't last long. My teacher had a younger sister who followed the path of heart dousing. She had an unfathomably loyal following. The headmistress, being the most powerful cultivator in the Red Dust Pavilion at the time, didn't pay close enough attention to her. She continued cultivating diligently until finally, she transcended."

Mistress Huang shook her head. "Ironically, her strength increased, but her freedom decreased. Her junior sister took the opportunity to consolidate her power and chase her out of the Red Dust Pavilion. My former teacher was forced to wander the continent like a vagabond, and I had no choice but to turn my sights on heart dousing. The new headmistress became my new master."

"How did it feel?" Hong Xin asked.

"How did what feel?" Mistress Huang asked.

"How did it feel to betray your teacher's ideals and completely change your heart?" Hong Xin asked. "Those who practice heart kindling believe in hope and salvation. Those who practice heart dousing are selfish and manipulative."

"It feels cold and uncomfortable, but you get used to it," Mistress Huang said. "By cultivating the Freezing Heart Sutra, you bury your heart in multiple layers of ice. Then the ice's quality changes and deepens from light blue to royal blue to navy blue. And finally, it freezes to purple, then purple-gold. It forms an impenetrable layer that bottles up your feelings so they can't escape. The discomfort vanishes soon after."

"I'll never be that way," Hong Xin said, her eyes regaining some of her former energy. "I've been down that hellish path, and I'd rather die than go back."

Mistress Huang shrugged. "You'll change your mind. Those with frozen hearts are pragmatic and calculative. Once you see loss on one side and benefit on the other, you'll surely chose the better path."

"But you'll never freeze my heart," Hong Xin said defiantly. "You've been trying but failing all this time."

"Is that what you think?" Mistress Huang said, edging closer. "I've been gradually wearing away at your heart flame, carefully making sure that it doesn't snuff out. Do you know why? It's because I want a frozen flame, not a snuffed flame. I want an unprecedented talent, not damaged goods."

Hong Xin's expression darkened. "You'll never succeed," she whispered.

"I always succeed," Mistress Huang said. "And I'm living proof of the process. In my heart lies a frozen flame, unmeltable and unchangeable. You're not an experiment. You're a second-generation product. I've experienced what you've experienced many times over."

Mistress Huang held out a slender finger and began tracing blue runes on Hong Xin's chest, carefully avoiding the black needles stabbed inside it. "It's time for another session. Stay strong, and don't disappoint me."

A wicked wind blew as Hong Xin opened her frost-covered eyes. Her eyelashes stuck together for a moment before finally coming apart. She glanced over to her sister, Hong Minyi, who was huddled in a thin blanket while trying to preserve as much body heat as possible. Four of their companions had already frozen to death. If no one came to their rescue, they would surely follow.

"Sister, I'm cold," Hong Minyi said, shivering. "And hungry. We haven't eaten anything for three weeks. We'll starve to death if we don't eat *something*."

Hong Xin glanced at the frozen corpses but pushed the revolting thought out of her mind for what seemed like the thousandth time. "Chew on your robe," Hong Xin said in a croaking voice. "It'll make you less hungry. Help is coming soon, I promise." She'd repeated it over a thousand times, though she didn't believe herself when she spoke the words.

"I've eaten so much snow my stomach hurts," Hong Minyi said, laughing hysterically. "Why do we need to care about them? They're dead, Hong Xin. Dead! We're alive, but they're dead."

Her outbursts are becoming more savage, Hong Xin thought. *Please don't let her lose her mind. Not like Lin Bai. I can't bear to have to kill my own sister.*

"Just eat some snow and go to sleep," Hong Xin said. Her younger sister nodded off in mere moments. Hong Xin watched her for a while before she, too, fell asleep.

A dull pain woke her some time later. The world spun as she looked around dizzily. A few breaths passed before her eyes focused on the source of the pain: Her sister, her only companion in this frozen hellhole, had just hacked half Hong Xin's arm off. Blood dribbled down the little girl's mouth as she ate the amputated flesh with a crazed look in her eyes.

"Why?" Hong Xin croaked.

Hong Minyi laughed hysterically. "They were cold. I tried to eat them, but they were cold." Hong Xin looked around them and saw chunks of frozen flesh splayed out over Lin Bai's corpse. "I needed something warm, and you're the only warm thing left."

And here I thought the most painful thing would be to kill my own sister, Hong Xin thought. *But now I that I'm dying, I know that's not the case. She's not my precious sister anymore. She's a monster.*

Hong Xin woke to a crackling sound. The ice in her heart turned purple and violently suppressed the small flame in the middle, which was now a tenth of its original size.

"The effect of that dream was far greater than I expected," Mistress Huang said. "This deserves a celebration." She placed a cup of hot wine before Hong Xin, who paused before picking it up and pouring the hot liquid down her throat. It warmed her body, but not her soul. "Just an hour ago, you said you'd rather die than drink wine offered by me. Now you're drinking it. Why?"

"Why would I refuse something to drink at this point?" Hong Xin said.

"Indeed, why would you?" Mistress Huang said, smiling. "Though it seems like you won't need to reach the fifth level of the Frozen Heart Sutra before completely succumbing. I anticipate that you'll only need a few more treatments."

"Just get it over with," Hong Xin said dispassionately.

"As you wish," Mistress Huang said. An illusion surrounded Hong Xin once more.

Hong Xin had a dream. In this dream, she was a member of the Imperial harem. She fought her way tooth and nail, using schemes to suppress her opponents as she strived for the emperor's heart. Eventually, she prevailed. The emperor came under her control, and so did his sons and grandsons. When she died, she died alone. But that didn't matter to her, as her heart had died long ago.

Hong Xin had a dream. In this dream, she loved a boy. He betrayed her and broke her heart. Then, being damaged goods, she found employment in a brothel, where she satisfied one man after another before eventually dying of illness. Not even the three children she birthed could give her joy in this miserable life.

A pile of ledgers appeared before Hong Xin. She looked them over with lightning speed before writing out three orders to her assistant, Tong Ya, who reviewed them and frowned. "Why would you order me to do such a thing?" she said hoarsely.

"We need to shut down these factories to cut the bleeding," Hong Xin said. "Their labor is too expensive to continue operating."

"But there are other ways," Tong Ya said. "You were at the family meeting just a few days ago. Some new machinery can help increase productivity and make these factories competitive again. We have the money—must we really make these people suffer?"

"And what next?" Hong Xin said. "I can spend the capital, but these machines are manufactured by my cousin, who'll use it to grow his influence. Furthermore, the amount of capital could be used to start many other businesses with much higher profitability. It's best that we shut these down."

"Can't you sell the factories to your family?" Tong Ya said.

"And create a competitor?" Hong Xin said. "You're too naïve. It's better to dismantle the company and sell the assets outside the family. At least this way I'll be able to salvage a bit of advantage out of this failed project."

"It's always about moving up, isn't it?" Tong Ya said. "You're willing to give up anything for the sake of your ambition." She sniffed and wiped tears out of her eyes. "I know a lot of these people personally. It's very difficult for them to find work. They all live from paycheck to paycheck. Many of them might not survive if you fire them."

"That's not my problem," Hong Xin said coldly. "They should have thought of that when they were younger. They should have gone to school and gotten better skills. Now they're saddled with untransferable skills in a dying industry."

"I can't do this," Tong Ya said, tossing the papers onto her desk. "You'll need to do it yourself."

"All right," Hong Xin said, taking back one of the sheets of paper. She wrote another name on the list: Tong Ya. "Your services are no longer required. Please leave the premises, as you're on private property."

Tong Ya left the room, sobbing. But Hong Xin was immune to this. She'd long since hardened her heart for success.

Years passed by, and she climbed over her cousins, brothers, and sisters one after another. By hook or by crook, she eventually took over the family business and consolidated her power. She ruled over everyone with an iron fist until she died cold and alone, a miserable existence.

Hong Xin suddenly woke in her cold cell. A hint of gold had appeared on the purple ice within her heart, a sign of imminent change to the fifth realm of the Frozen Heart Sutra.

"Who would have thought that this dream of all dreams would touch you so deeply?" Mistress Huang said. "Do you have a business background? Or a love interest who does, perhaps?" Hong Xin looked back in cold silence. "No matter," Mistress Huang said. "You're at the cusp of change, and I have the perfect story to tell you. I guarantee you that once you hear it, you'll lose all hope."

Hong Xin remained expressionless. Not a hint of her prior defiance remained.

"Do you know *why* we go through such great lengths to train students in the Frozen Heart Sutra?" Mistress Huang continued. "They must at least reach the third stage to graduate. By then, they've become cold and calculative and extremely pragmatic. They'll also be selfish. You must be wondering why in the heavens would we go through all this trouble to create manipulative, disloyal women who'd stab us in the back at a moment's notice?"

Mistress Huang leaned over to Hong Xin's ear and whispered, "It all relates to the headmistress's artifact—the Frozen Heart Oath Stone. By using it, she can compel others to obey her unconditionally.

But due to its power, the conditions are very strict. You see, one's heart must be completely frozen over for the oath to function. The reason for this is because of the oath's wording: *I swear on my frozen heart.* Those who don't have a frozen heart cannot swear on it.

"That's why, after the yearly performance, the headmistress will gather all the graduates and offer them a choice. On the one hand, she will offer them an extremely beneficial contract. As long as they swear an oath of obedience, they can enjoy great riches and power. On the other hand, they'll be tortured and executed. For those with a frozen heart, it isn't a difficult choice to make. Just like it wasn't a difficult choice for you to stay in this terrible academy when we hung up the corpse of one of your classmates when she tried to escape."

A single frozen tear dripped out of Hong Xin's eyes as she remembered the day she'd given up escaping the Red Dust Pavilion. Her heart flame flickered as she struggled to keep hope alive. Yet try as she might, the golden sheen was rapidly expanding.

I can't give up like this, Hong Xin thought. *I can't just let her win. My sisters need me.* Her flame shrank, little by little, until only a tiny purple wisp remained. As the outer ice completed its violet-gold transformation, the flame began freezing over.

One quarter, one third, one half. It froze from the outside in, until finally, only a tiny speck of unfrozen flame remained. It struggled for its life as its surroundings tried to suffocate it, locking away its light for all eternity.

I can't let her win! Hong Xin thought fiercely. She poured all her emotions into the budding flame. She poured her hope of saving her sisters into the feeble spark. She poured her yearning for the man who abandoned her into the dying ember. She poured her longing to see her parents into the warm spot that was swiftly icing over. The tiny flame shuddered once more before finally, a violet-gold strand appeared on it as it completely froze over.

"A success," Mistress Huang said, inspecting Hong Xin's core. She released the chains binding her. "Follow me to see the headmistress."

Hong Xin nodded and followed Mistress Huang. They exited the cell through a small wooden door and entered the courtyard, where

Hong Xin saw many familiar faces. Dozens of them were students whom she had helped before. They all wore icy-cold expressions as they dispassionately practiced their assigned hobbies.

They passed these students under the watchful eyes of the crimson trees in the courtyard. A couple of teachers scowled as they entered the smallest, northernmost building in the Red Dust Pavilion. Mistress Huang knocked on the door softly.

"Enter," a cold voice said.

They walked into a chilly room where a middle-aged woman in a red-and-gold dress sat. The woman scanned her core and confirmed it was fully frozen. "You succeeded," the headmistress said. "I knew you wouldn't fail me."

"I live to serve," Mistress Huang said, bowing.

The headmistress nodded and retrieved a blue jade stone. The temperature in the room plunged.

"This is an Oath Stone, child," the headmistress said. "I won't mince my words: You've a been troublesome student. The only way to avoid death is to swear an oath. You will repeat after me and speak exactly as I speak." She placed the blue jade stone in Hong Xin's outstretched palm.

"I swear on my frozen heart," the headmistress said.

"I swear on my frozen heart," Hong Xin parroted.

"To forever obey Hong Yinri," the headmistress said.

"To forever obey Hong Yinri," Hong Xin repeated.

"As long as I live," the headmistress said.

"As long as I live," Hong Xin completed. The blue jade stone glowed and resonated with her frozen core. Purple-gold shackles surrounded and bound it.

"Do you know Hong Yinyue?" the headmistress asked.

"She taught me heart kindling," Hong Xin replied.

"As I suspected," the headmistress said. "But as usual, she isn't cautious enough. She sent you into the lion's den thinking you'd survive, and she was wrong."

"It's as you say," Hong Xin replied.

"Return to your quarters and recover," the headmistress said.

"You'll be appointed as an instructor in the meantime. No use in wasting loyal manpower."

"Yes, Headmistress," Hong Xin said. She bowed and left the room. She didn't spare a word to the students she passed on the way back to the dormitories. Once she reached her usual accommodation, she sat on her bed and began the long process of mental recovery. Her soul had been badly damaged in the process of heart freezing. The temperature in the room plunged as she cultivated, but she paid no heed to the complaints of the students around her.

One week passed. She inspected her soul, whose heart was completely frozen through.

Then she smiled. In the center of her heart and the center of her core, the small frozen flame wriggled to life. Her core quickly became a mixed core once more, with purple-gold flame dancing in harmony with purple-gold ice. After basking in its warmth for a short moment, she had it retreat to a tiny speck in an otherwise-frozen ball of ice.

In comparison to its thick outer shell, it was undetectably small. Yet the purple-gold chains on her heart knew the difference. Their luster dulled and their links slackened.

Chapter 26: Jade Moon Garden

I s that Jade Moon Garden?" Cha Ming asked as they approached a gigantic jade archway. The intricate structure was one hundred feet tall and covered in many familiar runic fragments. The grand entrance led into a light-green shield that covered the lush valley like a weather dome.

"The one and only," Yu Wen said. "Built by the Jade Emperor to keep his daughter busy and out of trouble, if you'll believe it." She urged her ship toward the archway, which allowed them to glide in unrestricted. The moment they passed through, a set of rules appeared in their spiritual sea.

Do not break the restrictive formations.

Do not harm plants, nymphs, or forest spirits.

Do not kill other demons and cultivators.

Be nice to the garden, and it will be nice to you.

A group of tens of thousands of cultivators were gathered at an altar, while hundreds of thousands were camped beside the woods. "It's a far cry compared to the millions who made it out of the Bridge of Stars," Cha Ming said as they approached the shrine.

"Many of them were converted with devil seeds, while the remainder were conveniently slaughtered by both devils and fiendish demons," Yu Wen said. "Usually the number of cultivators wandering on Jade Moon Planet is around ten million. Now there's only a fraction of that number."

The camps near the altar were divided into many factions and sects. One of them stood out to Cha Ming. It was comprised of only four members. He waved at them as they approached on foot.

"Thank goodness you're safe," Han Jiling said. He sported a large greatsword on his back that oozed lightning-aligned transcendent might. "If you didn't make it, Lu Tianhao would have had my head."

"Of course we're safe," Cha Ming said. "We just had to take a detour. How are the others from the Alabaster Group?"

"Only a couple made it here alive," Han Jiling said mournfully. "I explained what happened with Song Min. Although they seemed to understand, they're a bit uncomfortable about the whole situation. They've allied themselves with a group that's historically been good to us. I think it's best if you don't see them until we get Senior Partner Lu to straighten them out."

"You're both lucky," Zhang Fei said grimly. "Our sect members didn't make it. That's why we decided to form our own elite team. Now then, what took you and Yu Wen so long?"

"Have a little tact," Fang Li said, winking. "I'd take my time traveling with a beauty like her as well." He winced as Mu Qianlin pinched him hard on the thigh.

"What are you all waiting here for?" Cha Ming asked, changing the topic.

"We're waiting for them to announce the contents of the examination," Zhang Fei explained. "Every year, many people come here with herb-gathering quotas. They're welcome to select whatever they like—except for top-grade herbs. Their supply is very limited, and priority on picking them is determined by the results of a two-part test. The first test determines eligibility and the second test, herb distribution. There is also a third test, whose reward is access to a restricted alchemical library. You can only take the second test if you pass the first, and so on."

Cha Ming looked toward the wood, where various cultivators were darting in and out of the trees, doing their best to avoid nymphs and wood spirits while they plundered low-grade herbs and fruits. "What about them?"

"They're people who've used their herb-gathering quotas and are trying their luck on low-grade herbs, which are unprotected by restrictive formations," Mu Qianlin said. "It's not technically against the rules, but it irks the elementals who administer the test. Given that the first qualifying test is usually arbitrary and bizarre, all of us are staying out of trouble until the contest begins."

"So that's how it is," Cha Ming said, laughing. "What are your plans?" he asked Yu Wen.

"I have something to take care of for the time being," she said. "Go ahead and keep them company. I have a feeling the test will be starting soon."

Seeing that she didn't want to discuss her task, Cha Ming left her to her own devices. He and the four angelic cultivators began playing *Xiqi*, a game like *Angels and Devils* that was played by many players on a spherical board.

"How interesting," Cha Ming said. "It's much harder than *Angels and Devils*, given that there are no edges to defend." He placed a blue stone on the wooden sphere, carefully protecting his growing group of stones."

"The best part is that openings and strategy aren't well defined," Zhang Fei said. "That way, smarter players can't get much of an advantage over me."

"I think smart players will generally find a way," Mu Qianlin said.

The larger man shrugged and continued playing his stones in a scatterbrained manner. It wasn't long before he was completely choked out of the game. Han Jiling followed soon after.

"Beginner's luck," Fang Li, who owned the game, said. He was still playing but was at a significant disadvantage.

"You can always side with me and take her out," Cha Ming said.

"Like you two did to me?" Fang Li said bitterly. The four others laughed. Winning was one thing, but to them, taunting Fang Li was half the fun.

Suddenly, the laughing died down. Cha Ming frowned and

looked around suspiciously. A cut-flower silence had covered the lush valley like a smothering blanket. The forest spirits, which usually sang encouraging songs to the trees, had halted their sacred words. The nymphs had stopped taunting the human cultivators, who began wantonly plundering their natural treasures. Overhead, dark clouds covered the starry sky and began forming a funnel, which descended onto the semitransparent green shield above them. The entire forest held its breath as the cloudy finger stretched out toward Jade Moon Garden's defensive shield.

Crack. A fissure appeared across the obscured sky. *Crack.* Another one joined it. Thousands of cracks appeared all around them as pieces of luminescent glass tumbled toward the valley from above. The cultivators near the shrine looked up fearfully at the powerful presence. Those near the forest, however, picked up speed and continued their plundering. The nymphs and forest spirits ignored them and chose to retreat to their shelters.

"You think you can do as you please in the Jade Emperor's sanctuary?" a voice boomed. A giant creature made of jade vines flew up from the forest. It placed its hand on the shield, mending it faster than it could break.

A black-cloaked figure appeared. Although it was difficult to distinguish it from the dark night sky, its black eyes stood in stark contrast to everything around it. "It was worth a try," the figure said. "But why do you bother? You and I both know you're incapable of holding out against me with the shield's power source.

"There's only one way to find out," the creature said. "I have sworn to protect this place, so I will fight you with everything I have. A wood elemental's dignity is inviolable."

"Suit yourself," the black-cloaked figure said. Over a thousand jade spikes covered in black runic fragments appeared at various positions above the dome. They whirled intensely as they accumulated their power. "Destroy!" the figure yelled.

The spikes stabbed downward at his command. Each one pierced a few inches into the shield, forming black runic lines across its surface. They joined together in an elaborate network that exceeded Cha Ming's comprehension.

"Your kind only knows how to damage and destroy," the elemental spat. It opened one hand, which contained a green spark. Then it opened the other vined hand, revealing a red spark. The spark was familiar to Cha Ming—it was the fire source that he and Yu Wen had retrieved from the volcano.

Does she have a relationship with Jade Moon Garden? he thought.

"No wonder you were confident," the black figure said as he saw red and green energies pouring into the barrier. They formed a counter-formation against the spikes, preventing them from eroding the shield further. "But you're just delaying the inevitable. I have plenty of time to counter this."

"Counter away," the elemental said.

The black-cloaked figure snorted and disappeared. The starry sky reappeared behind the black formation encapsulating Jade Moon Garden's original barrier, and peace returned to Jade Moon Garden. The wood dryads returned to tending herbs as they glared bitterly at the cultivators. The rogues shifted uncomfortably as they realized they'd likely stepped out of bounds.

The elemental looked toward the cultivators by the shrine as the black-cloaked figure disappeared. "Those of you who have waited respectfully will be taking the second trial tomorrow at dawn," it said. "Those of you who did not will now get their just desserts." It looked to those in the forest in anger. Tens of thousands of vines burst out from the forest floor and bound the men and women in place.

"Seeing that you care so much about these lesser herbs that you would plunder while we're in danger, your punishment will be to nurture them," the elemental said. It waved its hand, revealing hundreds of thousands of green sparks that shot into the offending cultivators. Wails of anguish filled the forest.

After observing them for a while, Cha Ming gingerly retracted his resplendent force, doing so out of disgust—the cultivators had all begun experiencing extreme and endless diarrhea. It oozed out from their orifices and leaked onto the lesser herbs, which greedily absorbed the premium fertilizer.

"For now, you will be fertilizing these plants," the elemental said. "Remember this lesson—you will have a chance to redeem yourselves later." He then flew back down to the forest. The cultivators let out a sigh of relief as the elemental's oppressive aura disappeared.

"I told you they were all fools," Zhang Fei said. "One year, on a whim, one of the elementals forced all the cultivators to pick weeds for a year. Only those who'd picked at least a million weeds were allowed to participate in the second trial. This time, the contents of the first trial was harsh but easy to pass. One simply had to be nice to Jade Moon Garden, and Jade Moon Garden was nice to them."

Cha Ming nodded, but inwardly, he had his suspicions. Was the first test was rigged in his favor? *Who knows,* Cha Ming thought. *All I can do is try my best tomorrow.* He sat cross-legged and awaited the trial with the few thousand remaining cultivators.

Yu Wen arrived just before dawn. "How did you like the first test?" she said, snickering.

I knew it, Cha Ming thought. "Who would have thought that you'd have connections with Jade Moon Garden's elemental? I take it Huxian and Xiao Bai are hunting for another source?"

"Yes," Yu Wen said. "But they should be fine on their own, and it's now very difficult to leave the garden. We can only wait and hope for the best."

Cha Ming nodded. "Will you be participating in the examination today?"

"I don't have much to do, so I might as well follow you into the library," Yu Wen said.

"The library?" Cha Ming said. "The test is related to learning?"

Yu Wen held a finger to her lips, and her voice lowered to a whisper. "I'm not allowed to say much. What I *can* tell you is that the second and third tests are related. It's best if you don't get distracted by other things in the library. I know that you're looking for a solution for your core, but you won't find it here. Only the alchemical library after the third trial has what you need."

"How did you know about my core?" Cha Ming asked. It wasn't something they'd spoken about.

"My space-time camera is a soul-bound treasure, Cha Ming," Yu Wen said. "I know more about you than you think."

Cha Ming forced a smile. "Are you sure I can find something in the alchemical library?" he asked.

"I asked a friend," Yu Wen said. "I guarantee it. Also, I have some good news for you. There is a Burning Samsara Lotus as one of the ten top-grade herbs this time around. As long as you finish in the top five, you should be able to obtain it."

"Why the top five?" Cha Ming asked. "Are there other, more valuable treasured herbs?"

"There are," Yu Wen said. "But I don't think you'll choose them."

"I don't need any others," Cha Ming said. "But I have to thank you."

"Thank me for what?" Yu Wen asked.

"For giving me hope," Cha Ming said. He tilted her chin and kissed her gently. At this moment, a gong sounded, and the green elemental from the day before flew up above the shrine.

"Only those who are competing should stay near the shrine," it said. "Though I encourage everyone to stay, as I'm in a good mood. With the help of those other cultivators, the forest is growing smoothly. Therefore, the test will be non-harmful in nature. Everyone can only benefit."

Many cultivators' faces brightened. After all, it wasn't unusual to be sent out on punitive expeditions against demon beasts for the second trial. Given the situation outside the shield, such a scenario seemed highly probable.

The elemental waved its vine-covered arm, summoning a large green portal. Beyond the shimmering surface stood a large building.

"Everyone who wishes to participate, please enter through this door into the Jade Moon Library. There, you will find billions of books on any conceivable subject. Weaponsmithing, alchemy, medicine, and cultivation—none of the basics are missing. Although the contents aren't as plentiful as those in the Sacred Jade Library, I dare say that it would be impossible to find such a comprehensive library on any of your respective planes.

"Your task today is simple. Each of you will answer ten questions in the archaic field of herbology. The final placing will be based on the completion percentage for each of ten questions at the end of three years. You have unlimited attempts, though remember that this is a once-in-a-lifetime opportunity. While only ten top-grade herbs are available, hundreds of thousands of high-grade herbs can also be obtained by participants. What's better—the selection of a few herbs or a treasure trove of knowledge?"

With these words, the elemental stepped back and walked toward the forest to tend to the latest crop of fertilizer. The cultivators began pushing and shoving to enter the library. After one hour, Cha Ming and Yu Wen finally entered the jade-green portal.

The moment they entered, Yu Wen sent him a mental message. *Bookshelves 1-74930231, 1-62930492, 1-17384940... and 1-10294810.* The ten numbers she gave him were all on the first floor. She then blew him a kiss before disappearing up a spiral staircase to the second floor of the library.

It took some time before Cha Ming reached the first bookshelf Yu Wen directed him to. The titles on the aged books were obscured by a thick layer of dust. He grabbed one of them and blew on it, revealing thin gold lettering. The book was titled *An Introduction to the Fundamental Principles of Herbological Dousing.*

The shelf had to do with the fifth question: "Provide an herbal remedy to douse an inflammation caused by Seven-Vices Fever Root." He paged through the book before quickly finding the answer. Then he memorized the book for good measure.

"What other good things can we find on this shelf, I wonder?" he said. He pulled out a random book and began reading. Given his strong soul, it only took him forty-five breaths to finish the entire book. He frowned once he finished it. "There's more than one answer?"

He quickly organized the knowledge he'd gleaned in his mind before confirming that there were indeed two answers to the problem. Just to be sure, he pulled out a third and fourth book. These did not provide any additional answers, but he discovered that they completed some gaps of knowledge he'd found in the first two books.

The fifth book, however, gave him a large headache. It contained no less than five additional answers to the problem, and one potential answer that was proven false using knowledge gleaned from the prior four books.

"How could I have thought the test would be easy?" he muttered. He was fortunate enough to have Yu Went as an inside contact to point him in the right direction. Others would need to wander through the library unguided. Then again, there were likely many multiples of the books he'd perused.

Seeing that there were no shortcuts to be taken, Cha Ming began reading through each book on the shelf, one at a time. He read anything that was loosely related to herbology. Ten days passed, and during this time, he read 20,000 books. Although his returns diminished with each book, he left nothing unread. This even included the loose research notes piled up on the shelf.

Finally, he spent ten days consolidating, reconciling, and reorganizing the information in his mind. Then, he poured the results into a jade slip that he titled *Dousing Using Herbs, Roots, and Fruits, A Summary*.

"One down, nine to go," he muttered before setting out toward the next shelf.

Chapter 27: Herbology

Months passed by in a blur. Cha Ming's long stretches of reading were only interrupted by Yu Wen's visits. Even then, they simply sat together on a nearby chair and read together. Time was limited, and they both knew it. After six months, Cha Ming finished the last of the books on each of the bookshelves. He spent another ten days reorganizing his thoughts before compiling the last of ten books.

"It's strange," he muttered as he held Yu Wen in his arms.

"What's strange?" she asked, snuggling closer.

"It's strange that the concepts I imagined for my runic poetry line up so perfectly with herbology," Cha Ming replied. "Fire is split into dousing and kindling, and earth into hardening and crumbling. Metal is split into sharpening and dulling, while water is composed of momentum and resistance. Just like my poetic talismans. If this isn't fate, I don't know what is."

"And what about wood?" Yu Wen asked.

"Wood is the most elusive of all to me," Cha Ming said. "Which is ironic, given that I've been studying herbology for six months. Herbology splits wood into life and death, but it's manifested in many ways. Killing and birthing, feeding and starving—the concept is much more multifaceted than the others."

"Perhaps it's because you don't understand the other concepts as properly as you think," Yu Wen said. "To me, it's not surprising at all that you've divided things this way. The five elements represent all of creation and destruction. This dual nature is at the core of the universe itself. Shouldn't it manifest itself in many ways?"

"But even in feelings and emotions?" Cha Ming said.

"Are we not creations?" Yu Wen replied. "Are we not part of this world? Feelings and emotions are a part of sentient creatures. They are intertwined, inseparable. Daoists often think they study objective truths, but by separating emotions from their studies, they sterilize the natural laws beyond recognition."

Cha Ming shook his head. "The more we talk, the more I realize I know so little about you. What else should I know, I wonder?" he teased.

Yu Wen's smile faded slightly. "You should know that I'm a precious treasure that's coveted by all the bad people in the world. Even the devil sovereign outside the barrier is after me. Now that you know that, do you still want me?"

"Come now, that's not something to joke about," Cha Ming said. "But even if that were the case, I'd still want you. I'd steal you away and hide you away from the rest of the world."

"And if they found us again?" Yu Wen asked.

"Then we'd run again," Cha Ming said. "As long as it takes."

"You know how to say sweet words," Yu Wen said. "But I like that about you." She kissed his forehead gently. "Now that you've finished studying these books, you should go answer the questions. I have something I need to do, so I'll come and see you later." She left Cha Ming with his books and disappeared up a staircase to the mysterious second floor, which no one else had yet successfully entered. He had also tried once but failed.

"Let's see what score reading all these books can obtain," Cha Ming muttered.

He walked for several hours before arriving at a hallway filled with testing rooms. There were hundreds of rooms and hundreds of cultivators lined up outside them. He lined up and glanced at a leaderboard. Only a hundred names were displayed, but the lower scores had the number 990 while the top fifty all had scores of 1000.

I wonder what the assessment criteria is? he thought. Hours passed before finally, he entered a dark room.

"To which questions would you like to submit an answer?" a voice said. "An appropriate human model will be provided."

"Question one, 'Provide an herbal remedy for growing a resistance to Withering Plague Flower,'" Cha Ming said.

A transparent human model appeared in front of him. "Apply seven-star flowers to the bottom of the feet as a salve three times a day for one week," said Cha Ming. A brilliant herb with silver-green leaves appeared in the air. It was crushed into a paste and migrated to the feet of the human model. The model's body was extremely feeble, on the verge of death. However, as time passed, strange green spots grew in the model's body. Little by little, these green spots began to attack a dark-green substance that pervaded its muscles. Before long, the situation was completely reversed.

"One point awarded," the voice said. "Continue with another question or provide another answer?"

As expected, Cha Ming thought. He proceeded to supply one answer after another. Some were straightforward cure-alls, while others were roundabout methods that somehow used principles of growth to treat the affliction. Finally, he finished the hundredth solution.

"One hundred points achieved," the voice said. "Continue with another question or provide another answer?"

There're more? Cha Ming thought. He sifted through the knowledge he'd accumulated before returning empty-handed. "Proceed to the next question."

Like this, Cha Ming answered all ten questions, giving him a total of 1,000 points and placing fifty-first. If this was a test of speed, he hadn't done badly, but he hadn't done well either.

But there's no way this test would be about memorization.

He ignored the automated voice's prompt and thought carefully for a moment about the current question: "Provide an herbal remedy using flow to relieve a cultivation block in the lungs caused by Miretoad Stagnation Root."

Although I've used all strict principles of flow, perhaps I can use something else to create flow? He ran through several scenarios before settling on a sharpness-based herbology treatment. Sharpness had to do with shape, so he selected several dozen herbs and applied them as pastes, powders, and juices to the model. Various shape changes took place in blood vessels, organs, and qi pathways. These localized changes didn't affect the health of the model much, but each one caused a small change in qi flow. Slowly but surely, these flow changes removed the stagnation effect near the lungs until finally, the obstruction was cleared.

"Using shape to induce flow successful," the voice said. "Three points awarded. Continue with another answer?"

The time limit for answering was ten breaths. Since he had had no immediate inspirations, Cha Ming exited the room, where the various contestants were in an uproar. Cha Ming's name had climbed to first place at 1,003 points.

Several people commented on the impossibility given their knowledge, while others frowned and sat in meditation. A few moments after he exited the room, another name shot up to second place. Li Fei, a beautiful girl in a red Daoist robe, exited one of the testing chambers. She frowned when she saw that someone had achieved this result before her but wasn't so surprised.

Cha Ming didn't waste time basking in his glory. His experience had completely upended the knowledge he'd gained over the past six months, and any improvements would be difficult to come by. He wandered the library, deep in thought, casually browsing through random books, looking for inspiration. At one point, he encountered a bookshelf on alchemy.

After some time, he found a book entitled *Cultivation Damage and How to Fix It.* Excited, Cha Ming read through the contents, but his expression turned ugly when he realized two things. Firstly, his comprehension of alchemy was extremely poor, so he could barely understand what was written. The second realization was that, according to what he'd read, the amount of damage to his core was irreparable.

Cha Ming adjusted his mindset before replacing the book. Although his curiosity gnawed at him from the inside, he turned away from the shelf and continued his search for enlightenment on herbology. After all, his time was limited. If he didn't finish in the top five for this challenge, he wouldn't stand a chance at obtaining the Burning Samsara Lotus.

I can focus on these other matters once I find a cure for Sun Wukong, he decided. He found a secluded location and began sifting and reorganizing his knowledge. A month passed by before he realized it.

"I still don't understand why you favor him so much," a human-sized creature made of green vines said. If one looked closely, one would realize that this was the same elemental that had deflected the devil sovereign's attack.

"It should be enough for you that I favor him," Yu Wen said. "Have you considered my request?"

"I cannot allow you to browse through the Sacred Jade Library," the elemental said. "These are the rules the master has set. You can browse all the alchemy books you like in the Jade Moon Library, but those in the Sacred Jade Library are fragile and rare."

"I'll just look. I won't take anything." Yu Wen pouted. "What about my other request?"

"I need to see if he's worthy of the resources," the elemental said. "I'll give them to him if he reaches the top five. Any boy who shows interest in my niece must meet a minimum standard."

"Thank you, Uncle," Yu Wen said. "You're the best."

The elemental sighed. "It may not matter. We could all perish here. This avatar of mine can't even communicate with my main body."

"It's part of the balance," Yu Wen said. "Heaven's luck couldn't last forever, and my luck has always been terrible."

"I know you're prophetic, but you mustn't speak such hopeless words," the elemental said. "It's not like you. I've known you since you were a little girl, and your faith has always been unshakeable."

"Sometimes life forces us to make choices," Yu Wen whispered. "I know the choice but not my decision." She looked to Cha Ming's figure in the scrying mirror. He'd just woken after reaching an epiphany. "It gets harder to make it with each passing day."

The elemental sighed. "Maybe top five is a little unreasonable," he said. "I'll let you help him once again."

"Really?" Yu Wen's eyes brightened. "I want to give him Shennong's Simulacrum."

"But that's a priceless artifact!" the elemental said. "Shennong would spit up blood if he knew a core-formation mortal was using it."

"What do you know?" Yu Wen said. "Uncle Shennong is all about helping people. Besides, the simulacrum has little practical value to immortals. It's just an old relic that's collecting dust in the library."

"But it's an antique from the dawn of mankind!" the elemental said. "Teacher Shennong is a revered elder of humanity. Anything he's touched becomes a priceless treasure."

"Who's more important, me or Uncle Shennong?" Yu Wen asked.

"You know it's you, but don't tell him I said that," the elemental said awkwardly.

"Then how important could his old toy possibly be?" she pressed. "I want to put it to good use, and Cha Ming will be an influential figure for humanity in the future. What better use could there be for Shennong's old toys?"

The elemental, not knowing how to respond to her onslaught, reluctantly gave in. "Fine. He can have it. But I'm not giving him any herbs. He can find them himself."

"Not a problem!" Yu Wen said cheerfully. Then she vanished from the room.

Why did she agree to that condition so easily? the elemental thought. *Does she know something I don't?* Then he shook his head. *It doesn't matter. If he has a way to use it, then so be it. Teacher Shennong will probably never ask about it.*

"Cha Ming," a voice said. "Cha Ming."

His eyes opened, revealing Yu Wen's beautiful face. He ran his fingers through her curly hair and kissed her lips.

"And where have you been?" Cha Ming asked as he got up and stretched his limbs.

"I've been here for a week, but you were too busy thinking to notice," Yu Wen said, pouting. "I finally couldn't bear it."

"It's my fault," Cha Ming said. "What's new and exciting today?"

"I found a new toy," Yu Wen said, grinning. "I thought it would be useful for you, so I brought it with me."

She waved her arm, and a large clear statue of a human appeared. It was a naked beauty, causing Cha Ming to avert his eyes in embarrassment. "Look again, silly," Yu Wen said, giggling.

Cha Ming cautiously looked up and saw that it was now the statue of a horse. The horse became a wolf, which then became a child, and finally, a giant.

"It's called Shennong's Simulacrum," Yu Wen said. "It's probably only a replica, but they say that Shennong couldn't bear using people or animals for medical experiments. Therefore, he created this simulacrum. It's able to perfectly replicate a living being's reaction to medicinal herbs, pills, and other medical treatments."

Cha Ming's eyes brightened. "Then this is a priceless treasure. If I had herbs to experiment with, I'd try right away."

Yu Wen rolled her eyes. "If only you had access to a spatial artifact. If only you had full control over said spatial artifact's world and could create mundane ingredients from scratch. How wonderful that would be?"

"How much *do* you know about me?" Cha Ming said, embarrassed. "It's like you're cheating at life."

"Life isn't always fair, Cha Ming," Yu Wen said. "It takes away as easily as it gives." Her voice contained unimaginable sadness and vicissitudes.

Cha Ming walked up to her and stroked her cheek with his hand. "What has life taken away from you?" he asked, concerned.

"It's taken away my destiny, my stability, and my good fortune," Yu Wen said. "But that's okay. Because it made up for it by giving me freedom, meaning, and power. It's given me the ability to see, and it's given me faith." She squeezed his large hand tightly with hers. "It's also given me you."

Complex emotions surged through Cha Ming. She seemed to know so much about him, but he knew so little about her and her troubles. And while he could sense that she considered meeting him a blessing, he felt that her last statement contained sadness. "You know my story," Cha Ming whispered. "So when will you tell me yours?"

She smiled and headed back up the stairs without saying anything. Sighing, Cha Ming pulled Shennong's Simulacrum into the Clear Sky World.

In the cold void, an aged, grandfatherly figure opened his eyes. He flipped open a device and sent a stream of consciousness inside it. After checking over the messages that had accumulated for the past million years, he settled on one that tugged at his heart strings.

"Fuxi University wants to borrow my simulacrum again as part of a special exhibit?" he said out loud. "That's great. And here I was worried that the old piece of junk was fated to collect dust for all time. It's time to go pay that old tree a visit."

Space shifted, and he appeared before a vast world. It was composed of seven platelike continents that were tethered together with jade bridges. Countless gods and immortals wandered through these worlds. Some were stoic while others were cheerful, but they all had one thing in common—angelic endowment, or at the very least, a substantial amount of merit.

Shennong shifted through space once more and appeared before a magnificent jade palace. The gates opened as soon as he arrived.

A butler greeted him at the entrance. "Will you be needing any refreshments, Master Shennong?" the butler asked.

"Your best wine," Shennong said. "But nothing I made myself. While you're at it, please tell Brother Yu I need his help fetching something."

"He'll be coming shortly," the butler said. "Please make yourself comfortable in the meantime."

Chapter 28: Consolidation

I t's been a while," Cha Ming said softly as he entered a white room and walked up to a bed of mists. On the bed lay a transparent figure—it was Sun Wukong's soul. Although it seemed unchanged on the surface, Cha Ming's soul was much stronger under the Jade Moon Blessing. He could now tell that Sun Wukong's soul was slowly deteriorating, thus his urgency in finding the Burning Samsara Lotus.

"I'm sorry I don't come to visit often," Cha Ming said. "It's just strange to visit an unconscious friend. I'm never sure if you can hear what I say, so who knows how much ammunition I could be giving you for when you wake up?" He sighed. "I'll be using the Clear Sky World to train again after all this time. Sorry in advance for causing a ruckus."

The world shifted around him with but a thought. The white bed disappeared and was replaced with a room containing Shennong's Simulacrum. It transformed as it saw fit, alternating between man and beast. After taking a deep breath, he approached the statue and sank his resplendent force into it. Operating instructions poured into his mind. With a few simple commands, he easily manipulated the simulacrum to maintain a constant human form.

"Let's see if this works," Cha Ming muttered. He imagined a plant sharing the same characteristics described in the book, the same theoretical properties. Then, as quickly as he'd wished for it, it appeared. He felt a small amount of high-grade spirit stone vanish from the Clear Sky World. "Well, the energy has to come from somewhere." Fortunately, he'd brought a literal small mountain of high-grade spirit stones with him.

After summoning the Seven-Vices Fever Root, he extracted its juices and sent it into the simulacrum's mouth. The entire statue rapidly turned feverish. Then Cha Ming caused it to freeze in time. Not only could he examine the simulacrum's body for modelled symptoms, he could also try different cures. To check this, he materialized five dousing flowers and collected their dew. The simulacrum ingested it. He observed as it snaked its way through the human body, entering the circulatory system before eventually diffusing through the meridians.

"It's a little different than in the books, but it's still effective," Cha Ming said. He repeated the process for all 100 successful methods, then did the same for the other nine questions. After carefully measuring the effects, he tested out ninety other techniques he'd postulated before. Surprisingly, only twenty of them were successful while the others failed.

Cha Ming wasn't dissuaded by these results. In fact, he was encouraged. Twenty out of ninety was an extremely favorable result as far as initial experiments were concerned.

Now I just need to find out why the others failed, he thought. He repeated them each a few more times, carefully investigating their mechanisms.

It's not that the theory is wrong, Cha Ming thought. *It's that other components interfere with the theory. While I'm using thinning nettle grass to enhance blood flow and increase cell growth, there is also a metallic component to the thinning nettle grass. It destroys the cells faster than they can grow. But what if I use it in conjunction with Silver Numbing Nettle? Wouldn't I eliminate this unwanted effect?*

He implemented this change and observed the results. There was a slight improvement. *But what about the ravenous lichen? It's targeting the lungs, but it's simultaneously harming the pancreas. What if I use a phoenixroot bark to activate the pancreas?*

One change after another was implemented, and soon, a four-element solution was successfully created.

"It looks like even four-element solutions are possible," Cha Ming muttered. "This will definitely shed some insights on interactions between herbs, and their relationship to different families of mechanisms."

He soon lost himself in his research. Days turned to weeks and weeks turned to months. Before he knew it, an entire year had passed since he'd entered the library. The cracking in his joints startled Cha Ming as he rose. After looking around for a moment, he walked back to the examination area, where Yu Wen was casually reading a book.

"Oh, I thought you'd forgotten about me," she said, not looking up as he approached.

"How could I ever forget about you?" Cha Ming said. "You know how I am—I have a one-track mind. Once I start thinking about something, it's hard to stop."

"It's not good to cultivate all the time," Yu Wen said bitterly.

"But I'd hate myself if I failed to save my friend because I wanted to relax," Cha Ming said, shaking his head.

Yu Wen's frown softened after hearing these words. "Over half your time is up," she said. "And the competition has long since surpassed you. They come here to validate their findings every few weeks or every month. Some of their points have already increased into the tens of thousands."

"That's reasonable," Cha Ming said. "My guess is that more complex solutions, more efficient solutions, and solutions with fewer side effects award more points. It's just very difficult to fine-tune solutions to get these results. However, enough trial and error will do the trick."

"How confident are you in surpassing their scores?" Yu Wen asked.

"This time?" Cha Ming said. "I'm not confident at all. The top ten all have scores over fifty thousand. Meanwhile, I've only come up with quantity by sacrificing quality. Everything this time will depend on how favorably the system evaluates my solutions."

"If you're already so far behind, how will you reach the top five?" Yu Wen asked.

"Don't worry, I have a plan," Cha Ming said. "This is just the first step—everything will be clearer after this validation."

"If you say so," Yu Wen said, returning to her book.

Cha Ming passed her and entered an empty examination chamber.

"To which questions would you like to submit an answer?" a voice said. "An appropriate human model will be provided."

"Question one," Cha Ming said. He listed off seven different herbs to be applied in a variety of ways. The transparent human figure changed and reversed its limb atrophy.

"Five points for a successful mid-grade solution," the voice said.

"Good, now try this one," Cha Ming said. He listed off almost the same list of ingredients, though he doubled the content of one. The transparent figure was cured much quicker than before.

"Repetition in solution, no points awarded," the voice said. Cha Ming, expecting such an answer, listed off twenty variations. Then, after some quick calculations, he adjusted the dosage again.

Finally, after hundreds of iterations, a soft ping sounded. "High-grade solution discovered. Adjusting solution value to fifty points," the voice said.

Encouraged, Cha Ming moved onto the next solution. It began by giving him one point, and soon upgraded to five points. Unfortunately, he wasn't able to improve this one past a mid-grade solution. Unperturbed, he moved onto the next one.

This continued for thousands of attempts until finally, a louder ping sounded. "Top-grade solution, adjusting solution value to 500 points," the voice intoned.

Cha Ming was overjoyed. He continued on until finally, he burned through 10,000 solutions. Roughly 8,000 were only worth one point at most, the subsequent interactions only being useful for data. Another 1,500 were worth five points, while another 450 were worth fifty points. Out of the 10,000 solutions he'd experimented with, only fifty were top-grade solutions.

"Continue to challenge questions?" the voice asked.

"No, I'll be leaving," Cha Ming said. He exited the room and saw that, after almost six months, he'd managed to break into the top ten with 64,000 points. Fifth place had 78,000 points, while first place had a colossal 160,000 points.

"How is that even possible?" he wondered. "You'd need to constantly hole yourself up in an examination room, even with my method."

"What do you know?" a cultivator said beside him. "I'll fill you in on some common knowledge. The one in first place, Fairy Sumei, is a perfectionist. While those before her were busy racking up 1,000 points before discovering herbal interactions, she had already realized this point. She didn't make an appearance on the leader boards until she'd perfected no less than five solutions, giving her 50,000 points."

"Perfected?" Cha Ming said. "There's such a thing as a perfect solution? And it gives 10,000 points?"

"That's right," the cultivator said. "We're all in awe of Fairy Sumei. Countless cultivators ask her to discuss the Dao, but she refuses all of them unless they gift her with an herb-gathering quota per hour of discussion."

Cha Ming hissed through his teeth. "I couldn't make so much money so quickly if I sold myself," he said.

"I'll buy you if you're so cheap," a voice said. Yu Wen walked up behind him, causing the cultivator he spoke with to awkwardly disappear off to the side. "Are you discouraged yet?"

"Not at all," Cha Ming said. "I'm just shocked that someone has already discovered sixteen perfect solutions. That's hard to beat—I don't even have a bit of confidence in achieving that."

Yu Wen laughed. "Will you be paying a fee to 'discuss the Dao' with her, then?"

"Heavens, no," Cha Ming said. "In fact, I'm just happy that she managed to discover perfect solutions."

"And why's that?" Yu Wen asked.

"Because it means I was right all along," Cha Ming said. "And that I didn't waste my time. I knew a lot of the solutions I tried were suboptimal and couldn't be improved. But I still tested them—do you know why?"

"Why?" Yu Wen said.

"Because I wanted data," Cha Ming said. "I theorized that it was possible to get more points for better solutions. Therefore, the first step was to acquire a bulk of data for baseline effects. The next phase is perfection."

"And how do you define perfect?" Yu Wen asked.

"You, of course," Cha Ming said. "Would you care for a cup of tea?"

"Yes, I'll have it with a generous helping of sweet talk," Yu Wen said, holding her hand out. Cha Ming took it and guided her over to a private room.

Cha Ming tapped the Clear Sky Brush on a notebook as he organized his thoughts using rough scribbles. It was inefficient to write, but it helped calm his mind. Hours passed as he puzzled over a problem. Finally, his eyes lit up, and he added to his solution. He tested it on the simulacrum and confirmed its success.

"With this development, I've cut down the number of herbs required significantly," Cha Ming said. "Moreover, I no longer use high-grade or mid-grade herbs. All of these are low-grade." To him, the epitome of herbology was not the most effective solution but the most efficient. If one could cure an affliction or fix a problem with dregs, why use fresh tea leaves? It was similar to Li Yin's philosophy on medicine, which advocated a minimalist approach with respect to treatment resources.

That wraps up the framework for the last round of solution optimization, Cha Ming thought as he stowed his brush and exited the Clear Sky World. Unfortunately, his knowledge of herbs was theoretical. Therefore, what he could simulate using his Clear Sky World was also limited. The models in the examination rooms were far more accurate, so he would fine-tune any solutions there.

"It's about time you woke up," Yu Wen said. She was seated beside him while flicking through pictures. Cha Ming recognized them as moments from their volcanic adventure.

"You really like looking through these pictures, don't you?" Cha Ming said. "And here I thought taking them was a waste of time."

"I just like capturing my happiest moments," Yu Wen said. "Speaking of which, I have a favor to ask."

"All right," Cha Ming said. "What's the favor?"

"After the examination ends in six months, I want to go see some nice things with you," Yu Wen said. "It'll be a vacation, a rest from all this cultivation and studying, with just the two of us. We don't have a lot of time left together on Jade Moon Planet, and I think I'd be a lot happier with more pictures once we head back to our own worlds."

Cha Ming swallowed and nodded. "I'd like that. But you make it sound like we'll be separated forever," he said.

"Who knows," Yu Wen said. "What if I die tomorrow? Would you regret not spending more time with me?"

"All right, I promise," Cha Ming said. "But I need to hurry for now. The examination ends in six months' time, and I have a lot of ground to make up."

"Knock 'em dead," Yu Wen said. Cha Ming gave her a quick thumbs-up before making his way to one of the many empty examination rooms in the larger foyer, where thousands of cultivators were busy chatting about the latest results. He didn't bother looking at the leaderboards. Knowing where he stood wouldn't change what he did one bit.

Cha Ming substituted yet another herb, one that was part of a set of a hundred with similar properties but whose secondary properties he wasn't fully aware of. The test was one of a thousand failures, but he didn't give up. Instead he moved on to the next component. He continued until the results took a favorable turn and changed his experimental model to account for it.

Soon, 10,000 experiments were fully completed. And while he'd managed to upgrade the final result to a top-grade solution, it was just a drop in the bucket. True success would come when he managed to find a perfect solution.

Cha Ming trudged on. Out of the initial 450 high-grade solutions, he burned through 150 optimizations. One hundred had been dead ends while forty-nine had been optimized to new top-grade solutions.

As he administered yet another cure to the model, a soft hum sounded within his mind. "Congratulations on discovering a perfect-grade solution to Question 2. Points for this solution updated to 10,000."

Counting the other solutions he'd discovered, he now had 95,000 points.

Continue, he thought. He wouldn't stop until he either ran out of time or until he ran out of experiments. He wasn't sure which would happen first. He burned through another twenty-nine solutions, none of which could be upgraded past top grade. Then, on the thirtieth, he was surprised with another perfect-grade solution.

Again! Months passed, and before he knew it, only one month remained in the three-year time limit. By then, he'd completed his optimization of all 450 initial high-grade solutions. A total of 200 had been upgraded, yielding 191 top-grade solutions and nine perfect solutions. His points had increased to 237,500.

"Only two percent of high-grade solutions could be upgraded to perfect-grade ones," Cha Ming thought out loud. "But perhaps the top-grade solutions will be easier to optimize. I refuse to believe that I can't squeeze out at least two or three perfect solutions from the last fifty."

He wiped the sweat off his brow and continued issuing instructions.

Outside the examination room, and near the rankings stele, cultivators were excitedly discussing the results.

"It looks like the first-place contestant will be Fairy Sumei with 490,000 points," a blue-robed cultivator said. "She's been producing one perfect solution after another at regular intervals. It's only recently that she's started slowing down."

"First place is a no-brainer," a yellow-robed cultivator said. "I'm more interested in the rest of the top ten."

"The remaining top ten is much more exciting," the blue-robed cultivator agreed. "Even tenth place has accumulated 200,500 points. The top ten are all monstrous talents in herbology."

"Most of them are alchemists by trade, the only exception being Fairy Sumei," a red-robed cultivator said. "She's a prodigy in a transcendent-grade influence. I heard that she had a head start on everyone due to the sheer size of their library. The others—well, they used their knowledge of alchemy and modified it to succeed."

"What about the current dark horse in eighth place, Cha Ming?" a brown-robed cultivator said. "He's only 5,000 points below seventh place, and 20,000 points below fifth place."

"Him?" the blue-robed cultivator said disdainfully. "I asked around and found out that he's from a low-grade mortal plane. His background isn't even in alchemy or herbology. He's only a talisman artist."

"But I heard he caused a commotion on the Bridge of Stars," the red-robed cultivator said. "I spoke to one of the seven other survivors from the final massacre. Every one of them obtained a transcendent treasure, and I heard his rewards were the greatest of all. Could he have obtained something that helped him in this trial?"

"Impossible," the blue-robed cultivator said. "No one has ever obtained anything other than treasures, techniques, and formulas. Besides, his ranking hasn't increased much recently. While the others are inching up by 500 points every day or so, his scores have stagnated." As he spoke, the current seventh-place contestant, Hong Fa, increased by 500 points. "See? What did I tell you?"

"You should look again," the red-robed cultivator said.

Cha Ming's name suddenly blurred and appeared one step higher. It had increased by 10,000 points.

"Wait, did he just discover a perfect solution? Is that why his rate of discovery stalled?"

"Don't forget his rather aggressive climb in the top twenty," the brown-robed cultivator said. "I'm really glad I bet on him when his odds were higher. I'm bound to win thirty herb-gathering quotas and some change at this rate."

The blue-robed cultivator's expression turned ugly.

"Who did you bet on?" the brown-robed cultivator asked him.

"I bet on the current fifth-place cultivator, Su Ming," the blue-robed cultivator said. "As long as he maintains his position, I'll break even. I refuse to believe he'll get kicked out."

Suddenly, Cha Ming's name switched places once more. He was tied for fifth place briefly before Su Ming gained 500 points and displaced him once more. The blue-robed cultivator wiped sweat off his brow. The next half month would be a nerve-wracking wait.

Chapter 29: Loyalty

Cha Ming was unaware of the commotion he was causing on the outside. Nor was he aware that he was running neck and neck for fifth place. Instead, he was wholeheartedly pursuing perfection within the testing chamber.

"My success rate is pretty good," Cha Ming said as he completed his twenty-fifth set of trials. "Out of twenty-five, I've succeeded in two. Although it might just be luck, it's better to be lucky than good sometimes." At least, according to Feng Ming it was.

As his rating stagnated outside and Su Ming steadily climbed past him, he performed thousands of experiments. Finally, after sifting through another ten sets of trials, he succeeded in yet another perfect solution, bringing him back on top. Then, nine sets later, he succeeded once more. Given Su Ming's current rate of success, it was a toss-up who would manage to remain in fifth place.

I only have time for one more set of trials," Cha Ming thought, looking over the five remaining ones. Only one day remained. *Which one should I pick?* Four of them seemed most promising, while another one seemed like a dead end. He quickly discarded it.

Suddenly, the Clear Sky Brush vibrated. Cha Ming frowned. He summoned the artifact by his side, but it showed no additional movement. "It must be stress," he muttered. He continued examining the four remaining ones before discarding another two.

The Clear Sky Brush vibrated again, this time more violently. *Just what do you want?* he said to it. The brush ignored him and stood still like before. Yet just as he was reaching out to the final two solutions, the brush dashed out and painted black lines on them, causing them to crumble to ashes.

"Just tell me what you want," Cha Ming said, massaging his brow. The brush darted out and ripped the other two solutions to shreds, leaving behind only the least-likely solution he'd first cast away. "And why do you think that's a good idea?"

The brush trembled for a moment before swiftly painting a pattern in thin air. A black star appeared, followed by a white circle. They superimposed and faded. Then the brush painted out the same thing once more. This time, however, the black star faded and the white circle stayed. A puff of gray floated in the middle.

Cha Ming's closed his eyes and tried to make sense of the situation. "There must be something different about this solution," Cha Ming thought out loud. "But what is it?" He recalled the alternating black stars and circles. He reviewed each of the five solutions in his mind, carefully poring through every detail. Them he compared them to the previous twelve perfect solutions.

"Are the other ones too skewed?" he wondered. "Are they not balanced enough?" Thinking about it, the other twelve solutions all followed a similar pattern. Firstly, they used a four-stage treatment. They weakened several functions in the body before bringing them all to equilibrium once more. Then the process was repeated, bringing the body's functions closer to perfection. However, doing this was difficult, as one had to incorporate the initial upsetting herb into their solution.

"Does the brush dislike these solutions because it's difficult to achieve this balance? Or is it because they can't?" Cha Ming reviewed the solutions and discovered that, through following an empirical approach, these top-grade solutions were indeed effective. However, they were more skewed toward one element or another. Balancing them would be difficult. However, the first solution was different. Although its effects weren't as good, the solution was close to a perfect balance. It would only require a bit of tweaking.

This will take too long, Cha Ming thought. *I'll have to simplify the initial set of experiments to mimic the final solution for the other twelve.* He quickly modified his approach and discarded three quarters of his planned experiments.

Cha Ming worked quickly. One after another, he weakened several functions in the model body. The herbs wreaked havoc on it, bringing it ever closer to the brink of death. But Cha Ming continued. A few more herbs created a balanced creation cycle and healed the ailing body. Only a minor amount of the original poisoning herbs remained. Therefore, he continued another round of fighting poison with poison before finally bringing the body back to equilibrium with one last creation cycle.

"Congratulations on discovering a perfect-grade solution," the voice intoned. "Would you like to continue submitting solutions?"

Cha Ming shook his head. "I'd like to leave. I don't have enough time to accomplish anything."

He exited the room and was greeted by cheering and jeering. He looked up to the board, and to his surprise, his name, Cha Ming, stood in fourth place with a solid lead over fifth. It would be impossible for the fifth-place cultivator to catch up without discovering a perfect-grade solution. A few moments passed, after which green light flooded the chamber, and everyone was transported back to the shrine in Jade Moon Garden.

"The competition is over," the elemental said, appearing once more. "Selection of top-grade herbs and high-grade herbs will take place over the next six months, starting with first place. The third examination will begin in six months' time." A green light enveloped them once more, and Cha Ming soon discovered he was in a room with nine other people.

"Sumei, please come select your prize," the elemental's voice echoed in the chamber. A dignified beauty in white robes stood up and walked through a small door. She returned a quarter hour later with a smile on her face. Second and third place followed, after which Cha Ming was finally called through.

He entered a large chamber that was fully crafted with alabaster, save for conspicuously tinted windows on three sides. They depicted scenes of war and heavenly carnage. Angels fought devils while saint beasts fought fiends. Righteous gods fought evil ones while Buddhas fought evil spirits. Each window revealed the bloodshed and chaos that enforced the delicate balance between good and evil.

A lone figure was seated in the middle of the chamber. "Greetings, young one," the figure said. Judging by its voice, it was the same elemental who was administering the exam, though much smaller than its original form. His upper body was thirty feet tall, and he sat cross-legged on the alabaster floor. "What do you think of these murals?" he said, gesturing to the walls.

Cha Ming shook his head. "It seems unfair."

"Unfair?" the elemental said. "One could argue that it's perfectly fair. Good and evil created for perpetual battle. Every side wants victory, but neither can obtain it."

"I think it's unfair for good people to be trampled upon by scum," Cha Ming said. "Why should they be punished for wanting to help others?"

"And why should devils be punished for pursuing their own benefit?" the elemental said.

Cha Ming shrugged. "It's something you need to believe. It's a starting point. It's faith. I can't use reasoning to argue with you. No one can."

"You're right." The elemental grinned. "Many people try to rationalize good and evil. That's impossible. Everyone has a starting point, and it's difficult to change a person's heart. Now tell me, which herb would you like?"

"I heard from Yu Wen that a Burning Samsara Lotus is available," Cha Ming said. "I'd like that one."

"Yes, Yu Wen mentioned that you'd come for it," the elemental said. "But I really think you should consider your options. Your potential is endless, and it would be a shame to let it get ruined by something as silly as a shattered core."

"Is there a cure in the Sacred Jade Library?" Cha Ming asked.

"There is," the elemental said. "If you can find it. But I won't let Yu Wen guide you to the answer this time. It's a gamble, you see. However, I have the perfect solution here. You're in luck, because if you'd gotten fifth place, you wouldn't have had this option."

The elemental held out two large green hands. Two exquisite green formations appeared in the air, and within these formations floated two herbs. One was the familiar Burning Samsara Lotus. Its dew caused his soul to tremble despite the formation that isolated it. The other, however, looked like a simple green vine. Despite its plain appearance, its very presence caused a soothing sensation to permeate his core.

"You already know about the Burning Samsara Lotus, so I won't introduce it," the elemental said. "But the herb on your left is known as a Saint Ascension Vine. It will allow anyone who consumes it to instantly enter the rune-carving realm with something known as a Saint Ascension Carving. Amongst the many transcendent realms, such a rune carving will easily allow one to approach immortality. Given enough luck, you'll be able to reach the highest realm of existence."

"And I suppose the damage to my core wouldn't matter?" Cha Ming said.

"That's right," the elemental confirmed. "It will allow you to continue your journey of cultivation as though this setback had never happened. And while I understand that you wish to heal a friend with the Burning Samsara Lotus, other cures exist in transcendent realms. They might be rare, but if you fight your way to the top, they are not unattainable. I'll give you an incense time to consider."

"There's no need," Cha Ming said, shaking his head. "My friend's soul is dissipating. I'll take my chances in finding a solution in the library."

"Have you thought of your fox brother?" the elemental pressed. "Yes, I know all about him. In fact, I've met his father before. He has limitless potential. Will you endanger his life to heal your friend's soul?"

"He'll understand," Cha Ming said firmly. "He knows the value of friendship and loyalty. I would never fault him for risking my life to save his friends. It's a two-way street. We understand each other."

"But you can save countless innocents if you reach rune carving," the elemental said. "If you don't, the amount of good you can do in the world will be limited to the 500 years of your short life."

"If that's the case, then so be it," Cha Ming said. "If I don't save my friend now, who knows if his soul will last until I can find a solution. And if I can't enter the library, at least I know that a way exists. If it exists, that means I can find it myself. I refuse to believe that it's impossible."

"Is that your final answer?" the elemental said.

"It is!" Cha Ming replied.

"Don't regret it," the elemental said. He waved his hand and summoned an herb-gathering quota from Cha Ming's body. One hundred slots were instantly used up, and the jade slip crumbled to dust along with a green formation. A soft jade orb remained around the Burning Samsara Lotus.

"You should remain here to use the lotus," the elemental said. "Otherwise you'll risk exposing your soul-bound treasure. Although the devil sovereign isn't here for you, he won't hesitate to destroy you if he finds out what you possess."

"And what is he here for?" Cha Ming said. "Why has he chosen now of all times to attack Jade Moon Planet?"

The elemental looked up to the windows depicting the battle between angels and devils. He looked to one of the smaller murals, where a lone angel surrounded by a jade halo stood holding a small white winged animal. Unlike most angels, however, her wings weren't jade. But neither were they ochre like a devil's. Instead, they were gray. Nine pairs of gray wings floated behind her.

"The most tragic part about this war isn't the countless victims," the elemental said softly. "Nor is it the fact that peace is unattainable." He shook his head. "Instead, it's the fate of a single person. She's doomed to be chased throughout her many lifetimes. Some people might experience thousands of years, or even thousands of generations of peace. But peace has never lasted for more than a single day for her. It never has, and it never will."

The elemental walked toward the doorway. "Oh, I almost forgot." Two objects appeared in the air. One was a dense green sphere while another was a vial of thick green liquid. "Yu Wen asked me for a favor. Seeing as how you're not useless, and that you're a man who treats his friends properly, this Wood Essence Core and Wood Source Marrow are yours."

Cha Ming appeared in the small white room in the Clear Sky World once more. He appeared before the Monkey King's bed and took out the jade orb containing the Burning Samsara Lotus. The orb dissipated under his direction, causing an intense soul-strengthening aura to fill the room.

Cha Ming used his resplendent force to gently harvest the dew on the flower. It wriggled on contact and sent a large dose of power into his spiritual sea. He held it back with all his strength, and after a few moments of fighting with the dew, it left the lotus. Its red-and-white petals immediately withered and crumbled to ash. Its entire life essence was in the dew, and it would only be born once more if the dew was planted in fertile soil.

Resisting the urge to immediately devour the dew, Cha Ming spread it out on the Monkey King's soul as a thin layer. Upon detecting this wounded soul, the dew immediately seeped into it. Not wanting to waste any more of its essence on himself, Cha Ming abruptly left the Clear Sky World and entered his spiritual sea. His soul rapidly broke through to the peak of the Resplendent Soul Realm before finally glowing with jade light. His resplendent vestment glowed brightly before bursting into tiny runes that dug into his soul, which sat cross-legged.

Its eyes shot open. Then, despite having never moved since its appearance in his spiritual sea, Cha Ming's soul did just that. The jade-colored spirit body grew to double its original size and stretched out its limbs. Every inch of its body was covered in mysterious jade runes that Cha Ming didn't understand. However, the moment his soul stood up, he knew that he'd broken into the Transcendent Soul Realm. From now on, his soul had the ability to detach from his body and wander as it pleased. In addition, its sensory range was extremely powerful. He was awestruck by the amount of power a simple soul could have.

Then, as suddenly as the flood of power came, it disappeared. His soul crossed its legs just as an intense suppression appeared in the form of a jade net. Jade Moon Planet had previously been blessing him. Now it was suppressing him. His soul could now only exert the power of peak resplendent soul.

Sighing, Cha Ming returned to the Clear Sky World. Then, seeing that Sun Wukong's soul was growing increasingly corporeal, he stood up within the alabaster chamber. He shot one last glance at the picture of the gray-winged angel. Though he'd never met her personally, she gave off an air of freedom and delight, a presence that couldn't be hidden no matter how hard one tried.

Then he noticed something he hadn't before: a background of jade and ochre manifesting as a gentle hand and a nefarious claw. The hand held her firmly, while the claw was biding its time, waiting for the right moment to strike.

"Brother Shennong, it's been too long," the Jade Emperor said. He took a seat in front of his good friend and removed his jade crown before serving them tea. They were both saviors of humanity, and there was no sense in putting on airs with each other. "To what do I owe the pleasure today?"

"I'd like you to contact Jade Moon Planet and have my old

simulacrum delivered," Shennong said. "Fuxi wants to borrow it for his university again."

"Easy," the Jade Emperor said. "Give me a second." He tossed out a jade orb and entered a set of spatial coordinates. The device rang several times, but no one answered. The Jade Emperor frowned. "He always answers my calls. And his consciousness can literally branch off many times, so there's no need to interrupt what he's doing."

He input a different set of spatial coordinates. A giant green elemental appeared as a hologram above the transmission orb. "Do you need something?" he asked.

"Why didn't your clone on Jade Moon Planet answer my call?" he said. He shot the elemental a displeased expression, as he'd lost a lot of face in this exchange.

The elemental frowned. "Strange. I just tried reaching out to my clone, and while I can sense its existence, I can't communicate with it. It's like it's isolated by a special field of sorts."

"Could it be a spatial storm?" Shennong suggested. "They've been known to interfere with inter-realm communications."

The Jade Emperor shook his head. "I don't believe in coincidences. Yu Wen recently went to Jade Moon Planet, and I've been having nightmares. I think that old goat is up to something."

"You mean…" Shennong said, his eyes widening.

"That's right," the Jade Emperor said. "I need to leave immediately. Even traveling by space-time transmission takes a while."

"I'll go with you," Shennong said. "It's been far too long since I've gotten some exercise. And for that despicable fellow to try hurting my niece again… Well, let's just say I won't let him off easy this time."

A portal opened in the room, and the Jade Emperor and Shennong immediately hopped through it. The giant hologram of the elemental was left standing in midair, unsure of what to do. However, before it could say anything, an arm reached out of the portal and grabbed the communication orb. The elemental's hologram winked out of existence.

Chapter 30: Ancestral Communion

"Quick, we're almost there," Xiao Bai said as their team of five rushed through the woods.

Silverwing casually flew to a nearby treetop, where he caught a fiendish monkey in his claws and crushed it to death. He greedily gobbled its demonic core, adding to his communal demonic essence pool. Lei Jiang and Gua, not wanting to be outdone, used lightning and acid to dissolve it in passing.

"I don't know if you were planning on keeping this a secret, but I'm pretty sure they know where we're going," Huxian said. Projections of light and shadow casually snuck out from his body and devoured two nearby fiendish mice. They fought for every inch of land as they worked their way toward a mountain in the distance.

"If they know where we're going, they know where we're going," Xiao Bai said. "Fortunately, they're busy doing many things at once. They have a strict time limit if they want to break that shield. They can't just throw everything at us."

"If this isn't everything, I'm concerned," Huxian said. "It took us years to get here. *Years.* Besides, can't they just catch you and end it all?" Huxian said worriedly.

"Do you think I'm so easy to catch?" Xiao Bai said. "Perhaps only your mouse friend is as quick as I am among demon beasts. There isn't a snare in this world that can catch this jade rabbit." As she spoke, the forest thinned. A mountain range appeared on the newly revealed skyline. Its multiple dull protrusions clustered around a conical monstrosity. It oozed mountainous demonic energy that grew thicker as they approached.

The five demon beasts zipped between the mountain's crevices, using rocky protrusions to propel themselves up its towering surface. It wasn't long before they passed a jade barrier that was completely impassable by devils and fiendish demons. It contained a dense white mist that extended toward the mountain peak. Huxian was surprised to discover that it was laced with flecks of jade light meant to weaken fiendish demons and devilish cultivators.

"There is a safe zone around each core area of Jade Moon Planet," Xiao Bai explained. "There are five safe zones in total, with two of them being on the other side of the planet and completely unreachable in a reasonable amount of time."

"The demonic power here is extremely dense," Huxian said. "I take it the ancestral altar you mentioned is up at the peak?"

"That's right," Xiao Bai said. "Though are you sure you want to use it? You only get one shot in your lifetime, and you're less than ten years old."

"We need extra firepower, and fast," Huxian said. "This happens to be a great place to get it. I refuse to believe that a Godbeast like me can't complete something as mundane as an ancestral communion."

Hours passed as the five beasts made their way up the misty mountain. Rocky demonic creatures avoided them as Huxian and his three friends emitted their Demon-Subduing Intent. After a long and boring journey, the mists finally thinned, revealing a conical mountain peak. Despite the dense demonic qi bathing the area in a purple glow, the ancestral altar was nowhere to be seen.

"Who dares disturb my slumber?" a grating voice suddenly said.

The five demons looked around but discovered no one. There were no humans or devils, only an omnipresent demonic aura.

"There's no need to look," the voice said with a chuckle. "You've been looking at me all this time..." The mountain trembled as the voice spoke. Sharp cracking sounds came from the mountain peak before them as rocks shifted into the shape of a face. "It's been far too long since you've visited, little rabbit," the mountain said. "To what do I owe the pleasure?"

"I'm afraid my visit won't be pleasurable in the least," Xiao Bai said grimly. She flicked out a jade slip that emanated inviolable power. "The time has come. I'm here to gather the earth source, including its core and its marrow."

The face remained unmoving for a few moments before speaking. "Very well," it said. "I have been waiting for this moment for ages. However, you must know that fiendish demons are gathering around the mountain. They are assaulting the barrier with strange means, and I believe that it's only a matter of time until they enter the safe zone. I must not be stopped as I harvest, and without my help, the jade mist's power is far from enough to stop them from ascending."

"We can stall them," Xiao Bai said. "On a side note, is it possible for my young friend here to use the ancestral altar?"

The mountain's gaze shifted and focused on Huxian. Its demonic energy surrounded the small fox and probed him. Huxian devoured it as soon as it intruded his personal space.

"I assume you are aware that most demons require a full year to complete an ancestral communion?" the mountain elemental said. "My harvesting will be complete within six months. I don't think it's a very wise decision to squander your one and only chance with insufficient time remaining."

"How hard could it be?" Huxian huffed. "I'm a Godbeast. An ancestral communion should be a piece of cake for me."

"Then proceed to the altar," the elemental said in its gravelly voice. A large crackle sounded as a fissure opened beside the face on the mountain. A dense purple mist oozed out from the fissure, which Huxian devoured as he entered. He walked forward cautiously against a blinding purple light that only grew brighter as he approached. Just when he thought that he couldn't take it anymore, his surroundings changed. He saw a large structure in the distance that was surrounded by a thick layer of purple mist. Despite being completely isolated from his friends, he could now see them faintly through the mountain walls. To his surprise, they were moving around much more quickly than before.

"Is this a time-delayed environment?" he wondered. As he spoke, a black-and-white mist appeared above the altar and congregated into the gigantic phantom of a black-and-white fox. It was unfathomably powerful, causing Huxian to tremble despite its weak presence. The fox had eight flowing tails, each with its own trigram. Further, its appearance was blurry and appeared to be present in eight places at once. The resulting image was that of a gigantic fox with sixty-four tails.

"Correct," the black-and-white fox said. "Descendant, you may call me Ancestor Hushao. As our descendants are few, only I, the founder of our bloodline, can appear for ancestral communion.

"The Ancestor?" Huxian said, gulping. "Great! Can we skip the test, then? I'm in a bit of a hurry, you see."

The giant fox's eight bodies laughed simultaneously. "In your dreams, little pup."

Ninety-nine circles materialized around the altar. Each one was composed of intricate runes. While he recognized the runes in the first sixty-six circles, as they pertained to light and darkness, the other thirty-three runic circles remained a mystery to him.

"To accept my inheritance, you must cross these runic circles and touch the altar. But be sure to hurry—you'll find that within this trial, time will slip through your claws like an intangible river. Only by transcending this river will you be qualified to accept my legacy."

The eight phantoms merged into one and lay down on the altar and began napping. Glancing hesitantly at his ancestor's imposing figure, Huxian firmed his resolve and charged into the first circle. He crossed it without any issues.

"Well, that was easy," Huxian said. He looked back, but to his surprise, the ninety-ninth line wasn't there. When he looked forward again, it had returned. "Well, phoenix turds," he said before charging in once more.

Hong Xin's fingers moved slowly as she played her red-and-gold flute, filling the room with a gentle melody. She did so as a dozen excited but worn-out students entered the room. They were the latest batch of new recruits, and she was to be their teacher. Although she was still technically a student, and her hairpin was red with four black stripes, she had sworn an oath with the headmistress. The cold woman had wasted no time in assigning her cruel new responsibilities.

As the students whispered, she continued playing. She played a calming music that dampened their expectations and caused them to hesitate. She observed them as she played and reviewed their information. Two dancers, three flutists, three zither players, and four singers. There were no *Angels and Devils* players like Bai Ling, but one of the dancers was unusual. She was a blade dancer, one who used her sword arts to mesmerize. Her eyes shone with a fierce fighting spirit, an unruly flame that would be difficult to douse.

She's the one, Hong Xin thought.

"How did you like my music?" Hong Xin asked them after some time. The students shifted uncomfortably, quietly discussing amongst themselves before one of the singers spoke up.

"It was wonderful," the student said. "I felt my anxious heart calm down as soon as I entered the room. Tell us the truth, did you bewitch us?"

Hong Xin smiled. "Call me Teacher Hong. And yes, I suppose I did. And how do you think I did it?"

The girl frowned. "It must take a fierce level of skill. And a great deal of passion and love toward your profession."

"You'd think that, wouldn't you?" Hong Xin said. "Truth be told, I've only played the flute for two years. Further, I'll tell you another secret." The students inched toward her. "I hate the flute." Her voice contained a powerful dousing force that extinguished the curiosity in their hearts. As her voice landed, ice-cold hooks dug into their foundations and caused them to shiver.

She held out the flute gingerly. "To control and manipulate a heart, one's own heart must first be cold and unfeeling. The first thing one must do is discard what they most love." She looked to the student who'd spoken. "As a singer, you must be very proud of your voice. However, this pride will prevent you from achieving your full potential. Xi Jia, your new hobby is dancing. You are now forbidden from singing."

Hong Xin tossed her a pair of ice-cold black-and-crimson slippers. She exerted her resplendent force, intimidating the student into wearing them. The moment she put them on, the seed of cold Hong Xin had planted activated and sent even more hooks and chains into her core. Her doubts began to multiply, and her expression became meek and subdued.

She moved from student to student until finally, she settled on the blade dancer. "You, Lan Ying, are outwardly strong. However, to pursue even greater ambition, one must first stifle her emotions. From now on, you are forbidden from dancing or practicing the sword. Furthermore, your new hobby is the flute."

Hong Xin summoned an icy black flute with crimson runes and handed it to Lan Ying, who struggled for a moment before ultimately accepting it. Unlike the others, her eyes were still defiant, despite her miserable situation. This wasn't surprising—she was the most talented student in the batch. "I will *personally* instruct you in playing the flute. It won't be long before your fiery little heart is as cold as mine."

Then, Hong Xin did something that Mistress Huang hadn't done. She sent out twelve balls of icy mist that plunged into these cultivators' spiritual seas, slightly freezing them over. Their eyes dulled as they complacently accepted their fate and filed out of the room on their own initiative.

"That was a very cruel thing you did," Mistress Huang said, walking out from a side of the stage. Hong Xin wasn't surprised by her appearance.

"It will help accelerate heart dousing and make them more compliant to orders," Hong Xin said dispassionately.

"But it will lessen their will," Mistress Huang said. "Although we want obedience, will and initiative are also important. Otherwise they will never be able to work independently when required."

Hong Xin shrugged. "If you disapprove of my methods, you may petition the headmistress," she said. "Without her direct order, I see no need to change my ways."

"I see," Mistress Huang said. "It seems I misjudged you. You're still just as full of fire as before. Which is strange, given your... condition."

Hong Xin's eyes flickered momentarily before regaining their focus. "Ambition is not prohibited by the headmistress. Rather, it's encouraged."

"Oh, I didn't mean ambition, my dear," Mistress Huang said. "I meant that, among the mistresses, not a single one dares to contradict what I say. It's a very interesting experience when someone talks back, especially when they've been through so much with me."

"Then perhaps everyone else's experience with you is different from mine," Hong Xin said. Then she looked toward the retreating students. "Don't worry about the results. I have everything under control."

"I hope so," Mistress Huang said. "If you don't, you'll find yourself the most pitiful mistress in the history of the Red Dust Pavilion." She then walked out of the performance hall, leaving Hong Xin standing on stage.

Hong Xin waited for a while before wiping the sweat from her brow. Despite the airs she'd put on, what she'd done to the students was extremely taxing. Not only had she infected their hearts with a seed of dousing, but she'd left a hidden surprise as well. And it wasn't leaving this surprise that was difficult but hiding it from the headmistress and Mistress Huang. If she wasn't careful, all the work she'd completed over the past few months would go to waste.

Silverwing let out a massive gust of wind as he flew overhead, slicing apart dozens of fiendish demons as they climbed the mountain. They made up for their weakness in the jade fog through sheer numbers. For every fiend he killed, two took its place. As another wave approached him, he let out a vicious caw. The sound waves traveled through the wind and ruptured the fiends' internal organs, leaving seemingly unharmed corpses to litter the mountain. Only a few dozen stronger monsters remained. Lei Jiang darted in, destroying these remnants with divine lightning.

Try as they might, however, their valiant efforts were nothing compared to Xiao Bai's fearsome presence. The demonic rabbit was the most vicious creature they had ever seen on the battlefield, wasting no time in biting through skulls to consume cores. She wasn't like this in the beginning, but her rage upon realizing that she'd broken her moon-cake-eating streak by accidentally devouring a demon whole hadn't yet subsided. Wherever she landed, a giant gray maelstrom of devouring energy spread out and consumed the surrounding fiendish demons to replenish her energy.

While the original members of the team took an active role in the battle, Gua played an insidious one. Pits of corrosive acid appeared throughout the battlefield, herding them into traps that reduced their movements and sapped their strength. Instead of killing fiends directly, he simply made everyone else's job easier. They weren't fooled by this false show of subservience, however, as they made sure to remind them of his contributions at every opportunity.

"Their attacks are getting more and more frequent," Silverwing shouted from above. "We need to cede this first outpost or they'll rush past us toward the mountain elemental." The fiendish demons were now attacking in irregular but organized waves. Their numbers had reached a critical mass where they could dictate the rhythm of the battle.

"Withdraw!" Xiao Bai shouted.

Silverwing, Lei Jiang, Gua, and Xiao Bai used their superior speed to zip past intercepting parties of fiends, cutting through them like blocks of tofu. They ceded one third of the mountain's height, but in the process, they greatly diminished the amount of land they had to guard. Up at the one-third mark, they were joined by smaller mountain elementals, the "children" of the ancient existence at the peak. They threw boulders and directed gravitational fields to suppress the opposing beasts, making it impossible for them to take to the skies.

"Silverwing, I think boss needs a hand," Lei Jiang shouted. The formation surrounding him glowed and drained his strength, diminishing his combat prowess by fifty percent.

"I told him he can take half for now, but he needs to give it back later," Silverwing said. "The earlier he comes back, the better."

"Can't he take care of his own ancestral communion?" Xiao Bai said. "What a wimp."

"He told me his ancestor is pretty unreasonable," Silverwing said. "Apparently, time decelerated by five times for him," he added. "No, make that six now."

"He's still a wimp," Xiao Bai reiterated. Yet a glimmer of worry appeared in her eyes as she redoubled her efforts. She was fully aware that as the devil sovereign's other missions wrapped up, increasing amounts of manpower would become available to supplement their siege.

The first thirty-three were hard, but this is just ridiculous, Huxian thought as he dashed through various illusory formations. As he ran, worlds of light and shadow intermingled. He sometimes split into light and dark clones and sometimes recombined, fully using his instinctual understanding of light and darkness to his advantage.

Unfortunately, it had become extremely difficult for him to progress further. The illusory world projected an intense suppression on him, making it necessary to draw on Silverwing and Lei Jiang's power to increase his own. His speed increased accordingly, and he now crossed two rings in the time it took to cross one.

"An interesting technique," Bagua Hushao said suddenly. "Borrowing the power of your generals to bolster your own. But I wonder how long they'll be able to hold out with their drained abilities?"

A projection of Xiao Bai, Silverwing, Gua, and Lei Jiang appeared. Seeing that their relatively accelerated figures were barely able to hold on, he eased on his power draw slightly, enabling them to barely overpower their opponents.

Seeing Huxian's reaction, Bagua Hushao grinned. "I predict you'll be able to borrow their power for ten of their days. Then you can drain them dry and finish the test in one fell swoop. What a meticulous plan."

Huxian didn't reply. Instead he ate a moon cake and pressed on with everything he had. His friends' lives depended on it.

Chapter 31: Game

An intricate pattern appeared in the air, a continuous bright green string filled with the vitality of a world tree. Simply being in the same room as the Wood Source Marrow caused Cha Ming to feel invigorated, and it was even more so when converted into runes. These marrow-refining runes caused the space around them to distort as they expressed their sovereignty over the world.

Only a few days passed before the lengthy string of script ended with a small dot. Then the 1,080-character-long script of Wood Source Marrow burst apart and dove into Cha Ming's bones, where they began infusing them with endless vitality. His marrow took on a green hue as its properties fundamentally changed. It rapidly began producing new blood, which immediately flowed through his body and enhanced his senses and his regenerative abilities. His physical prowess went above and beyond what had already been granted by the Jade Moon Blessing, something he hadn't thought possible.

The wood-based runes had barely used up any of their power by refining his marrow. After accomplishing this preliminary task, they immediately dove into the small voids in his bones, entering the seemingly endless space where Cha Ming drew his additional mass. A portion of the vitality was absorbed by the small worlds that had sprung up in the void, while the rest began floating around in the blackness of space as an endless green mist. Strange plantlike runes began growing on the worlds. Then they began dying off one by one, only to be absorbed by the others. They split in turn and continued the cycle.

With this transformation, Cha Ming's regenerative abilities greatly increased. Hidden injuries in his organs healed while tiny imperfections in his body were automatically fixed. His strength remained unchanged, however, as it was still being blessed by Jade Moon Planet. But his regenerative abilities weren't part of this blessing, and these saw a substantial increase. Previously, a sharp gash or stab would be healed in a matter of breaths, but now, having his hand hacked off wasn't a serious issue. But Cha Ming wasn't satisfied with this development. He immediately retrieved the Fire Source Marrow and began writing out a fiery script.

Ruby runes of burning vitality flowed from the Clear Sky Brush, forming a complementary script that was independent of the original wood one. He built up the ruby script in increments of 120 runes, infusing it with the power of runic fragments he'd learned on the Bridge of Stars.

A few days passed before finally, the script was completed. The 1,080 lava runes rushed into his bones and refined his marrow once more. Green coexisted with red and further enhanced his senses. The fire runes then followed the wood runes' lead and traveled into the void. A red mist spread out through space while fire runes appeared on the various worlds. His blood boiled and seethed as his marrow replaced the old inefficient fluid, strengthening his body once again. As his strength increased, the blessing decreased. With his newfound vitality, he discovered that even if he lost a leg, it would completely recover within seconds.

Then, within the voids in his bones, a new form of life took shape. This time, it was a life of fire and ashes. Flame runes lit up and extinguished with each passing moment, creating an endless cycle in this world of wood and flame. Fire then mixed with wood, creating a tenuous balance favoring the fire element. Yet the overall vitality in the universe was greater with this union than it was beforehand.

Finally, after completing these two marrow-refining steps, Cha

Ming left his small dwelling in the woods, where Yu Wen was waiting for him near a calm lake.

"Can we finally go now?" Yu Wen said, letting the ball of water she'd been playing with rain over the rocky beach.

"We can go," Cha Ming said. "Huxian ran into some trouble, so I needed to prepare for eventualities. Even if we can't leave the shield, who knows what we'll have to face." He gave Yu Wen an apologetic smile and held out his hand. Yu Wen took it, and together, they walked toward a nearby waterfall.

Thousands of cultivators meditated beneath it, flew before it, and bathed in the river above it. But Yu Wen and Cha Ming's goal was neither of these—instead it was the fish swimming in the humid air above them. Each fish was only three feet long, and their bodies were covered in iridescent scales.

"I've heard the nearby cultivators whisper that it's impossible to touch them," Cha Ming said. "The moment one gets close, the fish burns its blood essence to turn into a rainbow and escape back to their nest at the back of the waterfall."

"That's because they're scared of being eaten," Yu Wen said. "But if you know their secret, they'll let you touch them. And if you can touch them, they'll reward you with a single scale."

"Are the scales useful?" Cha Ming asked.

"They're a transcendent-grade mediating agent for alchemy," Yu Wen said. "There are many buyers but hardly any sellers. Many alchemists would trade a small fortune for a single one, as they greatly increase the concoction rate for pills up to and including transcendent grade."

"Then by all means, convince them," Cha Ming said, motioning toward the small school of 100 fish.

Yu Wen smiled and floated toward them. Then she yelled at them in a voice that carried across the river and waterfall area. "Flying friends, let's play a game!" she yelled.

The school of fish immediately stopped and looked toward her. A small fish that measured two feet at most swam before them as their representative.

"What kind of game, and what are the stakes?" the fish asked haughtily. Its companions whispered excitedly as Yu Wen pulled out an herb-gathering token.

"We'll play a game of chicks and eagles," Yu Wen said. "Fish are the chicks, and humans are the eagles. Our buy-in is one herb-gathering quota for a week of play, but for every chick we catch, the eagles will take two scales."

Several larger fish huddled around the small one. A moment later, the small fish popped out. "We can do one scale, with the falls as the playing field. Two scales are too many. "

"Then in that case, we want the herb-gathering quota to be refundable," Yu Wen said. "Any eagle who catches a chick will get their quota back, and you're not to use blood-escaping arts."

"Blood-escaping arts are banned, of course, but non-players have to vacate the field," the fish said. "Lethal techniques or strikes are forbidden. Only clean touches count."

"It's a deal," Yu Wen said. A mass of green vines burst out of the surrounding water and land, creating a thorny fence. A booming voice spoke to the nearby cultivators. It was the wood elemental's voice, a voice filled with boundless authority.

"All cultivators, either provide your wagers or vacate the premises," the elemental said.

The cultivators, with their sharp senses, had naturally heard what transpired. Many of them gritted their teeth and left, as they had already used all their gathering quotas. A few thousand, however, remained in the fenced-off area. A jade token flew out from each of their bags of holding onto an outstretched green wooden table.

"The wagers are set," the elemental said. "Are the chicks ready?"

"We're ready!" the smallest fish said.

"Are the eagles ready?" the elemental's voice boomed. The cultivators nodded and assumed fighting poses. "Then begin!"

The rainbow fish instantly spread out across the chaotic battlefield. Some flew in the air while others dove into the water. The smallest fish, however, flew tauntingly close to Cha Ming and Yu Wen.

Cha Ming and Yu Wen grinned as they jointly rushed at him, diving through the throngs of cultivators to catch the little miscreant. Yu Wen threw out solid silver strings that formed multiple snares along the fish's pathway. It lazily dodged her techniques but narrowly avoided a small ice wall erected by Cha Ming at the other end. Cha Ming rushed to catch it but was interrupted by another cultivator's movements. They both scowled as they realized that their respective chicks had cooperated to evade them.

Cha Ming looked back to discover that Yu Wen had given up their pursuit midway to catch another fish in passing. She held a small rainbow scale in her right hand. Her token also flew back from the green wooden table and into her bag.

"Let's see how many of you can escape," she said, pulling Cha Ming alongside her to execute their next tactic. They laughed as they evaded countless tricks, decoys, and teamwork. Their own teamwork progressed by leaps and bounds as they played.

Six days came and went. During this time, Cha Ming and Yu Wen had captured a total of seventy-eight scales. Although to them, the game was easy, few other cultivators felt this way. Out of the few thousand of them, only two thousand scales had been secured by perhaps two hundred individuals. They could only hopelessly chase after the mocking fish, who clearly reveled in this gambling game.

"It's getting more and more difficult," Cha Ming said as they flew down to the base of the waterfall.

"That's because we've run out of tricks, silly," Yu Wen said. "They never fall for the same one twice. I'd say it's a miracle we've caught so many scales."

"Formations and talismans are good for variation, if anything," Cha Ming said cheerfully. As he spoke, he looked toward a few dozen cultivators that had recently allied themselves against the fish. Their means were growing increasingly sophisticated, and it was only a matter of time until a fish was caught.

Suddenly, Cha Ming spotted a glint of gold as a flying sword stabbed toward a flying fish. It tried to evade the strike, but the sword managed to sneak past its defenses and slash its side. Dozens of blood-soaked scales flew out from the wound and were caught by a smiling cultivator. "That doesn't count, give them back," the fish yelled.

The cultivator shook his head. "It wasn't a lethal strike at all," he said. "But if you're so stingy, I won't quibble with you. There's no need for you to *give* me any scales. I'll take them myself." His sword struck out once again, wounding yet another fish. This time, Cha Ming ignored the spray of blood and scales and focused on the cultivator's aura.

"He's using a transcendent weapon infused with immortal jade," Cha Ming said. "How dirty."

Yu Wen frowned as well. "They signed up for a game, not to get hurt. This guy is skirting the rules. If things keep going this way, the fish will never want to play with humans again. It's like killing the chicken that lays golden eggs."

Cha Ming looked at the glittering scales in his hand. "I feel a bit bad for ripping them off. How about we repay the favor?" He didn't have a good impression of the aggressive cultivator. Although it wasn't thick, a light-yellow aura hovered around the man in sharp contrast to the predominantly meritous cultivators.

"Be careful," Yu Wen said. "A transcendent weapon is no laughing matter."

Cha Ming nodded and flew up to the cultivator, who'd just finished sending out his sword for the third time. "That's about enough, don't you think?" he said. "The fish are scared, and you're ruining this for everyone."

The cultivator looked at Cha Ming coldly. "You'd best mind your own business," he said. "You might be a prodigy in herbology, but that means nothing in the cultivation world."

"And you might have a transcendent weapon, but many others

do as well," Cha Ming said. "I know of at least a half dozen others who've refrained from using theirs. The fish are playing a game, not fighting."

As he spoke, Zhang Fei and the others approached from a distance. They had been avoiding Cha Ming and Yu Wen to give them some personal space.

"Let's see if you can stop me, then," the cultivator said, smiling wickedly. "Slaughter is forbidden in Jade Moon Garden. You might be able to block me a few times, but can you keep doing it?"

His sword flashed toward the two-foot fish. Cha Ming's eyes narrowed, and he summoned his Clear Sky Staff and struck out with Splitting the Heavens. The staff screamed as it rushed to the sword like a predator. The white blade of wind struck the sword and bounced it back. Transcendent power oozed out of the blue metal sword through a small nick as it limped back to its pale-faced owner.

"You broke my weapon!" the cultivator exclaimed.

"You threw it out when I warned you," Cha Ming said.

"Let's see you block this one!" the cultivator yelled furiously. The sword left his grip once more. This time, however, it headed straight for Cha Ming, its aura chaotic. Although its exterior was fine, Cha Ming knew that the Clear Sky Staff had completely damaged its internals.

A feeling of dread overcame Cha Ming as the weapon inched closer. He quickly realized his opponent's intent.

He wants to detonate his useless weapon and try to cripple me? Cha Ming thought. Although killing someone was forbidden, maiming them was not. *Fortunately, I'm not other cultivators. But isn't this guy a little crazy? Doesn't he realize the collateral damage he'll cause?*

Cha Ming quickly rushed forward and spread out his Dao sigils, encapsulating the weapon in an inward-facing shield. He then reached out with his hand and grasped the blade. Small cracks appeared on his bones, which were as hard as half-step-transcendent treasures. He quickly sent his resplendent force out like a sharp blade, aiming to sever his opponent's connection with his weapon.

"You fool!" the man yelled. Just as Cha Ming's blade was about to sever the man's connection to his weapon, his opponent decisively caused it to detonate. Instead of retracting his hand, as any sane cultivator would, Cha Ming held firm and fortified the Dao sigil shield, containing the explosion around his arm. Cha Ming screamed as his bones shattered and his nerves severed, leaving him with only a short stump attached to his forearm. The explosion, which should have encompassed hundreds of cultivators and fifty or so fish, stopped just short of the two-foot rainbow fish.

Yu Wen rushed over to Cha Ming and supported him as his stump rapidly regenerated, to the amazement of the other cultivators. The crazed cultivator had already left during the explosion, burning his blood essence to quickly escape the premises.

"I wonder what got into him?" Cha Ming muttered as his friends rushed over to check on him. He clenched his fist and circulated his qi, confirming that the new hand was fully functional.

"The same thing that always happens," Yu Wen said sadly. "Jade Moon Garden is no longer safe. The devil sovereign may not even need to break the shield to accomplish his objectives."

"What *are* his objectives?" Cha Ming asked.

Yu Wen simply sighed and flew toward the huddled group of fish. Everyone had long since stopped playing. The vine fencing retreated, and the tokens flew from the table and back to the cultivators.

"Our school is tired, so we no longer wish to play this game," the two-foot fish said. "Your fee is refunded, and you may all leave." Although the fish hadn't asked for the scales back, the cultivators all shifted uncomfortably. "You, staff wielder and friends," the fish continued. "You're all invited back to our nest as guests. Unlike most humans, us rainbow fish return kindness with kindness. You saved many in our school, so we are in your debt."

Although the many cultivators envied Cha Ming and his companions, they could only blame themselves for not intervening. They wandered off in shame as six humans followed hundreds of fish through the rainbow-colored falls and into one of Jade Moon Garden's forbidden zones.

Gong Ying gasped in pain as the side effects of burning his blood essence kicked in. "It shouldn't have gone this way," he whispered. "I should have been able to gather eighty-one scales without a problem."

You were too hasty, a voice whispered inside his mind. *The boy was brave and acted quickly.*

"I'll make that bastard pay," he spat. "I only have sixty-two scales. I can't get any more."

Sixty-two glimmering scales floated up from his hand and entered a crack in the void. A short moment later, a silver sword emanating transcendent might slipped through the crack.

"This isn't what we agreed on," Gong Ying said.

It's a partial reward for partial completion, the voice said. *I have one last job if you're interested. If you succeed, I'll reward you with a Saint Ascension Vine, as per our original deal.*

"What's the job?" Gong Ying said. Although he was bitter about the partial reward, the transcendent weapon was a timely replacement.

It's more dangerous than the last one, but you'll have company, the voice said. *And as a completion bonus, I swear on my very soul that should you accomplish this objective, all of you need not worry about the fiendish demons on Jade Moon Planet. These devils will disappear and never return.*

"I'm listening," the man said, kicking his lips. Although he didn't care about the other cultivators on the planet, he didn't mind being karmically owed.

Chapter 32: Hope

Rainbow-colored light filled the hallway as Cha Ming and the others followed the school of tired-looking fish. As they walked, the normally water-flooded corridor drained away, making the atmosphere much more comfortable for the human guests. The absence of water caused the light to reflect off the hall's crystalline walls even more brightly than they would have underwater. It was a sight that no humans had seen for millennia.

"Our ancestor was a good friend of the Jade Emperor," the two-foot fish explained. "Though it wasn't always that way. The first time they met, he caught her in a net and wanted to feed her to a crowd of hungry humans. Therefore, she made a deal with the budding new emperor. In exchange for sparing her, she would gift him with a special underwater herb that would be beneficial to humanity's cultivators. After completing their exchange, they didn't meet for ten thousand years."

"How did they meet again?" Cha Ming asked.

"In the most unusual circumstances," the fish replied. "An invasive species of aquatic fiendish demons had decided to displace her and devour her young. The Jade Emperor, who happened to be fishing not too far away, saw what was happening. He helped her evade the calamity without a second thought. When she asked him why, he said that her gift had saved countless lives, and he was simply repaying the favor. Our ancestor then struck a deal with him. Us rainbow fish would tend to some natural sea herbs in exchange for protection. The Jade Emperor readily agreed, and the rest is history."

The long crystalline hallway continued for a full nine miles before finally opening into a large cavern. Rainbow fish measuring only a few inches long swam around joyfully. Larger fish known as teachers tended to these young fish, raising them to become productive members of the school. The students were required to attend every day while the teachers drilled them on various subjects like ethics and the Dao.

As they traveled, Cha Ming looked around curiously. Though every rainbow fish was iridescent, the glow in the cavern was much more intense than their relatively dull colorings. Further, the crystals in the cavern were clear. After looking for a quarter hour, Cha Ming finally spotted what looked like a small fenced garden. A few thin strands of iridescent seaweed grew there under the care of watchful rainbow fish. The weeds glowed like incandescent lightbulbs, bringing light to what would have otherwise been a dark cave.

"Please follow me and don't touch anything," the two-foot fish said. "Mother doesn't like it when people disturb the nest."

They followed him into a small passage that continued for five hundred feet, opening up into a small cavern measuring barely a hundred feet in diameter. There, a fifty-foot rainbow fish was carefully inspecting a nest of small transparent spheres.

"We've arrived, Mother," the two-foot fish said respectfully. The large rainbow fish smiled and reduced in size. She made loud clicking sounds, after which dozens of fish filed into the room with small stools and a large table. They also placed large bowls and chopsticks on the table before retreating, leaving only the two-foot fish and its mother.

"Thank you so much for saving my Yu Gen and the others," the large fish said. "My name is Yu Ma, and I am the mother of all the rainbow fish on Jade Moon Planet."

"It was convenient to act, so we did," Cha Ming said. "We don't deserve any heavy praise."

"Alas, if only everyone thought so," Yu Ma said. "Inaction and indifference are far too common, even for those with merit glow. In a way, the greatest evil is indifference to the suffering of others."

She flicked her fin, and hundreds of rainbow scales flew off her body and floated before them. Cha Ming grabbed what looked like five hundred scales. He noticed that his pile was significantly larger than the others.

"This is my first gift to you," Yu Ma said. "Although it's inconvenient to shed these scales, they are very useful to human alchemists. I hope these will help you obtain what you need to transcend."

She then flicked her fin once more, and a few strands of the iridescent sea herb Cha Ming had seen outside landed in each of their bowls. A stream of hot water floated up from a nearby basin and entered the bowls, which began emanating a pleasant aroma. The broth was covered in a sheen of rainbow-colored oil.

"This is my second gift," Yu Ma said. "Please drink, and you'll understand the value of this gift."

Cha Ming picked up his bowl and sipped. The moment he did, a warm current gushed through his throat and entered his dantian. The rainbow-colored energy reached the center of his core and formed a small gray sphere. It didn't grow as he drank—rather, it became increasingly dense.

As he finished his noodles, he looked around the table and saw Grandmist Essence congregating around everyone in a thick gray cloud. Yu Ma refilled their bowls as they finished them, and they continued eating until the Grandmist no longer congregated.

The Grandmist Essence is beneficial to rune carving, Yu Wen sent. *When carving runes, every cultivator must borrow the mortal plane's Grandmist Essence. Having this reserve allows the cultivator to supplement it, therefore obtaining the plane's favor. Since the cultivator must no longer wrestle with the plane's will, the process is much more likely to succeed.*

Once everyone had finished, Yu Ma whisked the bowls away. The dozens of fish swarmed into the room at Yu Gen's direction and took away the stools and table, leaving them sitting cross-legged before the large fish.

"Your final reward is a consultation on the Dao," Yu Ma said. "Each of you may ask me questions about cultivation. Whatever gains you can consolidate are up to you." A moment later, Cha Ming saw Han Jiling close his eyes. He was clearly conversing with Yu Ma. Seeing that she was occupied, Cha Ming sat in silence, as he was unable to cultivate.

"You may ask your questions," a voice suddenly said from within his spiritual sea. Cha Ming directed his attention to his transcendent soul. A large fish floated before him, and in front of the fish, the projection of a beautiful woman with rainbow-colored hair appeared.

"I heard from Yu Wen that the soup you fed us is useful to rune carving," Cha Ming said. "Unfortunately, it will be difficult to reach that stage with my core like it is." Using a modicum of mental energy, he summoned the projection of an eight-colored sphere. Many cracks littered its surface.

The woman shook her head. "I truly don't know how to help you," she said. "Perhaps only the Sacred Jade Library holds a solution to your problem. That, or you could obtain a Saint Ascension Vine. To my knowledge, there are no other ways to fix your core."

"I thought so," Cha Ming said, sighing. "I really wonder what I did to deserve this. This karma thing isn't all it's cracked up to be."

"Is that how you think karma works?" Yu Ma said. "Then let me tell you a story to shed some light on the situation." She held out the palm of her hand, and images appeared within Cha Ming's spiritual sea. "There was once a virtuous man. He did good to all those around him, and in reciprocity, everyone treated him well. Whenever anyone asked him about the source of his success, he attributed it to helping his community, doing good deeds, and his faith in god.

"Truth be told, he'd accrued enough merit for angelic endowment," Yu Ma said. "But things weren't meant to be so simple for him."

The man's wealth, business empire, and family appeared on the palm of her hand. Then, one by one, they were burned to ashes until only he himself remained. He'd lost an arm and a leg and was on the verge of death. "Reality can be quite cruel. Do you know how the story ended?"

"It seems I've heard this story before," Cha Ming replied. "The man maintained his faith in God and regained everything he lost. This was all just a test of his faith."

"That's a children's story," Yu Ma said. "The true story is far different. He died a lonely wretch, yet he maintained his faith. The karma he accrued in this life could not be returned, so it materialized in his next life, granting him a fortunate foundation for spiritual growth. Unfortunately, he squandered it and became just another mundane character in the cycle of reincarnation."

"I'm not sure what you're getting at," Cha Ming said.

"Good things often happen to good people, Cha Ming," Yu Ma said. "But sometimes, karma just isn't powerful enough to help. Bad things happen to good people too, and that's life. In this web of karma, free will still exists. Misfortune might strike good people less often, but it still strikes. Otherwise, how could anyone possibly make choices? This variance is a consequence of free will.

"Therefore, the results are less important. The man might have lost everything and been crippled, but he kept his faith. He died a happy man, Cha Ming. Your situation is much better than his, so there's no point in feeling bitter. Keep your chin up and keep looking for a way. Live your life to its fullest, and don't blame karma for anything that happens. There are many beautiful things in life, so it would be a pity to miss them all to dwell on something so obscure as karma and fate."

Cha Ming paused for a moment as he adjusted his outlook. *Yes, if bad things didn't happen to good people, choice would be nothing more than an illusion,* he thought. "Thank you," he said.

"It's my pleasure," Yu Ma replied. Her incarnation left Cha Ming's soul. He opened his eyes and noticed that only he and Yu Wen were awake. The others were all deep in meditation. Seeing Yu Ma ignoring them and tending to her eggs, Cha Ming and Yu Wen bowed and made their way out of the cave and into the main cavern.

"Did you find what you were looking for?" Yu Wen asked.

"More or less," Cha Ming said. "But enough about that. We have a vacation ahead of us. There's no sense in worrying about anything else."

"Good!" Yu Wen said, grabbing his hand. "Let's leave the others here. I want to take you to a special place."

Moments later, they left the rainbow falls and flew toward the setting sun.

The last ray of daylight faded over the horizon as they arrived at a large forest filled with five-hundred-foot trees. Their giant, leaf-filled branches were large enough to completely obscure the land below from the sun and moon. Therefore, only mushrooms grew in the dark underbrush. They glowed light blue, illuminating the dark forest with a dull, eerie light.

A large deer appeared before them as they walked. It charged toward them, but as Cha Ming moved to dodge it, Yu Wen firmly gripped his hand. To his surprise, the deer passed straight through him.

"This is the Illusory Forest," Yu Wen said. "It's easy to get lost here while we walk. That's why, as real as these illusions seem, you need to ignore them and follow my lead." As she spoke, a herd of deer appeared behind the lone one and charged through them once more. This time, Cha Ming relaxed and closed his eyes. He simply followed Yu Wen as she guided him, completely trusting her directions. Hours passed in the darkness, with nothing more to lead him than Yu Wen's warm touch. Still, that didn't stop the many sounds he heard from tickling his imagination as they walked.

Suddenly, Cha Ming heard the rustle of many feet—human feet. He opened his eyes and saw twenty cultivators appear from the nearby woods. One of them looked familiar. He was the same cultivator who had attacked the rainbow fish. Although he thought to dismiss it as an illusion, both Yu Wen's actions and his instincts screamed that it wasn't.

"To what do we owe the pleasure?" Cha Ming said, stepping between the twenty cultivators and Yu Wen.

"It's nothing personal," Gong Yin said, drawing a peak-core treasure from his bag of holding. Several others followed suit. "You are free to go, but the girl has to stay."

Cha Ming's eyes narrowed. "I'm afraid that won't be possible. And I guarantee you that if you all choose to fight here, more than one of you will die." He summoned his Clear Sky Staff, which caused his opponents' weapons to let out hums of submission. These hums were soon quelled by their owners, who wrestled control away from him.

"You should go," Yu Wen said, surprising Cha Ming. "Their means are too powerful. I'll just drag you down."

A golden sword appeared before her. To Cha Ming's surprise, it was a soul-bound treasure. Including her cloak, she'd revealed a total of three soul-bound treasures thus far.

Cha Ming shook his head. "That's not how this sort of relationship works. I'm afraid I can't grant you your request." A thousand and eighty Dao sigils spread out around them, forming a protective shield of ice and snow. It rapidly grew and encompassed the twenty surrounding cultivators.

"Use everything you have to kill her," Gong Yin shouted. "Ignore the boy."

The twenty cultivators shouted in acknowledgement and began forming hand seals. An ominous aura gathered around them and funneled into three apparitions. These apparitions each wielded transcendent weapons and exuded a pressure that far exceeded the peak of core formation. The surrounding 100 feet shimmered and distorted as the natural laws were forcefully wrestled away from Jade Moon Planet.

"As I suspected, he found a way inside the shield," Yu Wen said, sighing. "These apparitions are too powerful for us. We need to run our separate ways. I'll distract them while you escape."

"I told you, it doesn't work that way," Cha Ming said. His face paled as the three apparitions' auras weighed down on him. He could barely hold on with the help of the Clear Sky Staff. As he converged his power and restored mobility to his limbs, the twenty cultivators surrounding them drew out long chains. They spread out around them and formed a circle, a deadly arena for them and the apparitions who'd just appeared. They rushed out with spears, sabers, and axes.

Seeing their approach, Cha Ming intensified his ice and snow formations, slowing their speed by half. He poured his creation and metal qi into the Clear Sky Staff and traced a white arc in the air. A horizontal line appeared and pushed back the three apparitions. White chains materialized from the white line and shackled them. Seeing an opportunity, Cha Ming grabbed Yu Wen by the hand and pulled her toward them. They ducked and weaved through the three apparitions, who shattered the white chains and threw out their weapons. They dodged, only to discover five cultivators' weapons flying toward them.

Five transcendent weapons? Cha Ming thought. *How?* Their original group might have obtained five transcendent weapons, but as far as he knew, this level of weapon was extremely scarce amongst those who'd finally arrived at Jade Moon Planet. Most sects weren't willing to send these precious treasures away from their mortal plane, preferring to use them to keep their home worlds safe.

Cha Ming deflected a saber and a sword with his Clear Sky Staff. Meanwhile, Yu Wen's golden sword cut a short arc, smashing through an axe before deflecting a second one. The fifth weapon, a thick staff, stopped just short of Yu Wen. A net of silver strings appeared, distorting and bending before finally breaking. Cha Ming quickly pulled Yu Wen out of the line of fire. He then threw out a Flow Talisman, causing the surrounding air to thicken and congeal around their enemies.

They kicked off together and rushed toward Gong Yin, who was linked to the twenty other cultivators with black chains. Cha Ming poured five-element qi into his staff and condensed it on a central point. He stabbed toward Gong Yin, who threw up a black talisman. A black runic shield appeared. As powerful as it was, however, it shattered under Cha Ming's Origin Strike. A point of gray stabbed through it and into Gong Yin's chest. A bloody hole appeared but was quickly regenerated as vital energy flew in from the black chains.

"Why do you defend her?" Gong Yin said spat. "If it wasn't for her, the devil sovereign wouldn't even be here. We could have gone through Jade Moon Planet's trial as we always have. Instead, a hundred times more people have died. The mortal realms have lost countless elite cultivators, all because of this one girl."

Doubts began to creep inside Cha Ming's mind. He thought about the intense chase with the devilish cultivators. Then he thought about her three soul-bound treasures. Then, seeing the rapidly approaching apparitions, he threw a Matter Talisman on his chest. It banished his doubts, enabling him to recognize the telltale signs of a curse.

It doesn't matter why the devils are here, Cha Ming decided. *If I save Yu Wen now, I can worry about the rest later.* As hope filled him, he pulled Yu Wen behind him and blocked three transcendent treasures with his Clear Sky Staff. His arms trembled but held strong as they pushed toward the circle of chains.

Cha Ming, I'll make an opening for you to escape, but I'll be greatly weakened, Yu Wen sent. *They're right. It's all my fault. If I die, everything will return to normal. You won't have to run or fight for your life, and everyone on Jade Moon Planet will survive.*

He looked toward her in shock. Her eyes were filled with tears as she shone with a gray light that poured into her golden sword. The sword disappeared before nine replicas reappeared in front of her. They focused on Gong Yin, who was still recovering from his wounds.

The surroundings seemed to freeze as all nine swords stabbed into the air around him. Runic lines spread like cracks in reality itself. They spread outward and toward the center, breaking apart Gong Yin and his weapon piece by piece. Yet only Cha Ming and Yu Wen could see this. While time wasn't frozen around them, the cultivators and the three devilish apparitions were moving impossibly slow. A few breaths passed before finally, a black hole appeared at the boundary of the circle.

Run, Yu Wen sent before collapsing. As she did, time began to accelerate around him while the hole began to close.

Silly girl, Cha Ming thought. He grabbed Yu Wen by the waist and ducked through the opening. It closed behind him, and he found himself five hundred feet away.

The moment he appeared, a giant green fist struck down on the circle like a hand of judgment. It crushed the cultivators and the three apparitions. Cha Ming didn't stay to observe their fate, and he rushed through the illusory woods. The scenery changed rapidly. One moment he was in a frozen tundra, and another he was charging into the maw of a dragon. He ignored everything despite the trembling in his soul. It struggled to hold on as his Clear Sky Brush constantly fed it with a stream of white healing light.

An unknown amount of time passed before they finally arrived at a small pond in a clearing. Seeing that no dangers were present, Cha Ming placed Yu Wen on the ground. Barely any color remained on her face. While her soul was strong, her heart was beating weakly. Seeing this, Cha Ming swiftly set up a wood-based vitality formation. Vines appeared around him and fed the formation, supplementing it.

"Thank you, Senior Elemental," he said before sitting cross-legged and focusing on the Myriad Truths Diagram.

Yu Wen's health continuously diminished. Three days passed until only a small spark of life remained within her frail body. At this moment, Cha Ming gained some insights and integrating water elements into the vitality formation. One hundred and twenty green sigils turned blue, and her condition stabilized. This was good enough for Cha Ming, who redoubled his efforts on studying the Myriad Truths Diagram.

Although I know nothing about life and death, I can use what I know to strengthen this vitality formation, Cha Ming thought. *Just now, I incorporated my knowledge of flow. Life isn't stagnant but flowing. I should be able to fuse this with the other elements.*

One week passed before 120 of the remaining green sigils turned gold. Further, the runic array rearranged itself in a particular shape. The flowing vitality inside Yu Wen reorganized itself into an optimal formation, increasing slightly.

While life has a flow, it also has shape and structure, Cha Ming thought. *Further, flow also has shape. Together, they create a framework that supports health.*

Yet another week passed before Cha Ming opened his eyes once more. One hundred and twenty sigils had turned brown, and her vitality stiffened. It gained substance and weight, a material resilience that was difficult to break. It was followed by yet another change from green to red. Energy spread throughout the formation and stimulated key points on Yu Wen's body. A healthy glow returned to her cheeks.

Her vitality began to climb, but just as quickly as it started, it stalled. Cha Ming probed her body and discovered nothing wrong. He directed his resplendent force to her spiritual sea, which immediately rejected him.

"Do you really want to die that badly?" he whispered. "Then forgive me for being selfish." Memories flashed through his mind. He thought of Yu Wen's gentle support and understanding. He thought of all the help she'd lent him, and the guidance she'd given him as he struggled to save the Monkey King. Every step of the way, he'd felt unconditional love and support. As they'd journeyed together, his feelings had evolved from a single emotional spark to a healthy fire.

As these thoughts swirled around in his mind, he poured them into his talismans. Shape, Material, Flow, and Kindling Talismans activated around Yu Wen's body and poured into her soul.

"You told me that doubt was the greatest enemy of good," Cha Ming said. "Please don't give up now. Even if things seem bleak, there's always a light at the end of the tunnel."

The energy in the talismans poured into Yu Wen's soul, and as they did, he felt her spiritual sea mollify. Then, little by little, her body's energy recovered. The glow returned, and her heart started beating again. The small spark of vitality began spreading throughout her limbs like a wildfire until finally, she opened her eyes. Seeing Cha Ming's exhausted figure, she smiled and pulled him by the robes and pressed his lips against hers.

As their intimacy continued, a green figure withdrew his vines and left the nearby woods to grant them privacy.

Chapter 33: The Promise

You're still in the mood for sightseeing after everything we've been through?" Cha Ming said as they made their way through the woods.

The illusory phantoms no longer hounded them but were now stranded behind an invisible boundary. The woods grew sparser, and they soon heard the sounds of trickling water up ahead. The scent of sulfur tickled his nose as they approached small pool in an open clearing. The sky above was free of clouds, the woods parting conveniently to reveal a symphony of stars.

"The first time I came to Jade Moon Garden, it was my birthday," Yu Wen said as she led him to the edge. "My father asked me what I wanted for a present, and I told him I wanted the warmth of the earth and the stars in the sky. After thinking about it for a few moments, he brought me here to this secluded hot spring. He cleared the surrounding trees and set down an illusory formation to protect it from intruders. From then on, no one could find it without my permission."

Yu Wen walked into the water and pulled Cha Ming down with her. The water was shallow, coming only halfway up Cha Ming's chest.

"He was right to choose this place," Cha Ming said, looking up. "The stars are beautiful, and the hot spring serene."

"That won't last much longer," Yu Wen said wistfully. "It never does."

Cha Ming hesitated for a moment before asking the question that gnawed at him most. "The cultivators, why were they chasing after you? And why were the fiendish demons and devils near the volcano pursuing you as well?"

"You must also want to know why I have three soul-bound treasures," Yu Wen said. "It's a bit of a long story."

"I have time," Cha Ming said. "I want to help you, but I can't do that unless I know what we're up against."

Yu Wen sighed before pushing herself backward. She floated through the water until she was stopped by a small outcropping in the shape of a chair. Cha Ming joined her in a similar rock formation just a few feet away.

"It's been this way as long as I can remember," Yu Wen said. "I've always been affected by something my father called a blessing. I call it a curse. You see, all the good people around me are lucky. They'll find random money, they'll make surprise breakthroughs, and they'll obtain lucky chances."

"That's hardly what I'd call a curse," Cha Ming said.

"That's only one side of the coin," Yu Wen replied. "The other half is that, while others around me are lucky, I'm supremely unlucky. My presence attracts devils, and even decent people will think up reasons to fall into depravity and pursue me. I bring out the worst in normal people—they'll look at me with greedy eyes and try to do everything they can to obtain me. Devils, on the other hand, are much simpler. They just want to kill me, and they'll stop at nothing to do it."

Cha Ming frowned. "Why would they want to kill a pretty young lady like you?"

Yu Wen chuckled. "I'm over a million years old, Cha Ming," she said. "Does it matter what the reason is? It's been this way ever since I was a child. I've spent every day, every passing moment hiding from despicable men and loathsome devils."

"A million years old." Cha Ming whistled. "You're seriously robbing the cradle right now."

"Care to say that again?" Yu Wen said sweetly. A powerful constriction enveloped him, making it difficult to breathe.

"My mistake," Cha Ming croaked. "You're a sweet young woman with many aeons ahead of her." The constriction lessened, allowing Cha Ming to breathe once more.

"I thought so," Yu Wen said. "But like I was saying, it's been this way for a million years. It was even difficult under my father's protection. His loyal retainers would suddenly become turncoats, or our home's protective formations would randomly stop functioning and allow for devil incursions. I left home because I didn't want everything I loved to become corrupted. My mother gave me her sword and my father his cloak, but even then, I was still forced to wander the world without staying in a single place." She sighed. "My life is filled with fear, but fortunately, it's also been filled with adventure. It's no wonder that my soul-bound treasure is a camera—with the amount of traveling I do, it's the most fitting companion."

"Do you know why they want you? Why they chase you?" Cha Ming asked.

"My father knows, but he won't tell me why," Yu Wen said. "His closest retainers know, but they've sworn an oath to never tell me. Even Xiao Bai knows, but her lips are sealed. Perhaps she thinks it will drive me to despair."

"I'm sorry," Cha Ming said. "I suppose it will be difficult to settle down, then. It'll be like a traveling relationship, sometimes long distance, but always on the road."

"Oh, Cha Ming," Yu Wen said. "Still a nice guy till the end." She looked up at the starry sky, and her gaze became distant and filled with sadness. "My space-time camera is special. With its help, I'm a bit prophetic. I can see glimpses of the future and likely outcomes from my decisions. I'm probably not going to survive Jade Moon Planet, Cha Ming."

Cha Ming frowned. "After everything we've been through, how can you give up? Wasn't it you who told me the root of all evil is doubt?"

"This isn't doubt, it's reality," Yu Wen said. "These past few years have been the best years of my life. I want you to be happy, but giving you false hope isn't going to do that." She sighed deeply. "That's why, if I survive Jade Moon Planet, we'll be going our separate ways. If we don't, you will die. I want you to have a bright future, Cha Ming, and you can't find that with me. I want you to promise me that once we leave, you'll forget about me and move on. You'll find someone else who can make you happy." Her voice quavered as she spoke, and tears streamed down her face.

"I can't promise you that," Cha Ming said. "I love you, Yu Wen. I can't just stop that on a whim."

"Love is a choice, Cha Ming," Yu Wen said. "Just like you can choose to love me, you can take that love away."

"That's not something that I can do," Cha Ming said. "If I did, I wouldn't be myself."

"Listen to me," Yu Wen said, her eyes red "If you don't give up on me, you *will* die."

Cha Ming smiled and swam up to her. He wiped the tears from her eyes and kissed her gently on her forehead.

"Everyone dies one day," Cha Ming said. "Why don't we stop thinking about these sad things. We're on vacation, Yu Wen. Let's take things one step at a time and enjoy these precious months we have together. We can figure out the rest when we leave."

Yu Wen nodded and pressed her head firmly against his chest. The waters of the hot spring splashed against them as they floated back to one of the seats to look up at the stars. They laughed as the celestial bodies put on a performance, adjusting their trajectories seemingly just for them.

Interlude: Full Circle

Tick. Tick. Tick.

Wang Jun's clock sounded its last in the Song Kingdom as Wang Jun stored it in a spatial treasure. "That's the last of my belongings," Wang Jun said to Elder Bai, who was standing beside him.

"Then that's the last of our office in the Song Kingdom," Elder Bai said. "Our temporary staff have all either packed up or decided to stay on permanent assignments. There are only a few formalities to take care of before management is officially handed over." He glanced to the cinnamon bark fireplace in the office. "Are you sure you don't want to take it? It's very expensive."

Wang Jun shook his head. "Consider it a small bonus for our new manager's loyal service. Speaking of which, he's here."

A thin mortal man walked into the room. He was frail. In fact, he could be killed if either of them exerted the slightest pressure. But Hong Ling's ability as a manager was far more important than his cultivation.

"Are you sure you're up for the position?" Wang Jun said. "It'll be dangerous, and you're more than welcome to follow us to Golf Leaf City."

"I'm sure," Hong Ling replied. "The Song Kingdom is my home, and although my parents and I are estranged, that doesn't mean I can't pull some strings in the dark to help them out. Besides, with

– 343 –

Xiao Li here, I don't think there'll be any danger."

A woman in a blue dress stepped into the room and stood beside Hong Ling. Given their positioning and dispositions, it was obvious that they had more than a working relationship.

Wang Jun sighed. "Not only do you choose to stay here, but you steal one of the best from my team. You're lucky you're a good manager, or I'd never let you get away with it."

"I'm grateful for all the support over the years," Hong Ling said. "But Xiao Li and I belong together. Even if I didn't say anything, she'd stay on her own volition. Before you leave, however, I have one last request."

"There's no need to say anything," Wang Jun said. "Perhaps one day I'll find her. If I do, I'll personally bring her back and reassure your parents."

"Thank you for everything," Hong Ling said.

"No, thank you," Wang Jun replied. He patted the man on his shoulder. "I left you some tea by the fireplace. Let me know when you run out, and I'll send you the best I have."

Then Wang Jun and Elder Bai left the room and the Jade Bamboo Auction House. They were joined by Protector Ren, who assumed his usual role in driving their carriage. Instead of a luxurious one, it was a caravan-style carriage meant for a few dozen people. It contained the best of the best, the core team he would be relying on in Gold Leaf City.

Suddenly, a soft buzz alerted Wang Jun to an incoming call. He sighed and activated his core-transmission jade. A jade hologram of Prince Lei appeared. "So, you're taking off without saying goodbye? After everything we've been through?"

"I saw you three days ago," Wang Jun said. "And it's not like we had much to talk about."

"If you don't care about him, surely you care about your niece," a voice said. Feng Ming appeared and pushed Prince Lei's apparition out of the range of the device. The tall armored man held a small baby in his arms.

"It's my fault," Wang Jun said, laughing. "However, the caravan's already moving, and slinking into the shadows is my style." An awkward pause ensued.

"When will we see you again?" Prince Lei said, edging his way back into the projection.

"Assuming I survive my family in Gold Leaf City?" Wang Jun said. "Even I don't know that. There's a war coming, and many things are up in the air. The entire continent is a giant powder keg, ready to explode at the slightest disturbance."

"Then I hope it's later rather than sooner," Feng Ming said. "We're weak right now, but given enough time, we can mount a substantial defense."

"We'll need luck in this war," Wang Jun said. "With you, we've got that in spades. Just don't forget to save some for me when I need it." The projection flickered out, leaving Wang Jun alone with Elder Bai in their personal compartment.

"Can the Song Kingdom really survive this war?" Elder Bai asked.

"It's why I said they needed luck," Wang Jun said helplessly. "They've only seen the tip of iceberg when it comes to the Southern Alliance's forces. It's only a matter of time before they find out why all these protective walls were erected around their kingdom in the first place."

Chapter 34: Validation

Jade Moon Garden was a flurry of activity. Cha Ming and Yu Wen landed before a group of cultivators who were excitedly discussing the contents of the next examination. This was all speculation on their part, but if humans knew how to do anything, it was gossip.

"Should I be worried?" Cha Ming asked Yu Wen as they approached the altar.

"I think you'll do fine," Yu Wen said. "I can't tell you what the third test is, but I can tell you that it will be quite hilarious. Senior Wood Elemental and I get to watch the performance on a big screen with snacks. Many of the wood dryads will be joining us."

"A performance, is it?" Cha Ming said nervously. He looked suspiciously toward the woods, where hundreds of thousands of cultivators were still suffering from the wood elemental's ire. A strange thought entered his mind before he remembered that the final trial was always linked to the second one.

Could it be practical examination? he thought. *Or will the elemental make us do alchemy with the herbology we've learned?* He sincerely hoped that this wasn't the case, as his knowledge of alchemy was rock bottom amongst the participants.

At this moment, the wood elemental appeared behind the altar. He stood there silently while waiting for the cultivators to quiet down.

"Are you all ready?" he asked everyone present. Seeing no one object, he nodded and summoned thousands of green spheres. "Then without further ado, I'll introduce the contents of the third examination. As many of you might have speculated, this examination will involve live herbological testing."

The cultivators broke into whispers as this was revealed.

"I'm glad to see you're all excited about this," the wood elemental said. "I'm also excited. Live testing is a great way to validate your theories on herbology. There are many variables to account for in every situation, and only through countless live experiments can one become a master in the subject. Unfortunately, there are many ethical considerations involved. My master, Shennong, strongly frowned upon using other humans, animals, or demons as test subjects. Therefore, he created his legendary simulacrum. But before the simulacrum was completed, he used what he saw as the most ethical test subject: himself.

"The third examination honors this tradition. You will all be poisoned and sent to random locations within Jade Moon Forest. Those who can hold out against the poison for the longest durations will be allowed entry into the Sacred Jade Library. First place will be awarded with a six-month pass, while second place will be awarded with a three-month pass. The duration will continuously be cut in half with decreasing rank, to a minimum of three days. Only the final thousand remaining cultivators may access the library.

"Now tell me, are you ready?" the elemental said.

The cultivators nodded grimly as they prepared themselves mentally. Thousands of green spheres flew out toward each of the cultivators, which were immediately immersed in a gray light that sent them to a random location in the woods.

"Go!" the elemental's voice boomed.

Cultivators dashed through the woods in search of useful herbs as their biological clocks ticked—literally.

"This trial is inhumane," Han Jiling grumbled as he grabbed a silver-leafed herb that was carefully concealed under a bush. A wood dryad chuckled in mockery as a spasm ran through Han Jiling's body while he picked. He clenched every muscle he could to counteract the poison's violent assault, and after a few moments of gut-straining effort, he managed to force it into remission. Then he combined the herb he'd just harvested with a few dozen others. They formed a paste that calmed the irritable symptoms of the poison when he applied it to his belly. "All that effort for just three hours of relief," he said, moaning.

It was a race against time. He ran past three helpless cultivators who could only assume the fetal position to delay the inevitable. Every second they gained could increase their standing in the competition and obtain library time. Only when they reached their limits would they shatter their antidote vials and accept their final ranking.

The herbs are getting increasingly scarce, Han Jiling thought. *I'll have to improvise.* He spread his angelic wings behind him, giving him a small boost of speed, but more importantly, an improved affinity with lightning. Electricity coursed through his veins as he propelled himself forward using his metal-based qi techniques.

An incense time passed, and as he walked, he suddenly stopped. "You can come out now," he said calmly toward a group of trees. A ragtag bunch of cultivators came out from behind them. "How honorable of you, resorting to such means to win out on this test of skills," Han Jiling said.

"They said weapons and lethal techniques weren't allowed," a blue-robed cultivator said. "There's literally no risk of you dying, not with the Jade Moon Blessing still active."

"I'm less worried about your combat abilities and more about what's in your hands," Han Jiling said.

"This?" the cultivator replied, gesturing to vial of purple liquid. "This is just an experimental concoction. You should try it out for us—perhaps it will cure the poison and save us all a lot of embarrassment."

"Stop lying through your teeth and get it over with," Han Jiling said stiffly.

"Do it," the blue-robed cultivator said.

The others joined together in attacking the lone angel, who expertly dodged the first few strikes with quick footsteps. Unfortunately, they weren't attacking him. As he avoided them, various restrictive techniques accumulated around him until he became completely entangled in a web of qi. The blue-robed cultivator then walked up to him and forcefully poured the contents of the purple vial down his throat. The older man grimaced as he tasted the bitter fluid that migrated toward the afflicted area: his bowels.

"What if it works, boss?" one cultivator asked.

"Then he can consider himself lucky," the blue-robed cultivator said. "But I'm not optimistic about his odds of success."

As the man spoke, Han Jiling focused on the changes within his body. His digestive system relaxed, and his stomach quieted. Then, to his surprise, his body returned to normal. It was as though he'd never been poisoned in the first place.

Han Jiling laughed loudly. "Serves you all right. I'm cured!"

"Is he really cured?" a cultivator said. He probed Han Jiling with his resplendent force before frowning. "I'll be damned."

"It's still too early to tell," the blue-robed cultivator said as he pulled out an old stopwatch. "Any second now."

Tick. Tick. Tick.

Suddenly, Han Jiling felt a stab of pain in his gut. Sweat beaded on his face as his torso spasmed and threatened to explode. "Let me go, I'll break my antidote vial!" he yelled. The cultivators released him and allowed him to scramble for his vial. He bit the cork off and spat it out before downing the contents.

Was I too late? Han Jiling thought. The spasms, which now came three times a second, lessened substantially. Two per second, one per second. He relaxed as his bowels returned to their original condition. Yet as he did, they also relaxed. A putrid scent filled the air as diarrhea oozed out from his robes and onto the forest floor. It was greedily absorbed by the many forest organisms.

Appalled at the huge loss of face, Han Jiling hastily retreated and used qi to wipe himself clean. He then applied a healthy amount of perfume herbs. "If any of you dare tell anyone, I'll kill you and your entire family!" he spat, before running away.

As Han Jiling and the other cultivators went wild trying to fight their embarrassment, Cha Ming remained calm. He slowed his breathing and blood circulation. Then he lowered his body temperature as he observed the various toxic substances in his bloodstream. A cocktail wreaked havoc on his various bodily processes. He soon discovered that, while hundreds of toxins were present, five different ones were the main perpetrators. He browsed through his knowledge of herbology before formulating a likely cure. Then he flew toward a nearby valley, where he sensed several herbs growing.

Fifty-three lesser herbs and seven mid-grade herbs, Cha Ming thought. He summoned a token from the Clear Sky World. Several dots appeared on the gathering quota before the formations disappeared and allowed him to retrieve the mid-grade herbs. He combined them in various ways before ingesting or applying them to his body.

An hour passed as the herbs worked their magic. The poison in his body lessened as he waited. A ninth, an eighth… soon, only a hundredth of the original poison remained. Seeing that his solution was effective, he quickened his circulation and breathing and directed his regenerative powers to bringing his body back up to full strength.

That was easy, he thought as he continued his journey, picking useful herbs as he saw them. Days passed as he harvested, and the other contestants dwindled one after another. It wasn't long before only a few hundred cultivators remained in the woods, and it was obvious that they, too, had cured their poison.

One day, Cha Ming felt an itching sensation on his leg. *Strange,* he thought, scratching it. He observed it with his resplendent force before discovering that the itch had turned to numbness and was rapidly spreading to the rest of his body. He turned his gaze inward and noticed, to his shock, that the original toxins in his body were making a resurgence. Moreover, the viral cocktail had changed. It was now feeding off his body to regenerate. *I knew it was too easy,* he thought.

Cha Ming quickly set up a concealment formation and sat cross-legged, entering a low-consumption state. *I need to find a better solution,* Cha Ming thought. *But for that, I'll need several experiments. And I only have so many herb-gathering quotas. That means I need to rely only on readily available lesser herbs. Otherwise I'll run out of herb-gathering quotas before I even have a chance at suppressing the poison.*

Seeing that time was of the essence, Cha Ming entered the Clear Sky World and summoned his simulacrum. His soul rapidly materialized various herbal remedies that could potentially solve the problem. First, he focused on quick, low-grade solutions that could make efficient use of his herb-gathering quotas. Then he thought up thousands of different solutions before discarding those with herbs that weren't present in the nearest hundred miles. Finally, he prioritized them according to ease of implementation.

There's just not enough time, he thought as he opened his eyes. He quickly ran to the nearest plot of herbs and plucked it bare before proceeding to the next one. As the pain faded, the numbness returned. He applied a mid-grade cure and forced the poison into remission. However, he knew it hadn't completely disappeared. It would soon return with a vengeance.

Seeing that his time was extremely limited, Cha Ming began a torturous cycle of experimentation. He constantly sifted through solutions and tested them on Shennong's Simulacrum as he fought the encroaching poison with stopgap solutions. Unfortunately, these solutions were growing less and less effective.

A decisive gleam appeared in his eyes as he summoned hundreds of lesser herbs from the nearby woods. It was time to begin live testing.

Huxian panted heavily as he breached the sixty-fifth circle. Illusions of light and shadow hounded him from all directions. Rather than being figments of his imagination, they were growing increasingly real. It was a fine line between illusion and reality.

Huxian jumped through a hoop of flame that transformed into a bird. He passed through it unharmed but walked carefully as he landed on a line of barbed wire. Halfway through, however, he glanced at the projection of his friends as they fought. Their wounds were growing increasingly deep, despite their renewed strength after they regained their energy.

"It looks like they can't take it anymore," his ancestor said. "You might as well drain them dry—it won't make a huge difference, but mosquito meat is still meat."

Huxian ignored him as he did the opposite, and his strength weakened by ten percent as he funneled it into his three companions. Although it wasn't a large amount split three ways, it was still enough for them to stave off the round of attacks and recover.

"Oh? You're not willing to give up these weak generals?"

"Quit yapping," Huxian said. "It's bad enough that you've made this test so difficult. Do you have to keep taunting me as I do my best to pass it?" He stepped off the barbed wire and plunged through a garden of shadowy flowers. They nipped at his fur, and he was forced to repel them with light-infused water, courtesy of the qi borrowed from Gua. Then, a raging fire roared toward him. He blew it back with blades of wind that pushed it back while simultaneously devouring it. Then it vanished.

"I'd hardly call this doing your best," Hushao said. "You've given up a substantial amount of your power instead of boosting it. It's a foolish decision, one that will hurt your odds of success."

As he spoke, Huxian passed the sixty-sixth circle. He grinned at Hushao, who shrugged. Excited, he edged his way toward a black-and-white ethereal boundary that was very different from the previous sixty-six circles. He cautiously walked through it, and to his surprise, the projection above turned to a familiar scene. It was from an hour ago, when Gua had received a vicious wound. Puzzled, he took another step. This time, the projection changed to a scene of Silverwing falling from the skies. Gua was dying, and Xiao Bai was combusting her life essence in a futile attempt to save him.

"You'd better hurry up. You only have an incense time remaining," Hushao said.

Frightened, Huxian took another step. The projection blurred, and he'd returned to the original scene where he'd just given back energy. His energy didn't change, but their situations had improved substantially.

"It's a time maze," Huxian whispered.

"A space-time maze, to be exact," Hushao said. "At any moment, you could lose time, and the trial will end. Conversely, you could gain time. It's all up to how skillfully you navigate these space and time laws. Should you err too far, your friends will die. Am I not merciful for telling you this in advance?"

Merciful, my tails, Huxian thought bitterly. *He's forcing me to walk on a razor's edge.* He stopped moving and began pondering the mysteries of the space-time maze. Or rather, he began to *feel* them. Demons were not very gifted at understanding natural mysteries, but they possessed a sixth sense toward them. Inspiration came easy, but deduction came with great difficulty. Fortunately, inspiration was currently what he needed the most.

Time trickled by as he felt the ripples and pathways pervading the nearby space. *If I want to preserve time, I need to find the smallest ripples,* Huxian thought.

His body and soul scoured his surroundings until finally, he detected a relatively calm area in the otherwise turbulent sea of light and darkness. He projected a clone in this direction and merged back with it. Then he looked up at the projection and saw that the effect on the outer world was rather miniscule. He'd also passed the sixty-seventh circle.

A good start, he thought as he continued the process. This time, the space-time turbulence was much greater. It took him longer to find a relatively calm area. By the time he'd spent an incense time discovering the solution, hours had passed in the outside world.

"So I've been fiddling around with that formation of yours," Hushao suddenly said.

Huxian looked up in surprise to his ancestor, who summoned a bunch of gray lines in the air. To his surprise, it was made of the various runic fragments they'd seen on the Bridge of Stars. They merged together and formed an outline around nine points, which suddenly glowed with black and white light. The yin and yang and the eight trigrams of the bagua appeared within the intricate framework.

"Is that my Friendship Circle?" Huxian said.

"No, it is definitely not your so-called Friendship Circle," Bagua Hushao said. "This is the new and improved Round Table Formation," he said proudly. "It's an upgraded version of your Friendship Circle, whose terribly wimpy name made me want to commit suicide out of shame. Therefore, I've renamed it the Round Table Formation. The name comes from a king who drew a mystical sword and had a bunch of knights fighting alongside him. Plus, in the story, there was the greatest wizard of all times, Mer—"

"I think I'll call it the Greater Friendship Circle," Huxian said, taking command of the new formation. He ate the central node, which rapidly superimposed with his old one.

"You didn't let me finish my story," Hushao started.

"No need, I'm sure that wizard was great," Huxian said.

"But I haven't told you why," Hushao started again. "The whole story revolved around him. He basically saved all of existence from the evil goddess. He aged backward in time, for heaven's sake!"

"As I said, I'm sure he was great," Huxian said, using his claw to tear a hole in the formation. He rushed forward to the next space-time circle and used his powers of light and shadow to block out his ancestor's annoying voice.

Chapter 35: Fighting Poison with Poison

A fishy substance oozed out from Cha Ming's pores as he knelt on the ground, panting. "Another failure," he whispered. Numbness spread throughout his body more rapidly than before, threatening to throw him into a coma if he didn't act quickly. "But I completed ten tests before needing to intervene," he said before throwing up several lesser herbs and a few mid-grade herbs. His energy stores replenished slowly until finally, he could stand again.

"Let's try solution 1,057 next," he said. A few dozen herbs swirled around him. Their various juices combined and separated. Several powders were formed, some of which were left that way and others which mingled together with liquid as a paste. His body was soon covered in various herbal concoctions.

A few minutes passed as they worked their magic and enfeebled the poison. Then he took out another batch of herbs and carried on a different experiment. This time, he strengthened his body's vital functions to fight off the remnants of the poison.

Another failure, he thought, looking at the suppressed but rapidly growing substance. *The grade of this solution was around top-grade. Does that mean that only a perfect solution will cure this poison? Is that the only way to completely purge it from my body?* He thought back to the way the poison manifested itself. After every cure, it drew on the five-element energy in his body to grow in potency.

But a perfect solution is risky, Cha Ming thought. *A perfect solution requires cyclical elimination. But given the nature of this poison, every destruction cycle could almost kill me. If I didn't have the Seventy-Two Earthly Transformations Technique's regenerative abilities, I would have died a thousand times over by now.*

He took another moment to analyze the data he'd collected before shaking his head. *There's no other way. I need to find a perfect solution, but I'll only get to try a few times. I only have a hundred or so mid-grade herbs remaining.*

His soul returned to Shennong's Simulacrum. Using the Clear Sky World's abilities, he performed hundreds of experiments over a few hours. By that time, he'd used a full third of his remaining mid-grade herbs to stave off the growing paralysis.

I don't have time to perform any more simulations, he thought. *I have three solutions, and whether I pass or fail depends on them.*

"Good, I gained time on this one," Huxian said as he stepped through the eighty-fifth circle. Only half of his original strength remained after he redirected another portion to Silverwing, Lei Jiang, and Gua. While they still bore many wounds from their vicious battle, they were surviving. In Huxian's current state, that was enough.

He took a step forward. This time, Lei Jiang was about to be devoured by a fiendish lion. He shrieked as he was crushed by the lion's maw.

"Lei Jiang!" Silverwing yelled before diving in. He was intercepted by a murder of crows that pecked deep gouges in his wings and caused him to plummet to the mountain. The lion, seeing that a second prey had arrived, went in for the kill. Silverwing shrieked and decapitated it with a blade of wind. Unfortunately, ten more lions took its place and jumped on the poor bird. He didn't survive.

Huxian howled mournfully and stepped forward. This time, Lei

Jiang and Silverwing were fine. *Thank goodness,* he thought, letting out a sigh of relief. *Wait a minute, I've seen many different futures with them dying, but they're still here with me. What does that mean?*

"There are many different branches in space-time, many different possibilities," Hushao said lazily, as though reading his mind. "One of these will come to pass, while the others won't. This has to do with free will. But forget about that for now. It's beyond you."

Huxian pondered the implications for a moment before grinning. "Great, so that means that those other futures don't exist," he said joyfully. He stepped forward and was greeted by another scene. In this one, Gua was about to be devoured by a fiendish badger while Silverwing was bravely defending against a swarm of fiendish bees. Huxian wasted no time in reversing the energy flow. His vitality soared to its maximum, but in the meantime, Silverwing, Gua, and Lei Jiang were drained to the brink of death.

"Why?" they called out simultaneously.

Huxian was overwhelmed by their grief, but he pushed this out of his mind and stepped forward. Time turned back, and though his friends were holding on, it was barely sufficient. He channeled ten percent of his energy, leaving him only with ninety percent. Their situation eased substantially. Then he used his newfound strength to forcefully resist the space-time turbulence and step forward with barely any change in time for the outside world. His energy greatly diminished as a result, but he didn't care. He stepped forward once more and arrived at another unfavorable time branch. He sapped these friends dry before returning and repeating the process. Soon, he'd crossed ninety rings, and he and his friends were better than ever.

"There are limits to what you're doing, you know," Hushao said from the side. "I mean, congratulations on discovering this great trick, but it can only help you so much."

"What do you mean?" Huxian said, using the same process to cross yet another space-time circle.

"I mean you should slow down and consider what's happening," his ancestor said.

"Can't stop, eating," Huxian said. He rushed through several more circles before finally stopping at the ninety-seventh. This time, he frowned. "Why is this one so similar to the one before?"

"If you would have stopped when I told you, you would know the answer," Hushao said coldly. "What you've done is what my master calls space-time reduction."

"Which is…?" Huxian said.

"You've forcefully plundered energy from several futures and delivered them into the present time," Hushao explained. "As a result, those futures have become unstable and collapsed. You are now left with fewer and fewer options."

"Use standard demon-speak please," Huxian said, confused.

Hushao smacked his forehead with his large paw. "You ate too many futures, so they're gone. Let's say you had thirty futures. Well, you ate twenty-seven of them, leaving you with only three. You weren't careful with how you picked—you just chose what looked nice, but now you're left with only three futures with very few differences."

"You mean…" Huxian said, paling.

"What, did you think you had unlimited futures to drain?" Hushao scoffed. "Wouldn't that make us the most powerful beings in existence?"

Huxian's head hurt as he processed the implications. He stepped forward and saw a vision of Lei Jiang being devoured by an eagle. Silverwing divebombed the opponent in grief, and Gua tried to save him but died while trying. Finally, Xiao Bai left the mountain in tears. The mountain elemental then collapsed under the pressure.

"Quick, go back before you run out of time!" his ancestor shouted.

Huxian stepped forward and jolted back. The projection played in reverse until it arrived at a precursor—a wave of demons far stronger than they expected.

"These are the consequences of your actions," Hushao said. "You're very gifted, I'll give you that. If you give them up, you'll undoubtedly pass my test. That would truly be the best choice for my lineage. But if you want to keep them, you need to give up on this test. There are only two choices before you, two forks in the road."

Huxian clenched his jaw and dropped his head dejectedly. "All right, I give up on the inheritance trial," he said without any hesitation. "Send me back."

"What?" Hushao barked. "And give up the opportunity of a lifetime? It won't come back you know."

"Who needs an inheritance?" Huxian said, looking up at his ancestor defiantly. "This isn't my fault. It's your fault. For setting such a ridiculously difficult test. In fact, I think you did it on purpose. You're a cruel-hearted fox who's trying to get me to choose between my friends and my lineage."

His ancestor said nothing to refute him.

Infuriated, Huxian continued his tirade. "If that's the case, I don't need you. I don't need this family, this power, or your stupid inheritance. My brother and I will make our own path, one that doesn't require us to make such heartless choices.

"You treat your generals like garbage. To you, they were nothing more than capable assistants who could be disposed of at any moment. They're your glorified cannon fodder that you could snack on at any given moment." His eyes turned red. "But to me, they're precious friends. I wouldn't give them up for all the power and tasty treats in the world. You might think it's a pity that I'm turning this all down, but I don't think so. Your system is terrible, and you can shove it where the light doesn't shine for all I care."

"As you wish," Bagua Hushao said.

A darkness suddenly surged out of the large fox's phantom and encompassed the ninety-nine circles. They slowly but surely disappeared, starting with the outer circles. Huxian panicked as he saw them disappear one after another, leaving behind only himself and the ancestral altar.

Seeing this, he sighed and charged out toward the fissure in the mountain where his friends were waiting.

"Lei Jiang, block the fiendish lions," Silverwing directed from above. As he did so, he sent out gusts of wind to disperse their formation and blow a quarter of them off the mountain. The elementals threw rocks at the falling creatures, completely decimating them as they struggled to slow their descent.

"I'm on it," Lei Jiang yelled. Dark clouds congregated above them, culminating in a fierce burst of lightning. It didn't strike the lions, but rather, Lei Jiang. The small mouse burst into thousands of smaller lightning-wreathed mice that wandered erratically throughout the crowd of frightened felines. Every time they contacted the fierce creatures, they burst apart. Their energy returned to Lei Jiang's main clone, who then reformed into his original body.

"You think you can escape me with these petty tricks?" a voice said. A black fiendish lion much stronger than the ones he'd just defeated appeared behind him. Its teeth bit down on the small mouse, who caught the fangs in midair. He used his whole strength to fight against the lion's maw as it threatened to clamp down on him.

"Silverwing, help!" Lei Jiang yelled.

"Coming!" Silverwing said. He dove down toward the mouse, but in the process, he spotted a crowd of ominous crows heading his way. The murder didn't express the usual caution against him. Instead, they let off surefire signs of self-detonation. The giant falcon increased his speed, using a convenient burst of energy from Huxian and bypassing the divebombing murder. He then generated extra wind currents that forced them to detonate without making contact.

"I can't hold out much longer," Gua said suddenly. An eagle had landed beside his hiding place and started pecking at the swamp-colored shield around him. "I can't die now," he said, moaning. "I haven't yet sired enough children. What will the world do if I die without passing on this beautiful face?"

The eagle, disgusted by his sudden outburst, sent yet another drilling peck toward him. His shield shattered, and the beak continued toward his heart.

Suddenly the void around Gua distorted as a black-and-white phantom appeared before him. It gobbled down the eagle and replenished Gua's energy. Then it sprung over to Lei Jiang, who was about to be eaten by the lion. The small rodent's arms trembled before finally giving out. Blood splashed as the lion's mouth closed down on him.

"Lei Jiang!" Silverwing yelled, letting out a furious shriek.

At this moment, however, something strange happened. As the black-and-white phantom rushed toward the lion, the lion's mouth opened. Yet instead of seeing Lei Jiang's mangled corpse, the blood flowed backward and into the small mouse's body. His fur stitched back together as the lion's teeth left him, and he returned to his initial struggling figure. The phantom transformed into a massive black-and-white fox that grasped the fiendish lion's head with two claws. Their sharp points lodged themselves into the lion's jaw joints, ensuring that it could never bite anything ever again.

Relieved, Lei Jiang jumped out. Huxian then crushed the hated lion's head, splashing blood all over the mountain. *After letting this lion kill Lei Jiang so many times, it's about time I get revenge,* Huxian thought.

"Silverwing, Lei Jiang, Gua, retreat up the mountain and converge on me!" Huxian yelled. "Xiao Bai, keep doing what you're doing!"

"Like I need you to tell me," Xiao Bai said, devouring a nearby crowd of fiendish demons. Her power was overwhelming, and whenever they managed to muster their forces to counter her, she used her extreme speed to escape and assault another disorganized group.

As they ran up the mountain, Silverwing and Gua shrank and joined Lei Jiang beside Huxian. Three trigrams superimposed on them as an intricate gray formation overlapped with them.

"Greater Friendship Circle, integrate!" Huxian yelled.

Silverwing groaned. "Can't we think of a better name? How

about we just call it the Silver Demon Battle Formation?"

"Ooo, how about the Thunder Judgment Circle?" Lei Jiang chimed in.

"Why don't we call it the Circle of Love?" Gua said.

Everyone glared at him.

"Because any circle with me is romantic by nature?" Gua suggested. Three claw marks appeared on his face as the formation locked on to each of them.

"It's the Greater Friendship Circle, and that's final," Huxian said. "The newest feature of this circle is limit breaking. Through the Greater Friendship Circle, we can transfer our strength beyond our normal capabilities. Because that's what friendship is—making each other better by being present, raising each other up as a group."

"That sounds incredibly corny," Lei Jiang pointed out.

"It's not, it's a great name," Huxian said. "As I was saying, we'll be able to better utilize our strength to defend the mountain elemental." Then he shouted toward the rapidly approaching rocky creature. "How long until you're finished?"

"Three days, perhaps," the mountain elemental said. It glowed with purple light that spread out toward its smaller selves. These clones suddenly melded together and formed spiky walls that strategically blocked off several access routes. "This is the last help I can give you. You'll need to defend me against any attacks until I'm finished."

"Leave it to us," Huxian said. "Xiao Bai, I need you to do something for me."

"And what's that?" Xiao Bai said.

"I need you to cook more moon cakes," Huxian said gravely. "As many as demonically possible."

Cha Ming sat cross-legged in the woods, his body looking like nothing more than a desiccated corpse. He trembled as he circulated qi throughout his body, bringing the medicinal components to selectively destroy all traces of poison.

This scene continued for three hours before he sent out dozens of herbs and prepared them with his resplendent force. He minced and cut, mashed and spread, powdered and juiced. Finally, he applied each of them to his ailing body, which rapidly recovered to his original appearance.

Having completed the treatment, he inspected his body before grimly concluding that the solution had failed. "It's like a cancer," he muttered. "The last two solutions were the least aggressive of the bunch. It seems as if to kill this poison, I'll have to nearly kill myself. I'll have to destroy my own vitality to starve it out."

A decisive gleam appeared in his eyes. Over a hundred medicinal ingredients appeared overhead. Each of them was mundane in nature, but when combined, they either made potent tonics or vicious poisons.

I'll lose some effectiveness by preparing them beforehand, but I can't afford to be distracted in the final moments, he thought. This was the last solution he could try, and the riskiest. If he failed, he might well die.

After a few moments of preparation and mixing, he stored half of the resulting ingredients in a contingent formation. Should the formation be triggered, it would immediately release the medicinal ingredients on his body. Then he looked at the other half of the ingredients solemnly. He lay down on his back before manipulating them with his resplendent force then injecting their juices into his veins.

Pain seared through his body as he forced the juices into every nook and cranny. The poisons coursed through his body and ravaged everything they touched. They doused his fires of life. They withered his lively cells. They stagnated the flows that sustained him. They dulled his vital senses. And finally, they crumbled the supports in his body.

His bones, strong as they were, shattered into tens of thousands of pieces as he withdrew his life force from them. The rest of his body put up little resistance as he retreated every ounce of vital energy into the voids in his bones. He screamed as his flesh dissolved and his bodily fluids evaporated.

Then the screaming stopped. Cha Ming lingered on the edge of consciousness. He waited for his fires of life to reach the critical level that would trigger the contingent formation. The moment it opened would be the most vulnerable in his entire life.

He struggled to maintain consciousness, hoping to see the formation open. Yet try as he might, he finally succumbed to his own medicinal concoction. What remained of his heart stopped beating, and the world went black.

Hong Xin dismissed her class as the lesson finished. "You're almost there," she said to the former sword dancer. The crimson runes on the flute showed hints of gold. Unlike the rest of the students, a small amount of fire remained in her disposition. But it wasn't hope. No, it was something all too common in the Red Dust Pavilion—ambition.

"Many thanks for your tutelage," the student said, taking back her flute. "I won't disappoint you."

"All of you should go to bed early tonight," Hong Xin said. "The annual performance is tomorrow, and your senior sisters will be displaying skills unlike any you've ever seen before. It will be an emotionally draining but eye-opening experience."

"Yes, Mistress," the students intoned. None of their initial zeal and enthusiasm remained. She looked on as they left the classroom. Once this batch was finished, the next would arrive. By then, with any luck, she'd be giving an entirely different lesson.

"Look at those sheep," Mistress Huang said, walking out from behind a dark curtain. "Only one of them has any ounce of ambition left, while the others are subservient. They'll at most be suitable for mundane tasks and assisting other sisters."

"Their luck was bad, and their talent poor," Hong Xin said. "As I've said countless times, if you disagree with my methods, you can talk to the headmistress."

"And spoil all your hard work?" Mistress Huang said. "If I know anything about you by now, it's that you hide yourself deeply. I doubt this batch of students is as simple as they appear."

"Hiding is also a strength," Hong Xin said. "Do you have any instructions, or are you just here for your usual banter?"

"I'm just checking if you need anything from me," Mistress Huang said. "Tomorrow will be an eventful but very stressful day for you. How do you feel about your closest friends graduating and sharing your fate?"

"It will be useful to have them with me," Hong Xin said. "They're stronger, much stronger than the other students I've seen. And I relate well with them."

"Do you now?" Mistress Huang said. "In secret, they tell me they hate you. They loathe you for what you did to them. You're directly responsible for their fate."

"I don't think you know what directly responsible means," Hong Xin said. "Their fate was a consequence of my behavior. In the end, the mistresses are the ones to blame for all this. Therefore, it's not surprising that they lie to you."

"Impressive," Mistress Huang said. "I felt doubt for a moment there. You almost shook me. But let me tell you, you're a hundred years too early to do anything to me."

"I have five hundred years," Hong Xin said. "I'm not in a hurry. Eventually, you'll get what's coming to you."

Mistress Huang shook her head. She walked over to a pile of black instruments in the corner of the room. These were enchanted items for the new students that would be coming shortly. "Your anger is misplaced, you know," she said. "I've only ever tried to help you. I've always had the best of intentions—within the strict framework of the headmistress's orders, that is."

"And why would that be?" Hong Xin said.

"Because I see a lot of myself in you," Mistress Huang said. "We had the same teacher, and the same talent for kindling. We're neither the most beautiful nor the most graceful. But we both have something the others don't have: hope."

"What hope could I possibly have left?" Hong Xin said bitterly.

"Where there's a will, there's a way," Mistress Huang said. "But no matter. Tomorrow will be a busy day, so you should rest. But before you go, I want you to remember one thing. If things get bad, and all hope seems lost, I'm the one person in the world you can count on in this cruel pavilion. Because like you, I also hide deeply. Like you, I also resent the headmistress to the core. And like you, I also haven't given up." She walked out of the classroom, leaving a perplexed Hong Xin alone in contemplation.

After some time, she left, but before leaving the locked door, she left a note on it. It was covered in three layers of glamour concealments using pass phrases known only to her closest friends. She then returned to her quarters and adjusted her condition. Tomorrow would be the day she risked it all.

Chapter 36: Heart of the Mountain

The first thing Cha Ming felt was an inhalation. It was painful, ragged, but a breath all the same. It filled his body with blessed air, enlivening his newborn cells as his bodily functions slowly resumed. At the same time, his heart started beating. His blood spread oxygen to every part of his body. His cells warmed his cold body as they shivered with excitement.

It worked, Cha Ming thought as he methodically took control of his sleeping body. He first moved one finger, then another. After all fingers were moving, he moved a full hand. An arm followed, and then another. He then flexed the muscles in his legs before activating his core.

Finally, he opened his eyes. Exhausted, he circulated his qi without sitting up. His life force gradually recovered as he replenished it with the energy of heaven and earth. Then, after confirming that the poison was completely purged, he tapped the voids in his bones, urging them to deliver the locked-away vitality back to his body.

His muscles and joints crackled as they readjusted. His bones let out crisp snaps as they mended back together in their gray, rune-covered structures. Cha Ming stood up. He summoned the Clear Sky Staff and executed crisp strikes and footwork, reestablishing the nerve activity he'd lost since being poisoned.

"Could you have made the test any harder?" he said.

"In all fairness, the test was never meant to be passed in the strictest sense," the elemental said, appearing behind him. "Yet while everyone else succumbed to the poison, you actually managed to cure it. I confess myself impressed."

"What are the odds that it gives me extra time in the library?" Cha Ming said.

"Zero," the elemental replied. "The access time has been limited by the Jade Emperor. What I *can* do is give you directions to the content you desire. But be warned: What you are looking for exceeds the boundaries of mortality. As such, it will be very difficult to memorize the pill recipes presented. You'll be able to retain three transcendent recipes with the current strength of your soul. Even then, you'll only be able to memorize things you understand, and that's something I can't help you with."

"When can I enter?" Cha Ming asked.

"As soon as you activate this token," the elemental said, handing him a slip.

Cha Ming didn't hesitate to pour his resplendent force into the token, causing a gray portal to appear in the woods. He stepped into it decisively.

"I wish you the best of luck," the elemental said softly. "Now where did that Yu Wen sneak off to?"

"How much longer?" Xiao Bai said as she bit through a demon's head. Her sharp front teeth shattered its core and converted it to pure energy. She then kicked out with her legs and pushed back a fiendish bull, sending it tumbling back down the mountain.

"Only a few hours," Huxian said. "There's not much we can do about it. We need to find a way to stall for time."

"You're on your own there," Xiao Bai said. "I don't have any more tricks up my sleeve."

"How about you guys?" Huxian asked his friends.

"I'm doing everything I can," Silverwing said. "And Lei Jiang too. We've been pinballing ever since we got moon cakes for quick recovery." He was currently floating in the skies, scouting while devouring pastries. Lei Jiang was a blur of activity. Ever since they'd resorted to this ultimate move, their kill rate had increased threefold.

"How about you, Gua?" Huxian asked.

"Is it my turn?" Gua said excitedly.

"You mean you've been holding back?" Huxian incredulously.

"Do you want me to act or not?" Gua said indignantly. "One shouldn't easily reveal their trump cards. Especially when it's as shocking as mine."

"You said that two trump cards ago," Huxian scolded.

"Being beautiful isn't a choice, it's a way of life," Gua said defensively. "One must wait for the most opportune moment to act in order to maximize their appearance."

"Please just do something, anything," Huxian said, moaning.

At his signal, Gua put a finger in his mouth and blew. He inflated like a balloon and floated out over the opposing forces, who looked at him strangely, stopping to cautiously observe him. After experiencing his trickery may times, they were careful not to trigger his deadly traps.

"Behold!" Gua said, shouting down to the mass of fiends. "I am your savior. For too long have you been relegated as disposable beasts of burden. For too long have you been enslaved under a devil sovereign's thumb. No more. Today, I will allow you to gaze upon my wondrous figure. My beauty will set you free."

Gua exhaled, regaining his original toady form. His face distorted slightly before revealing his usual ugly mug, with added rouge and red lipstick.

Huxian smacked his forehead. "What the hell is he doing?" he said. "He's asking to get hit. They're all furious down there."

"He's really good at playing the part," Xiao Bai remarked.

"What part, the joker?" Huxian said disdainfully.

"Bait," Xiao Bai replied.

As if on cue, the fiendish demons unleashed a flurry of attacks. Claws blades, needles, and spines flew toward the ugly toad before Huxian could react. Yet to his surprise, Gua's form vanished. It appeared slightly to the left, completely avoiding the various projectiles.

"You'll have to be faster than that if you want to catch Papa Toad," Gua said, laughing. He turned around and shook his butt. Contrary to their usual determined behavior, these beasts seemed less like controlled fiendish demons and closer to the original demons prior to their devilization. He'd slapped their faces, and they wanted nothing more than to smash him into pulp.

"How is he so fast?" Huxian asked.

"How are you so blind?" Xiao Bai said. "It's simple, really. What you see up there isn't Gua."

"It isn't?" Huxian said. To confirm, he reached out with his link to Gua. To his surprise, he discovered that the toad was currently ten feet underground, carefully observing his face in a mirror. His movements reflected those of the illusory body above. "Well, I'll be damned," Huxian said. "He's using a mirage to distract them."

"He's also using a subtle poison to influence their behavior," Xiao Bai said. "Effectively, this is a struggle for control with the devil sovereign. We can't attack now, or we'll waste his efforts. Any aggressive actions on our part will blow his cover."

Silverwing and Lei Jiang floated over beside Huxian and Xiao Bai, confused. "Why have they stopped attacking?" Silverwing asked.

"Gua is apparently a miracle worker," Huxian said. "He's even more infuriating than he lets on. He's actually modest when he talks to us."

"No way," Lei Jiang said. "Then what should we do?"

"Now?" Huxian said, thinking for a moment. He glanced at Xiao Bai before breaking into a grin. "Now we eat."

Two hours later, Huxian gobbled yet another moon cake, slightly enlarging his bulging belly. "This is the life," he said to Silverwing and Lei Jiang.

"I feel like I might just get taller if I eat more of these," Lei Jiang said. "It won't be long before I'm as tall as I am wide!"

"What a goal," Xiao Bai said sarcastically, stowing away her furnace. "Most people aim for a slender figure, but you aim to become a perfect sphere."

"A sphere is the perfect shape for combat," Lei Jiang said solemnly. "Your whole body becomes weaponized, and the muscles around your core become an impenetrable armor."

"Lei Jiang, that's not muscle around your core, it's fat," Huxian said. "But fat makes good armor all the same. I approve."

"It's muscle I tell you! Muscle!" Lei Jiang said.

"Guys, Gua's finally reached his limit," Silverwing cut in.

One by one, the fiendish demons began breaking away from the encirclement and abandoning their chase. Their eyes, which were previously covered in a muddy glaze, had now returned to their original pitch black.

"It's time for the final push," Huxian said. "Mountain elemental, how much time do you need?"

"Only a quarter hour," the mountain elemental's voice rumbled.

"A quarter hour? Easy," Huxian said.

Yet as he spoke, he heard a soft rumbling noise. The jade clouds below them suddenly shifted and revealed tens of thousands of forms that had finally ascended the mountain. The moment they arrived, Gua was forced to withdraw his mirage and huddle in the muddy ground. A large black hound walked at their forefront; its aura was suffocating and far exceeded that of a core-formation cultivator.

"How capable, forcing me to divert a portion of my devil seeds to cope with you," the hound said. "Your father would be proud," the hound said. He looked to the ground and slammed his paw down. Gua, who'd been hiding below him, suddenly squeezed up through the muddy soil and appeared beside Huxian. His body was covered in cuts and bruises.

"You really need to come up with something more original," Huxian said. "Do you remember the first time I met you? You talked about my father and then told me I'd get what's coming to me. And what did you do the next 100 times I killed some of your devil seeds? You did the same thing. Now tell me, what would you like today?"

"You'd better move out of the way and scram off this mountain, or—" the black hound started.

"Or I'll get what's coming to me," Huxian said. "Anything else?"

The hound bared his teeth. "I've wasted enough mental effort freeing myself from that hideous toad's mirage," he said. "I'm not about to bicker with you about a villain's presentation."

"Too late," Huxian said. "We're already bickering, and you started it."

"I *wasn't* bickering," the hound said angrily. "And now I'm not in a good mood. Instead of letting a future enemy escape, I've decided to get rid of you once and for all."

"I'm glad to hear it," Huxian said. "Let me know when you decide to attack. Detonate."

"What do you mean, detonate?" the hound said. Then his eyes narrowed as a whooshing sound came out from beneath his feet. He struggled to move but discovered that he couldn't. Which wasn't a surprise to Huxian—he'd already bound the hound's shadow in an assortment of restraints.

"Despicable!" the hound yelled as a purple ball of lightning suddenly appeared beneath him. A concentrated field of electricity expanded from the ball, covering the many fiendish demons surrounding the hound with a paralyzing force field.

"Now!" Huxian yelled. He split into thousands of foxes as he dove toward the tens of thousands of fiends.

"Kill the elemental!" the hound yelled. It slammed its paws into the ground, sending fissures toward the lone mountain creature. They stopped right before it. Instead of propagating further, a puff of sand was released into the air. "Ignore the others, charge at the elemental!" the hound yelled once more.

The fiendish demons crushed against Huxian's clones and resisted Lei Jiang's force field. A tenth of them passed through. But to their dismay, the moment they entered within fifty feet of the elemental, sharp gusts of wind lacerated them and pushed them back toward Huxian's clones. The clones perished in the collision but soon recombined in greater numbers with devoured energy. Meanwhile, some stragglers had managed to sneak past Silverwing. As they rushed to the elemental, Xiao Bai appeared and devoured any who approached. She was the gatekeeper, an invincible existence on the mountain.

"Change of plans, kill the fox," the hound said angrily. The fiendish demons adjusted their trajectories and aimed for Huxian. His clones were killed, and when the next batch of clones reappeared, they'd reduced in numbers. Seeing that his tactic was ineffective, the clones recombined, and Huxian reappeared in their midst.

He ate a moon cake and projected his force fields. His size grew to 333 feet long and his three tails whipped wildly in the air. The Greater Friendship Circle expanded around him and became superimposed with a central domain of light and shadow. It linked together with a domain of swamp, wind, and lightning. His Devil-Sealing Intent and Demon-Subduing Intent combined with them.

As this happened, Gua's, Silverwing's, Lei Jiang's, and Huxian's auras surged as their powers reinforced each other. He lunged at the black hound, who lashed out with his paws and met force with force. The mountain trembled as they fought, and hundreds of lesser fiendish demons flew off it in the process. Their power level had greatly exceeded these mere mortals and crossed into half-step transcendence.

"It looks like I have no choice," the black hound said. Its aura surged as several heads appeared on its fur and sprouted out. The gigantic hound now had five heads, each of them glowing with a different elemental color. Moreover, each element was laced with destructive black bolts of lightning.

"Be careful, Huxian," Xiao Bai said. "He's consuming his devil seed for a boost in power!"

"I'll be fine," Huxian said confidently. He moved to block the hound's approach, but as he did, he noticed that his normally impregnable fur was beginning to disintegrate. And so were his domains, and his teeth and claws.

"This is bad," Huxian said as he deflected a powerful blow from his superior opponent. He tried to recover from the ensuing numbness, but before he could, a paw coated in black qi slapped down on him. He quickly summoned his battle armor, which cracked under the pressure. It healed over slightly as he diverted energy from his companions and greedily absorbed the thick demonic energy on the mountain.

Chapter 39: Siege

Huxian continued his head-on collisions with the massive black hound. His armor of light and shadow was damaged in many places, and his domains weren't as strong as they used to be. Still, he slugged it out with the massive fiend. He knew full well that, should he avoid its blows, it would sneak past him and interrupt the mountain elemental's extraction.

How much longer? Xiao Bai sent to Huxian. A Grandmist Field, significantly smaller than when she'd started, sapped the life from a dozen fiends.

Soon, Huxian sent back. *I just need to last a few more exchanges before he reaches us.* At this moment, a few hundred fiendish demons emerged from the maze. Instead of joining their companions, they immediately disintegrated while channeling their strength into drops of black blood that shot over to the fiendish hound. *Crap, he's going all out.*

A paw strike containing twice the strength it usually did came crushing down on him. Huxian drew from Gua, Lei Jiang, and Silverwing to counter it. Despite this, Huxian coughed up blood that rained down onto the slick mountain peak. The hound lunged at his throat and bit down on it, causing the large bones in Huxian's neck to crack. Sensing a threat to his life, Huxian split into light and dark clones before recombining. The moment he reappeared, another paw came smashing down.

"You like this little disappearing act, don't you?" the hound said. Its five heads began to glow brightly. Their energy channeled into a small black orb, which grew from the size of a pea to tens of feet wide in a few breaths. As he did so, thousands of fiendish demons disintegrated and merged with it, further fueling the black orb of destructive energy.

"But will you disappear again? If you do, your mountain elemental and its earth source are doomed." Its five heads smiled wickedly as the black orb accumulated power.

He's right, Huxian thought. *If I can't block this, we're done. I need to bet it all on this one move.*

Huxian's fur drained to gray as he poured his light and dark energy into a black-and-white orb. The fiendish hound laughed as it saw Huxian resist. The black orb pulsed and launched forward simultaneously with Huxian's black-and-white one. Both orbs traveled frighteningly fast.

Yet as they approached, time slowed to a crawl. The small black-and-white orb suddenly expanded into a bagua diagram. Space and time fluctuated as it appeared, projecting a small field around the destructive black orb. It didn't stop it but slowed it significantly.

Xiao Bai! he sent, jumping backward. A trail of shadows followed him wherever he went. The trail curved off to the side of the mountain, where he promptly left it hanging.

Xiao Bai landed on Huxian's shoulders and poured her powers into him. His fur regained a black-and-white hue, which he immediately poured into his shadowy road in the form of black and white strings. They then connected the makeshift road to the black orb and anchored the road to the mountain just before the bagua trap faded. The black sphere continued as before, but this time, its trajectory curved. Space shattered as the sphere struggled against the black and white tethers that forced it away from the mountain and toward a smaller one in the distance.

"No!" the devil sovereign yelled. He urged what devilish qi

remained to try and correct its trajectory, but it was too late. The sphere rushed out toward the smaller mountain and exploded on contact, leaving a gaping hole where it had collided. Huxian walked up to him mockingly, licking his lips. "How dare you," the devil sovereign said venomously.

Huxian, not wanting to bicker anymore, sent out clones of light and shadow to devour the remnant devil seed. It howled in indignation as it struggled to salvage the situation by absorbing fiendish blood from its nearby companions. Unfortunately for the hound, it was too late. The fiends turned to ashes, and so did the hound.

"The core is almost extracted," Xiao Bai said as Huxian collapsed to the ground.

The mountain peak glowed with a dark-brown color. It surrounded the lone mountain elemental, who was seated at the core of a complex formation. The brown glow accumulated little by little. As it did, Huxian noticed a soft beating within the mass of energy. It continued to grow before finally solidifying and shooting out of the elemental's body. A brown orb surrounded by a brown liquid wandered over to Xiao Bai, who collected the earth source and flicked the Earth Source Marrow and the Earth Essence Core to Huxian.

That was its heart! Huxian suddenly realized. A wave of sadness overcame him when he realized that the mountain had sacrificed itself for them. *Did it have to be this way?*

In answer, the mountain elemental's face crumbled, revealing a small rocky egg. Seeing Xiao Bai shrug, Huxian received it inside his collar.

"Thank you for your sacrifice, Senior Mountain Elemental," Huxian said gravely. "I don't think it's a coincidence that you left the egg there. In return for your favor, I'll hatch that egg. I promise." Exhausted, he munched on a dozen moon cakes. They melted in his mouth and replenished his energy stores. "How long did it take us to get here again?" he asked Xiao Bai, who was beside him.

"Years?" she replied.

"Right," Huxian said. "I think I've figured out a way to get back faster."

"How much faster?" Xiao Bai said.

"With any luck, it should only take three months," Huxian said. As he looked toward Jade Moon Garden, multiple black and white threads appeared before him. He searched for a while before finding a convenient path through them. Xiao Bai hopped on his back while the others retreated to his tails.

"Full speed ahead," he said, pushing off. The air warped as they passed through it.

Huxian will be here in three months? Cha Ming thought as he walked through the Sacred Jade Library. He summoned his core-transmission jade and sent a message to Yu Wen before proceeding to the next book on the jade shelf. Like the one before it, it was old and dusty. Its vivid handwriting contained a mystical charm that conveyed far more than words but were especially taxing on Cha Ming's soul.

Like before, he read the book from start to finish, etching a portion of the contents into his spiritual sea. The writing in the book dimmed as he read it before eventually fading to near transparency. Once he could no longer read it, he replaced it on the shelf, which locked it in, and retrieved the previous book he'd read. The writing within it looked fresh and filled with life, much different than the previous time he'd looked at it. A single readthrough of the book retrieved the knowledge he'd missed the first time around.

Was it necessary to go into so much detail on even the most mundane topics? Cha Ming thought as he retrieved his core-transmission jade. He saw three new messages from Yu Wen indicating that everything should be fine with Huxian and the rest, and that she and the wood elemental would take care of receiving them in Jade Moon Garden.

Sighing in relief, he moved on to the next bookshelf, which contained more advanced knowledge. He pulled a book from the bottom shelf entitled *Cures to Cultivation Problems, A Primer*. It was a core-grade alchemy book, and the first time he'd tried to read it, he'd been knocked unconscious for a full three days.

Cha Ming took in a deep breath before flipping open the cover. Powerful handwritten runes came to life as he began reading the text one word at a time. He felt nauseous as he read, and a strong headache swiftly crept up on him the more time he spent on it. By the time he managed to read a few sentences, the world started spinning. He closed the book and returned it to the shelf before breathing deeply and allowing his body and soul to recover.

Although the books here are far more accurate and deliver much more content than Jade Moon Library, they're much more difficult to memorize, Cha Ming thought. *Further, memorizing advanced content is much too taxing on the soul without learning basic content. I can only take this one step at a time and learn as quickly as possible before my time is up. To be safe, I should try to learn everything I need within three months, in case Huxian needs help.*

Once he had sufficiently rested, Cha Ming picked up the second book on the first shelf. The writing faded as he read like before, but this time the knowledge was much easier to retrieve.

An hour later, he'd fully memorized the contents of this second book, bringing his total study time to a full day. Although the first shelf only contained twenty books, he was apprehensive about the second shelf, whose contents were overwhelmingly advanced.

If only I had a camera, he thought, as he began reading a third book. Unfortunately, it would be useless even if he did. A camera simply couldn't copy the charm present in the exquisite handwriting. He could only study in silence like a lone monk in a monastery, slowly accumulating the knowledge of his predecessors as the world around him crumbled into chaos.

Han Jiling passed many desperate cultivators spasming on the forest floor. Although he preferred not to see these men and women who suffered their punishment from the first trial, it was necessary to retrieve as many mid-grade herbs as possible before returning to the Ling Nan Plane. Dryads and wood spirits mocked the opportunists as he passed, gleefully making use of his presence to amplify their suffering. They only stopped once he reached a formation surrounded by nine cultivators, where he took out an herb-gathering quota to remove the mystical obstruction.

When did I become so useless that I need to use someone else's herb-gathering quotas while he goes to collect a reward? Han Jiling thought.

He activated a movement technique to zip through the woods toward yet another protected herb. "A Blood Ring Lotus!" he exclaimed when he saw a much larger formation surrounding a three-foot wide flower. It was a high-grade herb, and a rare one at that. While the flower couldn't be used to craft rune-carving pills, it could be used to create pills that simulated rune carving through the power of illusions. Its value far exceeded the ten points required to gather it.

What a stroke of luck, he thought as he began deciphering the formation.

Time trickled by as the flower's protection unraveled. *When did the forest become so quiet?* Han Jiling thought. The wood spirits no longer taunted the looters, and the looters no longer moaned. They shivered in unison, and Han Jiling soon joined them.

What's happening? Why do I feel threatened all of a sudden? He looked up to the formation-covered sky, and as he did, he saw several gigantic spikes floating above. And in the middle of them was a large black pillar that looked much like a battering ram.

Did they finish it? he thought. As he did, the air around the black spikes shivered. Energy danced around them, causing the void to crackle. The nine massive spikes stabbed down into the shield simultaneously, and unlike the 1,080 before them, they managed to dig several feet into the thick green obstruction before stopping.

"Thank goodness they didn't make it through," Han Jiling muttered.

But he didn't relax, as he noticed the pillar in the middle of the nine spikes pulsed and suddenly fell toward the shield. It accelerated for a moment before crashing into it. The collision caused the Jade Moon Garden to tremble. Tiny cracks appeared around the jade spikes but soon mended. Then the pillar rose once more. It wouldn't be long before it fell yet again.

"Your attention, please," the wood elemental's voice suddenly boomed. "All cultivators previously disqualified may now participate in a fourth trial for access to the Sacred Jade Library. Those first offenders who are fertilizing the forest may choose to participate and end their punishment early."

Cheers rose up in the forest when he said this.

"Merit will be based on contributions toward fighting the invasion."

The cheers died down.

"There is currently a requirement for formation energy gathering," the wood elemental continued. "Following this, we will organize a resistance force to fight against these invaders. Merits will depend on contributions. Deserters will get no rewards. Those who wish to participate, please announce your intent."

"Participate!" Han Jiling said without any hesitation after retrieving the Blood Ring Lotus. He suddenly appeared beside a few hundred other cultivators who'd immediately volunteered. Then over a hundred thousand others appeared. They looked gaunt and sickly after having served as a fertilizer source for years. Some had hands covered in cuts and stains but looked otherwise healthy; these cultivators had fully embraced their punishment and had been rewarded with weed-picking duty as an alternative.

"Why are there so few of us?" Han Jiling said to Zhang Fei, who had just appeared.

"You'll understand when you look up," Zhang Fei said dryly. Fang Li and Mu Qianlin appeared soon after. Han Jiling looked up and sighed when he saw that there was a note addressed to the inhabitants of Jade Moon Garden beside the pillar's imprint.

To those reading this message:

I don't want you. I never did. I killed many cultivators, but only to strengthen my overall plan. Now that we've reached the end game, I'd like to make a deal with you. I swear on my devilish heart that those who don't resist the invasion will not be harmed, not by me or my followers.

There are only three exceptions. First, the cultivator known as Yu Wen. Second, the demon rabbit known as Xiao Bai. Third, the wood elemental presiding over Jade Moon Garden. They are the reason I am here, and I will leave once they die.

Consider wisely. I don't give second chances.

Han Jiling shook as he realized that the forces of good might be helpless in this struggle. Far too many of them had already opted for inaction, and likely many of those who'd been transported here would rather return to their punishment than risk their lives in a battle they couldn't win. Doubt weighed down on his heart.

"Are you sure this will work?" the wood elemental asked as he watched Yu Wen turn a small knob. She was currently fiddling with an enormous tripod set in the middle of a giant formation. Energy-gathering runes pulsed as they greedily absorbed a pile of purple crystals at her feet.

"It's better than doing nothing," Yu Wen said. "It might not block him completely, but it will buy us some time."

"What about his threat?" the elemental said.

"What can I do?" Yu Wen said, shrugging. "I already knew what kind of people they were. They're humans without a backbone, cultivators without virtue. They pay lip service to good because it grants them luck, but they'll turn on a dime as soon as something threatens their life. The truth is, I couldn't be bothered with those people. They're nothing more than trash."

"I think you're judging them too harshly," the tree said. "Their situation is difficult. They aren't caving in because they've given up, but rather they're retreating because they see hope from another direction."

Yu Wen ignored him and continued her work. She adjusted several knobs and wheels on the tripod before finally nodding in satisfaction.

"It's ready," Yu Wen said, mounting her space-time camera. The soul-bound artifact displayed a widescreen picture at the center of the garden. Yu Wen zoomed in and focused on the nine black spikes and the black pillar. She flicked across the screen a few times before pressing a button and retreating outside the range of the formation, which glowed gray as it absorbed the purple crystals. The space-time camera ravenously absorbed the energy as a small meter on its display filled up. This continued for a few moments before the formation collapsed and was absorbed into the camera along with the remaining crystals.

"Say cheese," Yu Wen said. The camera flashed, and Jade Moon Garden stood still. It unfroze a moment later, but one thing did not—the nine spikes and the black jade pillar. "Moving when you're trapped in a picture is easier said than done," she said, smiling.

A small two-dimensional print appeared beside the camera. She blew it off and admired the fine detail. Not only had it captured these objects, but it had also captured black and white threads of space and time around them. They'd obediently stopped moving to stay in sync with the picture. The pillar was struggling with all its might against the threads, but to no avail.

"That will buy us what—a few weeks?" the elemental said.

"A few months, if enough cultivators help us," Yu Wen said. "We might even gain enough time for Xiao Bai to return with the Earth Source. If we can do that, we're golden."

"How about we save those ones?" Huxian said, pointing to a group of attractive humans along the way. Their movements were uncharacteristically slow, a consequence of the warped space and time surrounding them. They wore looks of horror as fiendish demons closed in on them, ending any hope they had for survival.

"They're traps," Xiao Bai said. "I mean, not that kind of trap. They're bait to catch us on our way back and delay for time."

"But I'm so tired," Huxian said. "It's very draining to keep up this technique."

"Just shut up and eat your moon cakes," Xiao Bai said. At this moment, her ears twitched. She suddenly ran up to the top of Huxian's head and urged him to go faster. "This is bad!" she said gravely.

"What happened?" Huxian said.

"The devil sovereign's begun attacking the shield," Xiao Bai said. "He's also scared off anyone from helping to maintain it. Maybe a few hundred cultivators are even bothering, and the rest are hiding."

"That's humans for you," Huxian said. "After all the advantages they obtained from Jade Moon Garden, they're not lending a hand when it's needed."

"Humans are selfish creatures," Xiao Bai agreed. "That's the way they've always been. I've lived for over a million years, and I've seen few exceptions."

Seeing that time was of the essence, Huxian picked up the pace.

Chapter 38: Breakthrough

"Greetings, sisters," Hong Xin said with a fake smile as she sat down among the mistresses. In addition to their usual red dresses, they wore golden trim usually reserved for special occasions. Their table was located behind a large seating area, where all the students obediently sat. Their eyes were dull and emotionless, a testament to the pavilion's brutal training methods.

"We're not your sisters yet," Mistress Meng said as Hong Xin sat.

Hong Xin shrugged. "Is there a difference at this point? Aren't we all in the same boat?"

"There's no need to bicker," Mistress Huang said from beside the headmistress. "The headmistress has given her duties like the rest of us. And after today's formalities, she will have the same official standing as you all."

The others shifted uncomfortably at her words. They were very clear about Hong Xin's talent, and it was only a matter of time before her official standing outstripped theirs.

"It's time," the headmistress said in a soft voice that carried throughout the crowd. The teachers and students stopped speaking, causing the auditorium to sink into a deathly silence. "Mi La, you can go first."

A student who'd been there for six years rose and bowed. She calmly walked over to the stage and took out a zither. She played a soothing melody that calmed the nervous students and doused their fears. Gentle clouds formed as she played, stretching out across the audience like a dry mist. The performance finished five minutes later.

"That's a passing performance," the headmistress said after evaluating the effect of her dousing technique. "Note that I said passing, not extraordinary. You qualify for graduation. Please come sit by the mistresses and await the gifting of your hairpin."

A pleased expression appeared on the student's face as she walked toward them.

She thinks graduation means an end to this hellish place, Hong Xin thought. *If only she knew.*

"Meng Jie, you may go now," the headmistress said.

The student bowed and walked up to the stage. She danced a slow, soothing dance that relaxed the audience even further. Yet compared to the previous performance, it was lacking in substance. Not a single hint of gold appeared on the crimson runes of her black shoes.

"You may stop now," the headmistress said. "Try again next year." The student choked back her tears as she walked to her seat. This was her fifth year in the school, and the hard eight-year limit was growing ever closer.

Students performed one after another. A third of them passed, and the rest failed. Hong Xin noticed that most passing grades were from stellar performances of younger students. In a sense, older students were only the leftovers from prior generations, the runts of their respective litters.

"Lin Xiu," the headmistress said, prompting a student to run up to the stage nervously. The mistresses all focused on this student, who was originally a core member of the rebellious group. "Let's see how skilled she is after undergoing your procedure," the headmistress said softly toward Mistress Huang.

"I'm confident that she's still a very talented student," Mistress Huang said.

As she spoke, Lin Xiu pulled out a black-and-gold zither. She plucked its soft strings, causing everyone's hearts to stir. A small cat wandered playfully about the stage. The previously calm students laughed and began talking to each other softly. The headmistress did nothing; this was an essential part of Lin Xiu's performance.

"How very interesting that she'd perform a heart kindling," Mistress Meng said. "And such a strong one at that. If you told me she practiced the Frozen Heart Sutra, I'd accuse you of lying."

"Feel free to inspect her core," Mistress Huang said dismissively. "It's frozen solid. I also advise you to be less jealous of our talented members, lest they plot against you.

"How dare you," Mistress Meng said indignantly.

"I happen to think that heart kindling is very useful," Hong Xin cut in. "Though dousing is an excellent way to bewitch the mind, what of the heart? What about passion? Is manipulating people using their mind alone really the best method?"

"Well said," the headmistress said. "Heart kindling has its place. Everything is fine as long as it's under the careful guidance of a frozen heart."

The performance continued for an incense time before stopping. Lin Xiu, who was covered in sweat from the draining performance, bowed deeply to her audience. The students gave her heartfelt applause before realizing what they were doing and returning to their previously cold selves.

"What an excellent performance," the headmistress said. "Please join your colleagues beside us as you wait to receive your pin." Then the headmistress looked to the group of remaining students and picked an older one, Su Ling. She was not part of Hong Xin's original group.

What a cautious woman, Hong Xin thought as Lin Xiu approached. *She's spreading out my generation of students, despite the treatment they suffered under Mistress Huang.* Her soul tingled as she felt the senses of the other mistresses inspecting Lin Xiu as she walked toward them. She smirked inwardly as those senses returned to their owners empty-handed.

Sweat rolled off Cha Ming's brow as he put down a half-finished book. It was the last book on the second shelf, the same book he'd once gone unconscious trying to read. Having finished *Cures to Cultivation Problems, A Primer,* he now understood why it was so mentally taxing to read it—the concepts conveyed were at the very peak of mortal understanding, and without a proper foundation to guide the knowledge into its proper place, it could drive a mind to madness. Therefore, he read it in spurts.

Cha Ming chipped away at the book bit by bit. It was his fifth reading of the book, so each iteration perfectly finished the voids in his understanding. As he finished the book, he looked at the second shelf in confusion. The answer he was looking for wasn't there. According to these books, fixing his core was impossible.

Did I miss something? He might have read every book on the first shelf, but in his haste, he'd only read half of those on the second one. Unfortunately, his self-imposed three-month deadline was swiftly approaching, and he had a sneaking suspicion that he didn't have much time remaining.

At this moment, his core-formation jade pulsed. He withdrew it and saw a message from Yu Wen. According to the wood elemental, the knowledge he was seeking could be obtained by reading the first book on the third shelf and a pill recipe in a chapter of the fourth book.

Smiling, he picked the first book off the shelf called *Preliminary Transcendent Alchemy.* As he opened its cover, he was overwhelmed by the dense runic writing it contained. Transcendent might flooded from the writing. As he read, he realized that had his soul been any weaker, it would have completely succumbed to the text's overwhelming power.

"We're almost there," Xiao Bai said as they passed a fiendish demon patrol. The horrible creatures wrinkled their noses, causing Huxian to question the effectiveness of his void-traveling technique. He looked around before finally spotting a carefully placed immortal-jade formation plate. Using his Demon-Subduing Eyes, he saw natural energy circulating within ten miles of Jade Moon Garden's protective shield. It was an alarm of sorts, a detection array to prevent intruders from breaching the perimeter.

"The last of the journey's going to be an all-out fight," Huxian said. "There's an army of fiendish demons out there, and judging by their positioning, they're expecting us."

"We've crushed loads of fiends," Lei Jiang huffed. "How is this any different?"

"Quantity, for one," Huxian said. "Plus, if you look closely, you'll see several powerful avatars surrounding the shield. They'll jump on us the moment we approach. I don't care how strong each of you are, there's no way we'll stand a chance against nine half-step rune-carving devils. Even *with* Jade Moon Planet's suppression." He then looked to Xiao Bai. "Are they ready?"

"They've just finished their preparations," Xiao Bai said. "We'll need to strike the black formation from the outside as they attack from within. It's not going to be easy to pull off."

"Don't worry, I have a plan, and it's a good one," Huxian said excitedly. He quickly issued instructions. "All right, let's do this!"

The five beasts rushed out toward the jade barrier in unison. They were immediately detected as they entered the premises, but they ignored the initial wave and tried to make up as much ground as possible.

As they approached the two-mile mark, millions of black crows flew up into the air. They flew toward them at breakneck speed to chase them out of the skies.

"It's your turn, Silverwing," Huxian said.

The small bird cawed in acknowledgement. He grew to his largest size and channeled the combined power of their four to unleash hundreds of tornadoes. They crushed over three tenths of the crows, and the remainder angrily chased after Silverwing. The large bird continued flapping at them, repelling them away from the main group. Meanwhile, Huxian, and the rest continued to the four-mile mark.

"You dare intrude upon my territory?" a voice said as they arrived. A large black wolf appeared. It howled and summoned a hundred companions, bringing them to charge against Huxian and the others.

"It's my turn!" Gua said, jumping at the wolves. They shivered when they saw the horrifying toad, who unleashed a cloud of corrosive and foul-smelling vapor. The air thickened and hampered their movements. Blinded, they cast out their spiritual force, only to discover that it could hardly penetrate the thick air. It was like a bog had completely encapsulated them. "I need to stay here for best effect!" Gua said.

"Good job!" Huxian yelled. As they approached the six-mile mark, a group of vicious-looking cultivators appeared. They were gaunt and drained from their hard work maintaining the formations. Further, they were all infused with a dark miasma. "Lei Jiang, your turn," Huxian said.

"Yippee!" Lei Jiang shouted as he jumped into the crowd of cultivators. He sent out bolts of lightning laced with Devil-Sealing Intent. These attacks were extremely effective against the evil-infused cultivators, who were forced to cope with him.

Three, two, one, Huxian counted mentally.

"Who would have thought you'd be so stupid as to come back here," a voice said. A strong pressure bore down on him as a half-step rune-carving devil avatar appeared.

"Xiao Bai, give me a boost," Huxian said.

"You've got it, boss," Xiao Bai replied.

Huxian glowed bright gray as the small rabbit poured half of her energy into him. Huxian suddenly grew to 333 feet long. Three tails floated behind him, each one radiating a powerful suppressive field. Light, dark, wind, lightning, and swamp bore down on the devilish avatar, causing its might to weaken greatly. Then Huxian lunged forward and bit down on him. The avatar grasped Huxian's front teeth and forced his jaw open, barely resisting against the giant fox.

"You think you can run?" he said to Xiao Bai, who rushed past him and fled toward the jade shield. He moved to intercept but was restrained by Huxian. The fox's aura was far stronger than normal. Not only was he being strengthened by Xiao Bai, but he was drawing any extra power he could from Lei Jiang, Silverwing, and Gua.

As she approached the shield, Xiao Bai began accumulating her power. A gray cloud surrounded her as the energy poured into her two back legs. On the other side of the shield, a massive vine had appeared. Yu Wen stood beside it with a golden sword in hand, ready to unleash her power the moment it was needed.

"You think a paltry formation like this can stop the one and only Jade Rabbit?" Xiao Bai yelled as she rushed toward the black formation covering Jade Moon Garden's dome. She dodged two devilish avatars that appeared beside her and kicked out with all her might.

At the same time, the wood elemental struck out with its vine and hit the same spot while Yu Wen's golden sword flew out and struck the shield. Space distorted as the three forces collided on the black runic surface, causing a small hole to appear. It healed over in the blink of an eye.

"Retreat!" Huxian yelled as he saw the hole heal over. He swatted at his devilish avatar with a large paw and threw it toward the shield. He then flew at full speed past Lei Jiang, Silverwing, and Gua, collecting them as he passed. Xiao Bai appeared beside him, exhausted. The three devil avatars they'd faced earlier had returned to their initial positions and refused to chase them.

"There goes Plan A *and* Plan B," he muttered. "What do we do now?"

"We need more firepower," Xiao Bai said. "I just couldn't make a big enough hole, and Yu Wen is busy stalling the giant pillar on the outside. Meanwhile, offense isn't exactly that old tree's specialty."

Huxian frowned. He hesitated for a moment before calling out to the last person he wanted to bother.

Brother, we need you, he sent.

Cha Ming's mind was numb. His soul had grown slightly transparent from the effort he'd spent trying to learn the first transcendent tome. After a full week of learning, he still hadn't learned even a third of it. Who knew how long it would take to learn a pill recipe after the fact?

Brother, we need you, he suddenly heard.

What's the situation? he sent, placing the book back on the shelf.

We couldn't pierce through the formation, Huxian said. *I think our brute force is enough, but something's missing.*

You likely haven't hit a formation node, Cha Ming replied. *That, and the opening on the black formation would only last for a brief moment. It would be very difficult to pass through it before it closed again. I thought Yu Wen and the wood elemental had special means to deal with that, but it seems I was being optimistic.*

Then what can we do? Huxian said. *We're safe for now. They're playing a defensive game.*

Let me find out, Cha Ming said. He placed a call on his core-transmission jade, and Yu Wen's embarrassed figure appeared before him.

"There's a bit of a problem," Yu Wen said shyly.

"I've heard," Cha Ming said wryly. "And it sounds like you need my help."

"Not right this second," Yu Wen said. "I needed to put a spatial lock on a formation-breaking pillar to protect Jade Moon Garden, and that's tying up most of my strength. As a result, Xiao Bai isn't able to pierce through as planned."

"Did you try striking a formation eye?" Cha Ming asked.

"About that," Yu Wen said. "Did I ever tell you that the only reason I was in Fuxi's Library was because I enjoyed their food?"

Cha Ming facepalmed when he heard this. "I'll be out soon," he said, sighing. "How long can you give me?"

"Three days at most," Yu Wen said.

"It'll have to do," Cha Ming replied before hanging up. He picked up the fourth book and thumbed through it until he found what he was looking for: the Nirvana Pill Recipe. His soul burned as he scanned the contents once through before halting. To his surprise, his transcendent soul had turned fully transparent after a single reading. Sighing, he rested for half a day to recuperate, even with the help of moon cakes. He repeated the process when he was fully recovered. This time, he read the contents word for word. He made it a third of the way through before he was forced to set the book aside and replenish his soul once more.

Two days passed by the time he'd fully read through the recipe. He'd only retained a quarter of what he read, so he read through it once more. This time, he only took half a day to read the entire thing, and he retained half of the recipe's contents.

I can only try once more, Cha Ming thought. *After that, I can only piece everything together.*

He carefully read through the recipe word for word, grasping at each one carefully. His life depended on his success. By the time he finished reading the text, his soul was on the verge of collapsing. He resisted the urge to enter a deep slumber and reorganized the knowledge he'd gained while recovering his energy.

Eighty percent, he thought. *Not bad.*

Why don't you tell me more about the technique with the terrible name again? Cha Ming sent to Huxian as his soul recovered.

It's not a terrible name, it's a great name, Huxian sent. *Greater Friendship Circle is far better than what my ancestor wanted to call it.*

Something like the Round Table Formation.

Wait, you mean King Arthur's Round Table? Cha Ming sent. *With the Knights of the Round Table and the greatest wizard ever?*

Oh God, not you too, Huxian sent.

Wait, listen, Cha Ming sent. *The guy was amazing. Even if his name's not in the title, the whole story was basically about him.*

Are you going to blather on, or do you want me to tell you what I can do? Huxian said angrily.

All right, all right, Cha Ming sent. *Please enlighten me, great master of light and darkness.*

The air surrounding the nine black spikes shimmered as they struggled to free themselves from their invisible bonds. Every so often, they would shudder ever so slightly, a sign of its weakening restraints.

"You should dispel the space-time lock," the wood elemental said gently.

Yu Wen, exhausted from continuously blocking the black jade pillar, resisted one last time before finally giving up. The pillar smashed down on the shield as she circulated her energy to recover. The old cracks swiftly returned and spread out across the surface of Jade Moon Garden's shield.

"How long do you think we have?" Yu Wen asked, panting.

"One hour, if that," the wood elemental said. "Unfortunately, we have far too few recruits. They've been supplementing our energy stores for some time, but it's far from enough. I know it's hard for you to accept this, but if all else fails, you need run for your life. You might just last long enough for the Jade Emperor to come to your rescue."

"I can't," Yu Wen said. "I can't just leave them here to die. It's not hopeless. I know that with great certainty. I can save them all."

"But can you save yourself?" the elemental countered. "It's not just about you. Your blessing is an invaluable gift from the heavens. Think of the countless innocents you can save by surviving."

"But then I'd betray who I am," Yu Wen said. "I might always be running, but I'm not a coward."

"Is there anything I can do to convince you otherwise?" the elemental asked.

Yu Wen didn't reply. He sighed before heading back toward the shield and diverting as much of the impact from each blow as possible. He didn't mind his clone dying here, but if Yu Wen did as well, even the Seven Heavens would be affected.

The soft glow of the Sacred Jade Library faded behind Cha Ming as he exited the spatial portal. He entered the familiar Jade Moon Garden, whose outer shield was now covered in massive fissures. Black tendrils sought to pass through its shattered surface, and it wouldn't be long before its integrity was breached.

"What's the situation?" Cha Ming asked. The elemental appeared beside him, looking gaunt and exhausted.

"Yu Wen is currently recovering after having exhausted her energy stores," the elemental said. "She can't contribute much, so it's just you and me. Xiao Bai and the others are outside awaiting orders."

"Give me a moment," Cha Ming said. He activated his Eyes of Pure Jade and his Demon-Subduing Eyes, revealing a complex network of runic lines above the surface of the jade shield. The fiendish energies gathered together in nodes. He carefully sifted through them before finally discovering a weaker one.

"Mark this area," he said. The wood elemental shot out multiple vines and outlined a circular target. *Huxian, move out and strike the target.*

Roger, Huxian said. He observed the area outside the shield as

Huxian's team rushed forward as per their plan. As before, Silverwing intercepted crows while Gua and Lei Jiang intercepted their own groups of enemies. It wasn't long before a devil avatar appeared and tangled with Huxian. Just like before, Xiao Bai began gathering energy as two devil avatars rushed in to intercept her.

This needs to be my strongest strike, Cha Ming thought. He summoned his Clear Sky Brush and painted horizontally as Xiao Bai rushed forward. A white circle appeared before him, waiting patiently for his next instructions. As Xiao Bai zipped past the first devil avatar, Cha Ming painted a black line, summoning a destructive star that floated unstably within the white circle. They suppressed each other mutually, threatening to devour each other whole if he didn't do anything soon.

Finally, as Xiao Bai rushed past the second devil avatar, Cha Ming summoned his Clear Sky Staff in its pillar form. He poured massive amounts of five-element qi into the staff, which accumulated at the tip as a soft gray glow.

Seeing that she was about to reach the shield, Cha Ming pushed out against a vine that appeared beneath his feet. Dozens of other vines appeared beside him, pushing out toward the shield. They pierced the circle, sizzling as they made contact. Cha Ming followed up and struck the shield with all his might. The massive pillar left a giant gray imprint as it smashed down on the black runes. Gray cracks expanded from the point of impact and dissolved the evil black marks.

A man-sized hole appeared, but it was quickly resealed by the black formation. Fortunately, it was too little too late. Xiao Bai struck the weakened formation with her hind legs and crashed through it. The black formation tried to follow but was beaten back by the jade shield.

"It's your turn, Huxian," Cha Ming said.

A tiny black-and-white fox appeared from behind Xiao Bai's ear. Then, on the outside, a tiny Huxian appeared from inside Lei Jiang's fur, Gua's mouth, and Silverwing's feathers. Each of them snickered naughtily as their tails glowed with his friend's respective runes.

They disappeared into his tail, barely avoiding fatal strikes heading their way.

Then the small foxes disappeared. The massive fox fighting the devil sovereign also disappeared. The small fox beside Cha Ming grew swiftly into Huxian's original form, and his three friends appeared beside him.

"Old Tree, catch!" Xiao Bai said. She threw the glowing brown earth source to the elemental's shrine. A large green hand snatched it in the air and plunged it into the earth. Jade Moon Garden's shield glowed brown, and the cracks near the spikes and battering ram mended. Then, seeing that attacking was futile, the ram stopped. They all let out a communal sigh of relief.

"You think this is over?" a voice boomed above them. The nine avatars surrounding the shield swiftly merged together and appeared before the previously gaping hole in the shield. "You think I didn't want you to bring the earth source inside?" The evil figure grinned, and at that moment, the shield shook.

Cha Ming looked around and realized that, to his horror, dozens of cultivators were destroying the formation from within. Writhing vines appeared and instantly destroyed them, but it was too late. The fissures were expanding, and it was only a matter of time before Jade Moon Garden's shield was destroyed.

"Who would have thought it was all a feint?" the wood elemental said self-deprecatingly.

"Not a feint, a contingency," Cha Ming said. "What self-respecting devil would leave home without one?"

"What do we do now?" Huxian said anxiously from beside him.

"Now?" Cha Ming said, tightening his grip on his staff. "Now, we fight."

Bai Ling stepped to the stage and summoned her zither. She plucked its golden strings carefully, letting out soothing sounds to calm the conflicted members of the audience. Over the past several performances, their hearts had wavered between hot and cold, kindling and dousing. These repeated stages were taking their toll, and thus far, kindling was winning out.

As she played the initial soothing notes, she looked toward the headmistress, whose expression was cold and devoid of any mercy. Bai Ling smirked and increased the pace. Golden birds fluttered as her audience began murmuring in playful excitement. The birds flew between them, prompting many of them to try catching the elusive creatures.

It was a song of remembrance, a piece of their childhood that they'd all but forgotten in this hellish place. It was a song of defiance, a slap across the face of their oppressors. She sweated profusely as she struggled to maintain her tune while the headmistress oppressed her mentally.

I can't hold on for very long, Bai Ling thought. *It looks like I don't have a choice.*

Her gaze hardened as her outer frozen core melted to accommodate her inner one. The power of kindling surged and assaulted the members of the audience, whose cores began to melt under her superior technique.

Seeing this, several mistresses joined in to covertly smother her efforts. She laughed inwardly as little by little, her tune slowed. Finally, she collapsed on stage. With her lapse in consciousness, the students suddenly realized what had happened. Unlike the first few performers who'd tried kindling arts on them, Bai Ling had gotten somewhere no one else had. She had wedged herself into their hearts firmly. An unwillingness remained in their eyes as she was ushered off stage without a comment from the headmistress and relocated to a chair beside her and the teachers.

"Ji Bingxue, please come up to the stage," the headmistress intoned. "I'm sure you'll give an excellent performance, one that reflects the norms of this institution."

Bai Ling didn't hear these words, as she'd fallen unconscious in her chair.

"You'd better hope, for your friends' sake, that she doesn't do anything foolish like that one," the headmistress said, gesturing to Bai Ling.

"What friends?" Hong Xin said. "I no longer have the luxury of friends."

"Don't lie to me," the headmistress said. "I can read you like a book."

Hong Xin remained silent. Although what Bai Ling had done wasn't according to plan, it had brought them past the point of no return. Ji Bingxue stepped up to the stage and summoned her zither. She plucked the strings carefully, and soon the stage was filled with snow. Large fluffy flakes landed on the audience, reminding them of the coldness of winter and the frostiness of the Red Dust Pavilion. It covered their hearts in a fresh coat of coldness that was easily dispelled by their roused emotions. Instead of calming them, it made them more indignant. Their hearts rose in unison to fight off Ji Bingxue's dousing arts.

"You'll need to act personally after this," the headmistress said. "They'll be difficult to calm down. Fortunately, the girl heeded my warning."

"Yes, Headmistress," Hong Xin said.

"I can also contribute," Mistress Huang added.

"That won't be necessary," the headmistress said, dismissing her. "This is a test for Hong Xin as much as it is a solution. We'll see how far her dousing arts have come since her oath."

At that moment, the snow stopped. Ji Bingxue's tune came to complete stop. A high-pitched sound pierced the cold silence. A songbird appeared, but it didn't emit songbirdlike sounds. Instead it sang with a human voice. Ji Bingxue's voice. Her fingers plucked as she sang. Her rousing tune of spring added to the indignation of the students, whose murmurs were now loud to the point of drowning her out. Several students shot angry looks at the teachers before looking back to the stage.

"I swear, I had no idea," Hong Xin said, paling.

This wasn't according to plan, but it's working, Hong Xin thought. She reached out with her soul and detected larger cracks building up as the students' icy cores melted. A thick layer of boiling water was forming, threatening to undo everything the headmistress had done to them these past years.

"Teachers, with me," the headmistress said. They simultaneously circulated their cultivation bases and combined their spiritual force, suppressing Ji Bingxue. It took less than five seconds for her to collapse on stage with a trickle of blood flowing from her mouth. The headmistress motioned to the unconscious woman and floated her up to the teachers' seats like a sack of dead weight.

"Quiet, all of you," she said loudly to the students. "There is one last performance, and the rest of you will sit through it *without uttering a single peep.* Anyone who does will know the meaning of the word *pain.*" She then looked to Hong Xin. "Are you ready?"

"Yes, Headmistress," Hong Xin said, bowing. She walked up to the stage, and as she did, she passed her eight comrades who'd given splendid performances. Six of them had exhausted themselves and passed safely, while two of them had sacrificed their safety in the process.

Lotuses of ice bloomed behind Hong Xin as she walked. Students calmed down and shivered as she looked at them frostily. After all, her reputation as a vengeful student preceded her. As did her merciless disposition as a teacher. In fact, they wondered why she, as the foremost talent in their generation, still had to perform.

Hong Xin gazed at the audience from the top of the stage as she took out her flute. The black instrument with golden markings pulsed as she blew into it, drawing everyone into a winter wonderland.

Chapter 39: Samsara

A gray slit appeared in the void a few million miles away from Jade Moon Planet. It was located just outside a transparent gray membrane covered in black runes. Shennong and the Jade Emperor stepped out into the blackness of space, carefully inspecting their surroundings. Then they looked at a nearby planet. "You might as well come out. We know where you're hiding."

A black-cloaked man with pitch-black eyes floated out from behind the world and stood between the two heavenly sovereigns and their goal, Jade Moon Planet.

"It was so difficult to find her again. Do you think you'll be able to stop me this time?" A large black double-bladed scythe appeared in the man's skeletal hands. Black lightning oozed out of it, causing the space around them to shatter.

The Jade Emperor and Shennong's eyes narrowed. "You brought Black Death, Hell's protective treasure with you? You dare to risk it on this gambit?" The Jade Emperor drew out a jade greatsword. A blessed wind surged around him, causing a vast world of prosperity to surround the duo like a corporeal mirage. It complemented Shennong, who summoned a giant spear wreathed in boisterous flames.

"I could say the same to you," the black-cloaked man remarked.

"It's very daring of you to bring the Jade Wind Blade out from the Seven Heavens."

"She's my daughter, Curse Sovereign," the Jade Emperor said. "You might be stronger than me, but with Shennong here, you can't block me."

Both heavenly emperors rushed toward the black-robed devil, who slashed at them with his dual scythe blades. A giant spatial crack appeared where they fought; it extended to a nearby planet and decimated it. Billions of lives were lost in the process, causing massive amounts of sin to accumulate on the Curse Sovereign and residual amounts to drift to his two opponents.

"Do you dare fight with me here?" the Curse Sovereign said. "Countless lives will be lost as we fight in these lower realms. Even heavenly emperors like you will have trouble shouldering this much sin."

"It's a small price to pay for saving her," the Jade Emperor said. Although his heart bled for those around him, saving Yu Wen came before everything.

I just spoke with Empress Han, the Jade Emperor sent to Shennong. *With her mastery over space and time, she'll be here in less than an hour. All we need to do is tie up this old fogie to reduce his control over his avatars on the planet.*

Not a problem, Shennong said, splitting into four. A fiery incarnation grasped his flaming spear while his water, earth, and wind avatars provided support to both his primary combat form and to the Jade Emperor. They also used their strength to block out aftershocks of their epic battle. Neither them nor the Curse Sovereign showed any signs of weakness as they fought a life-and-death battle in the depths of space.

Thud. Thud. Thud.

The large black pillar pounded away at Jade Moon Planet's shield, sapping up what was left of its energy. Cha Ming and Yu Wen stared at it intently as it built up its energy for yet another strike.

Thud. Thud. Crash.

Millions of cracks spread across the jade shield in the sky. Giant shards of energy tumbled down but dissipated before they could land. The starry night sky appeared overhead, along with a black-cloaked, scythe-wielding figure. Hundreds of thousands of fiendish demons bellowed as they charged from the edge of Jade Moon Garden.

"To all of you who are undecided, my offer still stands," the devil sovereign said. "And to those of you who've chosen to resist—prepare to die."

Thousands of cultivators quickly flew back to the central shrine. Cha Ming and his angelic companions summoned their weapons as the wood elemental summoned terrain obstacles to choke off the flow of devils and funnel them toward the many defensive groups.

"Will you come up and die, or do I need to come and get you?" Curse Sovereign said to Yu Wen, who trembled before flying up. Cha Ming reached out and grabbed her wrist.

"You might as well come down and get her," Cha Ming said, looking at the devil sovereign coldly. He summoned his Clear Sky Brush and painted elaborate runic fragments in a formation around him. They then rearranged themselves and contracted into a suit of armor.

Nearby, Huxian and his friends did the same. Their black-and-white battle armors resonated with Huxian's Greater Friendship Circle as they augmented their abilities through it. Meanwhile, Xiao Bai bared her fangs and prepared to launch herself into the thick crowd of charging devils.

"Foolish mortal," the devil sovereign said. "Do you think you think a lowly ant like you stands a chance against someone like me? My true body could extinguish your mortal plane with a flick of its finger."

"But this isn't my mortal plane," Cha Ming said, brandishing the

Clear Sky Pillar. "And this isn't your true body. Who will win and who will lose is uncertain."

As he spoke, tens of thousands of runic lines shot out from the central altar. A small formation surfaced around the few thousand cultivators who had chosen to resist. Their cultivation bases increased substantially as the Jade Moon Blessing intensified. It retracted from the rest of the planet and focused on those few people who were risking their lives.

Myriad jade runes shot into each of the cultivators and imprinted themselves on the jade envelopes surrounding their cores. A hint of transcendent might appeared within their bodies as their cultivation bases were forcibly promoted to half-step rune carving. Encouraged, the group of cultivators let out a yell of defiance as they charged toward the flood of fiendish demons. Huxian, his friends, Xiao Bai, and the angelic cultivators joined them.

"Do you really think you can resist against a sovereign of the seven hells?" the devil sovereign said, floating down to Cha Ming and Yu Wen. He slashed down with a massive double-bladed scythe, and as he did, the world seemed to collapse around it.

In response, Cha Ming swung his Clear Sky Pillar horizontally. A white-and-brown line formed a rocky bridge in the air that met the scythe head on. Black and white canceled and vanished in a puff of gray.

"We won't know unless we try," Cha Ming said. His Dao sigils floated out and formed a Myriad Truths Diagram. Yu Wen's gray strings joined him in attacking the bewildered devil sovereign.

"A soul-bound treasure?" the devil exclaimed as the Clear Sky Pillar crushed through his black scythe and shattered his bones.

"Not just one," Yu Wen said. She drew a golden sword and swung it down on the devil sovereign's neck. A golden light propagated throughout its body, lacerating it until it looked like nothing more than a shredded piece of meat. The mangled body crushed down onto the earth, and the two followed after it.

"It can't be this easy," Cha Ming said doubtfully as they approached the body. As he spoke, strands of black energy rushed in from thousands of fiendish demons that had just been slain. The corpse stirred as the strands merged with it, healing it in the process.

"Of course it's not," the corpse said, grinning as the flesh on its face regenerated. "I'm undying, and this wretched world's suppression can't change that. Nor can Empress Han's sword, for that matter."

Now that the cloak was torn to shreds, Cha Ming could see the skeletal figure beneath it. Its pale, gaunt face and thin body seemed fragile and sickly. Its white hair seemed devoid of vitality. But anyone who fought with him could easily see that it was a facade; his wiry limbs and scrawny torso were a mass of concentrated energy, a body built for destruction and nothing more. All this power came from a single place—his black eyes, tainted with sin.

Not waiting to see the devil sovereign make a full recovery, Cha Ming slammed down the Clear Sky Staff with Crushing Chaos. The power of half-step transcendence poured into this strike through both his body and qi. It collided with the recovering figure, who flew back twenty feet before crashing down onto the ground again.

"He's getting stronger," Cha Ming said, noting that its bones didn't break this time around. He rushed up to him once more, but this time, he lifted his hands. A black double scythe materialized and blocked the Clear Sky Staff. "Yu Wen, help me!" he shouted.

She appeared behind the devil sovereign just in time to stab him in the back. When she did, he twisted his scrawny neck around and stared her in the eyes.

"How long do you both think you can keep this up?" the devil sovereign said. A few more black threads jumped into him before he grasped her sword and inched it out from his body.

Yu Wen retrieved it quickly before regrouping with Cha Ming. "I don't think attacking is going to work anymore," Yu Wen said.

"Then we can only stall for time," Cha Ming replied, deflecting an incoming black blade. It left a small cut on his cheek, which burned with an unreasonable amount of pain. Black lines poured out from the small incision and onto his skin. They stuck together in odd shapes, forming something Cha Ming was all too familiar with—curse runes.

The burnt corpse of a fiendish wolf fell to the ground before Han Jiling. Its putrid flesh reeked of evil as black filaments left it and jumped into a fresh body nearby, reinforcing the devilish might within it.

Are we even causing any damage to him? he thought as he summoned a bolt of diving lightning and burnt another dozen fiends to a crisp.

Bravery took many forms. In Han Jiling's mind, standing up against more powerful enemies, no matter the consequences, was the ultimate expression of this virtue.

Do what is right, no matter what happens, he repeated to himself over and over. A larger fiendish wolf commander attacked him; he met it head on without hesitation. Beside him, a companion joined in to fight it off together. The man had a pair of freshly sprouted jade wings that had appeared only a few minutes ago. Danger might bring out the worst in men, but it also brought out the best.

Just what is that boy doing? Han Jiling thought as he saw Cha Ming and Yu Wen fighting out of the corner of his eyes. Through his Eyes of Pure Jade, courtesy of Cha Ming, he could see a thick green aura around the boy. It wanted nothing more than to burst out from its confinement, and all it needed was a final push.

You don't have much time left, he thought as he turned to fight off another wave of fiends. This time, it was a wave of fierce porcupines wearing rows of sharp metal spikes. *It's sink or swim, and you need to find something to hold on to before the current sweeps you down.*

As he fought, lightning struck once more. It crashed down on the horde of porcupines. Despite this, they would soon overwhelm him.

Huxian and his three friends jumped into an army of fiendish bulls. As they did, the four friends simultaneously extended their domains, crushing thousands of fiends into mincemeat. Tiny drops of black blood shot out from these creatures and headed toward the center, where Cha Ming and Yu Wen were busy fighting the devil sovereign.

"You think I'll let you do as you please?" Huxian barked.

Time stood still for a moment, freezing the black drops before they had a chance to regroup. He swiftly sent out thousands of clones to devour the drops before they could flee. Time resumed soon after. Having witnessed the dreadful slaughter, the fiendish demons scattered to join the other attacking groups. The moment they saw Huxian approaching, they self-detonated to preserve their precious devil seeds.

Xiao Bai, they're catching on, Huxian sent.

Just do what you can, Xiao Bai sent back. *I felt them weakening a moment ago. Someone must be interfering with the devil sovereign's main body. If we hold out for a little longer, we'll make it.*

Copy that, Huxian said, rushing over to the next group of fiends. He happened to be an expert in buying time. Or eating it. Or whatever was needed to make sure time stayed on their side and not on someone else's.

Cha Ming resisted a blow from the devil sovereign with Crushing Chaos. It caused him to fly back tens of feet while simultaneously shattering the bones in his arms. As they regrew, he wondered whether his opponent was growing stronger or the curse seals were making him weaker. As he did, seeds of doubt rose in his mind.

Can I resist the next strike? he thought. *Am I skilled enough? Is it even worth trying?* He rapidly shut away these thoughts, only to see a massive black blade heading straight toward his head.

"Snap out of it, dummy!" Yu Wen shouted as she struck out against the scythe with her golden sword and a gray mist. She panted as devil avatar flew back. "I can only do that a few more times," she said. "The rest is up to you."

Cha Ming looked around at the nearby battlefield. The cultivators were quickly being overwhelmed, but as they fell, the rest were invigorated. Angelic endowments caused majestic phenomena to appear all around them.

Many of those cultivators used to be selfish, he thought. *But as we and the others fought, their guilt got the better of them. They joined us despite knowing it was a suicide mission.* As he thought this, a new wave of doubt came his way. *Can I be strong like them? Can I control my trembling body well enough to fight again? Will I be quick enough?*

He shook his head, trying to clear it. It was the curse seals again, working their magic on him. Doubt poured into him through every rune, one for every cut. His body was covered in hundreds of them.

As Cha Ming focused, he began noticing some similarities between these doubts and the ones in Crystals Falls. He thought of his weakened state and the return of his strength.

I am strong enough, he decided. *I'm hard enough to take whatever tries to break me. Whatever cracks they make, I can mend them over. I'm not a piece of porcelain. I'm strong, unbreakable.* As he thought this, the effect of the curse seals on his mind lessened. At the same time, the devil sovereign began picking himself up.

He's stronger but not more skilled, Cha Ming decided. *This is an avatar, not his main body. Whatever he tries, he can't pay full attention. But I'm different—this is my main body. I can focus one hundred percent without getting distracted.*

The curse seals eased once more as the devil sovereign grasped his scythe.

No matter what happens, it's all worth it, Cha Ming thought. *Yu*

Wen once told me that doubt is the source of all sin. But in my opinion, the worst sin is apathy. The worst sin is not trying your best because you think you can't make a difference. It's refusing to fight against a current because you think it can't be changed.

This thought caused the last of the curse seals to weaken. Something clicked in Cha Ming's mind, and at that moment, three runes appeared on his back. The bountiful amount of merit he'd accumulated rushed out from them and formed a transparent set of magnificent wings. He knew they were incomplete, as a large amount of merit had yet to rush into them, but despite this, he felt his body strengthen. His affinity with the elements deepened, and earth, water, and metal seemed far less distant than before. Creation and destruction also became much easier to control. It was like the world around him was aiding him in understanding these elements.

The moment his phantom wings opened, he spotted the devil sovereign slashing down. Cha Ming speedily deflected the scythe using Splitting the Heavens. A white line appeared in the scythe's path and entangled it. Cha Ming rushed forward with Origin Strike. A gray point appeared on the devil sovereign's chest and began draining energy away from him. The Clear Sky Staff let out a cry of excitement as it feasted on his vital energy.

A panicked look appeared on the devil's face. "How is this possible?" he said, grasping the Clear Sky Staff with both hands.

Not wanting to be outdone, Cha Ming tightened his grip and summoned an Earthen Suppression Formation. A large transparent mountain appeared above them and crushed down on the devil sovereign, making it difficult for him to muster his energy.

Then, seeing that resisting was futile, the sovereign cackled madly. "This is the first time that I, the Curse Sovereign, has ever suffered such a loss. It's a pity you'll have to die so soon."

"What do you mean?" Cha Ming said.

The Curse Sovereign didn't answer. Instead, his face broke into a wide grin, and from his mouth spewed countless writhing black runes.

"Sir Wood Elemental, how many have you got?" Huxian said.

"Perhaps a hundred thousand, give or take?" the wood elemental replied. "How about you?"

"Eighty thousand here," Huxian said. He and his companions ducked and weaved as they used their five auras to reap fiendish demons like gods of death. Every step they took felled dozens more, and every bite they took gathered hundreds.

"Sixty thousand here," Xiao Bai said. "But something feels strange. We need to hurry."

"Let's give it one last push," the wood elemental said. "Once he realizes his first plan won't work, he'll do something desperate. We need to take out as many seeds as possible before then."

At that moment, a powerful fluctuation erupted around them. Massive explosions appeared and forced the elemental and the four beasts down to the ground.

"It's too late," Xiao Bai moaned despondently. "He's already beginning."

"It's not over till it's over," Huxian said defiantly.

Time froze once more, and he didn't evade fiendish attacks like he usually did. His size expanded twentyfold as he reached 333 feet in length. Thousands of explosions peppered his body as he did, causing him severe injuries.

"You think you can escape from me?" he yelled. A massive suction surrounded him as his three friends fed him energy. A hundred thousand black specks of blood were sucked into the swirling vortex and converted into energy. Xiao Bai attacked one last time, felling a few hundred more.

Meanwhile, the wood elemental struck out with a massive vine that captured another fifty thousand. The ones they missed rushed toward the center and accumulated into a massive black orb. Huxian's eyes narrowed when he saw this.

He moaned. "Are we seriously fighting against the Curse Sovereign?"

Before he had a chance bring up relevant ancestral memories, a thick gray mist spilled out around them. He saw space distort and time begin to slow, and soon, he saw nothing but gray.

Cha Ming's heroic figure stood frozen in time. As did Xiao Bai's, Huxian's, and the angelic cultivators who were trying to resist this final destructive attack. Only the devil sovereign maintained some semblance of consciousness. The orb above them was expanding slowly but surely, threatening to destroy every living and unliving thing in the nearest hundred miles.

"I know you can escape," the Curse Sovereign said. "But will you? Will you really let the man you love, his friends, and these other humans die to escape me for a few more millennia?"

Dozens of images appeared above him as he spoke. Yu Wen recognized them—they were pictures of the many times he'd discovered her traces, and the many near misses she'd never known about. Then she saw pictures of Jade Moon Planet and the many precious moments she'd had with Cha Ming.

Yu Wen laughed self-deprecatingly. "Now I know why my father told me there were no good men in this world," she said. "It wasn't that they didn't exist, but that I wouldn't live long enough to enjoy their company. He just wanted to protect me."

"You're right," the Curse Sovereign said. "It's been this way since the Painter created the world, and it will continue to be this way until I break this world and remake it. But in the meantime, I'm afraid you need to die."

Yu Wen looked toward Cha Ming and toward the others. She

looked around at the remnants of Jade Moon Garden, the refuge her father had gifted her. The gray mist shuddered as it began to weaken. "Alas, it looks like we're out of time," she said.

"Choose quickly," the devil said, grinning.

Chapter 40: Parting

A flash of gray appeared before Cha Ming's eyes then immediately disappeared. When it did, all he could see was a black ball filled with malevolent energy. The devil sovereign had given up on trying to extract the Clear Sky Staff from his chest. He held it with one hand while madly diverting all available energy to the growing orb. Hundreds of thousands of black strings rushed toward the globe that devoured them, converting them to pure curse energy. As soon as he laid eyes on the destructive sphere, Cha Ming knew that there was nothing he could do to stop it.

I tried my best, he thought, closing his eyes and accepting his fate.

Then the black sphere exploded. He waited for the inevitable impact to destroy him. One breath, two breaths. After three breaths, he opened his eyes to the most beautiful sight he'd ever seen.

Before him stood an angel with nine pairs of fluttering gray wings. Each wing was three times the length of any others he'd seen before, and they floated around her like a protective shield. He'd seen her before, on the window in the secret room, where the elemental had given him the Wood Source Marrow and the Wood Essence Core. He knew her personally as Yu Wen, and that very same woman, the woman he'd grown to love during his time on Jade Moon Planet, was currently holding the black orb of curse energy in her bare hands.

Strands of evil curse runes flooded into her body from the sphere as the devil cackled madly. His body was nothing more than an empty shell. Half of it had crumbled to dust, while the other half would follow in a few breath's time. Cha Ming tried to force his way toward Yu Wen but was repelled by her. Frustrated, he grasped the Curse Sovereign's corpse.

"Why?" Cha Ming demanded, pulling it closer while simultaneously clenching its fragile neck. "Why have you chased her for so long and never let her rest?" His eyes were bloodshot and furious, but as much as he wished to, there was nothing he could do to this vanishing clone.

"Why did he paint the world in black and white?" the devil asked coldly. "Why did he create such an unfair world? If you want to blame anyone, blame the Painter and his folly. He's the reason why she is who she is."

"I don't understand," Cha Ming said, tears filling his eyes.

"And you never will," the devil said. His fragile neck snapped, and what remained of his feeble body disintegrated. As it did, the last traces of evil vanished from Jade Moon Planet as though they had never existed. All traces except the hundred thousand curse seals covering Yu Wen's body, which finally fell to the floor. Cha Ming caught her as she fell to the ground and sent his resplendent force into her body. Unsurprisingly, her vitals were failing, and her pulse was almost nonexistent.

Cha Ming stroked her pale, rune-covered cheek and kissed her forehead. "It'll be all right," he whispered. "We'll find a way to get you better."

"There's a difference between hope and wishful thinking," Yu Wen said weakly. "I know what I did, and I know why I did it. I'm going to die, and there's nothing you can do to change that."

Cha Ming wiped his runny nose as he supported her head. Huxian appeared beside him and dropped a small white rabbit beside her. Xiao Bai was also covered in curse seals, just like Yu Wen. Huxian whined, not knowing what to do. And for the first time in his life, the small fox cried.

"Don't be sad," Yu Wen said weakly. "This should have happened a million years ago. It was only by of a stroke of luck that I managed to last for so long."

"And moon cakes," Xiao Bai said weakly. "My moon cakes saved you. Many times."

Yu Wen laughed painfully when she heard this, and Cha Ming couldn't help but chuckle as well.

"Cha Ming, I want you to promise me you'll live a good life," Yu Wen said. "I want you to find someone who makes you happy. You don't deserve a wreck like me."

Seeing Cha Ming shake his head, she took out an object from her robes. It was her space-time camera, the soul-bound treasure she always carried with her. "I need you to help me with something," she said, holding it out.

Cha Ming nodded and grabbed the camera. The moment he did, he felt a strong repulsion toward it, like it didn't belong to him. Yet a moment later, the feeling vanished. It was replaced with something akin to reluctant acceptance. He instinctively knew how to use the artifact, and he knew that what he'd received was permission from its owner and a transfer of ownership.

"What do you need me to find for you?" he asked.

"You don't need to find anything for me," Yu Wen said softly. Her skin began turning translucent, and her gray wings began fading. "The space-time camera is yours. I know you'll be sad, but when the pain becomes unbearable, remember to look inside it and see the memories we made together. I want you to look through our time in the volcano, and our game of tag with the rainbow fish. I want you to remember our time in the hot spring, and our life-and-death battles together. And finally, after you've done all these things, I want you to read my letter. It contains the depth of my feelings and a hint of my heart. If you remember these feelings, then no matter what happens and no matter who you find later on in life, I'll be happy."

"Please don't go," Cha Ming said in a trembling voice. She smiled as what remained of her body vanished, and as it did, so did Xiao Bai's. All that remained were two jade balls of spiritual energy. They dove into an illusory yellow river, where a ghostly figure collected them.

Cultivators cheered and rejoiced at their survival, but Cha Ming and Huxian didn't have the heart for celebration. The man and the fox cried until they could cry no more, kneeling despondently at the site where Yu Wen and Xiao Bai had vanished.

"Cha Ming," Huxian said as he lay on his lap. Cha Ming didn't answer; he simply continued petting the fox between the ears as he had for several hours. "If I could give up all the moon cakes in the world and have Xiao Bai back, I'd do it in a heartbeat," he said.

The tears came once more.

"Cha Ming," a voice said.

He and Huxian opened their eyes. They looked around and saw freshly sprouted plants being tended to by ambitious dryads. Much of Jade Moon Garden had already healed over from the vicious battle, but its charm had already faded. It was like a garden without a soul, a tool without a purpose.

"It's time to go," the voice said.

He looked up and saw the towering wood elemental. Although most of the cultivators had already left, the powerful creature had allowed them to remain a little longer.

"All right," Cha Ming said despondently. "Let's go."

"Are you sure you don't want to meet Shennong and the Jade Emperor?" the elemental asked.

"There's no need," Cha Ming said. "There's nothing to say at this point."

"Then brace yourself," the elemental said. "The bridge will collect and deliver you to your mortal plane. Please have your friend collect the others before the bridge arrives."

"Already done," Cha Ming said.

The elemental sighed and shook his head. At his signal, a constellation dipped down and picked up Cha Ming and Huxian off Jade Moon Planet, whisking them into the starry sky. Neither of them had any desire to watch the planes wage war or the planets pass by. They simply closed their eyes and drifted off into a merciful sleep.

"It's done," the elemental said. He stood in a barren crater where Jade Moon Garden used to be.

"Good," the Jade Emperor said. "And the rainbow fish?"

"They like him, so they chose to tag along," the elemental said. "I'll miss her, though. She was the flower that made the garden worthwhile. I don't understand why you didn't keep it. At least you'd have been able to look at it every time you miss her."

The older man shook his head. "I'm not a hoarder like you are. My cloak is enough," he said, touching the green garment on his shoulders. "I lent her my soul-bound treasure for a million years. Knowing that it helped protect her for so long and allowed her to enjoy her short life is all I need." Then he tapped the golden sword at his waist. "This sword is enough for my wife. Knowing that it killed those who sought to harm her will bring her great joy whenever she wields it. As for the garden—consider it compensation. Both to him and to her."

"She wanted nothing more than to help him heal his core during his stay," the wood elemental said. "Would it have killed him to ask you and Shennong about it?"

"Everyone goes through tough times like these in their life," the Jade Emperor said, shaking his head. "I've just lost a daughter, so I can understand his feelings. He'll recover, but it will take some time. As for his core... let's just say my daughter wasn't so honest with you."

"What do you mean?" the wood elemental said.

"There's no need to spoil the surprise," the Jade Emperor said. "With any luck, we'll be seeing him momentarily." He opened a hundred-foot-tall gray portal in the air. "Are you coming or staying?"

"There's no point in leaving this clone here," the elemental said. "This place is nothing without the garden." He followed the old man into the gray portal. It closed behind them, leaving only a barren planet and tainted memories.

"And then, the devil sovereign broke through the shield," Cha Ming said. "We fought as much as we could, but it wasn't enough. Yu Wen sacrificed herself to save us, and here we are."

He motioned to Lu Tianhao's desk, and a pile of jade herb boxes appeared. "These are the things you asked for. I used the herb-gathering quotas I had left to get them for you. The Burning Samsara Lotus is gone, as are any other herbs or treasures I found. The rest I consumed to cure my poison during the trial." He thought for a moment before placing a transcendent-grade sword on the table. "You can take this sword as compensation. I have no need for it."

"This is too much," Lu Tianhao said. "But I won't refuse a transcendent treasure. It will be immensely useful in the war." He received the pile on the table. "Now what about you? How are *you* doing personally?"

"What can I say?" Cha Ming said helplessly. "I lost the most important thing I found on this trip: love."

"You didn't lose love," Lu Tianhao said sternly. "You need to remember that you lost a person, but the love for her still exists." He tapped Cha Ming on the chest. "It's still here, where you left it. And don't you ever let that disappear."

"Yes, sir," Cha Ming said. His gaze was distant as he recalled those precious memories. He remembered Yu Wen, her light curls, and her smiling face.

"Due to your substantial contributions, I've promoted you to junior partner," Lu Tianhao said. "It's only a matter of time before you reach peak core formation, assuming you fix your core. Failing that, you can always pursue body refining only."

Cha Ming didn't answer.

"Is there *anything* I can help you with. Anything at all?" Time trickled by in silence.

"I need some time alone," Cha Ming said suddenly.

"Whatever you do, keep your wits about you," Lu Tianhao said. "You have disciples to care for and much to teach them. You have the Southern Alliance to fight, and devils aplenty to kill."

"What's the point?" Cha Ming said.

"The point is that you need to pull yourself together," Lu Tianhao said. "Now, I don't know what works for you, but I find going back to my hometown helps me ground myself. I go to the place where it all began, and I trace my journey from there."

"I'll think about it," Cha Ming said. He walked out the door and through the main garden to where Huxian was lazing around. His four apprentices were there, waiting for him.

"Do you need any specific guidance on anything?" he asked them. They shook their heads in unison. "Then Huxian and I will be going on a trip. Get Zi Long to contact me if you need anything." He picked up the small fox and flew off into the sky.

To go where it all began, Cha Ming thought, peering through the misty air to a walled-off cave behind a large waterfall.

In his mind, although Green Leaf City and his hometown were important points in his life, Crystal Falls was the true turning point. It was there that he'd met Li Yin and found hope. It was there that he'd learned runic poetry. And it was also where he'd met Yu Wen.

Cha Ming slipped by scattered villagers and floated toward the waterfall. It parted and allowed him into a small outcropping. The walled-off area melted as he passed through it. It was a low-quality defense against a troublesome problem.

"Would you look at that," he said as he touched an old mining wall. His transcendent force and earth qi tunneled into the wall and mapped out the nearest fifty miles. Then they latched on to the many ores that were scattered across the tunnel. The impurities within them crumbled off into a pile of dust as the remnants of the spirit-stone vein drilled through the earth and formed a pile at his feet. "A hidden threat is still a threat, but now the village is truly safe."

After receiving these riches, he proceeded down the tunnel. Huxian trotted beside him curiously as he cleared away the rubble that led to a large empty space. They floated down to a small bluestone fleck that was reminiscent of the Bridge of Stars. The front gate opened as they landed, and they walked in to find the Custodian waiting for them patiently.

"It's only been a few years since you last came," the construct said. "No, wait, it's been more than that from your perspective. I can tell that your bones have aged, and your power is much greater."

"I just came to take a look around," Cha Ming said, his voice melancholy. "May I have a room?"

"Of course," the Custodian said. Their surroundings transformed into accommodations and refreshments. "Unfortunately, I can't allow you into the library until ten years are up."

"That's fine," Cha Ming said. "I'm not here to study. I'm here to remember."

Seeing that Cha Ming didn't want to be disturbed, the Custodian slipped away. Cha Ming scratched Huxian between the ears as he thought about the time he and Yu Wen had first met. Then he retrieved the space-time camera from its own storage dimension.

"Let me show you some things," he said softly to Huxian.

His small friend sat up and looked at the device curiously. Cha Ming summoned the first picture. Funnily enough, it was a picture that she'd taken inside Fuxi's Library without his knowledge—he was studying intently while ignoring her.

"She helped me back then without asking for anything in return," he said. "Meanwhile, I thought she was a custodian." He chuckled at the fond memory and her insistence that he call her teacher.

He flicked through a few more pictures. These were their adventures together through the Bridge of Stars. They captured the many runic circles Cha Ming had activated, as well as the many fights they'd had along the way. Han Jiling, Zhang Fei, Fan Li, and Mu Qianlin made appearances in several of them. Oddly enough, the end of the battle was missing.

She must have intervened back then, he thought. He flicked over to the next picture, which was their pursuit through the woods. Then came the lava serpent and the volcano.

"There were many interesting demons down in the volcano," Cha Ming said. "I want to take you there one day and show you the magnificence of it all. We had a lot of fun there, and it's where we realized our feelings for each other." The pictures included the obsidian corals, the strange life-forms, the lava sharks, and finally, their first kiss.

"I still have that talisman," he said, taking out a red slip of paper. "It contains our first feelings for one another, and it's something I'll never use."

He flicked forward again and saw pictures of the Jade Moon Library. These were mostly pictures of them studying side by side. Then came their game of tag with the rainbow fish and pictures of their wondrous nest. The series of pictures ended just before their secret adventure in the woods and their private hot springs. The picture of a note came after. Its elegant handwriting tugged on his heartstrings. He couldn't help but weep when he saw Yu Wen's last heartfelt words. He put the letter aside and took out his brush. It flowed slowly across a sheet of paper as he poured his sadness into it.

> *Disappointment douses the hearts of the needy;*
> *Man is left wanting and ever yearning.*

He called it the Dousing Talisman, and as he finished it, the flame in his heart snuffed out. All that was left was a cold numbness that began spreading throughout his body.

Sadness pervaded Hong Xin's audience as she played a mournful tune. The sounds of her flute made them remember all that they'd lost in the Red Dust Pavilion and the meaninglessness of what they'd gained. Three icy phoenixes flew overhead. Snowflakes fell from their mighty wings, bringing coldness to their formerly enlivened hearts.

A thin sheet of ice formed over each of their cores, thickening with each passing second. The last of their hopes were extinguished as they became numb inside and out. Hong Xin's tune finished, and they were no longer capable of regretting their miserable fates.

Chapter 41: Kindling

The audience heard a single person clapping. That person was none other than the headmistress, the ultimate source of their pain and suffering. The students refused to join her sadistic encore. They wished for her to die a thousand times for what she'd done to them.

Yet at this moment, something changed. The snow around them began melting. The ice around their hearts transformed into a rousing energy that invigorated them. They looked up on stage and realized that Hong Xin had started dancing while still playing the flute. The icy phoenixes hadn't disappeared, but six fiery ones had joined them as well. It was a symphony of ice and fire, a performance of vengeance and vigor.

The audience grew increasingly raucous as they voiced their frustration. As their feelings peaked, eight other auras surged near the teachers. Six of them were those who had obtained passing grades, and the two others were Bai Ling and Ji Bingxue, who burned their blood essence to boost their cultivation and break through their captors' restraints.

One by one, the cultivation bases of those in the audiences surged as a small spark within their hearts ignited. Hong Xin smiled as the seed of hope she'd planted in each student over the past six months suddenly sprouted, establishing deep roots within their hearts and souls. Two hundred students simultaneously broke through in their cultivation bases and reached the first level of heart kindling. As they did so, they linked together with their like-minded sisters, further spurring their rebellious mood.

"You dare?" a shrill voice said. The headmistress and her teachers flew into the air toward the podium. Their resplendent forces bore down on Hong Xin, who looked at them coldly.

"I do dare," Hong Xin said. "You've suppressed us and taken our joy. You've trampled on us and taken our feelings. You've killed our sisters and frightened us into submission. No more. We're our own masters, and we'll fight for our freedom."

A chorus of agreement rang out around her. These voices joined her performance, enhancing it. They combined into hundreds of fiery birds that flew out and shredded the teachers' assault.

"Join together and restrain them," Hong Xin said. "Today, we'll be free."

The flames intensified, and as they did, they bore down on the teachers' icy cultivations. Although dousing restrained kindling, so, too, did kindling restrain dousing. While their cultivations weren't as strong, their numbers exceeded their teachers by over ten to one.

"Kill them all," the headmistress suddenly said. She drew out a weapon—a prohibited item in the Red Dust Pavilion—and so did each of the teachers. They began hacking into the audience in unison. Agonizing wails tore into Hong Xin's performance, threatening to destroy it.

"They're just weapons," Hong Xin said. "I know better than anyone that each of us is a living weapon. We don't need these tools to take down our opponents."

Her dance intensified as flames poured out from her. They crashed against the mistresses, who hastily used their weapons to deflect them. Fire and ice rained down on the merciless teachers, causing some of them to cry out as they were burned black. Then, Hong Xin flew up to the headmistress. A fiery dragon appeared on her fist and crashed into a shield of ice.

"You think you can win?" the headmistress said. "You think you can fight against us on our home turf?"

Suddenly the Red Dust Pavilion glowed with an ominous crimson light. The many trees covered in crimson leaves year-round shone brightly with strange runic characters. They joined together in a runic pattern, causing the mistresses to grow in power.

"Everyone, fight!" Hong Xin said. "Fight for your life!"

As she renewed her assault, she directed their joint power of kindling to a nearby teacher. Her kindling powers wormed their way into the icy teacher's mind and sought for a modicum of resistance but found none.

How can this be? she thought. She tried another teacher but failed once more. *Do they truly not wish to be free?*

She tried each teacher, one after another, in quick succession. One by one, she found not a shred of resistance. Before long, only the headmistress and Mistress Huang remained.

Here goes nothing, she thought as she probed Mistress Huang. To her surprise, she didn't resist. The power of kindling poured into her tormentor's core, causing its outer layer to crumble. Finally, a large purple flame at the center flickered to life. The ice that once pervaded it melted and fused with it, causing her core to turn into a harmonized purple core of ice and fire like Hong Xin's gold-and-purple one.

Despite this change, Mistress Huang didn't act. She continued fighting against the students like nothing had happened, allowing the headmistress to close in on Hong Xin. Fire and ice clashed briefly as the headmistress used her superior strength to press against Hong Xin's protective shield of fire.

Frozen spikes jutted out of the earth, impaling the protective phoenixes floating around the younger girl. The headmistress thrust her hand out and grasped Hong Xin by the neck, causing vivid blue runes of restriction to form on her fragile body.

"You gave it a good shot, but you're still two hundred years early," the headmistress said. "It's a pity you didn't pick better companions. If they hadn't betrayed you, you might have grown into a real threat."

"That's the thing about trust," Hong Xin croaked. "To make

friends or lasting partners, you need to take a gamble. Otherwise, they're nothing but slaves."

"Slaves listen," the headmistress shot back.

"Slaves will stab you in the back as soon as they have the slightest opportunity," Hong Xin said. She grinned as a blue sword pierced out of the headmistress's chest and twisted.

The cold woman turned her head around slowly until she came face to face with her killer, Mistress Huang. She died with a shocked expression on her face. The thought of her best student betraying her had never crossed her mind.

All around them, the fighting stopped. The teachers, seeing that their master had perished, no longer put up any resistance. The chaos was instantly quelled, and the students rounded up the sullen teachers, who seemed to have given up on everything, including living.

"It's about time you took the hint," Mistress Huang said dryly.

"I was being cautious," Hong Xin said. "Besides, you made it rather difficult for me to believe you. Something about stabbing cold needles in someone's heart makes it very difficult for them to trust you from then on."

"You think I did all that to follow orders?" Mistress Huang said. "I did it hoping that you'd succeed where I failed. And it seems my gamble paid off."

Hong Xin kneeled down and retrieved the headmistress's bag of holding. She glanced inside it before confirming that the Oath Stone was still intact. Then she looked at the crowd of weeping students. They hugged the cold bodies of their fallen sisters and mourned those who hadn't even lived to see this day.

She sighed before walking over to a nearby group of students to direct them. There was a lot of work to be done, and someone had to step up and face the many challenges ahead of them.

Cha Ming wiped the tears from his eyes as he read Yu Wen's letter on the space-time camera again. Although it pained him to do so, this time he read the words out loud. Huxian listened intently to its brief but heartfelt contents.

Dearest Cha Ming,

This might come as a surprise to you, but I've known for a long time that I would likely die on Jade Moon Planet. I'm prophetic, you see, and as we grew closer and closer, my choice became a lot easier. If it was between me and the other cultivators on the planet, I'd choose myself in a heartbeat. But with you, it's not so simple. Cha Ming, I love you. And when you love someone, you jump out to save them, even though you're certain to die in the process.

By now, you've likely finished looking through the first set of pictures in my camera. You feel sad and lost, like life isn't worth living anymore. But let me tell you, even though I knew I would die because of it, I never felt more alive than when I was with you. When you look through these pictures, I want you to remember what we had. I want you to keep me in your heart and remember that this sadness comes from happiness. The root of your grief is joy, and the reverse can also be true. You can rise from this sadness stronger than ever. It can be the spark that sets it off for you, the drive you've been seeking your entire life.

I know you'll have trouble moving on, and I can't make that easier. I also know there's no guarantee you'll find someone else. Therefore, I'll settle for a smaller goal. Once you're done reading this letter, I want you to promise me to look through these pictures again. I want you to ignore the sadness and remember the happiness you see. And then I want you to keep looking through the rest of the album—there are a few pictures I never showed you. I promise that you'll feel better once you've seen them.

That's it. I've now run out of things to write. Please do me a favor and imagine all the other nice things I should say to you. You're good at it, and I like that about you.

Love,

Yu Wen

"I can do that," Cha Ming said, closing his tear-filled eyes. He opened them and returned to the beginning of the album. Instead of focusing on what he'd lost, he focused on what he'd gained. As he flicked through the pictures, he laughed as he remembered their playful moments. He cried tears of joy as he remembered their close encounters in the volcano and their playful game of tag with the rainbow fish.

"Is that us?" a voice said from within his Clear Sky Brush.

Unsure of how to react, Cha Ming sent his transcendent soul into the brush and saw a two-foot fish. He looked around and saw a lush garden in the formerly white space. Hundreds of rainbow fish were swimming joyfully in the rainbow falls.

Beside the rivers and lakes, dryads tended to rapidly growing trees and herbs. This scenery brought life to the memories in the pictures. He didn't question their presence, he simply continued looking through the rest of the album. Once he reached the missing pictures in the illusory woods and the hot springs, he remembered the things that weren't captured. He burned these memories into his heart.

Finally, he returned to the letter and flicked over to the next page. There he saw a transcendent pill formula entitled Nirvana Pill. He was familiar with this pill, as he'd already memorized eight tenths of its recipe. As for the ingredients required for the pill, they were all located within Jade Moon Garden, the same garden which had just appeared inside the Clear Sky World.

Excited, Cha Ming flipped over to the next page. It was the page of a textbook. He continued flicking through and realized that it wasn't just a page but an entire book. Seeing that the process could take years, he zoomed out from the full display and saw many tiny pages all lined up in a row. The camera contained tens of millions of pages that should have been impossible to copy so easily, given their magical nature. Yet due to the wondrous powers of the space-time camera, he now had full access to the first three shelves of the Sacred Jade Library. And at the end of these sheets of paper, he saw a final note.

I snuck into the Sacred Jade Library and took pictures of what you needed. Don't give up—I have confidence that you'll succeed. And remember: The source of all evil is doubt. I wasn't attracted to you because I saw a nice guy, but because I saw a man who refused to crumble, who refused to let the ages wear down his soul. I saw a man who'd fight against the currents of apathy and kindle the smallest flame to save it from the rain. I saw a man who would breathe life into a world of death, who would hold on to hope no matter what. That is who you are, Cha Ming. Never forget it.

Yu Wen

Her words were a hammer that struck a hot iron in his mind. At that moment, he gained inspiration on the Energy Talisman, which united the concepts of dousing and kindling. Dark-red and light-red energy merged together out of thin air and appeared in the shape of four lines.

Disappointment douses the hearts of the needy;
Man is left wanting and ever yearning.
Kindling the flames of love and caring;
Never questioning his devotion.

And at that moment, he realized that a figure stood behind him. He looked back and saw the familiar figure of a red-haired man. The man grinned as he walked up to Cha Ming and embraced him in a warm hug. His soul was much healthier than when they'd first met.

In fact, it was even more tangible that Cha Ming's own transcendent soul.

"I might have been sleeping, but I have some idea of what's going on," Sun Wukong said. "And she's right. You can't let this keep you down."

"I know that now," Cha Ming said. "I'm glad you're all right."

"If it's any consolation, I have some knowledge on how things work at the higher levels," Sun Wukong said. "I know that a god or an immortal is capable of many things. Specifically, I know that they have the power to awaken forgotten memories of past lives like the Buddhists do."

Cha Ming's lips trembled. "You mean that if I find her, I can make her remember?" he said. The flames of hope burned ever brighter in his heart. And as they did, his transparent jade wings appeared once more. This time, a fourth rune appeared. Its red lines merged into the jade wings that once again bolstered his body and his affinity to fire. Only a fifth of his merit glow remained.

"Piece of cake," Sun Wukong said. "And if you can't, I'll do it for you. It's the least I can do after all the trouble I've put you through."

"Thank you," Cha Ming said, hugging Sun Wukong tightly. "Thank you for everything."

Yu Wen, I promise I'll find you, he thought. *I'll protect you from those who want to harm you, and I'll become an immortal. I'll help you remember our precious memories, and I'll make you fall in love with me again. This I swear.*

Epilogue

It's been a while," Yama said as he looked at the twin jade souls in the palm of his hand. "Where will you two be going next?"

The two souls stared back at him dully.

Of course, he thought. *They don't even need Aunty Meng's potion. They're just blank slates every time.* Sighing, he summoned the threads of karma surrounding them. They were fading quickly, but as the most powerful man in the universe, it was a cakewalk for him to untangle them.

Five main threads, Yama thought. *One for enmity, two for parents, and one for friendship. And finally, one for love. That's new.*

He thought for a moment before appearing above the six gates of reincarnation. He walked through the gate of humanity and entered large space containing millions of portals.

"Same deal as before," Yama said. "You can pick whichever one you like. If you don't, I'll send you somewhere random."

The soul looked around in a daze. It looked at the five strings before choosing one of them. Yama performed some quick karmic calculations before flicking his finger and forcing the tethered souls into a large portal. This one led to a transcendent realm.

"I knew you'd pick that one," he said cheerfully. He then took out his phone and looked at the two messages that topped his SpiritChat app. One was from the Curse Sovereign, and the other was from the Jade Emperor. He sent them both messages of regret, informing them that he couldn't divulge her whereabouts, as that would be a gross violation of Diyu's privacy policy.

Then, for good measure, he flicked his sleeve. Millions of miles away, a small book that recorded every transaction in Diyu had a single entry redacted—aside from himself, perhaps only the deceased Pangu would be able to decipher it.

"I truly hope that you can find love again," Yama said, shaking his head. "You've had so much misery in your life. You deserve better."

A short while later, he opened his door and received his next appointment. It was Judah, his candidate for mayor. The campaign was reaching its final stretch, and things were getting serious.

A small pile of corpses burned, filling the Red Dust Pavilion's courtyard with a wretched stench. The headmistress was one of the corpses, and she had been joined by ten other teachers who'd ended up resisting. The rest were now imprisoned within the pavilion, and Hong Xin wasn't quite sure what to do with them yet.

The smell of burning corpses joined that of the burning trees, the strange guardians that had reinforced the headmistress's grip over the institution. They had eyes, she found out later. They were trees possessed by spirits, a gift from the Shaman Temple in the south.

"It's done," she said to the assembled crowd of students. "Please go back to your dormitories while I think of a path forward for all of us. If anyone has any ideas, please come discuss them with me."

No one lingered, preferring to retreat to their own accommodations. A small group of them, however, gathered in the central courtyard and began playing music, singing, and dancing. Others watched the revelry as they stared up toward the starry sky.

Hong Xin sighed. "Was this your plan all along?" she said. A beautiful woman in a thin red dress walked out from behind a tree.

The woman was none other than Hong Yinyue, the one who had changed her life. But now that she'd reached her current realm of mid-core formation, Hong Xin could vaguely sense an intangible aura around her. It was none other than an aura of transcendence.

"I hoped that you'd find a way," Hong Yinyue said. "For the sake of everyone in the pavilion, and for the sake of my old apprentice."

"You could have killed the headmistress with a flick of your sleeve," Hong Xin said bitterly.

"I could have," Hong Yinyue admitted. "But the cost would have been high, and I would lack that energy to interfere in the upcoming war. The role we transcendents play is a delicate but vital one. It's a balancing act, where we weigh each action carefully."

"Is the situation on the continent so bad that you can turn your back on hundreds of young women?" Hong Xin asked softly.

"More than you know," Hong Yinyue said. "In the south, although most of them are free, millions of people are slaves. It is a result of their cruel society, where power and wealth rule above all else. My goal isn't to save a few young girls, but rather to save those poor people. Regrettably, the Red Dust Pavilion is but a small speck in the grand scheme of things."

Hong Xin walked up beside Hong Yinyue, who was gazing at the Red Dust Pavilion with affection. "What next?" she said. "What do we do with all these young women who've been through so much? They're no longer fit for normal society; not after what they've been through."

"I leave that up to you to decide," Hong Yinyue said. "I'm no longer fit to lead these people. Besides, you're their spiritual leader. They'll follow you wherever you go." She then turned her gaze north. "But speaking of a direction, I've heard that your old love has returned to Gold Leaf City. Do you want to see him again?"

"Perhaps," Hong Xin said, fondling the purple hairclip that had replaced the previous red-and-black pin. "But if I go see him, I don't want a repeat of the last time. I need to be able to stand my own ground."

"I also hear that a substantial amount of Red Dust Pavilion members had previously been assigned to that same city," Hong Yinyue said. "If you're game for cleaning messes, it's a good place to start."

Hong Xin smiled. "It's as good a place as any. After we burn this wretched place down, we'll need somewhere to stay."

Having said her piece, she left Hong Yinyue in the woods and returned to the Red Dust Pavilion to join the festivities.

"So let me get this straight," Lu Tianhao said. "Now that you've learned talisman arts and formation arts, you now want to split your focus *yet again* and dabble into alchemy?"

"Not just dabble," Cha Ming said. "What I did with Mo Tianshen before was dabbling. I want to *master* alchemy. There's a big difference."

They were seated in the older man's office. The plants previously growing there had already been harvested by Grandmaster Yao and were currently being refined into Transcendence Pills and other beneficial items.

"I know a place," Lu Tianhao said. "It's the holy land for all professions, a neutral territory in the sea. I can write you a recommendation letter for Haijing City, and with your skill, you shouldn't have any issues joining."

"Good," Cha Ming said. "I'll be taking my disciples along with me. It'll be a good training experience for them."

"When will you leave?" Lu Tianhao asked, putting a brush to a piece of paper.

"Tomorrow," Cha Ming said decisively. "There's a lot to do, and not much time remaining."

None of the previous despondency and depression remained in

his eyes. Hope shone brightly within them, a flame far stronger than the love that had kindled it.

– End Book 6 –

A Note to Readers

If you've enjoyed this book, I would greatly appreciate it if you left a rating on the site where you purchased it. Ratings lead to credibility in this competitive marketplace, and by leaving one, you signal to the world that this book is worth reading.

As some of you might know, I release each book as I write it. It wasn't necessary for you to buy this book, but your support is greatly appreciated. If you are so inclined, you can continue reading as I write at:

https://royalroadl.com/fiction/16320/painting-the-mists

I can't promise fully edited or proofread content, but I will do my best to continue maintaining frequent and high-quality releases.

If you would like to receive bimonthly updates on writing progress, releases, and the life of Patrick Laplante, subscribe to the Painting the Mists newsletter at:

http://eepurl.com/dymvO1

You can also find a link to the newsletter at www.paintingthemists. com. As a bonus for subscribing, you'll receive exclusive biography sketches for each of the key characters, starting with Huxian!

Other ways to contact me or keep in touch:
Facebook: https://www.facebook.com/RedMiragePtM/
Twitter: @RedMirage_PtM

The Cultivation Systems

Qi Cultivation
- Qi Condensation – condense the qi of heaven and earth into a liquid in your dantian
    - Stages 1-3: form a qi pool
    - Stages 4-6: form a qi lake
    - Stages 7-9: form a qi ocean
- Foundation Establishment – form pillars from your qi, setting a firm foundation for your future cultivation.
    - Traditionally, a cultivator forms between one and nine pillars, which are affixed to the bottom of the qi oceans.
    - The liquid qi in this stage is more viscous, its quantity and quality is dependent on the number of pillars.
    - Pillars are grown from the bottom up, gradually forming the foundation with which to form your core
- Core Formation – condense your foundation into a core, the basis of your future growth
- Rune Carving – ???

Body Cultivation
- Body Strengthening – basic body strengthening and purification. Typically, the body is fed with qi and then refined with an opposing qi, removing any impurities
- Bone Forging – bones are the basis of strength and durability. The strongest body is nothing without strong bones supporting it.
- Marrow Refining – marrow is the basis of your blood, which feeds the remainder of your body in turn.

Soul Cultivation

- Innate Soul – cultivators are born with an innate soul, and it grows as the cultivator advances in qi condensation. Eventually, the soul will make a rapid breakthrough into incandescence.
- Incandescent Soul – the soul begins to shine with incandescent light. Advanced soul manipulation of objects and mental communication is now possible.
- Resplendent Soul – wrap the soul in a resplendent vestment
- Transcendent Soul – A single realm spanning all of transcendence. A transcendent soul can now leave the mortal body and operate independently.

Acknowledgments

As I continue to write, I find that this list of acknowledgments grows. There are far too many people to thank—if I missed you, I'm sorry; it wasn't intentional.

A special thanks goes out to my fiancé, Xing Wen, who recently accepted my proposal for marriage. Please wish us luck in the upcoming year. I'd also like to thank my parents and hers, who were present for the engagement.

I'd also like to thank this book's beta readers: Denis Laplante (my brother), Dave Yeung (who has been providing feedback since the start of the series), Sarah, Psiioniic (RR), Astrael (RR), and Savane (RR).

Likewise, thanks go to my two brothers and my sister. Thank you once again, Denis, for joining the beta team, and thank you, Levi, for finally starting to read the novel.

Thank you to all my friends once again. We've kept in touch since moving to China, which has been a tremendous pillar of emotional support.

Many thanks to Crystal Watanabe for her excellent support while editing my novel. My writing continues to improve with her help, so I'm glad to have her on board.

Thank you to Petros Stefanidis for great cover. I look forward to the eventual set of 9 frames that we are working on, and the eventual reworking of Book 1–4's covers.

Last, but not least, thank you to my readers. I write to tell stories to people, and a story is worth nothing if it isn't shared.

About the Author

Patrick Georges Laplante was born in a small town in the Canadian prairies in 1987. He began publishing *Painting the Mists* online under the pseudonym RedMirage in January 2018.

An engineer by trade, he graduated from the University of Alberta in 2009 and completed his master's degree in 2011. While writing and engineering have little in common, he actively utilizes his experiences and attention to detail in fleshing out a vivid world and answering the "whys," which are often left unanswered in Xianxia fiction.

As an avid vegan, he aims to prompt internal reflection in his readers through various themes like non-violence, choice, and begging the question: Is personhood restricted to humanity? And what is proper conduct, morality, and love?

His work is inspired by a combination of Western fiction, *Dungeons and Dragons*, Chinese web novels, and various Japanese, Korean, and Chinese comics and illustrated novels.

www.ingramcontent.com/pod-product-compliance
Lightning Source LLC
Chambersburg PA
CBHW051510250626
47156CB00001B/37